SOUL'S FIRE
THE NORTHWOMEN SAGAS

SUSAN FANETTI

THE FREAK CIRCLE PRESS

Soul's Fire © 2017 Susan Fanetti
All rights reserved

ISBN-13: 978-1542602914
ISBN-10: 1542602912

PRONUNCIATIONS AND DEFINITIONS

To build this world, I did a great deal of research, and I mean to be respectful of the historical reality of the Norse cultures. But I have also allowed myself some creative license to draw from the full body of Norse history, culture, and geography in order to enrich my fictional representation. True Viking culture was not monolithic but instead a various collection of largely similar but often distinct languages, traditions, and practices. In The Northwomen Sagas, however, I have merged the cultural touchstones.

In this installment, which takes place primarily in a fictional version of Anglo-Saxon England, I have likewise fictionalized history, culture, and geography, exploiting and stretching history to create story.

My characters have names drawn from that full body of history and tradition. Otherwise, I use Norse words sparingly and use the Anglicized spelling and pronunciation where I can. Below is a list of some of the Norse and Anglo-Saxon names and terms used in this story, with pronunciations and/or definitions provided as I thought might be helpful.

NAMES:
- Åke (*AW-kyuh*)
- Birte (*BEER-tuh*)
- Bjarke (*BYAR-kyuh*)
- Eadric (*EE-drik*)
- Eira (*EYE-rah*)
- Håkon (*HAW-kun*)
- Jaan (*YAHN*)
- Leif (*LAFE*)
- Leofric (*lee-OFF-rik*)
- Solveig (*SOL-vay*)
- Vali (*VAH-lee*)
- Ylva (*IL-vah*)

TERMS:

- Dwale—*(DWAH-luh)* an anesthetic potion made of belladonna
- Hangerock—an apron-like overdress worn by Viking women.
- Hnefatafl—*(NEH-va-tahpl)* an ancient Viking strategy game, vaguely like chess.
- Pleasaunce—*(PLEEZ-awnce)* a garden designed to be pleasing to the senses.
- Skause—a meat stew, made variously, depending on available ingredients.
- Skeid—*(SHIED)* the largest Viking ship, with more than thirty rowing benches.
- Thing—the English spelling and pronunciation of the Norse *þing*. An assembly of freemen for political and social business.
- Úlfhéðnar *(OOLF-hyeh-nar)*—a special class of berserkers who took the wolf as their symbol. They were known to be especially ferocious and in some sagas are identified as Odin's elite warriors.

THE NINE NOBLE VIRTUES

This story is organized into nine sections corresponding to the "Nine Noble Virtues" of Norse culture. These virtues were organized into this list in the twentieth century; however, despite that recent organization, they were taken from the ancient Norse eddas such as the *Hávamál* and might be considered to reflect a true Norse warrior's code.

The virtues appear in this story in the order that best corresponds to the theme and/or plot of the part to which they are assigned, but they are most commonly listed in this order:

Courage
Truth
Honor
Fidelity
Discipline
Hospitality
Self-Reliance
Industriousness
Perseverance

CONTENT WARNING

The Northwomen Sagas takes place in a brutal, combative world, and, as is sadly always the case, women in such a world suffer in particular ways. The leads of these stories experience things that reflect the realities for women during this period of history. Even by the harsh standards of this series, Astrid's story gets quite dark. She suffers badly through a few chapters. It is always my tendency not to go into much specific detail about the hard things that happen while they are happening and instead focus on the aftermath, and that is the case here. I don't dwell long on such events, but I do dwell on their consequences. *Soul's Fire* is a romance, and Astrid's story ends happily, but if you thought *God's Eye* and *Heart's Ease* had some tough moments to deal with, this one will likely be even tougher.

So have your shield and armor at the ready.

For my fellow survivors of sexual assault and abuse.
Our fire is our own, and no one may take it from us, try
though they might.

Many thanks, as always, to Lina Andersson, for her help with
Viking history and culture—and for making sure the Swedish
lines say what I want them to.

PROLOGUE
TRUTH

SHIELDMAIDEN

Astrid kicked on her mother's door. The move jostled the girl in her arms, and she moaned.

"Mother! Are you there!"

From behind the slatted wood, she heard, "Usch! I'm here! Why all the yelling and pounding, just open the—"

The door swung open, and Geitland's healer—her mother, called Birte—stood there, her face flushed and her hair stuck in wet sweeps over her forehead. She had been at the fire, probably boiling some new potion.

"Öhm!" she exclaimed upon seeing the girl Astrid held. She moved her substantial body out of the way, and Astrid pushed through, carrying the girl to the cot in the main room of her mother's house. When she laid her down, the girl moaned and clutched her side, where blood soaked her tunic.

Birte dried her hands and pushed Astrid out of the way. "Another? You push these girls too hard, daughter. If you are not careful, one will die from your training soon."

"If they would die in training, then they are not fit for battle."

After she turned eyes full of weary displeasure on her daughter, Birte bent to the girl and plucked at her tunic. "Let me see, child." She lifted the coarsely woven fabric and showed a wide, deep wound. She had been slashed with a true sword, sharpened for battle.

Astrid had been training shieldmaidens for years, and she knew her work. There was little to be learned batting sticks at one another. She taught her charges the way she had been taught: with sharpened weapons. They learned because their lives depended on it.

Her mother knew that, and also knew that Astrid's shieldmaidens had brought great honor on themselves and on her. But it was true that this year, there had been more injuries. Astrid blamed the crop of new fighters, who were softer than any she'd known before. In the past, young women had come to her with some fighting skill already. All boys, and many girls, in their world were taught to defend themselves as soon as they could wield a weapon.

But in the past few years, with Geitland basking in great prosperity, people had grown soft. They had only raided once each of the past three summers. Each raid had brought so much treasure that everyone had more than they needed, and the appetite for the fight had dwindled as warriors grew rich and drunk and made their women fat with their children.

If not for the sneak attack during the winter from an inland clan, which had shaken all of Geitland up and awakened their bloodlust as well as depleted some stores, Astrid doubted the people of Geitland would have had the interest to raid at all this summer.

But they did. In fact, Leif, Geitland's great jarl, and Vali, the jarl of Karlsa, Leif's good friend, and his northernmost ally, planned to raid again together this summer, in a daring journey to the other side of the fertile land they had plundered so fruitfully for the past four summers.

Anglia.

For this new, bold raid, a long voyage in new water, to new land, her shieldmaidens could not have any softness in them. They would need all their wits, all their strength. They would need to turn their hearts and bodies to stone and iron.

As Astrid had, long ago.

She watched as her mother pressed her fingers along the girl's wound. When the girl whimpered, Birte shushed her, her voice and breath both crooning softly. These soft touches and sounds were not the kind of mothering Astrid had grown up with, and she felt a pluck of irritation at the bleeding girl.

Then her mother pushed a finger into the wound, and the girl screamed.

Astrid scowled at the sound.

Her mother sucked the blood from her finger. "You are fortunate, child. There is no greater damage than this slice. I will close it, and you will heal." She turned back to Astrid and waved her hand toward the door. "Schas, daughter! I have no need of you. You have done enough, I think."

Dismissed, Astrid left without another word and headed for the great hall. She had no more need to be there than her mother had need of her. The girl was of no more interest to her. She would make no shieldmaiden.

A true shieldmaiden closed her mouth against her pain.

~oOo~

Winter had crept away, and the afternoon bore the warm promise of dawning summer. The door and windows of the great hall had been thrown open. The night would likely freeze again, the sun was still young and its warmth did not last long, but for now they could enjoy the air and light.

As Astrid came to the main doors, a trio of young goatlings trotted out on their stiff legs, bleating. Right behind them, laughing as he tried to catch one, was Magni, Leif's son, born of his second wife, Olga. He had five years, and he had grown wilder with each of them. He was a goodhearted boy, and robust, but he was undisciplined.

Astrid had never borne a child, and she cared not to do so. She had never had a husband or a man promised to her, and she cared not about that, either. When she wanted a man, she had one. When she was done with him, she went away from him.

She wanted no man to seed her. A shieldmaiden who mated and bore children was a shieldmaiden no longer. A mother was bound to the hearth, to tend to the needs of others during her years of greatest strength. Such was not the life for Astrid.

Her lack of experience about children or parenting did not stop her from judging the parents she knew, however. She kept her mouth closed, but she judged nonetheless.

Leif and Olga, in her estimation, were soft. Olga's mothering was sweet songs and gentle kisses. Leif's fathering was play and laughter. Having five years, Magni was old enough to begin to be taught the ways of their world, which was a harsh place of long winter and cold iron and steel.

Instead, he was being shown a world of love and warmth and joy. Without hard training to forge his will, he would make no good jarl to sit in his father's place one day.

Astrid doubted that Leif would ever be challenged for his seat; he was revered as jarl, he had earned the seat in battle, and he would hold it until his death. But he was not immortal, and his son—if Magni were not challenged even before he could claim his father's seat, Astrid believed he would be challenged shortly thereafter. And he would be killed.

Unless he found his stone and iron before that day.

She watched the boy dive for a goatling, his blonde hair flying. He missed, landing in the dusty dirt with a gleeful shout, then jumped up and ran again. All around him, people at work made way for the jarl's son, his only living child.

Leif had put in the ground six children, his first wife, and the unborn son she'd carried. Olga had thought herself unable to bear Leif a child, until she'd borne their son. Perhaps there was good cause in that for the way Magni was indulged. Good cause, perhaps, but not good sense.

Astrid shook her head and went into the hall to discuss with Leif their upcoming travel to Karlsa, where they would make their plans for this great raid.

~oOo~

Vali, Jarl of Karlsa, strode down the pier to Leif, and the two men clasped arms and then embraced warmly. Though Leif was a large man among their people, Vali stood taller and wider. He was the largest man Astrid had ever known. His size and power, his ferocity and skill in battle, and his endurance had made him a renowned warrior. His steady hand, keen mind, and warm heart had made him, like Leif, an esteemed leader.

Vali's wife, Brenna, known as the God's-Eye, who had once been a legendary shieldmaiden, stood behind her husband, their three children around her. When Vali and Leif had made their greeting, Leif moved on to Brenna, wrapping his arms around her. She released the hand of Ylva, her youngest, so that she could hold him. At the same time, Vali embraced Olga, who, with Magni, had joined them on this brief journey north.

Then the women embraced and cooed over their children. Brenna and Vali's oldest, a girl, Solveig, had six years. Håkon, their son, was only half a year younger than Magni, so had

15

near five years. The three of them greeted each other like old friends and ran off toward town, their parents calling after them warnings to be careful, as if every eye in the town would not be mindful of the jarls' children.

Brenna and Vali's youngest, Ylva, still bore the round cheeks and wispy locks of infancy and could not have had more than three years. With wide, still eyes, she studied the adults as they spoke together. Vali swept his youngest girl into his arms, and she tucked her fair head under his dark beard.

Still in the ship, Astrid watched all that friendship and family with an evaluative eye. There was no denying the greatness of either man, or of Brenna. But the men were building on their legend, adding tales to their story. Brenna had given over to breeding and had not raided for many years, since they had traveled for the last time to Estland. There, they had met Olga, Leif's wife. And there, Vali had wed the great God's-Eye and turned a shieldmaiden into a broodmare.

She did not understand the impulse. The children were well-made and good-featured, yes, and she supposed there was the drive to leave one's blood behind after death. But she had admired the God's-Eye as a great warrior, and here she stood, in a hangerock fastened with bejeweled brooches, smiling up at the man who had sheathed her sword when he'd sheathed himself in her.

At the intimate image that accompanied that impatient thought, Astrid scanned the people of Karlsa who stood along the shore, watching the welcoming of the Jarl of Geitland. She did not see the face she wanted. When she joined Leif in Karlsa, she coupled with Jaan, with whom she'd often coupled in Estland as well. He was good company, well built, and a fine rut. Usually, he was at the shore for the welcome, but on this day he was not.

She found herself disappointed. No matter; she was sure he would show himself.

Vali handed his daughter to Leif, then turned and smiled at Astrid. "Will you stand there glowering, my friend, or will you join us?"

He held his large hand out as if he meant to help her onto the pier. She gave him the smile he sought, and she joined her friends, but she did not take his hand.

~oOo~

"Again, you would have us be farmers? Was not our failure in Estland lesson enough?" Astrid slapped her hand on the hide before them, covered with thin lines and small pictures. A 'map,' it was. She was still skeptical of them. It seemed to her that to use such a thing for navigation was to trust someone they did not know to create an image of a place they had not seen.

The sun and the stars. The wind. Her own eyes. Her own feet. These were things she could trust to show her the way.

Vali leveled sharp blue eyes at Astrid. "Estland did not fail because we could not farm. Estland failed because we were betrayed. By the jarl *you'd* sworn fealty to."

"Leif and your wife had sworn to him as well." She should not have brought up Estland. Vali always harkened back to Åke when that time was raised in disagreement. But he wanted to carve a settlement from this new raid, and that was folly. Astrid tried another tack. "To the point: none among us is a farmer. We were not farmers in Estland. Why would we settle land we do not know?"

"We *do* know it. We have explored well inland and taken great mountains of treasure from these kingdoms of Anglia. We know it is lush and green." Vali leaned back. "You are right. I have no wish to be a farmer. My duty is here, in Karlsa. My home." He reached over and took his wife's hand. "*Our*

17

home. But there are those among us who would seek to make a life in that greener, warmer place. Raiders who *are* farmers, and would rather sow the earth with seed than with blood."

Then they were not raiders, not truly. No matter their skill with a blade.

Astrid turned to Leif. "And you? You think this is wise?"

"I think that we should see what we see in this new place. With each raid, resistance has grown, and the battles have been harder won. So we move to the west, where they might not expect us. If we can take the land we need, we should take it. We take all that we can claim. Why would we not take the land as well?"

"Because we are not people of that place. It is not our home." The words churned from Astrid's mouth, through teeth clenched in frustration. Their last attempt at settling had been a terrible disaster, one she meant never to see repeated.

"It shall be, when we make it so."

Brenna had spoken those words, and Astrid turned her frustration on the God's-Eye, "*We?*"

The woman who had been a great shieldmaiden turned a look on Astrid that would have made a softer soul quake, full of fire and fury. The God's-Eye stare. Brenna's strange right eye might well have held the power of the Allfather, and Astrid gave it the respect it was due. She could not hold Brenna's gaze.

"Yes, *we*. I shall raid with my husband, my friends, and my people."

The God's-Eye would be a shieldmaiden once more? Was she fit, after so many years with a child at her teat?

It wasn't a question Astrid would ask. If she was not fit, then she would die in battle, and that was none of Astrid's concern.

As long as Vali wasn't weakened by his concern for his woman.

Astrid could meet Vali's eyes, so she did, though she was faced with a furrowed brow as he agreed with his wife. "Brenna's mother will tend to the children, and Bjarke"—he nodded at the man beside Leif—"will hold Karlsa in our absence. His woman is bringing forth their child soon, so he will not be with us."

"Ah!" Leif exclaimed and slapped Bjarke on the back, changing the mood of the room at once. "That is good news, friend."

Bjarke grinned. "I am sorry to miss this raid, but I am honored to have your trust to lead in your stead, Vali."

And again, Astrid was surrounded by people celebrating the thought of a coming child, with no concern that they had lost a strong warrior to that endeavor.

~oOo~

That night, in Karlsa's great hall, which was far less great than Geitland's, the people of Karlsa feted Leif and Olga and the rest of their guests. After a few horns of mead, Astrid began looking in earnest for Jaan. She was restless and irritated, and she wanted to expend some of that energy.

Wandering through the hall, pushing away drunken hands that sought the same thing she did, Astrid pulled up short as Solveig, Magni, and Håkon ran across her path, holding hands like a chain and giggling.

She tried to remember if she had ever played as these children always seemed to. If she had, her mind could not recall it. She had been raised in a house that had been always full of the ill. She had been raised to be quiet, to be helpful, or to be sent away. And when she was sent away, it had been to her father, a cart maker. With him, she'd learned hard, physical work, and to be stoic in any discomfort.

Her parents had tended her well, kept her fed, clothed, shod, and warm. Though they had been disappointed to have had only one child and a girl at that, she supposed her father had loved her in his way, and she knew her mother did in her way.

But no, she did not think she had ever run giggling through the hall.

The mead had made her thoughts maudlin. She needed a good rut. But Jaan was not in the hall, and there were no other men of as much interest as he would be.

She went outside, into the bright light of a nearly full moon. The night was warm enough that her breath didn't plume from her mouth. This summer might be long. That was good; this year, she hoped for more than one raid. Her joints felt stiff with idleness.

She took a long, deep breath and let it out, blowing it toward the heavens.

"Astrid."

She wheeled and saw Jaan in the shadows along the side of the building. With a smile of pleasure anticipated, she went toward him. "Jaan. It has been a long while."

"A long while, yes. You look well."

He'd taken a step back as she'd neared. Surprised, her battle senses tingling lightly at the suggestion that all was not right, she stopped. "As do you. You have been keeping yourself from me today. With purpose, I think." Understanding had dawned as she'd spoken, while he lingered in the shadows, holding himself off.

"I am wed."

She laughed. Of course. Why not he, as with all others in her life. "Then glad tidings. I wish you and your beloved many fat babies. Good night, Jaan."

Feeling a sour turmoil in her belly that she didn't understand, Astrid turned and took a step toward the hall. She would find one of the men with the grasping hands and mount him. One ride was as good as another.

That wasn't true, of course. But it would be true tonight. With enough mead, it would be true.

"Astrid, hold."

She stopped but didn't turn back.

"I'm sorry to tell you in this way."

"It matters not, Jaan. I hope you are happy."

"I am."

There was nothing more to be said, so Astrid left him in his shadow and went back to find a horn of mead and a man to mount.

PART ONE
COURAGE

1

Ulv charged at Astrid, bringing his sword around high, going for her shoulder. She threw up her shield and ducked, slashing at his leg. He aborted his swing to block her blow and then reeled back, panting and grinning.

Astrid glared at him—he wasn't supposed to be enjoying this—and turned to her charges. "If you turn your back on your opponent, or if you swing your blade too wildly, then you make of yourself a target. As women, we have an advantage: we're smaller. Men think that makes us the easier opponent, but they're wrong. They underestimate us. And their greater size makes them slow. We can be quicker. Do not serve your heart up on a platter. Blades and shields front. Steps to the side. Make yourself compact. Go under. Bring his legs from under him, and then deal the killing blow."

Pacing along the line of young shieldmaidens before her, she formed her face into a fierce scowl, the expression she used in battle. She stopped before a particular woman and focused her battle face on her. "The next of you who swings her blade so wildly that she turns her back to her opponent will fight me. Unshielded."

She stepped back. "Now. One on one. Again."

As the untested warriors turned on each other in pairs, Ulv stepped up behind her. His broad body made a shadow over her shoulder.

"You are hard on them."

"I am always hard on them. Soft warriors are no more than corpses that have yet to rot."

"Harder on these than most, I think."

Perhaps she was. They had come to her softer than most, and if they meant to join them soon on this great raid, then they had to harden more quickly. Irritated that Ulv, who himself was more scholar than warrior, found himself with so much to say about her training, she turned from her trainees and gave him her battle face.

He laughed and stepped back. "I meant no offense, Astrid."

"What have you to say about the way I train? You who would rather sit in the hall than join us."

Like Bjarke in Karlsa, Ulv would take Leif's place in in Geitland. In truth, not even that. Olga would lead while her husband was raiding, but she did not feel that she had the knowledge to address every possible concern that might arise, so Ulv had been tasked as her advisor.

Ulv was the last surviving adult son of Åke, the jarl who had been defeated by Vali and Leif after he had betrayed them all. Ulv's older brothers had been relieved of their heads in the coup, but Ulv had sworn to Leif and been spared. Not only spared, but brought into the hall as a trusted friend.

Years had passed since his father's ignominious death, and Ulv had, Astrid supposed, proved himself both loyal and worthy. He was a good warrior, smart, strong, and brave, but he did not relish the fight. He preferred to use his mind rather than his arm.

Neither was his temperament suited to battle. The fire in his belly was well banked. Astrid could not recall a time that she had seen him truly enraged or impassioned. He was steady and calm, far more likely to laugh than to roar.

Thus, he didn't take umbrage at her sharp words. Instead, his grin settled into a patient smile. "I would. You have enough lust for battle for us both." His smile quirked up, and he leaned in. "But I have other lusts I would share with you."

Ulv was a handsome man, and Astrid enjoyed coupling with him. Unlike some men who sought her out, he had the same interest in her that she had in him: as a friend with a comely body. His heart was engaged elsewhere and so no trouble for her.

He was in love with his stepmother, Turid. His father's youngest widow, Turid was younger than Ulv. She had left Geitland with her fellow widow, Hilde, after Åke's defeat and death.

Ulv had searched more than a year before finding his stepmothers and their young children, his half-siblings. Now, he went to them once a season and brought them supplies to keep their lives steady.

Astrid held back a quarter of her trust from Ulv on this point. Though he had sworn to Leif, his youngling siblings, Hilde's four daughters and Turid's two sons, had not. When they grew old enough to mount a fight to avenge their father, their connection to Ulv, and his connection to Leif, might well be trouble, whether Ulv intended it or not. His love for the boys' mother would only complicate the problem and indict him.

The children were yet young, so for now it was a problem to know, not to solve. But Astrid never let herself forget it. Leif actively rejected her reservation, which was folly. Men could be so arrogant and complacent in their own sense of rightness and trust. So she would keep Ulv close, and she would pay attention. And in the meanwhile, she would enjoy his body when the wish moved her.

But now, she had other concerns, like the women flailing at each other with swords.

With her hand on his chest, she shoved him back. "Seek me later. For now, I have no more need of you."

He put his hand over his chest in a gentle parody of hurt feeling and stepped back. "You deal me the killing blow, shieldmaiden." Then he turned, his loose, golden hair swinging, and sauntered away.

~oOo~

While Astrid considered her next move, Magni fidgeted on his father's knee. Leif picked up one of the pieces he'd claimed from Astrid and handed it to his son, who began to bounce it up Leif's arm as if it were a toy man. Astrid focused on the game and closed off her irritation.

"Watch, Magni. Do you see what Astrid is trying to do?"

Lifting her eyes from the board, Astrid glared at her jarl. "She would be doing it, if your father weren't trying to distract her. He's not playing with a fair hand, Magni."

Leif chuckled. "And I thought you believed that winning was the only rule, in battle, life, or Hnefatafl. Is that not your great wisdom?"

"What is *wisdom*?" the boy asked.

Astrid moved and put Leif's king in jeopardy. She leaned back with a smirk, but Leif's attention was on his son.

"Wisdom is knowing what you know and also knowing that you cannot know all. It's seeing as far as you can see and knowing that there is more to see beyond that. It's knowing when you can succeed on your own, and when you can succeed only with friends at your back and at your side. It's knowing who your friends are, and who might be made friends, and who will never be friends."

28

Magni gave his father a serious look for a moment, and there was the glimmer of the quiet, watchful infant he'd once been. For a moment, Astrid saw the man he might someday become, more like his father than she might have thought. A man who would make such an answer, who would understand wisdom in that way.

Then he walked his toy over his father's face, and the moment was broken.

With his turn up, Leif shifted Magni on his knee and focused on the board. After he'd considered it a while, his forehead creased in a frown, and Astrid couldn't help but smile. They'd been playing Hnefatafl together for as long as Leif had been jarl. Often, while they played, they discussed problems in the town or plans for the future. Though Astrid had minimal interest in the minutiae of leadership, Leif liked to work out his thinking on the ears of people he trusted, and take all of their thoughts and reactions into consideration. Olga was his most trusted advisor in town matters, and Astrid his most trusted in matters of raiding and battle.

More than once, she'd wondered whether Leif worked out his battle strategy on the board itself.

He won their contests far more often than Astrid did— Hnefatafl was a game of strategy, and she was a fighter; strategy made her impatient—but she had wedged him into a predicament on this board. Lately, she had wearied of losing so often and had made an effort to slow down and see more than the fight directly before her.

He looked up. "You are changing the way you play this game."

"Are you worried?" She couldn't resist the grin that lifted her cheeks high.

"Watch that you don't become smug. There is fight left in me yet." He moved, protecting his king for another turn, possibly two, but Astrid thought this game might fall her way in the end.

"Mamma!" Magni shouted and scooted off his father's lap. He ran to the front of the hall, and Leif stood, smiling. Astrid turned to see Olga walking in from the front door. One of the servant girls came in behind her and then moved past, her head tipped in respectful deference, on her way to the kitchens.

Astrid believed that people should strive to be the best at what they did and to be productive among their people, thus she had a great respect for Leif's wife. Olga was a small, slight woman, and no warrior, but she was strong in a way of her own, and she strove to be the best help she could be to those around her. She had been a healer when Astrid had first known her, and she had been also a slave. She had given aid and succor to all who needed her, even those who had bound her with rope.

Now, as Leif's wife, she'd become an important counselor to the people of Geitland. All knew that if they came to the jarl with a problem, he would give them good aid. But his wife would give them understanding and empathy and soothe hearts as she offered advice. It was a thing Astrid had no talent for herself, to put herself in a stranger's place, but she admired it greatly in Olga, and she admired the effect she had on their people.

That was not to say that the effect she had on their jarl was not often frustrating. Olga's very presence drew Leif to her like a beacon.

As Leif followed his son, Astrid complained, "The game is not over!" knowing well that it was. She shoved at the board, jostling the pieces from their places. Which mattered not.

~oOo~

That afternoon, Astrid felt the need for solitude, so she took her axe and sat near the shore, at the point where the forest claimed the coastline.

Though she enjoyed the company of her clanspeople, and she enjoyed drinking and carousing, she didn't enjoy aimlessness. Even in feasting and drinking, even in rutting, Astrid had to find a purpose in it. To expend restive energies. To celebrate. But not simply to fill an empty space. Empty spaces were the marks of indolence.

When those around her caroused because they thought they had nothing better to do, Astrid became impatient, and she sought solitude and activity.

Putting her back to the drone of a town shifting from work into aimlessness, she drew the blade against her whetstone.

Though the sword was a raider's first weapon, the weapon that could gain history and legacy and be passed down from one generation to the next, Astrid preferred her axe in battle. She was as deft with a sword as any man, but with an axe in her hands, she felt as though she were made of water and air, fluid and untouchable. The cutting edge might be smaller than a sword's, but it was more precise, its blows more decisive.

Behind her, the crunch of pebbles told of someone encroaching on her quiet moment, and she cast her eyes over her shoulder. Leif approached, alone. She offered no word of greeting but watched as he neared. He offered no word, either, and sat on the log beside her.

She went back to honing her blade. Leif looked out over the Geitland harbor, and for long minutes, they were simply quiet.

"You are vexed," he offered eventually.

"I'm not."

He didn't reply, but his chuckle served as rejoinder enough.

Though she had no need to be the last to speak, or the first, Astrid was not one to hold her tongue when speaking would serve her better. So she set her stone on its leather pouch, she laid her axe across her thighs, and she turned to her jarl. Her friend.

"I am tired of quiet. I need a fight."

"We sail in days, Astrid. A fight is coming. If this will be like our other western raids, the spoils will be magnificent."

"I care not about the spoils. We have enough already. We have too much, and it has made us less. We have grown soft here."

"We were not so soft that we were overtaken in the winter."

"But we were soft enough that a chieftain with no story thought he might try."

Leif sighed and turned back to contemplate the water. "What would you have me do, Astrid? We raid to bring health and wealth to our people. Would you call our successes failures instead?"

He was right, of course. People wanted this prosperity. This was what they had striven for, and it would be lunacy for Astrid to wish away her people's plenty so that she would not be bored. But it was much more than her own agitation.

"No. You are a great jarl, Leif. You have made Geitland great. We are all warmed in your light. But being warmed by you, the fires in people's own bellies have gone out. Well-fed warriors have no hunger. Without the will to kill, they will be killed."

"You think we're not battle-ready?"

"I think our warriors are well trained. I believe the gods sent the chieftain and his clan to us as a spark, to remind us that we aren't invulnerable and that we must be ready to fight. But are we? Some of us, yes. The core of us. But I fear that core will be ringed by the fallen bodies of those who fought without hunger."

"Would you have us stay home?"

"No. If we have need of nothing else, we have need of that lesson. But I would tell you to prepare to take many losses."

Astrid had returned her attention to her axe as she'd spoken, drawing a finger along the honed edge until she bled. She didn't turn to Leif, but she could feel his eyes on her.

"You are my strong right hand, Astrid. I esteem you as a great friend and a mighty warrior. And I know you're not so cold as you pretend. You would not sit here ready to sacrifice your clanspeople, your fellow warriors, for a lesson. But I think you know, in your heart, that you're wrong. We conscript no raiders. They come of their own will. Any who would volunteer for this raid would do so with fire in their bellies, even if those bellies are full of meat as well. And any shieldmaiden you would send forth will be fierce and bold as the best of the men. We are ready. We will be bold, and we will bring glory home."

He had said the thing that she truly feared, the thing she knew was at the heart of her disquiet. Now she turned to Leif and faced his dark blue eyes. "There was a time, before Vali and I carried that first great golden shield home to you, before Geitland was so powerful, before *you* were so powerful, when you spoke of honor, not glory. It was Åke who sought glory. Are you not better than he?"

33

Before Leif could answer, Astrid picked up her weapon and her stone and left him sitting alone at the edge of his empire.

~oOo~

In the hall, Astrid found Ulv. He was sitting amongst other men of an age, deep into their mead. She strode up, pushed herself between him and another man, and grabbed the horn from his hand, draining it. She had a need tonight to stop thinking. What she wanted instead was a drunken rut.

Ulv smiled up at her and didn't complain that she'd taken his drink. When she held it out, he hailed a servant girl to fill it full again.

She had been harsh in her words to Leif. He was not like Åke. In Åke's hall, the servant girls had been slaves, and the men had had free rein to take what they wanted from them. Though the full holding of Geitland still kept people in thrall, the town itself did not. Leif had freed his own slaves before he'd wed Olga. Once they were wed, Olga had campaigned hard, in her soft way, with the Geitlanders against keeping slaves. In the town, she had prevailed, but the farmers and people of the villages had been intractable.

Of his own accord, without his wife's guiding force, Leif had banned the raping of women and the harming of children and oldsters during raids. That had been an edict, not a consensus, and it had not gone down smoothly among warriors trained under Åke's lax eye, men who believed that it was as much a warrior's right to bury his sword of flesh into a vanquished body as to bury his sword of iron or steel.

There had been some harsh corrections of men who would not heed. Leif didn't make his sole word into law often, but when he did, he didn't countenance disobedience.

His only other edict was that any slaves that were taken might only be able-bodied and hearty men and women. Children could not be held in thrall. Neither could they, or the old or infirm, be slaughtered.

If their raids had not been so wildly prosperous, Astrid thought Leif might well have met an early challenge for his seat. But they had been. He had brought them great wealth and honor, and there were few grumblings now among men who had no thralls to force to their will.

Because freewomen could not be forced. A man who forced a freewoman, who treated her ill in any way, would know the wrath of the woman and the town behind her.

Astrid marveled at the women in the places they raided—weak and useless, the lot of them. Especially the women of Anglia, who were frail and limp, who cowered and wept when she and her clan came. Faced with a foe brandishing a blade, they didn't fight. They dropped to their knees and slammed their palms together. They turned their eyes up to the sky or the ceiling, and they spouted gibberish to their strange dead god, whose naked corpse they hung on their walls.

Those women could not know how lucky they were that Leif Olavsson and Vali Storm-Wolf led the raids that leveled their homes. Any other jarl would have taken far more from them. Any other jarl would have taken everything.

They could only have been luckier if they had lived in a world that expected them to fight and be their own strength.

After another horn of mead, Astrid pushed Ulv's hands to his sides and straddled him. His eyes flared wide, and his hands found her hips.

"You're hard for me, Ulv Åkesson."

He nodded, but he frowned. "I am. But I would you would not call me that."

35

He disliked that she so often drew notice to his lineage. But she would not forget who his father had been. "Is it not your name?"

"You know how I feel to be son to a man such as he. I would it were not my name."

"Then earn for yourself another. The Storm-Wolf wasn't born as such. He earned his name. He is another who wanted no connection to his past." She opened his breeches and found his sex, hot and thick. Their friends had continued to drink and talk and laugh, ignoring them. It was nothing for their people to couple in company. They did everything in company.

He groaned. "Still your mouth, woman." Fussing at her lacings, he threw his hands out in frustration. "Why will you not wear a hangerock? I would be deep inside you if I could get to you."

With a single exception—when Vali had wed Brenna in Estland—Astrid had not worn a gown since she had first picked up a sword. As Ulv well knew.

She bit his ear. "Grab a fur and carry me outside. The night is warm. We can be under the stars and I'll let you have me like a beast."

He groaned and stood up, taking her with him. She worked his sex while he shambled to the door, reaching down to take up a fur along the way.

When he laid the fur down on a soft patch on the berm near the pier and dropped with her down onto it, Astrid flipped hard, putting him on his back with a grunt. She would take him in like a beast, but first she would make him beg for it.

This was better. It did not warm her or soften her—Leif was wrong; she was exactly as cold as she seemed—but it satisfied her. And that was enough.

2

Leofric drew back his bow, sighted on the buck before him. He took the breath that would lock his aim. At the precise moment that he loosed the arrow, Dunstan whistled at his side.

The buck jolted at the sound, and the arrow that would have taken him in the eye buried itself in a tree instead.

Pulling another arrow from his quiver, Leofric nocked it, drew, and turned in the saddle, sighting his grinning friend. "I should kill you for that. A man who cheats has no honor, and a man with no honor has no claim to breath."

Without the slightest sign that he feared for his life, Dunstan shrugged. "Not cheating, Your Grace. *Conserving.* I only mean to be sure there are beasts left to be hunted." With a loaded lift of his eyebrow, he turned away from the arrow pointed at his face, to the gamekeeper behind them, his heavy horse pulling a litter with three bucks already. Two of which were Leofric's.

The Duke of Orenshire, second son of King Eadric of Mercuria, unnocked his arrow and returned it to the quiver. "I suppose greed doesn't do. And I've bested you in any case. Shall we return to the castle, then?"

At Dunstan's wry nod of agreement, Leofric slung his bow and turned his horse. With the gamekeeper following at a respectful distance, the Duke and the Earl of Tarrin began the hour's ride home.

~oOo~

Leofric laughed at his friend's moaning. "Well, she's a comely lass, at the least. And I suppose you're not an ogre."

In truth, Dunstan was renowned in the kingdom for his personal beauty. The young ladies of the court threw themselves at his feet even before their noble parents could heave them at him. He was considered more of a catch than Leofric himself was. Dunstan's parents had finally negotiated a match with the Duchess of Avalia. Though his intended was very young, it was an excellent match for him, and a fine one for her as well.

"She's frail and pious, and she'll spend all her time on her knees—and I don't mean at my feet."

"That, my friend, is what kitchen wenches are for. And certain ladies in waiting."

Both men laughed, but Dunstan was not yet finished with his complaint. "I don't see how you've escaped the wedding noose for so long. You've near thirty years!"

"It's the blessing of the second son. My father's attention is on my brother."

Dunstan shuddered. "My sympathy is with the prince."

The crown prince, Eadric, son of Eadric, had married and buried three women. The first, a match of love as well as politics, had died in childbirth and taken the child, a son, with her. The second had lived for nearly two years before she'd taken a fever. She hadn't been seeded in that time. The third had choked to death at the wedding feast.

A legend, more like a superstition, had risen up around Leofric's older brother, and finding a likely match for a fourth wife had proved difficult, even though he was heir to the throne. Noblemen thought their daughters might be better matched with men of perhaps slightly lower standing with a higher chance that their daughters would live.

Three years had passed since the last princess's death. Their father was consumed by the mission to get his eldest son married and producing an heir.

The king had not much interest in Leofric's fate on that point. His second son was not pious enough, or serious enough, or anything enough to warrant much attention, except to increase his urgency in getting Eadric an heir. Once Eadric had issue, Leofric was half sure he himself could wed one of the kitchen wenches and his father would barely notice, so long as she'd been baptized.

He had no intention of marrying a kitchen wench, or any other wench, for that matter. He would have to eventually, he had no doubt. But so long as he could dodge duty's long claws, he meant to remain his own man and rut where he wished to rut.

Dunstan fell into a morose silence as he contemplated his eventual fate at the altar, and the men rode quietly through the woods for a long spell.

They weren't yet in sight of the castle walls when a flurry of activity—quick and gone—caught Leofric's attention, and he pulled up his horse. Dunstan stopped as well.

Leofric took his bow and nocked an arrow, but before he could draw, he heard a small sound that he recognized at once. With a glance at Dunstan, who shook his head and rolled his eyes, Leofric put away his weapon and dismounted. He heard Dunstan send the gamekeeper on and then dismount as well.

He sneaked into the brush, picking his way carefully, until he came upon the clump of flowering shrub at which he'd placed the sound. Reaching over, he grabbed hold of coarse wool and pulled.

As he lifted her from the ground, the girl squealed and then giggled—a muted version of that giggle was the sound he'd heard.

She was filthy, dressed in tattered peasant's rags, her long, honey brown hair snarled and festooned with leaves and bits of twigs. Leofric set her on her feet, and she grinned up at him.

"Dreda," he scolded his sister. "Someday, Father will act on his threats, and you'll live out the rest of your childhood locked in the tower."

Dreda was much younger than her brothers; she hadn't yet seen her tenth year. She'd been born late in their mother's life—too late. Her birth had been the end of the queen.

Their father had named her for the mother she'd never known, and he doted on her almost as if the spirit of his beloved had entered their daughter. She was indulged shamelessly by all the men in her life—and she was wild and intractable because of it.

But she was a delight to them all, and none had the will to see any emotion in her eyes but joy. So her predilection for slipping the attention of her governess and escaping the castle's protection had gone largely uncorrected, except for the threat that she'd be locked away in a tower—and for her governess's fretful certainty that some day her own head would be lost.

Leofric scanned the woods around them and saw no other sign of life. "Are you this far from the castle entirely alone?"

"No one would come with me this far." Once free of the castle, she played with some of the peasant children, none of whom were, it seemed, as intrepid as she.

"Does it never occur to you that the caution of others might do you, as well?"

"You're out this far."

He crouched down and picked the twigs from her hair. "I am a man grown, I'm armed, and I'm not alone."

"If you would take me with you, then. I'd be good, I promise."

Brushing the dirt from her nose, Leofric stood and lifted his sister into his arms. "A hunt is no place for a fine lady such as yourself. And where did you get these rags?"

Under the dirt, her cheeks pinked. "They were on a line. I wanted to be harder to find."

His admiration for her sneaky mind was tempered by surprise. "You *stole* them? You stole from a peasant?" He put as much censure as he could muster into his words.

And saw it all strike its target. She blinked, and then recovered. "I left my dress and shoes! They're worth much more than these! The shoes have pearls!"

With a great, dramatic sigh, Leofric conveyed his disappointment as he carried Dreda back to his horse. Dunstan, who'd held their horse's reins, forced the grin from his face and bowed as if he were at court. "Your Grace."

"Lord Tarrin," Dreda answered, trying and failing to sound regal. In that moment, she was simply a little girl who'd been caught misbehaving.

Leofric set his sister on his saddle and mounted behind her. By the time he was settled, he could no longer withstand the sad looks, so when she fussed about being placed sidesaddle, like a proper lady, he relented and lifted her so she could sit astride.

He put his arm around her and held her close, and when she asked to run, he kicked his horse to its fastest stride. She laughed, her mussed hair flying in his face, and he held her more tightly and laughed with her.

~oOo~

At the castle, Leofric left Dunstan to hand off the horses while he whisked Dreda in through a service door and delivered her to her frantic governess.

"Does his majesty know?" he asked the woman.

She shook her head. "She was resting. I thought she was having her afternoon rest! When I went to wake her, she was away. I've been looking. I was…I was on my way to tell the king. *Please* forgive me, Your Grace."

Leofric suspected that the governess would have combed every single inch of the castle, the stables, and the bailey—twice—before she'd have risked the wrath of the king again, and he didn't hold it against her. Dreda was a handful, and it was only in hindsight that she cared for the impact her actions had on others. Then she cared deeply.

He set a comforting hand on the governess's shoulder. "Fear not. All is well. We will all be well served should His Majesty be kept innocent of the day's adventure."

"Thank you, Your Grace." She curtsied low. "You have a good heart, if I may say it."

He crouched to his sister. "You should be clean and proper and lovely by dinner, don't you agree?"

Dreda nodded. "Yes, Leofric." She threw her arms around his neck, and he embraced her. "Please may I ride with you again soon? That was wonderful! My belly felt like fire!"

He couldn't tell her no. "Someday, poppet. Go now, and wash. Be kind to your governess, who has had a much more trying afternoon than you."

~oOo~

After he left Dreda, Leofric skulked through the service passages of the castle, seeking to avoid his father or his brother, or any other man who might feel the need to address him if they met. He was headed to his own chambers to wash and dress for dinner.

Just as he arrived at the service door to the corridor of the royal residence, that door opened, and young Edith came through. Seeing him, she nearly dropped her load of soiled linens in her surprised haste to curtsey.

"Forgive me, Your Grace," she mumbled. Women were falling all over themselves on this day to seek his forgiveness.

"Edith. I should be asking *your* forgiveness. I am in your way."

"No, Your Grace. Never."

Edith was a lovely young thing, with wisps of soft yellow hair peeking from her prim head covering and a lithe, pert body under her servant's gown. He'd seen all of her on a few bold occasions when he'd pulled her into his rooms and kept her far longer than he ought to have.

Today, he had no more time for that than she. But he was feeling high-spirited, from the successful hunt on a lovely day, and from riding with Dreda, not to mention being a paragon of chivalry and goodheartedness, and standing before him, with her head kept deferentially low, was a likely wench at his beck and call. More than that, she was willing.

He pulled the linens from her grasp and tossed them to the stone floor of the stairwell.

"Your Grace," she protested mildly, but didn't offer more than that reluctant gasp.

"Correct," he said and turned her around, putting her to the wall. "I am your grace."

With one hand, he lifted her skirts, and with the other, he unlaced his breeches and released his sex. Kicking her legs wide, he pushed a hand between her legs and made sure his passage would be easy. He grinned when he found that it would be, and he pushed into a slick sheath, covering her gasp with a groan.

He took her hard and fast. When he spent, he pulled out and did so over the pale globes of her bottom, then picked up one of the linens from the discarded pile and wiped her clean.

He was a gentleman, after all. And chivalrous and goodhearted as well.

He sent her down the stairs with her bundle restored to her arms, and he went smiling to his chamber to dress for dinner.

~oOo~

The evening meal on an unremarkable day such as this one, with no guests at court of especial note, was a comparatively relaxed affair. There were no speeches or great toasts, no meticulously designed program of bards and troubadours. Simply the king's musicians, playing in the careful way all court musicians seemed to cultivate, to be both entertaining and unobtrusive. The bishop gave his blessing, and the king opened the meal, and the nobles at court proceeded to fill their faces with the king's food.

Always there were people at court who sought the king's attention, or sought to avoid it, and Leofric, from his vantage at the head table, watched the political acrobatics. Everyone arrayed before them—and, as the head table was set on a dais, below them—was in some way performing. No one who sat before the king in any capacity forgot that fact for even a moment—and on those few occasions when some hapless lord went too far into his cups and did, he rued the day. If he were lucky to live long enough to do so.

His father was a godly man, who took the counsel of the bishop above all others, and this court was sedate compared to others. A man too far in his cups had likely already taken the ill notice of his father.

It was why Leofric had been considered such a disappointment for as long as he could remember. He did his duty to God, gave his regular confession and did his regular penance. It was only that his confessions, and his penance, were typically…*longer* than most. He enjoyed a good time, and that good time was not spent on his knees. Not unless there was a lovely pert bottom before him.

Without clear proof, Leofric was quite certain that Father Francis, known more formally as His Excellency, the Bishop of Mercuria, did not find the seal of confession as sacred as one would hope. The king seemed to know much more about his adventures than was otherwise reasonable.

Father Francis, in Leofric's opinion, was an overblown prat who wielded far too much influence over the kingdom. But the realm had been in peace for some years now, allied with its neighbors and protected by distance and difficult seas from the barbarian invasions their more eastward fellows had suffered. When their allies had been beset, they'd sent soldiers to their aid, Eadric and Leofric included.

The result, however, of the weakening of their allies was the strengthening of Mercuria. Without mounting any offensive, without losing any alliance, King Eadric had become the most powerful monarch in Anglia. He gave glory to God— and by extension to Father Francis—for that.

So the fat priest in his rich robes sat at the head table with the king's family, and Leofric tried not to be caught, by anyone but Francis himself, sneering at the lout's bulbous red nose that spoke of too much time 'blessing' the communion wine.

A gentle tug on his sleeve drew his attention to Dreda, sitting at his side. She was dressed now as the young princess she was, in a gown of pale blue and crème silk with silver stitching. Her hair was done in an intricate braid, with tiny pearls woven into the strands. A marked improvement over the urchin he'd sneaked into the castle that afternoon.

"What is it, Your Grace?" They were whispering and probably needn't have stood on ceremony, but he enjoyed needling her when she was dressed as such a proper young miss.

"I don't like this." she whispered, poking with a golden knife at the aubergine stuffed with…something. He didn't like it, either. But he knew that a royal who didn't clean his plate was saying something to, and about, the cook who'd prepared the food on it. He liked the cook. He liked her daughter, Edith, even more.

"I don't like it either, but it would hurt Mildred's feelings if we sent back plates with food."

"Can't we leave it for the hounds?" The hunting dogs got the scraps from each meal.

He shook his head. "Look at all the people before us, Dreda. Do you see how often they look up at our table?" She looked, and then nodded. "We are the royal family. They look to us to know what is good and what is right. So everything we do, they take a message from. Would you say to them that Mildred is a poor cook whose food is only fit for dogs?"

She turned to him, her eyes wide. They were the dark blue of stormy seas. Their mother's eyes. And his own. "No. I don't wish to make Mildred unhappy. She makes me honey cakes whenever I ask."

"I like Mildred, too. So we must eat the food that she toiled to make for us, even if we wish it were honey cakes instead."

Dreda sighed at her plate, then cut a small piece of aubergine and put it in her mouth. Leofric watched as she chewed daintily and swallowed, and he saw her understand without being told that she shouldn't pull a face.

"Well done, little sister. You will make a fine queen someday."

"I don't wish to be a queen," she whispered back. "I want to be a pirate!"

In her elegant dress and coiled hair sprinkled with pearls, with her big blue eyes and tiny bow mouth, that declaration sounded charmingly, positively ridiculous, and Leofric laughed, full and loud, before he could catch it back.

Dreda smiled in the vague, faltering way that said she had not quite understood what was so funny, and that made him laugh still more. Below them, the people at court began a halting chorus of laughs, too.

He despised that. They had no idea what he'd laughed at, but they were so conditioned to share the emotions of the royal family that they picked up whatever sign they might get. Since it had been he who'd laughed and not his father, the chorus never took over the whole room. For a moment, there was confusion. In the way that it died out into silence, he knew that when he turned to his father, he would meet a scowl.

And he did. Two scowls, both of them named Eadric.

His brother asked, "Would you share with us the jape?" and Leofric wanted to kick him under the table. He was only four years older than Leofric, but he was the dutiful son, pious and studious. Even as a young boy, he'd never found trouble. Indeed, once Leofric had been old enough to find it, his brother had usually been the one to expose him for it. That remained true.

Their father, aware of the eyes on them at all times, did not countenance strong showing of feeling in public.

Mercy, Leofric missed his mother. The queen had softened all their father's hard edges. She had been light and sweet and loving, and she'd pulled the best of her husband out into the fresh air. Since she'd died, the king, a good man and a great king nonetheless, had turned nearly to stone.

"Forgive me, Papa," Dreda said. "I told Leofric about puppies I saw playing in the bailey today, and I made him laugh."

Leofric was properly stunned. She had lied for him. She had shown the intuition to know why their father was scowling and how to change the tableau.

Oh, she would be a great queen indeed if she was learning to manage social drama so well already.

In public, they were to address each other formally. Only in private might they use given names and informal address. But the one crack in their father's stone was Dreda. His scowl melted away, and he smiled instead. So did Eadric.

"Well enough, then, my light. But let us hold back such stories for a better time from henceforth, yes?"

She dipped in her seat, a piece of a curtsey. "Yes, Papa. Please forgive me."

"Of course I do."

They all returned to their meal, and the buzz of the room returned to its normal flow. After a moment, Leofric felt a tug on his sleeve again, and he leaned down.

"Will you take me to Father Francis after the meal?" she whispered.

"Why?"

"I told a lie. What if I die in the night? I need to confess."

The little girl who wanted to be a pirate, stole peasant's clothes, sneaked away from her governess and otherwise ran circles around the rules was afraid of the tiny untruth she'd told to protect him. He might have laughed again if not for the real worry on her face.

An intense wave of love for his sister moved through him. She had been brave to lie, when the sin of it frightened her so.

"You will not die tonight, I promise. You will live a long and wonderful life full of adventures, I promise. And God doesn't mind lies told to protect another person. That is a kindness, and God doesn't punish kindness. You have nothing to confess, I promise."

Not if she didn't think the rest of her day worthy of a prayer or two.

"You're certain?"

He put his hand over his heart. "I solemnly swear."

"That's all right, then." She sighed and went back to her aubergine. "I wish there really had been puppies."

3

The ships—four majestic, beautiful skeids that Leif and Vali had commissioned for their first westward raid the year Magni was born and that had carried great bounty home every summer since—were laded and ready. On the shore, the raiders trained together for the last time before they would set sail in the morning.

Though the sounds of steel and iron clashing and colliding on linden shields thundered and rang through the air, this training was more play than anything, Astrid noticed. Anticipation for the coming sail, for the feast that would precede it and the raid that would follow it, had spirits high. Even those who would wait behind in Geitland were feeling glad and hopeful. No raider had found Valhalla for three summers, and the people were beginning to feel invulnerable. There was little worry about sending even the young raiders off for their first glory.

Astrid remained concerned, but she had expressed her opinion, and Leif had heard it. Their preparations had been more serious since she'd spoken with him at the shoreline, and Leif's tone among them all had been as well. He spoke again of honor, and of Valhalla, and the raiders had trained with more intent.

But today, with the sun shining brightly over sparkling blue water, and the skeids gleaming at the piers, the sound of swords, axes, and shields clashing made a chorus of celebration.

Rather than engage in the play herself, Astrid prowled the edge, watching her shieldmaidens, satisfying herself that those about to raid for the first time were as ready as she could hope they would be. Each successive raid had seen more women aboard the ships, and this year was no different. Astrid was, to some extent, responsible for them all—she certainly felt she was.

The young ones, and the seasoned ones as well, had been dazzled to find the God's-Eye in their midst. Brenna was no older than Astrid, but her renown had made her esteemed above all shieldmaidens living and most dead. Yet it had been years since she'd raided, and Astrid had had her doubts.

She'd kept them, for the most part, to herself—and for that she was glad, because Brenna was near as fit and agile as Astrid could remember her being. Watching her now, sparring with Vali, Astrid smiled. Though they sparred with sharpened sword and axe, there was a decidedly erotic cast to their movements, even to the locked look in their eyes. She wondered if the God's-Eye had kept her form by all manner of wrestling with her warrior husband.

Olga walked up and stood next to Astrid. At first, she simply observed the training and said nothing, her eyes turned toward her husband.

Leif was sparring with Jaan, both of them bare-chested like most of the other men, and Astrid had been trying to keep her eyes elsewhere. Not only was Jaan wed, to Karlsa's flame-haired healer, Frida, but she was with child.

That news had infuriated Astrid, though not for reasons most would think. She wanted neither husband nor child, but she had enjoyed Jaan, quite a lot, and not merely for his body. He had an impatience with society's trivialities that she understood. It vexed her to see him bound now, like all the others, to the mundane concerns of the nest.

But he was manifestly pleased, so she supposed she was happy for him, too.

Olga laughed. "You're not raiding yet, Astrid. Is there need to look so fierce?"

She hadn't been aware that she looked any way in particular, but her face in repose was not known for its sweetness. Rather than answer Olga's teasing question, she simply said, "We might be ready."

"I hope so, as you leave with the dawn. Leif said you had concerns. Do you still?"

It was unlike Olga to insert herself in any way into a discussion of such matters. She was not of their people, and she had never fully understood or appreciated their warlike ways. She thus deferred to her husband on those topics and focused her attentions on the things she did understand and appreciate: people.

But she wasn't asking about raid preparedness, Astrid suspected. She was asking if her husband would return to her. If Magni's father would return. The boy who played with friends in the yard before the hall, swinging wooden sticks at each other in a parody of the raiders.

"Leif will be home again, Olga. For him I have no concern. He is strong, and he and Vali will have at their backs the strongest of us."

One corner of her mouth quirked up in a grateful smile. "But you are concerned still. For the others."

"Concern is not a bad thing. It leads to watchfulness and care. This will be a great raid. Perhaps the greatest of them all."

The smile faded from Olga's face, and she turned and watched her husband put Jaan on the ground, then offer his hand to help his friend to his feet.

"So much war. To take more when we already have so much. I don't understand."

For Astrid, it was the war itself that appealed, the fight and the victory. She had little more need or use for riches than she had for a husband. But for others, for most, it was the looting and taking they wanted. Flush with gold, they now had appetite for land. "It's our way, Olga."

"Yes, I know. The way of things," she muttered and then turned away, headed back to her son.

~oOo~

They sacrificed a great boar to the gods to ask their blessing for a raid of which stories would be told, and then they feasted long into the night, and even so, most of the raiders were spry as they loosed the skeids from the piers and rowed toward open water. Two ships bore the sails and shields of Leif Olavsson, Jarl of Geitland, and two of Vali Storm-Wolf, Jarl of Karlsa.

The wending course to Anglia was the most challenging that Astrid, or any of them, had ever run, and each year had brought some new challenge. Even so, they had grown accustomed to that route over the years they'd sailed it. This course, to another part, farther, of that land, one they'd only seen on a 'map,' would be more challenging yet. But the sun was bright and the wind was favorable, and on the first day, and the second, it seemed that the gods had heard their plea.

Clouds took the sun on the third day. Storms crashed over them on the next, and they huddled under the sails, left to the whim of Ægir and his wild sea. They lost two men and a woman to the wind as they lashed a torn sail. Their first raid losses in years, and they hadn't yet struck land.

Those who'd been long raiding had been through worse seas, and they battened down their wills as they did their supplies, and they rode out the fury of the gods. When the storms subsided and they could unfurl the sails again, the raiders opened their hope, too. But Astrid saw that the storms had weakened some of the new raiders, in will and body both. If their courage flagged already, they would be a liability in a fight.

With the sun shining again, they pored over the sunstone and the 'map' and oriented their ships, with the hope that they had not been thrown too far off course.

When they first found land, it offered them no beachhead. Tall, looming cliff walls faced them, forbidding entrance.

And then the ships were framed by cliffs on either side—and at that, the raiders rejoiced. They were on course.

The journey had taken days longer then they'd planned, and by the time they put their feet on land again, they were hungry and weary, but they had found the world they'd sought.

It was verdant and aromatic, and not far from their landing, they found a village with the telltale symbol atop a roof: the crossed bars that told of the house the Christian god kept in every village. Where he stored his treasure.

A rustle went through the raiding party, the sound of a whoop held back for stealth, and then they descended the lush green hill to take the town for their own.

~oOo~

The raiders always surprised the Christians, taking the little places along their edges which no Christian king thought to defend, and moving inward from there, meeting with soldiers somewhere on the road to their great stone castles.

Astrid, like many of her clan, found these kings and their kingdoms repugnant in every way. They left the poor at a distance, in broken huts too small to hold any life well, while they themselves sat behind high stone walls in massive stone mountains far too big for the life they held. It had been the same in Estland. They set out their poor as fodder to feed their enemies and distract them, then sent their shiny armies to meet them in the forest before their walls.

But this time it was different. For a small village, unremarkable from all the others they'd ransacked over the years, this one was shockingly well guarded. The raiders hadn't even made the Christian god's treasure house, which was always at the center of every village, before guards in mail were on them, at least a score of them, fighting as if they themselves kept homes in the tiny huts.

This king had learned the lessons of the kings before him, those who'd handed over vast cascades of their treasure to send the raiders away. This king had protected even his humble villagers. More likely, considering where they found the greatest concentration of soldiers, he had protected his god's house, and the villagers were an afterthought, but no matter. There were strong soldiers ready to defend this place.

She was glad. There was little satisfaction in taking a village when the hardest fight came from their smith, and most of their opponents fought with scythes and pitchforks. But a soldier, one trained to fight and armed to do it, that fed the fire in her belly.

The guards near the village's edge fought well and hard but were drastically outnumbered and fell quickly, and the raiders stormed through the town toward the center, killing any who would raise arms and marking good loot to return to after the residents had been cowed or killed.

But when they arrived at the center, they found the treasure house all but surrounded by guards in full armor, their swords and shields at the ready.

Vali and Leif called "HOLD!" nearly in unison, and Astrid moved to stand with them and with Brenna. They scanned the area. Except for the sounds of fear and suffering that they'd left in their wake, the moment was perfectly still.

Without a word, the four of them—Vali, Brenna, Leif, and Astrid—knew that they were thinking the same thing, and they all nodded. Leif gestured with his hands, and the rest of them repeated his movement. The raiders, keeping their eyes turned on the guards and their ears turned behind them, began to move out into the center, spreading out their ranks—which was a weakened position should they need a shield wall, but it seemed they would not.

The raiders had landed in their great skeids and left only the essential workers back to set up camp. Many score warriors and shieldmaidens had stormed the village, and none yet had been lost in this fight. The guards holding this house were outnumbered at least four to one. And they had their backs to a building, with nowhere to break away and regroup, now that the raiders had surrounded them. Their defensive position was terrible.

It was as if their god were actually in the building at their backs, and they were making his last defense. Astrid wondered if he might be.

The guards shifted warily as the raiders spread out but didn't attack. Astrid found that strange; she would have attacked a force moving into position rather than waited for it to have taken that position.

But then the door of the god's house opened, and a man in a long dress stepped out. Their seer. This one seemed young. He held out his hands, his arms wide, making himself a perfect target. He began speaking in the Christian language.

To Astrid, it was babble. She'd learned the Estlander language when she'd spent nearly a year in that land, but she would not learn the Christian words. Her disgust for these savage people, who kept their women like helpless children and fed their poor to their enemies, while they knelt to a god who claimed all power to himself and preferred sacrifices of shiny baubles to one of hot blood, knew no bounds, and the taste of their language burned her tongue. Leif had taken some words over the years, and Vali a few, too, but they seemed to understand this seer no better than she.

At the moment her impatience for the standstill became critical, a spear went through the seer's chest, and she didn't have to look to know it was Vali's. He roared as his strike sent the seer's body back through the still-open doors, and the raiders charged forward.

Astrid went for the nearest guard and swung her axe. He showed none of the surprise or hesitation so many of these Christian men showed when they faced a shieldmaiden, and he blocked her blow deftly. He was bigger than she and probably stronger, but she could use that against him. When he swung his own sword, narrower than a raider's longsword and more pointed, she blocked him with her shield and swiped her axe low at the same time, cutting him across his legs.

He wore armor head to toe, so her blow was not perfectly disabling, but her axe was heavy and sharp, and the metal around his calves dented deeply. The guard's knees gave just enough to upset his next strike and force his head back as he regained his balance, and Astrid swung high, dragging her honed edge across his throat. When his blood gushed into her face, she closed her eyes and allowed herself a single heartbeat to savor the hot wash.

Then the fierce shout of another shieldmaiden cut into her brain, and she turned and found more fight.

They'd lost two shieldmaidens and two warriors to the fighting, and had seven whose injuries would keep them down until it was time to sail again. As raiders carried the dead and wounded back to their new camp, the rest of them, led by Vali and Leif, and Brenna and Astrid, went into the god's house to see what was so precious that it had been heavily guarded.

Nothing.

Not even a golden cross on the wall. But for a wooden cross on the table at the back, the church was barren.

"The floor," Leif said, and Jaan and two others moved the table. They'd discovered that most of these houses had doors in the floor and dark holes underneath where they kept their best treasures. And bones. Many bones, in boxes. With more crosses.

Such a strange people these were.

The dark hole was empty, too, except for bones.

They stood in a loose circle in the middle of a building they'd fought hard to take. A building utterly empty of anything worth taking. This village held nothing of value, yet it had been defended nearly as if it were at the doors of the castle itself.

"I don't understand," Brenna said, her hands on her hips. "Why fight so hard for this?"

"A trap." Vali stalked to the door and looked out, an axe cocked in his hand. Vali fought unshielded, wielding two axes. He also fought bare-chested, as the *Úlfhéðnar* he was.

His back and chest were streaked and smeared with blood and sweat.

"There is no one," he said at last and came back to them.

"They could not know we'd landed." Leif went to the hole in the floor and frowned into its depth. "Even a lookout couldn't have brought soldiers to this place before us. They were already here. Guarding nothing."

"Waiting for us, then. They weren't guarding. They were waiting," Astrid offered.

Jaan came to Astrid's side. "But why?"

She shrugged and stepped away from him. Her body was fired from the fight, and so was his. She didn't rut with other women's men, but she might tonight, with him, if she were not careful. Best to stay clear.

"To take our measure and thin us out." Brenna's tone was decisive; she'd seen the sense of this baffling development. "Did any flee? The peasants? The soldiers?"

Because they didn't kill all they came upon, in the heat of the fight it was likely that some had fled the village. Brenna knew as much and didn't wait for her question to be answered. "We've lost eleven fighters, and this small battle has given them more time to mount a force against us. This king was ready."

Leif nodded. "You're right. We should return to camp and prepare to defend it."

~oOo~

The camp had the curious feel of defeat in victory. All the raiders were agitated. They'd taken the village and looted it to its rafters, but there was little good treasure in it, and no satisfaction. They'd taken a few slaves and left the rest with nothing but their wooden cross.

And now they hurried to bolster a camp they'd only just staked. When they'd returned, Leif and Vali had explained the disappointment of the god's house and their suspicions about the reason, and even the ransacking of the village had taken on a murky shade, as if they'd been made to fight for it and then allowed to have it, tricked into giving away too much of themselves in the bargain.

It was a dangerous mood, and they were already bickering amongst each other. Full-out fighting might not be far behind.

As the afternoon light began to deepen and make the green fields of this place glint gold, Astrid left the camp alone to find a tree to squat behind. She went with her axe and her dagger, and she kept her eyes and ears sharp for signs of scouts.

A night attack would be unlikely; these woods were dense, too dense for even an army familiar with them to be mobile in deep dark, and there would be no moon tonight. But scouts—a scout, or a team of them, could take away crucial information. Astrid knew there would be some in the woods tonight, and she would love to find them and silence them.

As she finished and resettled her breeches, she heard a rustle at a fair distance. Crouching low, unsheathing her dagger, she crept toward it. Within a few feet, she knew it could not be a scout—or it was the worst scout ever to hold the position—because he made no attempt at stealth. She did, however, sneaking forward until she saw the back of a raider behind a shaking bush.

Just as she understood what the partial scene before her meant, a soft, heavy *thud* sounded. The raider reared up, clutching his head, and Astrid knew him at once: Vidar.

An older raider, Vidar had once been sworn to Åke, and he had been among the last of Åke's men to accede to Leif's more temperate way of raiding. Vidar carved a line into his own chest to mark every kill, and his chest was covered with those marks. He had massive lusts for the spoils of victory.

Now, he roared and picked up the rock he'd just been hit with, slamming it down on the body beneath his.

Astrid came quickly around the bush and put her dagger to his throat before she had entirely understood the scene she'd come upon. Instinct had made her draw on her own clansman in defense of an enemy. A *Christian.*

She almost backed off in shock at herself, but before she could, she understood the scene entirely.

Beneath Vidar was a girl. A small girl. A child. A peasant, in tattered rags. Those rags had been rent from her body, and her bare skin was covered in blood.

As it splashed onto her frail little belly and thighs, Astrid understood that it was not her blood, but Vidar's. The little thing had opened his head with a rock—more than once, by the look of the blood.

And he had bashed hers in with the same rock. Blood pulsed from a dent in her head, staining her long, matted, honey-brown hair.

"Leif will take your head for this," Astrid hissed in Vidar's ear.

"She hit me!" Vidar growled, then grunted as Astrid pushed the point of his blade into his skin until blood beaded up around it.

"A child. You would claim that you were forced to defend yourself from a child? And why do you sit astride her naked body?"

His only answer to that was a grunt. Then he threw his body backward and dislodged her. Spinning, he came to his feet and pulled his dagger. He hadn't brought any better weapon. And his breeches were fastened, so he hadn't yet unsheathed the weapon he'd meant to use.

Astrid kipped up to her feet and faced him, taking her axe from her back.

"If I'm to die, you'll have to kill me, Astrid. I'll die in a fight. I'll not go back to kneel before the jarl for taking what should be mine to take! What other spoils are there here?" He sidestepped unsteadily; the girl's blow with the rock had shaken his head some, it seemed.

The little one had been a fighter. She might have been a shieldmaiden someday, if she'd been born to a people who knew women's strength.

Vidar swung, wildly, and Astrid dropped and took out his knee with the poll side of her axe. When he collapsed with a shout, landing on his knees, she broke his arm as well with another blow.

"You will kneel, Vidar. And die a coward's death." One more blow, this to the head with the flat of her blade, and he fell unconscious.

With a sigh, still keeping alert for scouts, Astrid bent to the work of dragging Vidar back to camp.

She left the little body where it lay. Such a tattered, matted little thing would probably not be missed overmuch.

PART TWO
HONOR

4

"There is one among them…" the soldier's words faded away. "Your Highness, he cannot be born of man."

Leofric chuckled, but his brother shot him a corrective glance, then returned his attention to the young man—a boy, truly—whose job it had been to observe the barbarians and return. The alarm had gone out long before he'd made it through the forest, and Eadric and Leofric, as well as Dunstan and the other lords at court, had their base set up well outside the castle walls. They had no intention of letting the barbarians within an arrow's distance of the bailey, but they were willing to let them encamp and take their leisure.

"He cannot be born of any other, lad," Eadric said. "He might be no better than a beast, but we know he cannot be one. Why would you think him so fearsome?"

"He is…" Again, the young soldier's words failed, and he instead threw his arms up, high and wide, as if he were describing a mountain. "And he wore no armor! Arrows bounced from his bare chest, and swords sparked and glanced away! He roared like a lion! And he was not all! Many giant men—and women, Your Highness! There were women with paint on their faces, and they shrieked and flew over the soldiers and slashed them to bits! Their swords go through armor like through air!"

Eadric pushed away from the chart table and stalked to the soldier, who cowered in the shadow of the Crown Prince. "You blaspheme to tell such a tale as a truth, boy. We know the work of the Lord our God on this earth, and there is none such as you describe. So tell me true or lose your head as a blasphemer."

"Your Highness," Leofric cut in. "The boy is affrighted. We should not have charged one so young with the reporting."

His brother turned his head just enough that Leofric could see he hadn't appreciated being interrupted or redirected. But he did step back. "Leave," he commanded, and the boy nearly tripped in his hurry to back respectfully from the tent and their company.

"We have nothing of sense in his report," he complained, returning to the charts. "We lost a unit and a *priest*, and we have nothing."

Leofric watched through the tent opening as the poor boy walked backward far longer than necessary before he spun and ran. He turned to his brother. "I disagree. We know that your strategy thus far is working. The loss of the young priest is regrettable, but he understood the sacrifice he might make. As did our soldiers. Standing firm against the bishop's bilious wails and convincing the king to empty the church and then guard it heavily gave us exactly what we hoped."

That had been a hard fought debate, among Eadric, Leofric, their father, and the bishop. Eadric commanded the king's army and had developed a defensive plan against the chance that the raiders would make their way to this kingdom as they had so many others.

Father Francis had been appalled at the idea that the church should be denuded of its treasures and had argued long that to worship the Lord in nothing more than a hovel smacked of blasphemy. Eadric had quoted scripture at him, reminding him that the Lord was present wherever the faithful worshipped.

Their father had focused on the 'waste' of a full unit, left to languish in the village for an indeterminate time, against a threat he didn't agree was so likely. The Northmen were a seafaring kind, and Mercuria's coastline offered few points of welcome.

Eadric and Leofric had persuaded their father that, in this time of peace, it did no harm to send a unit to Garmwood. Their best case was made, to king and priest alike, when they argued that should the horde arrive and they were ready, they might be the only kingdom to defeat them. Though Mercuria had never yet been invaded, the lands abutting the kingdom, all to the east and the north, had, and they were weaker for it.

The king was already considering ways to overtake the claims of his neighbors and unify the realm under his own banner. Defeating the Northmen would make him all the more fearsome. If King Eadric stopped them, then none would dare stand against him when he sought to unify.

The Northmen had had their way with Mercuria's neighbors, and whole legends were rising up about the rampaging hordes of wild men from the sea.

The heathen barbarians crashed onto a shore, stormed through a land, taking everything, and often everyone, of value and destroying anything they left behind. They desecrated churches and went through defending armies as if mail were vapor, and then they sat outside castle walls, astride stolen horses, and waited for chests of gold and jewels to be rolled out to them. And then they went away—until the next time they had a taste for the blood of good Christians.

It was little wonder the scout had seen monsters surrounding the church in Garmwood. Leofric had a difficult time himself imagining this horde as made of man.

He had heard the stories of women fighting, but he had an even more difficult time picturing that. He knew no woman who could wield a longsword or broadsword, much less do so well.

What kind of savages put their *women* in harm's way? Had they no kind of honor at all, no sense of responsibility, even to their own kind? Even the greater of the animals respected each other. Yes, it might be blasphemy to believe them true monsters, but it was no easier to believe them men.

Eadric considered the charts before him. After a moment, he nodded. "Then we proceed with the plan. We confused their first attack, so we let them encamp and take them in the night."

They meant to go without the aid of moonlight, sending stealth and range soldiers ahead and then coming through with torches to set the camp ablaze.

When one's enemy did not understand the concept of honor, the cause lessened to fight with honor oneself.

Leofric believed that wholeheartedly, but he knew his more pious and honorable brother had felt turmoil over a decision to fight like sneaks and ignore the rules of engagement. Even the king had felt more right with the plan than his son who had devised it.

Eadric sighed and looked up at Dunstan. "Ready the men."

Dunstan bowed. "Your Highness." He backed from the tent and went to do as he was bid.

Before Leofric could think of a thing to say that would settle his brother's mind, Dunstan was back. He ran in, forgetting his courtesy. His complexion was deadly pale. He said nothing, but stared wildly into Leofric's eyes.

He carried a bundle in his arms. Leofric couldn't understand what he might have found that would have induced his friend to charge into the royal tent in such a way.

"What? Duns—oh, no! Our Father in Heaven, let it not be!" Eadric wailed and grabbed the bundle from Dunstan's hands.

As he did, a dirty, blood-stained hank of long hair fell from one end of the bundle.

Leofric blinked.

Underneath his brother's weeping, he heard a thin, wispy sound, like a whine. The bundle moved, ever so slightly.

"She lives?" Eadric gasped and fell to the floor, pulling the covering—an officer's cloak, it was Dunstan's own cloak—back and exposing a sweet face with a bow mouth.

Leofric's legs gave, and he landed on his knees. "Dreda?"

"She lives!" Eadric whipped his eyes to Dunstan's. "The healer! Bring the healer NOW!"

Dunstan ran from the tent.

As Leofric crawled to his brother and sister, Eadric rocked her and cooed, "You're safe, sister. You're safe now."

"Dreda?" Leofric repeated. There was no other word in his mind.

She whined again, and her eye fluttered as if it might open. Only one eye; the other had been pushed inward, its socket destroyed, and the pretty cheek caved in.

There was no healer who could make that right.

But her eye opened, its stormy blue center resting in a vile sea of red. "Lee…Lee…"

"I'm here, poppet. I'm here." He opened the cloak and found her hand. He also found that she was bare and bloody, and rage and horror filled his chest. But he took his sister's slack hand gently and bent his head so that he could kiss her fingers, and then her forehead, and her lips. Her skin was cool already.

"Was…bad…need…c-c-c-….conf-…"

Tears surged from him. She knew she was dying and wanted confession. "You have nothing to confess, poppet. You have never been bad in your life. The Lord is waiting for you. He'll take your hand, and you'll meet our mother in Heaven. She's been waiting to hold you in her arms."

Eadric grunted fiercely as if to protest, but he didn't speak. Dreda trembled, and Leofric realized that it was their brother's shaking body that made hers quake.

"I…wanted…to see…"

"I know, sweet girl. I know."

They waited in silence for her to say more, but there was no more. Her eye did not close. Her hand remained slack. Eventually, they understood that she had left them.

~oOo~

Dunstan returned with the healer only moments after, but it was too late, and after allowing him to make certain, Eadric sent him away.

"Take her," he said and lifted the bundle that had been their sister to Leofric. As the prince stood, Leofric remained on the ground and cradled Dreda to his chest.

"Tell me what you know," Eadric commanded of Dunstan.

Leofric didn't want to hear the details of what he already knew, what he could see. Dreda had slipped the guard of her governess again and gone off to run wild. Perhaps she had somehow overheard word of the Northmen. He thought she must have, and they were what she'd wanted to see. The little girl who wanted adventures and had not enough fear in her to keep her safe.

He'd promised her a long and adventurous life. Leofric laid his cheek on her broken head.

Dunstan cleared his throat and answered the prince. "The scouts returned with her. They found her in the woods, near enough to the Northmen's camp."

"And in what state?"

A pause. "As you see her, less my cloak. They carried her back covered in the pieces of rags they found nearby, but I could not bring her to you in such a way."

Eadric stormed back to Leofric and ripped the cloak back, exposing their sister's lifeless body. Blood spatters covered her, with thick streaks and dried pools over her belly and legs. Into the crease between her pale thighs.

The prince roared and wheeled back. Stunned with grief, Leofric covered her again and held her even closer.

"If I may, Your Highness," Dunstan began, quietly, "We are ready here. If you would take her to the king, we can proceed in your absence. Your word commands us."

"No." Eadric's voice showed no sign of sorrow's weakness. "Brother, if you would take her, you have my leave. But I will be at the vanguard when we set the savages on fire."

Keeping Dreda close to his chest, Leofric stood. "As will I. But we cannot send her to Father without us. He will need us. We must be the ones to tell him." That was private family talk, but Dunstan was as near to family as could be without blood.

"Then we leave her here. Under guard. And get Father Francis."

"No." Leofric carried her to a chaise and laid her on it.

"Brother?"

"Francis will snoop and sneak to Father while we fight. He shouldn't know before the king."

"One of the lesser priests, then."

"No. They obey Francis in all things."

"She needs the Rites!"

"She's dead already. The Rites will not ease her way."

Eadric's eyes narrowed. "You balance on a thin thread, Leofric."

"Yes. But I am right."

The prince went to the chaise and crouched at their sister's side. He drew a finger lightly over her pert little nose. "She was a great gift to come from such sorrow. A light to lead us from our grief for Mother."

"Yes." Leofric blinked back fresh tears. He felt a hand on his shoulder and turned, surprised. He'd forgotten that Dunstan was in the tent with them. Tears streaked his friend's cheeks, too.

Eadric stood and wheeled around, his brow creased deeply. "I want to see these filthy barbarians in the light. Leofric, will you ride with me?"

"I will."

~oOo~

Against emphatic protests by Dunstan and anyone else who saw what they intended and had the spine to object, Eadric and Leofric, the only heirs to the realm, dressed in common soldier's garb and rode out that afternoon alone through the forest toward Garmwood and the raider camp.

They were silent and watchful on the ride, moving in as much haste as care and quiet would allow. When they were near enough to the place the scouts had named as the raider camp, the brothers dismounted and left their horses to await their return.

The forests of Mercuria were known for their dense underbrush and thickly clustered trees, both of which made speedy stealth more difficult. But if one took one's time and knew the way, one might be all but invisible.

Eadric and Leofric knew their way, and they took as much time as their roiling hearts would allow.

The closer they came to the camp, the more Leofric's eyes wanted to seek out bushes for signs that Dreda had lain there. The scouts had found her alone, under a bush near the camp. Alone and bare, bloody and broken. Defiled. Destroyed.

It was his fault. He had condoned her escapes and helped her to keep them from their father. He'd protected the governess who could not keep control of her one and only charge. If he'd done what he should have done, what Eadric would have done, and told their father, Dreda would be alive right now, sitting in her chamber, dressed in fine silks, with her pretty little feet on a satin tuffet, learning to stitch.

Not dead in a tent, naked and bloody and wrapped in Dunstan's cloak.

He had indulged her foolish fancy, and now she was gone.

They heard the camp before they saw it. They'd come in obliquely and were on a rise, above the camp. When it emerged from between the trunks of the trees and the branches of the brush, the brothers crouched low and went still.

Even in the crush of his grief, Leofric found room for fascination. He'd never seen a camp like this, or men like this. He couldn't discern a hierarchy. All the tents seemed alike, or alike enough, and the camp was erected without an intentional shape that he could see.

The tents were rough hewn and made of hides and furs, and the people seemed dressed likewise. Nearly everyone had long hair in braids, even the men, and the men wore massive beards, some of those braided, too. Many of those without long hair had oddly shaved heads. Some had both long hair and shaved heads. Many had black drawings on their skin, and some wore paint on their faces.

And women. The women wore the same clothes as the men. They wore breeches and boots and leather chestpieces. Warriors—just as the stories said.

"There." Eadric yanked on Leofric's arm. "That must be the one the scout spoke of. He is a big one at that. But nothing more than man."

Leofric found the one his brother meant—the biggest man he'd ever seen, with a back so broad and muscles so carved it was as if boulders filled his skin. He had both long hair and a shaved head, and dark pictures over his shoulders and arms and back. Which was bare.

A young lad watching that man fight in a bloody battle might well wonder if a monster hadn't crept from the sea.

He stood with another large man and with two women, both blonde and elaborately, though messily, braided. They seemed small in the company of the giant, but Leofric thought they were both taller than the women he knew. One woman wore a sword and shield on her back. The other had an axe under her shield.

These were the warrior women who shrieked and flew.

"I want one of those women alive." Eadric snarled quietly. "I want her to feel what Dreda felt."

"Eadric?" Leofric couldn't have heard his quiet, pious brother correctly.

"One of those." He nodded toward the group talking below. "They are important to the giant, and I think he is their leader. I want one of those women alive. We will take her to our father and let her carry the burden of his grief. And of our own. All the rest of the savages will burn tonight, but one of those mongrel bitches will be made to atone for their sins against our sister."

As they watched, the giant hooked his hand over the neck of one of the women, drawing her close. The gesture was tender and possessive, and Leofric understood that she was his woman.

"That one," Eadric said, obviously seeing what Leofric had. "I want her."

~oOo~

They returned to the camp and prepared for the attack. Dreda's body lay in the tent, so Eadric met with the captains outside, leaving the tent to serve as her resting place for now. The guard at its entrance was ignorant of whom he protected, but he needed no knowledge to keep his duty. The Crown Prince had said his task was the most sacred, and so he had not moved.

The plan was uncomplicated: they would move through the forest during the near dark hours, stopping well away from the camp until full dark descended. The range units would move forward from there, sending flaming arrows into a quiet camp, and the riders and foot soldiers would charge in to exploit the chaos the fire would create. Any scouts they might encounter would be speedily and permanently silenced.

There had been quiet rumbles of distaste when the plan had first been laid out to the men. This was not the way honorable men fought. Men of honor faced each other on a field of battle, and they limited their battle to that field. There were rules of engagement to be followed. Foe or not, there was no honor in stealing into a camp, where innocents worked and men slept unarmed, to kill someone not prepared for his own defense.

That was murder, not war.

But these Northmen were not men of honor. They flouted even the laws of God. They were barely men at all.

So the honorable army of Mercuria would stretch the rules of engagement and send them on their way to Hell.

5

"It's good you brought him back alive," Leif said, staring off at Vidar, on his knees and tied to a post.

"Is it?" Brenna asked, her tone suggesting that the answer to her question was *no*. "How old a girl?"

Astrid shrugged. "Young. Small, but many of these people are smaller than we. Her chest was yet like a boy's, however."

Vali growled and took two fierce steps toward Vidar. Astrid reached out and grabbed his arm. She held him back, but only because he allowed it.

"His fate wasn't in my hands, and it shouldn't be in yours. It should be decided among us all." She turned to Leif. "Should it not? Is that not what you mean that it's good I brought him back alive?"

"Yes. Vali, the raiders of my clan were not all so pleased to have their appetites curbed. When the treasure was great, they were appeased, but if more here than Vidar feel resentment, we must deal with it now, before we make another assault."

"You would let him live, if the people will it?" Vali had taken Vidar's actions personally, as had Brenna. Their eldest, Solveig, was about the same age, and they seemed to be thinking of their girl when they thought of the young urchin in the woods.

"It falls on us to ensure the people will his death. If they move to take his head for what he did, then we are all of an accord. The disappointment of the village might fracture us unless we can unite around something. Let it be Vidar."

That was Leif's strategic mind at work. Astrid had thought no further than her conviction that a jarl should not act unilaterally unless he had no other choice. Their people were not subjects to any king. They were freepeople who used their voices in their own governance. Leif had power because he had earned it. If he took more than he earned unto himself, then their world wobbled.

But he had thought beyond that and saw both the danger here and the possibility. They had come away from their first foray all but empty-handed, and they had lost fighters to the effort. Many among them had never before experienced a disappointment in a raid. If others felt as Vidar did, that any spoils, even the flesh of the innocent, were better than none, and Leif executed him for it without trial, then they could well find themselves facing a war within the camp.

Vali's raiders were different. Karlsa was different, smaller and more humble, and the jarl before Vali had been like him. They had never known a time when raiders were free to satisfy any lust. But those who had known Åke remembered a time when Vidar might have brought the body of the girl back to camp and crowed over what he'd found.

Leif was right to let Geitland's raiders have their voice now. If he presented the question to them well, they might be influenced by the will of Karlsa, and their voice would turn Leif's edict into a compact instead.

Astrid grinned. She was impressed. "Yes. It should be that."

"Only if you can shape their will with your words. He'll get his chance to speak as well." Brenna crossed her arms over her chest and glared at Vidar. Astrid saw the man bow his head, averting his eyes from the legendary God's-Eye.

Leif smiled and set his hand on Brenna's shoulder. "I am almost as good with words as your man is, and far better than Vidar. Let's do this as we should, so we can return our attention to the raid. There is treasure here, and we are standing on the greater share of it."

The land under their feet. Astrid looked between her boots. It was not so magical. She preferred the land of home.

~oOo~

With the exception of those on lookout duty, all the raiders came together near the main fire for an impromptu thing, at which they would decide the fate of Vidar, accused of attacking a child in the woods.

Leif and Vali stood together, the two jarls allied, but it was Leif who spoke. "We are come together because Vidar Arvidsson is accused of attacking a peasant child. Astrid brings the accusation."

Astrid strode forward and scanned the group, trying to know the feeling behind the faces before her, but they seemed simply interested, for the most part. She had their respect, she knew, and that would carry her voice well. So she spoke. "I came upon Vidar in the woods there"—she pointed in the direction—"he had a small girl beneath him. He had stripped her bare. Her body was so young it was still like a boy's. Vidar bashed her head in with a rock. I found him thus and brought him back to the camp to meet the justice of the thing."

At the last, she had turned to face Vidar straight on and burn her gaze into him. He stared back and leapt into his defense before her own mouth had closed. "The girl came at me and hit me with a rock!"

A rumble of surprised chuckles greeted that assertion—which Astrid believed to be a falsehood. She believed wholeheartedly that the girl had first struck out from the ground, in a brave attempt to defend herself. At the chuckle, though, Vidar understood that he'd taken the wrong tack. A claim of self-defense against a child was not a warrior's claim.

Someone in the group called that out in words: "You could subdue a child no other way than with a rock?"

Another voice rose. "Why was she unclothed?"

Vidar blinked and glanced around at the men and women surrounding him. He changed his approach. "What does it matter? She was a peasant! We ransacked the village and found nothing of value! It is my right as a warrior to take the spoils I find!" With the arm Astrid hadn't broken, he slammed his fist into his chest.

"That is your defense, Vidar? That raping and killing the child was your right?"

"It *is* my right. You are no king, Leif Olavsson. You are no god. You lead us. You do not rule us."

He didn't deny the rape, though Astrid knew he had not gotten so far. She began to wonder at that, and then understood—he had decided that it stood his manhood better to have taken the girl than to have had Astrid deny him the chance.

Men. They behaved as if their mind, heart, and soul all resided in that one small piece of their flesh. In a man such as Vidar, perhaps they did.

When Vidar was finished, a long moment of quiet took over the group. Leif let it settle around them before he stepped forward again. "Vidar stands accused. He doesn't deny Astrid's accounting. Instead he claims that taking and killing the child was his right. And there was a time when that was true. He also reminds me that I am not a king, nor a god. I know this to be true. I have no wish to rule you. But I hope I have earned your trust to lead Geitland. As Vali has earned the trust of Karlsa, and as we together lead this raid."

He walked in a near circle, around the group. "Now it comes to us all to decide Vidar's fate. Is his defense honorable? Is it just? Should he—should any of us—have the right to take absolutely anything we have the strength to claim?

He stopped and scanned the group. "Or should there be more to us than that? Is treasure taken from the weak treasure that brings us honor? Do the gods look down on Vidar today and see that he is strong and mighty? Are they proud? Do they toast his claim in Valhalla tonight? I wonder—are the gods pleased with any of us? Are they glad of the easy way we've had these past few years? Or do they see us growing fat and soft in our plenty, and mean us to take a lesson?"

As the warriors registered that surprising question, Leif walked back to stand at Vali's side, then turned and went still.

"As Jarl of Geitland, I am daily asked to give counsel. I give it now. We all knew disappointment today. We took a village that was too poor to be worth taking, and we lost strong warriors in the effort. But our enemy fought hard against us, and there is honor in that victory, despite the lack of treasure. We faced a worthy opponent. For this raid to bring the honor that we mean it to bring, we will face this strong foe again before we leave. If we would regain the gods' favor, then we must *earn* our treasure. We must wrest it from the mighty hands of a king, not slide it from the frail arms of a child.

"That is my counsel. My opinion. But this decision is not mine to make. We all must decide together. If you would see Vidar struck down for his actions today, raise your arm ring."

There was little hesitation. From where Astrid stood, it seemed that the decision, with the single exception of the accused, was unanimous.

Vidar looked around at his clanspeople and allies in shock. "You would have my head over a *Christian child*?!" The group was quiet. Vidar spat on the ground. "You think the gods will be pleased with you for that? For putting that little scrap of filth over me? I have nigh twenty raiding seasons!"

A Geitland raider named Karl stepped out from the group and punched Vidar in the face. When he fell to his knees, others came from the group and restrained him.

Leif turned to Astrid. "The honor is yours, unless you do not wish it."

She absolutely wished it. Pulling her axe from her back, she went to Vidar. "You can kneel and accept your fate, and hope the gods are mollified enough to remember what honor you have and open their doors to you, or I can bind you to the stump like an animal, and you can go the way of one. Make your choice."

He glared at her, trying to find courage to clear the terror from his eyes. He went still, and, after a moment, his restrainers stepped back.

"An honorable choice." Astrid stood before him and looked him in the eyes. She swung her axe and struck true.

~oOo~

As the sun began to set and raiders were well fed on meat and mead and leiv bread, Astrid sat with the jarls, and Brenna, and a few others who were close to either Leif or Vali. Jaan was among them, but Astrid's mood had tamped her appetites for all things, so she wasn't vexed by his presence.

They were discussing their next move. Scouts had located the castle and found soldiers well away from the walls. This was another unusual thing. Kings tended to cower inside their walls and send soldiers out through the gates in groups to be slaughtered before they sent treasure out instead.

But this king had sent a large group of armored men to make a stand away from the castle, near the far edge of the forest.

"I cannot fathom how it serves his purpose to put the soldiers away from stone walls," Jaan said. "It only makes them more vulnerable, does it not?"

Jaan was an Estlander, brought up a peasant outside a prince's great stone wall. He could imagine nothing stronger, even after years raiding with Vali.

Vali leaned toward his friend but directed the answer to them all. "The walls limit their vantage for attack and focus their enemies. We know to send our arrows to the top and our blades to the gates, and no soldier will come from anywhere but those. This king has learned that lesson as well."

"But they are still dressed in their shiny metal," Jaan countered. "They carry their silken flags and sleep in silken tents. The spies found their camp, even in these woods, from more than mile's distance. This king hasn't learned all our lessons."

"We took the village," Astrid reminded them. "They'll send a man to parley. If this king is like the others."

"This king has yet to be like any other, as I understand." Brenna, who had not raided in these lands before, had been quiet through the discussion, but the point she made now was made well.

For a moment, the friends and leaders were quiet, considering that truth.

"Brenna is right," Leif said, repeating what Astrid knew they'd all been thinking. "We should not wait longer than we must. We know where the castle is, and we know where the soldiers are. At first light, we go. We will fight as if they were our own kind, and would fight alike. On the run. Archers at the fore. Shields and blades at the ready."

~oOo~

That night, as full dark took over the camp and most of the raiders had settled down alone or with each other, Astrid sat alone at the banked fire. She was unsettled, for no cause she could find. Vidar's death had meant nothing to her. He had earned that death. The little girl in the woods—she'd had a thought or two for her, but not more than that. She couldn't even say it had been a life wasted. Not among these people, where the girl had had no chance to make a better fate for herself than the toil and struggle she'd been born into. Astrid had seen enough of these Christian people now to know that to be a peasant woman here was no better than to be a slave among her own people. No rights, no will, no voice, no life but that which a man—a king, a father, or a mate—allowed.

Leif had worked a marvel with his words during the thing. He'd unified the raiders as they'd begun to fragment, and he'd done more than that—he'd made them see their honor and find their fire. He'd reminded them of Valhalla, where honor was the greatest treasure, and strength and courage the greatest weapons. He had made the last of Åke's warriors into his own.

So it wasn't the events of the day that had her spirit stirred, but stirred it was. The hairs on the back of her neck danced, and not merely from the breeze. Again and again, she went still, sending her ears out as far as she could, listening for something that was not there. No horn had sounded from the watch. The night was safe in these lands.

These Christian kings attacked in daylight only, on wide fields, in neat rows. Again and again, king after king, they'd confronted the raiders in that way and were confounded by the first shield wall.

This king had made no other move like his fellows, and yet the night should still be safe. This night especially, with no moon or stars. The woods were dense and forbidding here, and though this king might have learned some lessons, his army had been trained long, she knew, to fight a certain way. There was no path in these woods for armored knights to form their lines.

Yet she couldn't be still. With a huff of agitated breath, she stood and paced the perimeter of the camp, squinting into the dark beyond the wicked boundary of planted spears. There was nothing. She looked up the steep rise to the south, where the forest loomed like a wall of the darkest black in an already inky night.

There was nothing.

Or—

She squinted again. Was there a lightening of the air along the ground? Walking farther from the low fire, putting her back to the camp and the few torches still lit, Astrid went perfectly still and stared. She allowed herself to blink so that her eyes wouldn't conjure ghosts, but otherwise, she didn't move.

Yes. A faint wavering of light. The barest trace. In the moment she took to be sure before she raised an alarm, the trace took on color.

A reddish-gold glow. Fire.

"ATTACK!!" She spun back to camp and ran for her axe and shield. "ATTACK!! FROM THE SOUTH! ATTACK!"

As Astrid grabbed her weapons and Vali and Brenna charged toward her, an arrow of fire struck the top of the tent at her side. It struck from nearly straight above.

They meant to ride down the rise. In full dark. As fiery arrows rained down on their wooden shields, Astrid knew that there would be plenty of light for the king's men to see their way into the camp.

~oOo~

Leif had been right to expect these soldiers to fight like raiders. But they had not expected them to break what had seemed to be their sacred rules, and they had not expected anyone to have undertaken the risk of crossing that forest in the black night. Only the smallest band of raiders might have tried something like it in their own land. But an army galloped down the steep rise behind archers who had set half the camp afire and killed a score of raiders as they'd done it.

The spear fence took the first run of mounted soldiers, and the raiders' archers sent arrows into many of the rest. But the bodies of dead and dying steeds helped foot soldiers surmount the fence and meet raiders in their own camp.

Raiders charged forward, warrior and shieldmaiden, seasoned and green, and met the soldiers with the fierce sense of protecting their home.

As she fought furiously, swinging her axe again and again into the mail and plate of these soldiers' armor, Astrid heard Vali's *Úlfheðinn* roar, and she saw him, bathed in dancing firelight, leap over a mound of bodies, his axes raised high, and bury them both into the body of the last mounted soldier, who had somehow made his way into the camp while still in the saddle. His axes buried in the soldier's armor, Vali went down with him, off the horse, into the midst of a melee on the ground.

Astrid knocked a helmet from a charging soldier and swung again, taking off the top of his head. He stood, surprised, and tried to lunge with his sword. Instead, he fell forward, and Astrid turned back to the place she'd seen Vali go down. She saw Brenna running in that direction, without heed of danger around her. Astrid yanked a spear from a dead soldier and heaved it, striking the one about to take Brenna down.

She was no good with a spear, and the strike glanced from his shoulder—but it was enough to pull Brenna's attention and to distract the soldier, and the God's-Eye slashed her sword low, opening his belly. Another soldier was on her then, but Jaan was there with her, and Astrid left them to their fight.

If Vali went down, the raiders would lose. If he remained standing, they might beat any odds. He was more than a jarl, more than a leader, more than a great warrior, more even than a legend. He was a symbol, as was his wife. The Storm-Wolf and the God's-Eye. They two were their strength and their valor. Their honor in the eyes of the gods.

She ran toward Vali, but then the foremost tent collapsed in a fiery puff and blew sparks into the air. Astrid breathed in fire and fell to her knees in sudden agony. So great was the pain in her mouth and nose and throat that the battle around her seemed to fade away. She almost dropped her axe and shield so that her hands would be free to claw the fire out, but she caught her wits back and struggled to her feet again.

What had happened inside her would not matter if the raiders took this camp. So she forced air into lungs on fire and hefted her axe again.

Before she could find another fight, pain exploded in the back of her head, and for her, the night ended.

6

Leofric had never fought men like these before. And he'd never fought women at all. He'd never even raised a hand to a woman, and something deeply ingrained in him made his sword feel heavy in his hand when a shrieking woman with wild red hair and a face full of freckles charged at him. He barely managed to block the strike of her sword, and she batted away his return as if she were swatting away a fly.

He blinked and set his will. She was no woman. She was a barbarian warrior, his enemy, and she would kill him if he didn't kill her first. He blocked her next slashing blow, caught her blade with his shield, spun, and buried his sword in her chest.

He didn't dwell on the sight of a woman dropping to the ground at his feet. Instead he turned and found another savage to kill.

All around him, the air was an inferno of heat and reddish light, redolent with the stench of searing hide and wood and flesh, and clamorous with the crash and thud against steel and wood, and the crackle and whoosh of fire devouring all it could eat.

Their attack had been executed exactly as planned, and they'd taken the Northmen by surprise. And yet this was no rout of an enemy camp. The savages fought like animals—no, more fiercely even than that. They fought as if they had no fear at all of death, indeed, as if they *sought* it. Most of them unarmored, having had no chance to prepare, they fought without caution or sense.

Twice Leofric had seen raiders disarmed and then seen them use their hands and even their teeth to keep fighting. There were raiders who fought while their bodies were on fire, burning soldiers with them.

They simply did not stop until they were dead.

No wonder the legend around them had grown so high. No wonder naïve scouts raved of monsters. No wonder they'd stomped through most of Anglia and taken what they would.

But no more.

The big one, who seemed to be their leader, fought nearly naked, in only breeches and boots. He had five soldiers on him, and as Leofric charged in that direction to help, he watched three of his men cut down. A fourth went down. When he arrived to make his first attack, the fifth soldier's head flew past him.

The barbarian's eyes turned to Leofric, and for a brief moment, he quailed. He had been a soldier since he had been old enough to fight. He had fought in wars against other kings, and he had fought for allies in their wars. He was a man of courage and honor. He might engage in the satiation of a few lusts, but he was no coward.

And yet he knew fear. The barbarian was massive, a full head and more taller than Leofric, and he was bathed in blood that was clearly not his own. In the strange light of the conflagration, pale eyes blazed from that wild face, with gore dripping from a dense, long beard.

Leofric had just seen him cut down five well-trained soldiers as if they had been children playing.

In that brief moment when Leofric faced the truth of his looming death, the world stopped and went silent. Then the barbarian raised his arms—he wielded a battle axe in each one—and roared. It was no kind of human sound, and yet the rage and hate in it was pure human emotion.

In that sound, Leofric heard victory for Mercuria. They had already beaten these savages, even as they fought on. Not on this night—this skirmish, even with the edge of surprise, would end in a draw. The only way to defeat the raiders decisively on this night would be to kill them all, and Leofric could see that they had lost too many of their own soldiers to press the point much further.

But the raiders would take what was left of them, climb back into their odd ships, and leave Mercuria's shores, and they would do so broken and empty-handed.

No other realm in Anglia had accomplished such a thing.

Those thoughts came in a blink, and then the barbarian leader lunged for Leofric. He spun an axe in his hand and swung, bringing the poll side in. He meant to do harm before taking the kill. Leofric blocked the blow, and yet its force was so powerful that it took him off his feet, throwing him sideways and back. He hit the ground hard, his breath leaving him in a gust.

The barbarian would kill him. This was the time of his death. But Mercuria would still be victorious.

"LEOFRIC!" Dunstan's voice rang out over the din, and then there was a body between Leofric and the massive Northman. As Dunstan struck a blow—it clanged against the blade of an axe—Leofric got to his feet. And then they two stood against their enemy.

Suddenly, a call ran through the night. "FALL BACK! FALL BACK! FALL BACK!"

Eadric was calling the soldiers off. At the same moment, another tent fell, and a cloudburst of sparks flew up. The barbarian must have seen something behind them, because he simply plowed straight through them, knocking Dunstan to one side and Leofric to the other, as if they'd dropped so far beneath his notice that he hadn't even felt them.

Leofric turned and saw him fly at a woman on fire, bringing her down to the ground and covering her with his body.

The woman. That was the woman they were meant to take. He took a step toward them, but Dunstan grabbed his arm.

"We fall back, Your Grace."

"The woman."

"We have the other. His Highness took her, and she's already been sent back to the castle."

They were in the middle of the enemy camp, so Leofric let any argument drop. He nodded, and he and Dunstan ran, fighting through the last of the raiders as they went.

They had achieved all the aims of this attack.

Now it was time to take their sister home to their father.

~oOo~

After dawn, still wearing the blood of their enemies and reeking of smoke, Eadric carried Dreda's body, wrapped in Dunstan's cloak. Leofric walked at his side. They brought her through the castle gates, across the bailey, and into the castle. Though they would bring Dreda to their father in the private quarters, they had no intention of sneaking her in as if there were shame in her death.

There was no shame for Dreda, and Leofric would cut down any who might say otherwise. She had been young and innocent and lovely. She had been good and ebullient and kind. No matter what had been done to her, there was no shame for her.

A wake of silence trailed behind them. The people they passed, soldier, peasant, and lord alike, stood in quiet respect. Some had already known who Eadric carried. Others learned as they watched. They stood with their heads bowed and their hands at their hearts because there was no shame for Dreda.

The gossip would come, but Leofric would ensure that no shame would go with it.

Inside the castle, the steward stepped forward with a bow, and the brothers stopped. "Your Highness, Your Grace, the king—" his eyes fell on Eadric's bundle, and his words died away.

"Mercy, that is not—" He recovered himself and bowed again. "Cry your pardon, Your Highness, the king has missed the princess. She slept not in her bed." His shaking hand reached to the bundle and then dropped away. "Let that not be her!"

Ignoring his informality and his question, Eadric walked past him and took the lead, climbing the main staircase to the family quarters.

"Is he in the residence?" Leofric asked before he followed his brother.

"Yes, Your Grace. Awaiting word."

They climbed the stairs and walked silently down the corridor, side by side, toward the double doors at which two guards stood at attention. Leofric saw one of them register first confusion and then shock at the bundle Eadric carried.

The guards opened the doors, and the brothers entered their home.

King Eadric, in a heavy silken dressing gown, paced the room. At his sons' entrance, his first expression was of paternal relief. He'd sent two sons into the wood to face an enemy, and, even in his worry for Dreda, he was glad to have two sons return.

Then his eyes found Eadric's burden.

"No." The word had the sound of royal decree. "No."

Eadric stopped walking toward him. "Father…" His voice broke.

"No!" The king staggered backward, abject terror twisting his features. "NO!" He tripped and fell into one of the vast armchairs at the fireplace, then slid to his knees. "NO! GOD IN HEAVEN, PLEASE!" He slammed his hands over his face. "NO!"

Eadric stood where he was, holding Dreda's stiff body, his shoulders shaking as sobs took him over.

Leofric went to their father and dropped to his knees before him. He tried to put his arms around him, but the king pushed him away and crawled to Eadric.

He crawled. The sight of the king crawling and weeping was so shocking and so desolate that Leofric thought he would be ill. He doubled over, clutching himself as his tears soaked his beard.

"Give her to me. *Give her to me!*" Their father yanked Dreda from Eadric. The wild emphasis of the act pulled the cloak away and exposed her bare, filthy, bloodstained body, gone stiff and grey in death.

Their father screamed. He tried to clutch her to his chest, but the earthly form she'd left behind was unyielding. Finally, screaming again and again, he held her as Eadric had been carrying her. On his knees, he rocked her.

Leofric had the presence of mind to look beyond the scene and ensure that the doors had been closed behind them. They had been; the family was in privacy.

Eadric picked up Dunstan's cloak from the floor and draped it over her again.

The king's wails quieted, and he sobbed whispers into Dreda's matted hair. "You cannot leave me, my light. You are the last I have of your mother. You are everything. Please, O Lord in Heaven, I beseech thee. Please do not take her from me!"

"Father," Eadric said gently. "There is no hope."

"There is always hope! There is nothing He cannot do. Francis! We need Francis!"

Leofric began to protest—he did not want that porcine prig in the midst of their family sorrow—but Eadric cut him off with a shake of his head. "We do. She must have the Rites. I will summon him."

~oOo~

Father Francis had no conduit to a miracle, but he did perform the Last Rites. Eventually, Eadric and Leofric persuaded their father to let Dreda go, and Francis summoned two lesser priests to wrap her and carry her to the chapel so that they could prepare her for vigil.

Thereafter, while Leofric watched the sunlight move through the room as the day aged, King Eadric stayed where he was, kneeling on the floor where he'd last held his daughter. Leofric and Eadric sat quietly and waited.

Leofric mused on the governess, his emotions cycling from guilt to rage and back again. She should have been able to keep her charge safe. That was the very definition of her position. But Leofric bore fault as well—for Dreda's wandering and for the governess's laxity. He should have insisted that the king know about each event. He shouldn't have been so amused and gentle with her when she got up to mischief.

He'd seen himself as a child in her, and he hadn't wanted to quash that high spirit. He'd been proud of her for breaking free.

And now she was gone.

"How did it happen?"

They were the first words their father had spoken in hours, and they'd been uttered without any affect at all. Leofric turned; the king hadn't moved.

Eadric stood. "She was attacked by raiders in the wood."

"You know this to be true?"

"Her body was found near their camp. She was…as you saw her. Yes, we know it to be true."

"And she was alone in the wood."

"Yes."

"Arrest the governess."

Leofric almost said something, but he stilled his tongue and let Eadric leave the room to do their father's bidding.

While he was gone, the king stood. He brushed his knees and straightened his dressing gown. Then he came and sat in the chair he'd fallen into earlier. Facing Leofric, his expression impassive, he said, "Tell me what happened last night. I sent you out to prepare a defense, and instead you return to me reeking of smoke and carrying your sister's body."

The King of Mercuria had returned. He'd put away the grief of a father and pulled the duty and power of a king over his shoulders.

Leofric described Eadric's plan and their execution of it. When he was finished, his father stared at the empty fireplace.

"That you left any of them alive is a defeat. What they did to your sister—nothing but their annihilation will suffice. You must go back and finish them off."

Though they had dealt a devastating blow to the raider camp, they had taken heavy losses themselves in the attack last night, and for that, and for Dreda, now was not the time to attack again. In reckless fury, they might turn victory into defeat. But there was an outlet for their father's vengeance. Eadric had seen to that.

"If I may, Father—we took one of their warrior women. A leader among them. She is in the dungeon now. Eadric means for her to bear the burden of Dreda's death."

A light of interest fired in the king's eyes. "This is Eadric's wish? And you?"

Leofric didn't answer. Savage or not, a woman could not have defiled Dreda. He would rather they had found the one who had. But his father stared, waiting for his answer. "I understand that there is a fitness to it."

"But you don't like it."

"She is a woman."

His father sneered. "No more than a hound bitch is a woman. I want to see this warrior wench." He stood. "Come. We'll dress and then to the dungeons."

~oOo~

The lowest part of the dungeon, known as the Black Walls, was where things happened that were unutterable and went unsaid. No one who was locked away in the Black Walls ever saw the sun again. Leofric had only known two men in all his lifetime who had been subjected to the trials found here.

And now one woman.

She was stripped naked and bound hand, foot, and neck, lying on the stone floor of an empty cell. Her blonde hair was filthy, and its many tight braids, both elaborate and somehow unfeminine, had loosened so that her hair was like a bird's nest.

When he, his father and brother, and the warden filed into the dank cell, the woman glared up at them and growled.

There was no fear in her eyes. Nothing but loathing and threat. From the filthy floor, naked and bound at their feet, she managed to convey a threat.

The warden's bandaged face offered evidence to the threat she posed, even as their prisoner. She had bitten his nose away—and then eaten it, spitting out the gristle before the guards had knocked her senseless again. She'd injured three other guards as well, though none other so…memorably.

Her body was like no other woman's body Leofric had ever seen. Her stomach undulated with muscle, and her arms and legs, her shoulders, her back, every part of her was contoured like a strong man's body, albeit smaller. If not for the round globes at her chest, and the smooth, nearly hairless wedge at her thighs, her body might have been a man's.

Like the men he'd seen with dark pictures embedded in their skin, across their chests, their arms, their backs, over their scalps, this woman had such a picture as well—coiling up her thigh. A dragon, Leofric thought.

She growled again, and this one ended with a rough cough.

The king was right. She was more animal than human, more man than woman.

"We want her to suffer for Dreda," the king said at last, using the royal pronoun. "We would she suffers long. Do what you will, but do not kill her or precipitate her death until we wish it."

The warden bowed. "S'you wish, Sire. The men'd have a go at her, if it wouldn't offend." Without his nose, his voice had a thick, stunted tone that might have been comical if there had been any humor left in the world.

Standing at his father's side, Leofric saw a spasm of furious grief tighten his cheeks. "It is meet that they should take her, yes. But do not spend in her. No child should come of that."

"Would she be alive long enough to bear a child, Sire?" Eadric asked, surprised.

The king stared down at the tense form on the floor. "Mayhap. We would see her suffer until our grief is cleansed."

He walked from the cell. Leofric met his brother's eyes. If their father meant to keep the barbarian woman alive until he no longer mourned Dreda, then she would suffer a very long time indeed.

"To me!" the king summoned, and Leofric followed Eadric into the center chamber, where their father waited.

The warden slammed the oaken door shut and turned the iron lock, and Leofric knew their prisoner had been left in perfect darkness.

"Where is the governess?" the king asked.

"Not on this level, Sire," the warden answered. "She's in the light."

"Take us to her."

They climbed to the level where the gentler prisoners were kept—not nobility, but those who moved among them. These cells had humble but comfortable furnishings and small but airy windows.

The warden opened a window in a cell door, and the king looked in. Again, Leofric saw an angry spasm tighten his father's profile.

He wondered if that anger would be directed his way were his father to know that he had shielded both Dreda and her governess from his censure on more than one occasion.

"Summon the executioner. Her head was too empty to keep her focus on her charge, and so we will take it from her shoulders."

He turned, then paused and turned back. "She is fair-haired."

"Aye, Sire." The warden cocked his head at the king's stray observation.

Leofric, unable to see into the cell, wondered if he'd ever known the color of the governess's hair. Always he had seen it covered, in the way of women of her station.

"The savage bitch is a leader, you say?"

Leofric looked to his brother, who seemed as baffled by these random comments from their father as he was.

"Leofric, did you say so?"

"Yes, Sire. She seemed to be a leader among them."

"She will be missed, then. They will come for her."

"Mayhap, Sire," Eadric answered. "But there are not many of them left. We will turn them back long before they reach the castle."

"No."

"Sire?" Eadric asked.

"Father?" Leofric asked at the same time.

But their father turned to the warden and slammed the window closed. "Have her hair braided like the savage's before you take her head. When it is done, take the eyes and crush the face so that she might be any yellow-haired wench."

He spun on his heel and faced his sons. Leofric had never seen such a look in his father's eyes before. It was more than grief or rage. It seemed like madness—and it seemed madness, too, to desecrate the body of a Christian woman, no matter her sin or her station.

"You will take the head back to the raider camp, and you will throw it at them. Let them know we've taken their woman, and let them think her dead. Let them feel it. Then let them run. Deny them their deaths in battle. Make them flee."

~oOo~

105

They rode under their father's gold and blue banner, a full unit of soldiers behind them. Eadric had collected the barbarian woman's axe as well, thinking to return it with the battered remains of the governess's head, thereby strengthening the ruse.

Weary and desolate in spirit, Leofric felt no satisfaction as they came upon the still-smoldering remains of the raider camp. The stench of death filled his nose and lungs. The bodies of their own soldiers and their mounts, left behind when they'd fallen back, were still strewn over the ground.

The raiders' dead were piled like firewood. Little was left of the camp. But as Eadric, Leofric, and Dunstan rode up, the Northmen picked up their weapons and stalked forward, ready to do battle again.

At Eadric's signal, mounted archers spread out, making an arc around them. They nocked and drew, and then waited.

Eadric dismounted, and Leofric followed. With the leather bag over his shoulder and the axe on his back, his brother strode forward. Resting his hand on the pommel of his sword, Leofric kept his brother's back.

The giant yet lived, as did his woman. The woman's arm and chest were wrapped in heavy bandages, but she walked up with her mate and the blond warrior, who also showed bandages over his chest.

The giant seemed unscathed.

"Do any among you speak our language?"

The blond man stepped forward at Eadric's question, and the giant followed, hefting an axe in his hand. When the woman made to join them, the giant stopped her with a hand on her shoulder.

The blond spoke. "Speak some."

"I come with a message from Eadric, King of Mercuria. You are not welcome here. Do you understand?"

None of the barbarians answered. They only glared. But Leofric thought they understood.

Eadric continued. "The king commands many more soldiers than these we have brought. If you have not quit our land by the next day's break, this fate shall be the fate of you all."

He opened the bag and pulled out the head by its braided blonde hair. It was filthy and bloody and barely seemed human. Eadric threw it at the one who'd spoken. In a move of obvious reflex, he caught it and beheld what he'd caught.

His eyes came back up, wide and full of shock and rage.

Eadric stalked forward, within a mere few paces of those huge, furious, fierce men. He pulled the woman's axe from his back and dropped it to the ground. "You go, by day's break. Do you understand?"

Again, there was no response. But Eadric turned on his heel, putting his back to the enemy, and walked calmly back to his horse.

A roar filled the air, and the giant charged. The first archers loosed their arrows. All three arrows struck the giant in the chest, and he went down.

He was not invulnerable after all.

PART THREE
DISCIPLINE

7

As a child, Astrid had been terrified of the dark. She'd been tormented by horrifying nightmares, vivid stories charging through her young, sleeping mind, clawing at her until she would burst from sleep howling and sobbing. Even during her wakeful hours, when the dark got too deep, the fearsome, inexplicable creatures from her sleep would creep and slither at the edges of her sight.

In their world, darkness was a steady companion. For the long months of winter, especially in the weeks nearest the solstice, darkness was all but constant. Her fear had been a source of shame and anger for her father and of impatience and consternation for her mother.

When she'd had seven years and still would not tolerate to be left alone in the night, her father had taken her by the hand one afternoon, during a time of the year when the darkness lasted only the length of a good rest. He'd led her into the woods, beyond the sight of Geitland, under the pretense that they sought a particular night-growing herb for her mother's potions.

With the town out of sight and out of hearing, as the sun began to sink beneath the ground, Astrid's father had bound her to a tree. He'd walked away, deaf to her screams and wails and pleas.

That night was Astrid's clearest memory.

She'd screamed herself hoarse, and then she'd screamed until something had torn in her throat and she could taste blood.

She'd wept until there were no more tears inside her, and then she'd wept without tears.

She'd wet herself. She'd soiled herself. She'd vomited.

Though the night had been hours shorter than the nights of winter, it was the longest night of Astrid's life. The animals of the wood had come to play with the creatures of her imagination, and she'd fallen into a black, bottomless chasm, delving every moment into a deeper place of terror.

And then she'd found the bottom.

And then the terror had fallen away.

Her father had returned to her in the dawn. He'd unbound her, and she'd stood. When her body had exploded with painful prickles, she'd jerked her arm from her father's stabilizing hand and had gripped the tree instead. The prickles had subsided, and she'd walked ahead of her father through the wood and back home, where she'd cleaned herself up and gotten on with her chores.

Her love for her father had never recovered, but he'd done what he'd set out to do. She'd never feared the dark again.

She'd never known fear of any kind since that night.

And she did not know it now.

Despite all the hours she'd lain bound and ignored in this dungeon cell, her eyes had found no hint of light to grab onto. There was no sound, either, not even a drip of whatever moisture kept the cell damp. Only the sounds she made herself as she shifted in the minuscule ways she could, and as she coughed against whatever ills the fire she'd breathed in had left inside her, assured her she hadn't gone deaf.

She might as well have been blind, and she might have thought she was, had she not been visited by her jailer and three other men, who'd stared down at her and talked in their strange words and then left her. The jailer had carried a torch, and after a moment's pain from the sudden glare, she had seen the men, three of them in gleaming costumes that spoke of their wealth and power.

And she'd seen the jailer, in his humble woolens and his hateful eyes. His nose had been a vile meal, but she'd enjoyed the sight of his bandaged face.

They had done nothing to her yet but beat her, strip her, bind her, and leave her. They'd bound her for maximum discomfort, her hands and feet in contact at her back, and the bindings at her neck tightening subtly with each movement more than a twitch. If she had the mind to do it, she could end herself in that way, drawing on her arms and legs until the rope at her throat throttled her. But that was no way to be welcomed to Valhalla. So she would live until she escaped or was rescued, or until they killed her. Either way, she would be free.

Why they'd taken her, she'd yet to discern. She doubted they intended to press her; even if she'd been a traitorous coward, she had none of their words to say, and by now they must have come to understand that. They'd taken her for some other reason.

They'd leered as they'd stripped her and pawed at her body, pinching and probing. When she hadn't reacted as they'd expected her to, they'd become more emphatic and brutish, shoving their fingers wherever they could, biting her, slapping her. That had been her opportunity to hurt them back, and every blow they'd dealt her after they'd managed to restrain her again had been worth the satisfaction of making them bleed.

These men seemed to want her to be ashamed of what they did to her. She'd seen it in their eyes, that they'd thought they were abasing her in some way. She'd seen it, but she hadn't understood it. Her body was no source of shame, and what other people did to it could not possibly bring shame unto herself.

These Christians had bizarre ways of thinking and being. They seemed to disgust themselves almost as much as they disgusted her.

They caused her pain, however, and that she would remember. At every opportunity, she would repay injuries dealt her.

She didn't know the fate of her people, but she felt strong hope that they'd been victorious, even against that sneak attack. She imagined Leif and Vali opening the cell door and unbinding her, and she let that vision fill her blank sight.

And then she imagined her retribution.

If the Christians had won, however, she would die in this place. They would hurt her, or they would leave her where she lay and let her starve. Either way, she knew they would kill her.

She knew that, but the knowledge carried no fear and no self-pity. If this was to be her end, then she would meet it with her eyes open and her mouth shut.

And she would fight at every slightest chance.

~oOo~

Using her body's signals—its need to void and its need for nourishment— to mark time, Astrid judged that she'd been left alone in the pitch black and perfect silence for near two days when she heard the deafening clank of a lock being turned. The cell door scraped open, and she slammed her eyes shut at the stinging glare of a torch.

Until the golden glow through her eyelids no longer bit into her eyes, Astrid did not open them. When she did, she saw the jailer's bandaged face wavering behind the torch flame. He made a gesture with his free hand, and two other men pushed into the cell past him.

She recognized these men as those who'd stripped her and pawed at her. They both bore the marks of the fight she'd put up before they'd managed to subdue her and bind her.

She smiled and saw the leering satisfaction on one face falter.

Bound as she was, she couldn't fight, so she lay still while they stomped up to her. One of them made a show of sniffing deeply and saying something to his fellow. Astrid didn't understand the words, but she supposed them to be making a jape about the filth she lay in. Again, they expected her to feel shame, but her body's need to void was not a shameful thing, and it was not her fault she'd had no other choice but to void where she lay.

One of them brandished a crude dagger, and Astrid tensed. But he reached back and cut her bonds. Then, while the other began to unwind the rope from her, he leaned in close and pushed the blade under her chin, letting the point sink into her flesh.

He spoke snarling words at her, his breath reeking of old meat and poor ale. She glared back.

The second she felt that her arms were free, she rolled, disregarding the brief, shallow slice of the blade through the underside of her chin, and slammed her hands over the ears of the man who'd wielded it. He roared in shock and pain and fell back, landing on his end with a crack.

Slowed by stiffness and weakened by hunger and thirst, Astrid saw the other man's fist coming for her head but could not manage to avoid it. She felt the blast of pain at her temple and sagged, and then she felt fists and feet crashing into her.

~oOo~

She woke in a room so bright she nearly thought she was outside. But no, she was in a different cell, still dank and rank and windowless, but illuminated by torches on every wall.

They had bound her to some kind of table, her arms and legs spread wide. She could lift her head to look around, but she didn't. Instead, she focused on her body and let it tell her what it could.

The way the air—sluggish and tepid—seemed to move over her skin, she didn't think the table was of a typical shape. It seemed to be formed like one of the Christian crosses, except split at the bottom.

She was surrounded by men, at least six of them. They were all filthy, sneering rotting mouths at her. The jailer was among them. His bandage was soiled, and there was a smear of yellow over the wound where his nose had been. Astrid, daughter of a healer, knew that yellow was a bad color to come from a wound.

Good. She wished to see his face rot off.

Letting her eyes drift around, she also saw a man in a dress, like one of their seers. Fat, with a large red nose. His hands were laced together over his big belly. He stood back, near the door. The other men seemed to defer to him.

Their eyes met, and his expression did an interesting thing: First, he smiled. Not kindly, but smugly. Then the smile twitched and became a sneer like all the other men in the room. And then his face went completely blank. All but his eyes, which glittered with rapacious interest.

The seer spoke, and then the jailer spoke. And then all the men except the seer put their hands on her.

At first, they simply touched her. There was no gentleness in them, but neither was there an obvious intent to hurt her. It was as if they expected her to be different from their own women and were testing out her body to see if she was.

Then one of them grabbed her breast and twisted it savagely, and that emboldened the others.

Astrid understood. She was meant to be their plaything. That was the torment that they had devised for her.

Such simple, stupid men. With no weapon but their own bodies, they could hurt her, but they couldn't do her harm enough even to linger in her memory, let alone break her.

She lay still and stoic, casting aside the hurts of her body and focusing her mind on the image of Leif and Vali opening the cell door.

The men babbled and laughed, but words she couldn't understand were meaningless.

When they took their turns with their little worms, she met their eyes and didn't blink.

When they bit her breasts, she sought out their seer and memorized that leering face. That watcher seemed worse to her than these dumb animals rutting in her.

When they spent their seed on her, on her face, over her chest, her legs, she stared up at the rough ceiling and thought of home.

When one of them tried to force himself into her mouth, she bit down, swallowing his blood, relishing his screams, until a blow to her head loosened her jaws and brought dark to her mind.

~oOo~

Again and again, they took her to the room. Again and again, the men took their turns. Sometimes, they would bind her to the strange table. Other times, she would wake with her belly over a saddle and her wrists and ankles bound, and the men would take her that way. Again and again. Even as she knew contempt for them and no shame for herself, her body ached with the ill use.

But it wasn't long before Astrid learned to be relieved when the men filled the room. Their rutting was the least of the torments.

When they weren't abusing her, they kept her bound in the black, silent cell. They offered her water by dumping it over her face, and food by shoving small bits of bread into her mouth, once each day, she guessed, after they were finished with her.

They talked but almost never at her, and never with any expectation that she would answer. She understood few of their words, but she understood the men. Their only intent was to cause her pain, as much as they could without killing her. That had become quickly obvious.

They meant her to suffer, and they meant her to do so for as long as they could manage it.

Sometimes, the window in the door would open. Astrid knew that someone was watching, someone besides the seer who stood in the room and always watched. She could see only darkness in the space, however, when she could see anything at all.

It was never one thing they did to her, and she never had any idea how long they would press her before they tired of their games for the moment and returned her to her cell.

Sometimes, after the leering men left the room, another man would come in, and it would be only him. One man and the seer, always standing at the door, watching. Those times were the worst. That one man, dressed all in black, knew of ways to make hurt that would have impressed Astrid had she been standing at his side and not strapped naked before him.

There was a kind of device made of many strands of soft hide. At the end of each strand was a metal barb. The man in black would raise his arm and strike down, sending all those barbed strands over her bare flesh, sometimes over her front, and sometimes over her back. Again and again and again he would strike, and Astrid would feel the blood oozing over her skin. Then he would rub a kind of ointment into the wounds, but not a healing salve. Something that turned her flesh to fire.

There were times when the man in black would use the leather strands on her for days in a row, each lash over already devastated flesh digging that much more deeply into her abyss of pain.

There was a thin, pale switch, little more than a twig. Sometimes, she would be strapped face-down on the table, and that switch would sing out over her flesh. Other times, he would strike the bottoms of her feet only.

That was the worst pain but for one other.

The very worst times were when they hung her by her wrists in iron shackles and walked away. They'd leave her there for a timeless eternity. As she dangled over the floor, every wound they'd made, every muscle they'd bruised, every joint they'd strained would scream in agony. Wounds that had managed a tentative healing would break open.

Astrid knew that if she broke, it would be while she hung from the shackles. That was the time her mind could not go away, could only stay and feel every pain.

She tried to focus on Leif and Vali. Though she could no longer mark time—she spent too much of it unconscious, and when she was being hurt, she worked too hard to turn her mind away—she told herself that it hadn't been as long as it seemed. Pain and loneliness had a way of making all time endless. She remembered that infinite night in the woods, when hours had seemed years, and she told herself that when she was free, this time would be but a blink in her life.

Leif and Vali would come. If they could come, they would come. And if they couldn't, if they'd been killed, then she would see them in Valhalla, as long as she died with honor. As long as she didn't break.

When she was young, just about the time she'd had her first blood, Jarl Åke had executed a traitor. The man had been a valiant warrior and an ally chieftain. He'd been well loved in his clan and in Geitland as well, until his treachery. In light of the honor the man had known for most of his life, Åke had performed the Blood Eagle.

In that manner of execution, the condemned's back was opened with a sharp blade. His ribs were then hacked free of his spine and splayed outward. From the opening, his lungs were pulled and draped over his shoulders. Death came after all that had been done, while the lungs struggled to fill with air until they could do so no longer. It was an exquisitely painful and gory way to die, and a man who could withstand it without crying out would retain his honor and his seat in Valhalla.

The chieftain had barely flinched. Astrid, standing between her mother and her father, had watched carefully, seeking any sign that he felt pain. All he'd ever done was, occasionally, take long blinks. When his lungs had finally stopped, he'd dropped his head. His body hadn't even sagged.

To Astrid, that had always been the epitome of an honorable death. Although he'd betrayed his friend's trust, no one could ever say that he was anything less than a true and valorous warrior.

If that man could withstand pain of such magnitude, then Astrid could, she told herself, withstand the petty trials these ignorant Christians could devise.

So she never screamed. A true shieldmaiden closed her mouth against her pain.

When they came to take her, she always fought until they knocked her senseless, but still, each day, she had less fight left in her bones. She was weak, and she was ill. Corruption had settled into her wounds, and her body was failing her. She would not be able to fight forever.

But she would not be broken.

8

In the weeks following Dreda's death, especially after her vigil, everything around the castle seemed to turn grey.

Grief was taking the king's sense. He refused to dine even in the company of his sons, and Leofric thought that he was eating very little in any event. He barely allowed himself to be dressed for each day, and he could hardly countenance the presence of anyone with him.

Beyond the necessary servants, only those closest to the king had seen him since Dreda's body had been put into the earth. Those closest, and the keepers of the dungeon. The men who worked in the deeps of the castle saw the king every day.

He spent the great bulk of his day dividing his time between two places: the chapel and the dungeon.

Most of the nobles had left court, as there was little reason to stay. The barbarians had been repelled, so there was no need for noblemen to don their armor. Moreover, the king had not offered his audience since the day his daughter had been killed, and the royal table was empty at dinner, so there was no gain to be had in being seen at court.

Even Dunstan had left, drawn home to prepare for his marriage.

Prince Eadric had taken on the managing of affairs that couldn't be avoided. There wasn't much; as all activities but the basic business of daily life ground to a halt, the people had little need of the royal family. So the family were left to themselves and their sorrow.

Leofric and his brother spent most of their time in the private residence. Their father wanted nothing to do with them or with anyone else, but neither Leofric nor Eadric sought solitude. They didn't want the company of servants or sycophants, but in these weeks, they gravitated to each other more strongly than they had since their boyhood.

While Eadric saw to those royal obligations that couldn't be deferred, Leofric wandered the halls and rooms of the residence, alone and lonely, more a ghost in the space than their sister was. He often sat in Dreda's rooms, untouched since the governess had been arrested. He'd hold something of his sister's and try to conjure her to sit with him.

The scent of her was everywhere still, and the *feel* of her. In her pretty dolls and faulty needlework. In her golden hairbrushes and pearl-tipped pins. In the hide rocking horse that still stood near her bed, though she'd been well past the age to ride it. She'd adored that horse.

Such a perfect young lass she'd been. So much promise. Beauty and poise and spirit. A lively mind and an open heart.

He understood his father's poisonous rage. He felt it in his own heart. But with each passing day, Leofric saw more clearly what his father could not see at all—that the poison had infected them, was crippling them, and when they fell, so too would Mercuria.

~oOo~

"Of course he's unhappy. Dreda was more than his daughter to him, and you know it. She was our mother's spirit. You cannot expect him already to have made his peace with the loss of her." Eadric slammed his knife down and picked up his goblet. They were dining alone, as usual, the table ponderous for the empty places at it. Their father had not joined them for any meal since Dreda's death. Leofric wasn't sure that he'd eaten at all since then.

"He is more than unhappy," Leofric countered. "This is more than grief. This is an evil."

Eadric's eyes narrowed dangerously. "Watch your words, brother. Our father's will cannot be evil, and you risk treason to say so."

Knowing how fine was the line he walked, Leofric took another step anyway. "How can this be a godly thing, to allow a woman to be treated in this way?"

Eadric chose not to answer that question. "She's a savage. What do you care of her?"

"I care nothing of her. I care deeply for the king. Our father is losing his way. What's happening to the prisoner is vengeance, and vengeance is not ours. Eadric, you are the one of us who best understands these things. You know your spirit. You feel God in you. Search your heart. Is it right, is it righteous, what we do?"

Eadric had lost his way, too. Leofric's contemplative, careful brother had absented himself entirely from the happenings in the Black Walls. He couldn't abide to think on it, but in that distance, he'd found a way to accept it. He had carried their sister's body to their father, and he had a taste for barbarian suffering, too.

Only Leofric had qualms. He was the more rash brother, the one more likely to fight and to play, to sin without care, but it was his conscience that had been pricked in the Black Walls. He saw the work of the sin on their father. Eadric saw only the work of grief.

But Leofric had been in the Black Walls. He had seen. If Eadric would sully his boots to descend the dungeon steps, he might also see, in that dark, more clearly.

~oOo~

Something had to be done. Eadric was wrong; they could wait no longer for the Lord's intervention on their father's misery. Convinced that he had to do something, that the weeks trapped in this dead grief were only killing them all, Leofric went in search of his father.

He knew where he would find him.

In the midst of a bright, warm day, Leofric left the residence and strode through the castle.

The stone walls echoed against the silence. The castle itself had become a crypt.

The only time in a day that his father showed liveliness or interest was when he went to the dungeon. He would stand at the cell door within the Black Walls, sometimes for hours, and watch what was done to the captive woman. Occasionally, he would call the jailer to him and command them to do something specific to her.

The king was obsessed. Something deep and primal inside him fed on the strange woman's pain.

But he knew it was wrong. How else to explain why he would leave the dungeon, pale and sweating, and go to the chapel and kneel on the stone floor, before the altar, beneath the cross, for hours?

Leofric had sought him out in the Black Walls often. He'd stood in the shadows, reeling with shock and dismay, and watched his father, King of Mercuria, peering through the cell door like a wayward boy peeping into a lady's chamber.

When he'd tried to call him away, he'd been ignored or dismissed.

Leofric was obsessed as well, with his father's precipitous decline. His own grief had been supplanted by his worry and his powerlessness. He didn't know what he could do to bring his father's focus back to the living.

And the bishop? The man in whom the king put his greatest trust, who might ease his heart and mind? He spent most of his days in the cell with the captive, under the guise of 'overseeing' the torments they subjected her to.

Leofric, who'd sinned well and often himself and traveled in the places to find all manner of them, knew Father Francis to be slave to a variety of sins, and he could see the bishop's venal interest in the woman. With his own sick fascination at the fore, Francis wasn't available to counsel or comfort a king who'd sought neither.

Even were the bishop to turn from his own depravity and do his duty to his king, Leofric didn't believe that there were hours enough left in the day or the night for his father to pray his way to rightness with what had happened in the wood, or what was happening within the Black Walls.

It sickened Leofric, what they were doing to the woman. Never before in his life had he known a prisoner to be treated thus. Even those two men who'd been locked in the Black Walls before hadn't known such constant, inexplicable torments, and for those two, there had been cause to what they'd been subjected to. The tortures had had a goal beyond the pain itself. Information or correction, there had been a reason and, thus, an ending.

If the goal for what was happening to the woman were truly to ease the king's broken heart, to cleanse his grief, as he'd said himself, then it could not have been less effective. Each day, the king dwindled more, pulled more deeply into a black caul of sorrow so heavy it sapped his sense.

And the woman—Leofric had never known of any like her. Through everything they did to her, every abasement, every agony, she was silent. He'd observed it himself, though he only rarely looked through that window and could not bear to look long.

He needn't see to know. The Black Walls rang out with the sounds of the lash or the cane or the cat o' nine tails, and the effortful grunts of the men on her, but she was silent. The men spoke of it, were frustrated by their inability to make her scream, and each time they tried something to break through her steely resolve.

Only in senselessness would she make a sound. When she lost her senses during a pressing, or when she'd been left in her cell and could sleep, then she moaned.

That was the window Leofric found himself peering into, though the black inside it was nearly impenetrable: her cell, when she had been left to herself. The unconscious sounds of her suffering made him ill, made him furious, but he felt admiration, too, or something greater even than that.

Awe. He felt awe.

Not for the men who'd done her so much damage, but for the woman who had taken so much and not lost her will. In those sounds she made only when she couldn't control them, Leofric heard tremendous suffering, exquisite agony. Pain that would break the strongest men he knew. That would have broken him long before.

But when she woke, she went instantly silent and made no sound again as long as she could lock her jaws.

They no longer bound her in her cell; after weeks, she had lost the strength to fight them. Her body was failing her. But her will was not.

Leofric had never known *anyone*, man or woman, with such strength. To break her, who was, as all were, God's creation, seemed a most grievous sin. She hadn't—she could not have—done to Dreda what had obviously been done to her. She was paying for another's crime.

She was an enemy, yes. A barbarian, a heathen, who had stormed their shore and trampled a town, so she was not innocent. She was a vanquished enemy. That earned her a death.

Not this atrocity, this endless evil.

After weeks of standing quietly by while his father settled into depraved madness and the bishop allowed it to happen, Leofric descended into the Black Walls, expecting to find his father there.

He did not. But before he could turn and climb back to the light to seek him in the chapel, the door of the torture cell opened, and Father Francis stepped out. Behind him came the warden, and then the executioner, whose assigned tasks extended well beyond beheadings and hangings. He carried the captive slung over his shoulder. She was senseless, and her body shook and swayed with his steps.

Leofric had not seen the woman clearly in weeks, and he was shocked into wooden silence. Her blonde hair was black with grime. Her face was discolored and misshapen with bruising. Her skin was smeared with blood and filth. Her sleek, wondrous muscles had wasted away. She was little more than a hide-wrapped skeleton.

The greatest horror, however, was none of that. The thing that turned his stomach was the state of her wounds. Her back and her legs, her arms—they were nearly shredded with ragged gashes, the work, he knew, of multiple lashes repeated over many days and then left to fester. Or worse, to be filled with what the warden and cottars called black fire, some kind of unguent that burned and ate at the raw meat of wounds.

A sudden, powerful urge gripped Leofric's body, and he nearly stepped forward. He wanted to take the woman from the executioner. He wanted to gather her to his chest. To protect her from these men.

He caught himself and stood still.

The executioner dropped her body in her cell, and Leofric heard her moan.

How the woman was alive, he could not imagine. What had her will been forged of?

He felt more than sick for this woman's suffering, more than worry for his father's soul, more even than grief for the loss of Dreda. The vengeance that had been in his own heart, which had stilled his tongue from protesting this from the start, from saying something in those moments when their father had stood up from the floor in the residence and pulled his regal bearing back over his shoulders, before he'd come to the Black Walls and been overtaken by this madness—the vengeance that had made Leofric complicit in this horror was gone from his heart. Now he felt...he didn't know.

"Enough of this," he said without thinking. "Enough."

The three men who'd come from that room all looked at him. For the hundredth time, Leofric marked the oddity of a holy bishop so comfortable in a dungeon.

"Your Grace?" the bishop asked, and Leofric heard no respect in the address.

What was happening here was under his father's orders. The king. He had no authority to stop it, and he transgressed badly to assert such a challenge. But he didn't back down. That urge that had almost compelled him to wrest the woman from her tormentors drove him yet.

"I'm sending a healer to her. And proper food and drink. You've played your games, and now this is done."

The bishop bowed his head. "Your Grace, I would obey, but I cannot. We are under orders from the king your father."

"I will speak to my father. You would have done well to counsel him away from this sinfulness in the first place."

Hard light glinted in the bishop's eyes. "I think you are not the one to say what is sin and what is not, Your Grace. The Lord uses me as his tool here."

That was terribly convenient for the bishop, then. Leofric set his jaw. "Leave her alone."

Father Francis bowed and managed to show no obeisance. "I shall speak to the king as well, and we shall know."

There was no point in quarreling with the man, so Leofric turned and sprinted up the steps. He would have to impress upon his father that the time for this horror was over.

~oOo~

As he entered the chapel, Leofric didn't know what he would say. The father he'd known all his life would know reason. But that man would have had the captive woman killed as soon as it had become clear that she didn't know their language and couldn't be pressed for information. He would never have tortured anyone, man or woman, for so long, for no purpose but to cause pain.

This man had been twisted and stretched by grief, one doubly deep because it claimed two losses.

The queen had died while she'd held Dreda in her arms for the first and only time. Leofric didn't know what exactly had happened, but childbirth was a dangerous thing, and often women died bringing new life into the world.

His parents had been married in the way royals were always married: to forge an alliance between realms. They'd barely known each other before they were husband and wife. But the queen had been beautiful in face and in spirit, and the king had been steady and kind, and they had grown to know deep love.

Leofric vividly remembered the day of Dreda's birth and their mother's death. Though he had been a man grown, he'd wept wild tears. He still felt the loss of their mother even now, and he knew that Eadric did as well. Her unconditional, unreserved love and devotion would always be missed.

But in the midst of that gaping loss had been a tiny, perfect girl. Their father had come from the queen's chamber with his eyes full of sorrow and his arms full of hope. "She is not gone," he'd told them with a quaking voice. "She is with us in our daughter. Meet your sister. She is Dreda."

Their mother's name.

The newborn princess had been calm and curious, her eyes open wide already, and Leofric had believed his father's words. Their mother's spirit had wrapped around her daughter and stayed with them.

Their loss had been eased, and every sweet thing that Dreda did—her smile, her laugh, her sighs in sleep—every new thing she learned, even the stormy blue of her eyes, reminded them all of the mother she'd never known.

In losing Dreda, they'd finally lost the queen.

Leofric knew that. He felt it himself. But none of them could be reclaimed from their pain by causing it to another. That would have been true even if the woman in the Black Walls had been the one to hurt his sister. Nothing they could do to the captive would change their loss in any way.

The king knelt at the end of the aisle, before the altar, beneath the golden crucifix. He wore only breeches and a linen tunic, not even a brocaded doublet. His iron grey hair was wild around his head. He might have been a trespassing peasant.

Leofric blessed himself in the font and walked down the aisle, his boots striking the stone floor, making his footsteps echo through the high-ceilinged sanctuary.

His father didn't acknowledge that he was no longer alone. When he arrived at the altar, Leofric genuflected and then knelt at his father's side. He didn't speak. He put his hands together and made an effort to pray.

The words wouldn't come at first, but as his thoughts circled the trouble of the castle, the grief, the anger, the vengeance, the horror, he understood that he was praying. He opened his mind and waited for the words to come to him that his father needed to hear.

He didn't want the woman to die. That would be the most expedient solution, he knew—to tell his father that it was right to treat her as an enemy warrior, to take her head. It was the proper solution. Her suffering would end, the vengeance would be done, and they could turn again to life.

But he didn't want her to die. Kneeling at his father's side, he understood that truth—he wanted to *save* her.

Why? He didn't know. How? He didn't know. It was hopeless, of course. Nothing would induce the king to save the life of a woman he'd spent more than a month torturing. What purpose might she have? Her people had been driven away; they had no more need of information. And she couldn't speak their language, so what information she might have was locked behind her barbarian tongue.

Nevertheless, the thought that rose to the top, that grew until it silenced all the others, was that he wanted the woman to live. To be released from the Black Walls and restored to that fierce, sleek strength she'd had.

That was folly. It was madness.

The king sighed heavily and stood. Leofric stood as well. His father looked at him, his eyes weary.

The man before him was broken, and it broke Leofric's heart to see it.

"Father, I would speak with you, if I might."

The king inclined his head, and Leofric took that for permission to continue.

"I would speak with you about the captive woman. I think she might be of use." The words were there in a rush, and he spoke them as they came. It was as if they were being poured into his mind from the mouth of God Himself. "She was a leader among her people. She has information about their ways. She is a warrior. She can explain to us their ways of fighting."

"We drove them away," the king said, showing a glimmer of interest. "And she doesn't speak. She never speaks. She never screams. I don't understand why she will not scream."

Leaving that rambling unaddressed, Leofric continued with the idea that now charged through his brain. "And if they should come back? Mayhap she can be taught to speak with us, and prepare us for barbarians better prepared for us."

The king blinked. "She is a savage. An animal."

He wasn't dismissing him out of hand. Leofric realized that the king had been *ready* for this challenge. Perhaps he'd been seeking a way out of the cycle. Something he couldn't see for his own benightedness.

Leofric sent an angry thought—or maybe that, too, was a prayer—toward Father Francis. The soul of the king was the bishop's first charge, and he'd let it fester while he'd sated his own prurient interests. Any one of the lesser priests in the kingdom would have been a better guide and guard for the king's soul.

"Father, she is not an animal. She is a woman, heathen or no. She is God's own child, like any other. And she is smart enough to lead and fight. She is strong enough to survive. She can be taught."

Turning from him, the king gazed up at the golden crucifix. "I had the crucifix made so that the queen your mother might be wed under it. She didn't like it. We were wed years, we had our two sons, before she told me that she thought the Lord wouldn't like so well to be formed from gold. Humble wood befitted a carpenter, she said. But she wouldn't have it removed because we had been wed beneath it." He stepped to the altar and brushed his hands over its smooth surface. "Dreda was the last of her."

"No, Father." He closed the distance between them and rested his hand on his father's shoulder. "She is in Eadric and me. She is in your heart. She is in our love. Dreda is there, too. Here. With us." He set his hand on his chest, over his heart. "Mother wouldn't like what we've done in the Black Walls."

After a long, fraught silence, the king nodded. "No, she would not." He turned and faced his son again, and Leofric was heartened to see life flickering deep inside his father's eyes. "And you would have me free her?"

"Not free her. Tend to her. Offer her comfort. Bring her back to health. She is alone in our world now, and she understands nothing. After everything she's suffered, kindness might be a balm. And if she is no help or use, then kill her as our enemy."

"And who would be her tutor in this endeavor? Who would we trust so much with such a loose tether on a prisoner who would tear my heart from my chest with her teeth?"

"I would, Sire. I would teach her. I would build her trust."

A spectral smile fluttered over the king's lips and disappeared. "Do not exchange one kind of sin for another, my son. You would do better to keep your trust with the kitchen wenches and chambermaids."

Leofric blushed and smiled. There had been a glimmer of his father in that scolding—the godly man who bore his son's dalliances with aggravated patience and disappointed affection.

"No, Father. My interest is in making of her some use. Healing her wounds and ours. Righting what is wrong. That is all."

"Very well. Bring her to the servants' quarters. Keep her under guard. If she can be healed, do so. If she can be made to speak, do so. If she has knowledge, find it. But if she is dull, or stubborn, if she will not be useful, she dies."

9

Brenna God's-Eye had been a slave when Astrid had first known her. She'd sold herself into thrall to Jarl Åke when she was young, still on the cusp of her womanhood. Astrid, almost the same age, had been fascinated by the way people feared the girl, a mere slave.

But she was the God's-Eye as well, her right eye full of color and light and said to have been Odin's own. Not even the lowliness of thralldom could weaken the power of her eye.

Åke had taken great pride and power in calling the God's-Eye his thrall. Astrid remembered the nervous reverence the people of Geitland, warrior and craftsman, farmer and thrall alike, had paid to the girl as she'd moved through town performing her humble duties. Slaves were usually beneath notice, but Brenna God's-Eye had both attracted and repelled attention. She'd been a steady source of fascination.

Astrid had known real envy. For a slave. She'd wanted to be feared like the God's-Eye was feared. She'd wanted men to quail to look on her.

Then, two years or so after the God's-Eye had come to Geitland, the town had been attacked and nearly overrun. Åke and his warriors had defeated the chieftain—he who would come to know the Blood Eagle for his treachery—and the God's-Eye, who'd fought and killed the invaders who'd come for the jarl's family, had been freed to train as a shieldmaiden.

In the God's-Eye's strength, and in her change of fortune, Astrid had seen her own path. She would be a warrior, too. She'd taken up the sword at once.

For the first time in her life, her father had looked on her with something warmer than benign disappointment. He had seen that she might bring honor to her family after all.

But that had barely mattered to Astrid. The first time she'd hefted a sword and swung it true, she had felt a power fill her veins. She had known her calling, found her path. She had, for the first time in her life, seen who she was. Not a cart-maker's daughter. Not a healer's daughter. Not an only child who should have been a son.

A shieldmaiden. On the day she'd embarked on her first raid, she'd cast off her father's name, no longer claiming that she was Hanssdottir. She was simply Astrid. And someday, she hoped to earn a name beyond herself. Like Vali Storm-Wolf.

Or she might remain simply Astrid. Brynhilde had needed no extension of herself to be told of in the sagas and revered among all the Northern people.

Like the great Brynhilde, like the great God's-Eye, Astrid was a shieldmaiden. She was strong and brave and valiant.

A true shieldmaiden closed her mouth against her pain.

A true shieldmaiden closed her mouth against her pain.

A true shieldmaiden closed her mouth against her pain.

~oOo~

Her body was dying. Far away, on the floor of that black cell, her body was ending its use. She could feel it burn and throb, could feel the corruption dig deep, all the way to her bones.

There was no place in that body, from her cracking scalp to her swollen feet, that did not hurt, that was not dying. Her head was on fire, her belly full of molten lead, her joints and muscles made of jagged rocks.

The pain was so acute and so complete, so constant, that it had become its own presence, separate from her mind.

Her mind had moved far away. Into the past, sometimes, and into the future, sometimes. Never in the present. At any cost, not the present.

She could see the rolling winter hills of Geitland; she could smell and hear and feel and taste her home. She could watch her mother at her healing. She could see Olga and Magni.

She could see Leif. Her friend. He had made her his right hand when he'd taken the seat of the jarl, and she'd found a talent in herself for seeing the things he missed. He looked ahead, and she watched their feet, and together they kept Geitland on a steady path.

She could see the great doors of Valhalla, gleaming ahead.

Leif was not coming for her. He and Vali would not break the cell door down and pull her back into the light. They were dead, then. They would have come for her if they'd lived.

They were in Valhalla already. She would drink with her friends soon.

How soon, she didn't know. Time had lost all meaning. The signs of need in her body had gone silent as it progressed in its dying. There was only the black cell, and the bad room. The man in black, and the seer. The pain.

All she had left was to close her mouth and wait.

She would die with honor and valor, and she would join her friends.

A true shieldmaiden closed her mouth against her pain.

A true shieldmaiden closed her mouth against her pain.

A true shieldmaiden

Closed her mouth

Closed her mouth

Closed her mouth.

~oOo~

The scrape of the cell door wrested Astrid from a hazy dream of home and shoved her back into the black cell. A small voice somewhere inside her urged her to fight, and she made an attempt to move her limbs. They had long ago stopped heeding her commands, however, and she lay passive, not even blinking to try to clear her sight.

There was nothing she needed to see. They would grab her. They would heave her up. They would carry her to the bad room, and they would do what they would.

It seemed as if it had been longer than usual since they'd last come for her, but time was a broken circle, spiraling into nothingness. She closed her eyes and tried to return to the woods above Geitland.

Something hard and cool was pressed to her lips, and she felt wet spilling over her, into the cracks of her skin. A hand slid under her head—it hurt, pressing on swollen, broken skin— and she called up what focus and strength she could and forced herself fully into the horrible present. She yanked her head away, and, unable to hold it up on her own power, she let it fall with a rattling thud to the floor.

A man spoke, his voice quiet and soft. She didn't know the words he said. In her time in the dark, she'd learned a few of her tormentors' words, she thought, but none of them good, and none of what this man had said.

Again, he lifted her head, this time using both hands, and something happened—he shifted, and lifted her higher. Oh, it hurt, it hurt, it hurt, and she tried to close her mouth against her pain but her head was full of sparks and swirls. Images of the woods at home crowded in with the door to Valhalla and the flash of the lash and she didn't know which one was real or where she was.

She felt arms around her—they were gentle and strong. That wasn't real. There was nothing gentle in what was real. Gentle was a dream. But it was one she wanted. How long since anyone had been gentle with her?

Again the hard, cool press at her lips and the wet over them. A cup. It was a cup. That couldn't be real, either. No one had offered her a cup in the black place.

The soft, deep voice at her ear, very close, speaking words she didn't know. It didn't matter. Here in this dream place, there was water in her mouth, and soft hands on her agonized body, and gentle sounds of safety at her ear. She swallowed, and the water turned to broken glass and cut its way down her throat, but it was cool and good. It was good. There was something still good.

Shhh. The deep voice said in this dream. *Shhh.* She understood that. There were more words, but she didn't need them. Only the soft sounds. In this unreal place, she was leaning against a warm chest, and strong arms were around her, holding her tenderly, and she had water. Even if it cut her, it was water, cool and brilliant.

A woman's voice spoke in the strange words. Never had a woman been in the black place. What was this place? Had her mind conjured something new? Not past or future but something else entirely?

The man answered her. Then they conversed. Back and forth. Unable to understand, and unable to care, Astrid focused on the little good she'd found here in this new unreal place. She turned her head and felt cool skin on her cheek. She heard the deep rumble of the man's voice. He stopped, and she felt a whisper-light touch, like fingertips over her cheek.

Then there were different hands on her, small and sharp, probing at her legs, her arms, her back. Pushing into her wounds, tearing them open.

This was just a new torment, then. The worse one yet, offering her a reminder of comfort and then wresting it away. She found the last dregs of her will and strength, and she fought back, throwing her arms and legs out, wheeling away from the man's gentle touch, lashing out at all the hands on her, the soft and the harsh.

After a moment, the last of her strength faded away, and she collapsed again.

The voices continued, softly, man and woman, but they were far away. Astrid let her mind leave the black place. She couldn't fight. They would do to her body what they would.

Time fell into its void. Her mind spun, images shifting, memories and dreams, one over the other, and she didn't try to find one place to go.

A weight fell over her, soft and thick. She didn't understand what it was. It hurt, but lightly, a scant pressure over each wound. But something under the sting was new, was not pain, and she felt…eased.

Warm. She felt warmth. She had been bare so long that she hadn't remembered what it was to be warm.

The man's hands were on her again, gentle again. He lifted her, and pain snarled through her muscles. She tried to resist, afraid to go into the bad room again, but there was no fight left in her.

The man cradled her against his chest. She felt his voice rumble against her ear. He hadn't taken the warmth away. He shifted her in his arms, tucking her closely to him. She could smell the warm clean fresh of his skin, a scent so good and clear, so different from the rank reek of the black place, that it stung her nose.

He carried her from the black place. He carried her and carried her.

He carried her into the light.

~oOo~

The room was too bright, brighter than her eyes could see. It hurt, it burned, and Astrid wondered if the man had brought her to the sun.

Or Valhalla? Was this how a shieldmaiden was carried to Valhalla? Not the Valkyries but their brothers? She'd never heard of such a thing.

There was more talking, there were more voices. A crowd of them, all female. Yet the man held her, and she was soothed by the rumble of his voice, steady and firm.

Then the sound of water. Splash and pour.

No. No, not that. Not the freezing water dumped over her bare, broken body. She had no strength left to close her mouth against that. Where was Valhalla?

143

Had she cried out? Had she been weak? Was the man carrying her to Helheim instead?

Yes, that had to be it. She felt herself falling, falling, falling toward Hel.

She tried to fight and found that the brief moments of ease—how long had she been headed toward the sun?—had restored to her some small strength.

He held her firmly, whispering *Shhh, shhhh, shhhh* at her, but she struggled. She tried to find her battle cry, but only a croaking groan came from her ragged throat.

Then she wasn't falling any longer. She tried to see, but her eyes could only burn in the white light.

The man was arguing with a woman—the woman with the cruel hands. Astrid could hear the fight in his voice.

He moved, and she was falling again, and she heard the splash of water, but her limbs wouldn't struggle against it this time. To prepare herself for the bitter bite of the icy water, she untethered her mind from this white place.

But the water was warm—very warm. And the man had not let her go. She could feel him under her body, under the water with her. The water bit into her wounds, but the pain didn't torment her. There was ease in it. There was hope. This was helpful pain.

Healing pain. Were they healing her?

His voice at her ear, speaking unknowable words meant to soothe.

Hands at her head—small hands, but gentle. Pulling at her hair, but slowly. Undoing old braids that had been tangled into knots.

Were they washing her?

Had she been saved?

Was she home?

Again, she tried to see, and again her eyes gave her back only white light. "Leif?" she made her voice croak out his name.

Or was she with the healer? Her mother. Were those her mother's hands in her hair? Was she finally knowing her mother's gentle touch?

"Mamma?"

Soft, strange words at her ear. A deep voice. The scratch of a beard at her cheek. Lips—lips on her skin.

Not her mother. She knew no one who would touch her in such a tender way. She had not lived a life for tenderness. She had not wanted such a life.

She could think now of nothing she wanted more.

Valhalla or Helheim or home or just another cell, she didn't care. She would take this soft salvation for as long as she could have it. She let her body ease into the arms around her. She turned her head as much as she could and felt the quiet strength of the one who held her.

She tasted salt on her lips and didn't understand.

~oOo~

The man washed her, dabbing a soft cloth over her body as he held her. When he struck a spot where vivid pain lurked, he whispered in her ear and lightened his touch even more.

The hands at her hair worked endlessly, and then there was more warm water, and her hair was washed.

She could feel some of the pain wash away in the warm water. Other pains sharpened, but they didn't vex her as they might have. Calm was easing into her flesh.

Time still spun aimlessly, but her mind settled a bit. Though it was still full of fire and confusion, it wanted to be in this present, and she could catch purchase and know sense every now and then. The room began to go dim just as the man lifted her from the water and wrapped her in something warm and as soft as lambswool.

Then there was the glow of fire, and Astrid knew alarm. Was she in the bad room after all?

Her eyes flew open, and she could see—not well, but enough to make out furnishings. A bed. Chairs. Sconces on the walls. A fireplace. She was in a room like those in the Estland castle. There were windows, showing the darkening blue of new night sky.

She looked up at the man, her savior. She couldn't make out his features, but they were dark—dark beard, dark hair.

Was she still in Anglia? She was. Gods, no. She hadn't been saved.

Had she been sold? Was she a slave?

He carried her to the bed. Would he use her now? It didn't matter. Of all the harm that had come to her, men putting themselves inside her was by far the least.

He pulled a fur over her naked body, speaking some of his strange words. Then he brushed his fingers over her forehead. He laid his palm over the same spot.

He turned and said strange words to someone else in the room.

Astrid didn't care. She was weary and sick, her head burned and her mind reeled. Pain ravaged her body. But, for the first time in an eternity, she felt some comfort, buried under a fur, lying on soft linens.

She rolled to her side and wrapped her arms around the man's arm. If he had bought her, she was glad. He had taken her from the black place, and nothing else mattered. If he would only be gentle, he could use her as he would.

It wasn't pain that had broken her.

It was tenderness.

10

Leofric brushed his hand over the woman's damp hair, blonde again since the bath and Elfleda's careful attention to the filthy snarls and mats. Out of its braids and clean, it was long and the color of spun flax, too pale to be called gold. The strands still bore the kink of the braids, even after washing.

The woman had rolled to her side and wound her arms around the arm on which he'd propped himself, and he hadn't the heart to pull away. In her restive sleep, she whimpered quietly with each panting exhale.

She'd been delirious since he'd entered her cell, shifting from unconsciousness to an indolent insensibility to a frenzied, pallid madness, over and over again. She spoke in her language, and Leofric wished he understood her. Sometimes, it sounded like she called out names, as if pleading for friends to help her. Friends she didn't have here, who were far away from her now.

Once, she'd called out *Mama*, and he'd understood that. His heart had seemed to rend.

His heart had confused him since he'd entered her cell, since he'd settled on the floor to help her drink. Mercy, he was sad. Sadder now, perhaps, than when Dreda had been carried to him and his brother.

They had done all this to her, this woman, this warrior, who'd been sleek and powerful and was now wasted to nearly nothing. When he'd lifted her, she'd seemed lighter than Dreda had last been.

He brushed his fingertips over her full, cracked lips. An old scar ran through them, from her nose to her chin—a thin, straight, pale line. It was a fighter's scar. So odd to see it on a woman.

"She's too hot," he murmured. Now that she was clean, her wounds were all the more horrible, and her skin, what little of it wasn't open and festering or mottled with bruises, was a vivid red.

Elfleda huffed. The healer had behaved brusquely with him, giving him the barest respect due his station, since he'd insisted on getting into the tub with the woman.

But she had panicked badly when he'd tried to lay her in the water, and he couldn't bear the sight of this wonder of a woman in fear. So he'd toed off his boots and climbed in, fully dressed, her bare, broken body on his.

After a moment of frantic delirium, she'd calmed and turned into his hold. His embrace.

That was what it had become, as she'd settled with him and let them clean her: an embrace. When she'd begun to cry, he'd even kissed her cheek, and her head, again and again, without thinking.

Elfleda had seen it all and given him a stern eye.

"The corruption is terrible, Your Grace," she said now. "She is hot with fever because the poison in her wounds feeds on her."

"Make a poultice, then."

"A poultice for her whole body?" She shook her head and waved off the challenge he'd been about to make. "It matters not, Your Grace. The corruption goes too deep." Pulling back the fur—the woman moaned at the loss of its warmth—

Elfleda made a sweeping gesture with her hand. "You see the color? The seeping? Already the linens go dark with it. There is little to be done."

No. He couldn't abide the thought that she would die of illness they'd given her. "Little to be done is not nothing. What can you do?"

The healer pulled the fur over her patient and stood straight. "It would cause her terrible pain. Mayhap more than she's yet known."

He looked down at the woman beside him, at more peace than she'd been since he'd brought water and healer into her cell.

She was still unclothed—they couldn't dress her because her wounds were too many and as yet untended. She was still unfed—she'd vomited water repeatedly and could only keep sips down as yet. She seemed to be blind, or near to it—the consequence of weeks without sun and with only occasional torchlight. But now, she slept with a semblance of ease, her body quiet, her face in repose. Only the shallow panting of her ailing breath told that she suffered.

And her arms wrapped around his arm—cleaving to a stranger for comfort.

"What can you do?" he repeated. He wouldn't let her die. If the healing caused her pain, he would be here to offer her what comfort he could.

"What's rotting must be cut away, and what's left must be closed. Blade and fire, Your Grace. In all these rotting places. Do you understand the pain she would feel? Better, I think, to speed her way to her eternity."

"Can you not give her a dwale?"

"She is too ill, Your Grace. The potion could kill her."

There seemed not much risk in any event. "Then we will have speeded her way, yes? And she will be at ease when she goes."

Elfleda sighed and then nodded. "I shall seek out Brother Thomas. He is deft with a healing blade."

"No. No men. I want no men in this room but myself." The woman had been subjected to too many men over too many weeks. Other than himself and the guard outside the door, only women would tend her.

"Brother Thomas would not..." The healer was obviously scandalized even to think the thought she'd had.

"It matters not what he would do. It matters what she would fear. No men, Elfleda. You will do what you must for her."

She gave him a long stare pregnant with meaning. "Your Grace, if I may speak..."

"Go on."

"Is this woman not your father's enemy?"

He answered her question with one of his own. "What do you think of what we've done to her, Elfleda?"

She ducked her head, her first true showing of respect in this night. "It is not mine to say, Your Grace."

"You say much without using your tongue, woman. Now use your tongue and answer the question I asked. What do you think of what you see before you?"

"I think...I think if she was not the king's enemy before, she will be now."

Leofric was sure that was true. She'd turned to him for comfort in her delirium, but if she regained her strength and her senses, he was under no delusion that she would see him kindly then. She might not even remember that it was he who'd taken her from the Black Walls.

But that didn't matter. He wasn't doing this for her gratitude or her friendship. He was doing this because it was right.

"Prepare what you need to clean her wounds. Bring what assistants you need, as long as they are women. Give her a potion to help her sleep through what you must do. Do it now. And bring me dry clothes."

Elfleda nodded. "Yes, Your Grace."

She left the room, and Leofric settled at the woman's side, letting her keep hold of his arm.

~oOo~

The dwale Elfleda gave her was enough to keep her sleeping, but not enough to erase her pain completely.

They laid her on her front, and Elfleda and her apprentice spread her arms and legs wide on the bed. In her deep slumber, the woman moaned in protest, but she couldn't resist. Leofric sat on the bed and wrapped his hand around hers.

Though he'd been in battle and seen men separated from limbs, and he'd seen the gruesome work of a battle healer, Leofric felt ill watching what Elfleda and her girl did.

A sharp, hot blade sliced away flesh that reeked and oozed. Scores of corrupted gashes over her back, her arms, her bottom, her legs, her feet. Then a thin rod, heated in the fire

153

and glowing red hot, was laid over each sliced wound. The smell and sizzle of cooked flesh filled the air.

The woman whimpered and shuddered with each slice, each burn, mumbling desperately in her own language. Tears slid over her nose and wet the linens she lay on, and Leofric felt despair. He wanted to know words that could console her. He wanted to make her well in her heart as much as her body.

When Elfleda was done with her back, they turned her over and did it all over again to clean the wounds on her belly, her breasts, her thighs. The woman let loose a thin scream when the sealing rod closed a wide gash over her belly.

Leofric slid from the bed and knelt at the side. As he moved, her hand tightened around his fingers.

"I'm here, I'm here, I'm here." He repeated words he'd said hundreds of times in these hours. "I won't let you hurt more after this. I'll protect you. I'm sorry. Forgive me. Forgive *us*. Oh Lord, forgive us."

He understood that he was praying, and he bent his head to his hands, still wrapped around hers, and prayed in earnest.

~oOo~

For days, even after Elfleda's cleansing of the wounds, the woman lay in fever and delirium. Her pain remained acute—worse immediately after the cleansing than before it, as the healer had warned—and her times of swooning were a boon to her and to them all.

He sat with her most of each day, leaving only to dine with his father and brother and to wash and tend to his own needs. After a few days, he slept in his own bed, when Elfleda shoved him from the room and said he was like to make himself as ill as their charge.

Leaving her was difficult. Though she hadn't gained her senses, she had times of near wakefulness, and she always sought him out. Her eyes didn't focus, but they turned toward him, and when he leaned close or held her, she relaxed. She wanted his hands on her—holding her, stroking her hair—as if his touch itself eased her pain.

There were signs that she was healing. She gained enough sense at times throughout each day that she could take water, and some thin gruel, and after a few days managing a full cup of water, her breathing settled and deepened. There was still a strange, rough edge to each breath, but more air came in and went out, and that helped her calm.

Each day, Elfleda changed her many bandages, and the seepage dwindled and disappeared. When the dressings stayed clean, her skin began to cool. She was healing.

One morning, nearly two weeks after he'd carried her up from the Black Walls, Leofric went into her room and saw her sitting up in bed. Still dressed in nothing but bandages, but with her pale hair brushed, and holding a cup on her own, she turned and looked right at him, blue eyes clear and steady.

Her face had healed well. Most of the bruising had faded, and the cuts were reduced to thin red lines. Her beauty shone through the new scars. Her body would take longer, but on this day, he saw that she would be truly well. She would be strong again.

He smiled. "Hello! You look well!" She couldn't understand him, of course, but the words had come out without much thought, so glad was he to see her improving. And she'd understand his tone, he hoped, and his smile.

A smile she didn't return. He would have been glad to see what her smile might look like, but she only stared steadily at him, and Leofric knew that the need she'd had for him in her delirium was over.

He was no longer her savior. Now he was her enemy again.

She set the cup on the tray, and Elfleda's girl picked it up and carried it from the room, curtseying as she went by. He and the woman were alone.

Perhaps it was not yet too late. He went to the bed and sat on the side, as he'd done so many times during these weeks. When he reached for her hand, she pulled it away.

But there was something in those blue eyes that said she remembered how she'd needed him and how he'd been there. How he'd lent her his strength.

With the hand she'd rejected, he patted his chest. "I am Leofric." Then he pointed to her and formed his face into an expression that was a question. "Your name?"

She stared.

Again, he patted his chest. "Lee-*off*-ric. Leofric."

He knew she wasn't stupid, and he knew she wasn't deaf. She understood the question he was asking. No language barrier was so tall that names couldn't be exchanged.

She was stubborn. Willful. And mistrustful.

There was a small bowl of fruit on the table; the girl, who was always flustered around him, must have forgotten it in her haste to leave the room. He reached for an apple.

"Apple." He held it out to her, but she didn't take it. "Apple."

From his belt, he pulled a small blade, and she reacted strongly, going stiff and shoving herself across the bed, away from him.

"I won't hurt you." He sliced a piece of the apple off and ate it, then sliced another and held it out to her, balanced on the blade.

She stared at that blade for a long time. He held it out for just as long. At last, she reached out and snatched the piece of apple.

As she ate it, he saw the delight in her eyes, the savoring of something good and sweet. Her face remained impassive, but her eyes danced.

She let loose a long string of her own words. He didn't understand at all. Her voice was hoarse and choppy, from abuse and lack of use, but the language was lovely.

"I'm sorry. I don't know your words." He shrugged. "I would have you teach me, and I will teach you."

She eyed the apple, and he sliced off another piece for her. As he held it out, he repeated, "I will teach you. Apple."

She ate the apple slice and lay down, tucking herself under the cover and rolling to put her back to him.

He leaned over and laid his hand on her head, seeing her eyes close as he touched her. She didn't flinch away.

Resisting the urge to kiss her cheek, he said, "Rest. I will visit you later in the day. I'm glad you're gaining strength."

She didn't understand his words, but it didn't matter. He hoped she'd understand his tone.

~oOo~

Whether she understood his tone or not, she was like stone to him. She would not tell him her name, and after that single burst of words on the first day her mind had been clear, she hadn't spoken again at all. She allowed Elfleda and the servants to tend her, but she did so silently.

She ate and drank. She healed. She grew strong. But after a few days, Leofric left her alone with the servants, only checking in once or twice in each day. He wasn't doing what his father expected. He wasn't winning her trust or teaching her their tongue. Each day at the evening meal, his father and brother asked after his project, and each day he reported that she was still convalescing but that soon he would be able to work with her in earnest.

His father had returned to something more than a shadow of his true self and had resumed his work. There was not yet happiness in the private residence, but the pall had lifted. Leofric thought the woman had at least some part in the lighter air. No longer was a horror going on under their feet, and without that, and the vengeance that had caused it, their memories of Dreda and the queen could flourish. There was room in them for their light.

But the woman continued to resist him, and soon enough, he would have to tell his father that she was of no use.

When she was fully healed, he told himself, when she had no need of extra care, then he would be firm with her. He would make her cooperate with him. He would find some way to communicate to her that her only other choice was death.

But he didn't want to force her. He wanted her to remember that he had saved her. He hadn't thought he wanted her gratitude, but now he supposed he did. She had neither thankfulness nor patience for him, and it hurt.

One day, when the woman had been in his care nearly a month, Leofric returned to the castle from the stables, having gone to look in on a newly acquired stallion. He went back to the servant's quarters, intending to make the first of his twice-daily efforts to warm the woman to him again.

Elfleda met him in the corridor, her hands on her hips. An armed guard stood at attention, as always, just outside the door.

"There is a problem." He didn't need to ask—the healer's posture was pure frustration.

"Yes, Your Grace. I removed the bandages. She is healing well. All the wounds are closed and healed over."

"And how is that a problem?"

"She will not dress! The bandages no longer cover her, and she stands there as Eve in her sin, and she will not dress! I tried to make her, and she tore the dress from my hands and ripped it in twain! She truly is a savage, Your Grace, to stand so bare without shame."

"I will see what I can do."

"No!" As surprised at herself as he was, Elfleda bowed her head. "Your pardon, Your Grace. But she is bare. Completely. And knows no shame for it."

"I've seen her bare body, Elfleda. You were with me when I took her from the Black Walls. I held her in the bath. I sat with her while you cleansed her wounds."

"But...Your Grace..."

Pulling all his patience to the fore, Leofric sighed heavily. "What is it?"

"She is healed. She is stronger. No longer is she an invalid."

He thought he finally understood, and he grew angry. "You think I would take her? After all this?"

"No, Your Grace. Please...I think she would...entice you."

The healer honestly thought the woman would seduce him? She would barely look at him now. Though he was even angrier, feeling defensive for the woman and for himself, he forced himself to laugh. "A scarred savage? Elfleda, you wound me to think my tastes run so low."

Again, her head bowed. "Forgive me, Your Grace."

"Yes, of course. Is there something you want her to wear? I will make an attempt to persuade her."

~oOo~

He carried a simple, plain-spun servant's dress, folded into a tidy square, into the woman's room, with a pair of plain leather slippers on top.

She was sitting on the bed, as bare as Elfleda had warned. One leg was folded, and her sex was exposed. Except for the glossy tresses on her head, she was nearly hairless everywhere. Between her thighs was only the scantest bit of silky down.

He imagined it was silky. He had imagined it often. But he'd been careful never to touch it.

As he lingered at the door he'd just closed, holding the clothes like an offering, she stood.

Her body was terribly scarred, from head to toe, but most especially from her shoulders to her knees. The elaborate drawing on her thigh was broken by scars. He knew the very worst of it was her back. She was covered with the red welts of fresh healing.

And she was still skinny. Her shoulders stood at sharp angles. Each rib carved itself into her flesh. He might well have been able to hang from her hip bones the dress he held.

But she stood tall, perfectly straight, and the fierce fire in her eyes was likely to burn him.

Her breasts…even scarred, they were lovely. Softly round, with nipples of the faintest pink.

She did indeed entice him.

He walked to her, and she stood still, except to lift her chin in defiance as he neared her.

"You must dress. Elfleda assures me these will suit you." He hefted the light bundle in his hands, and she knocked it away, the blow enough to send the dress to the floor, several feet away. The little shoes clattered off even farther.

She spoke a string of words. Even in her clear contempt, he heard music in her language.

Leaving the dress in its new wad on the floor, Leofric smiled and attempted persuasion in a light tone. "I wish I understood. I wish I knew your name. Your *name*."

As he had many times now, he patted his chest. "Leofric." He pointed at her chest and lifted his eyes in question.

She pulled a face of pure disgust and dropped back to the bed, sitting again in that decidedly unladylike, decidedly alluring pose.

A bolt of sensation went through him as he imagined getting onto the bed with her and putting his hands there, the place she seemed to be offering him.

But he knew she wasn't offering him anything. She was merely sitting and, if it were possible, unaware of the affect she might have to sit in that way.

Elfleda had been absolutely right to caution him against coming in here, because he wanted her. He wanted her badly.

And she wouldn't even give him her name.

For something to do besides leer at her, he gathered up the dress and brought it back.

"You must dress. You're well enough to be out of bed, and you cannot"—feeling foolish, he waved his hand over her nude body and shook his head, then held the dress out to her and nodded.

She stared at the dress. Then she took it. She shook it out, laying the fabric over the bed. She stood up.

Had he managed to convince her?

She picked up the dress and held it up to her body. Leofric nodded, smiling, hoping to encourage her.

Turning to face him directly, she smiled—and he'd been right. It was beautiful. She'd lost two teeth in her ordeal in the Black Walls, but none in front. Those were straight and pearly.

Then she grabbed the dress by the neckline and yanked, rending it down the middle. As she discarded the ruined dress, she let loose another string of musical words, these fiery and furious, and she slammed her hands on his chest.

She did it again, and said something else. She dropped her hands and slapped his hips, his thighs. More words he didn't understand.

He didn't think she was trying to hurt him. She was telling him something. She slapped his thighs again, the leather of his breeches making a sharp sound against her palms.

Then she slapped her own thighs. His thighs again, then her thighs. Her chest, then his chest.

She wanted clothes like his. Breeches. A tunic.

His father would be outraged. Her only chance for survival was to become a part of this world, and in this world, women did not wear breeches. They did not wield weapons and fight in wars. Women were demure and subdued. They knew their place. She could never leave this room in men's clothing. It would mean the end of this project and her immediate death.

Without a way to explain all that, he said what he could. "No." He shook his head.

She very obviously understood that. She shoved at him again, this time meaning to hurt him, and he took a few surprised steps backward to keep his balance.

Then she ran for the door. Completely bare.

She wouldn't get far; there was a guard immediately outside the door, but Leofric didn't want him seeing her unclothed. That imperative—to keep her from any eyes beyond this room—superseded all others, and he leapt for her, catching her around the waist.

He'd moved too quickly, with too much force, and they fell to the floor.

She was under him, fighting at once, in a feral frenzy, though he'd knocked her breathless.

But she was only a few weeks removed from more than a month of steady torture and starvation, and her strength had not returned enough for a fight. Leofric grabbed the hands that sought to punch and scratch, and he held her down.

On the floor. Her bare body beneath him, writhing. He couldn't help what his body did with that.

He saw it when she felt his sex harden in his breeches, against her, so near the place he wanted to be. Her eyes narrowed. They went dark. And then they dimmed. She went limp. In that moment, he could have taken her if he'd wished. She would not have fought him.

But in her darkened eyes, he saw not surrender but betrayal.

She'd had some trust left for him after all, and he'd killed it.

He pushed himself to his knees and then his feet. When he was standing, she rolled and stood. Without looking at him or speaking another of her words, she went to the bed and got on it, pulling the fur over herself.

"Forgive me," he said before he left the room.

In the corridor, he found Elfleda waiting. "Let her be bare. She cannot leave the room, but inside it, let her be bare."

He walked off before the healer could respond.

PART FOUR
SELF-RELIANCE

11

Astrid stood at the window and looked out on the castle grounds. People were at their work—farmers and craftsmen bringing supplies into the yard and driving empty carts from it; workwomen carrying baskets and buckets; stable boys and kennel boys, and all manner of people moving back and forth past her small, distorted view of the world outside.

The windows in this room were tall and narrow, not even the width of her shoulders. She was above the ground some short distance, like the Estland castle but not so high as the room she'd had there. More like the rooms for the servants. If she could jump, she didn't think the landing would do her unbearable harm.

But these windows were full of some kind of smooth, translucent material, almost like horn, but clearer, and cool like the surface of a looking glass. There was too much of it, and it was too clear, to be any kind of glass she'd ever known. A kind of metal joined pieces that made a pattern. They opened—the woman who tended her, Elfleda, had opened them on several occasions and let fresh air and lively sounds into the room—but Astrid had not sorted out the how of it.

They were too narrow, in any event, she thought. Her body was smaller than it had been, but she wasn't sure it was small enough to ease through the stone sides and jump to the ground below.

The windows were not a likely means of escape.

Neither was the fireplace—she'd peered up into the stack above and found a black hole. She thought she would have fit, but what would she have done on the roof of the castle, nearly bare, and unarmed? No, that was no use, either.

The door, then. It was the only way. They didn't lock it, but there was always a guard standing just outside. She'd paid close attention and discerned a pattern. Three guards: one large, almost as tall as Leif, and quite fat, who guarded her during the night; another small, shorter than she by perhaps as much as a head, who was outside her door in the afternoons, and a third, the size of what she supposed was average for these men, about her own height, who stood watch in the mornings.

Always, one of them was there, whenever the door opened. She'd opened it once herself, in the middle of the night, and the big guard had swung silently into the threshold, dropping his weapon, like a metal-shafted spear, across the opening. He hadn't spoken. He'd simply eyed her, his eyes lingering over her bare body before lifting again to her face, as he'd blocked her way, until she'd closed the door. Through the heavy wood, she'd heard him return to his guarding position.

When it was women coming and going, Astrid often found the guards turning to look through the open door at her bare body. Only when it was women, though.

If she would escape, she would have to neutralize the guard. With the big man on duty during the hours of dark, she would have to do it in the daylight, when one of the smaller guards stood watch.

Assuming that she had the strength to take either of them. She didn't know. She had no opportunity to test her strength or her skills. No weapons, no training. Nothing but this room.

Her body felt different. Smaller, yes, and frailer, too. More than that—she felt different inside her skin. The way her legs and arms moved, the way her weight felt on her feet—it was as if, somewhere in the black place, they had changed her body to another.

It was a problem greater than her mind, still bleary and unwell, could manage.

She was worried about her mind, in fact. It didn't work as it once had. She was often confused, and things felt wrong all around her.

Her fear of the dark had returned, for one thing. She was forcing herself to face it, to bear it, to sit up at night in the dark and let the creatures cavort in her mind's eye, but it wasn't like the night in the woods, where her terror had found its bottom and then crumbled away. Now there was no bottom. There was only her will, refusing to give in to the fear. But the fear was there, and she despised it.

Fear and weakness was what she knew now, and she despised herself for it.

The door opened, and Astrid turned from the window. Elfleda came in, carrying a new bundle of women's clothes and shoes. Every few days, she changed out the bundle that Astrid ignored.

She would not wear the clothes of their women, with their heavy skirts and inconvenient sleeves, and the strange covering over their hair. Better she stay bare. These people treated their women like slaves, like beasts of burden and breeding, and they would have to kill her before she would bend to that. Put her in the black place again if they might…

The shudder that went through her cut off the thought, and she slammed her fist into her thigh. She was broken. Gods, she was. After everything she'd endured, they'd still managed to break her.

Because she would wear that blasted dress and be their slave beast if they threatened to put her in that place again. She would stand up to death, but not to that. Not again.

But until they threatened that, she would stand up. They wouldn't give her men's clothing, so she refused clothes.

He wouldn't give her men's clothing. Leofric.

Except for the tunic she now wore, which he'd brought to her the day after he'd knocked her to the ground and shoved his hard sex against her. He'd brought her that, and she'd agreed to wear it. She wanted boots and breeches and a chestpiece. Or a soft, heavy tunic like those he wore, made of some fabric softer than wool and more robust than linen. But she'd agreed to the white linen tunic.

It skimmed high on her thighs, and the neckline was wide enough to drop from a shoulder when she moved. It wasn't what she wanted. She wanted to be dressed as the warrior she was. But he seemed relieved to have her agree to wear a man's shirt, at least.

And she'd felt something strange at the smile he'd given her when she'd pulled it over her head. She didn't understand it, but she'd nearly smiled back at him.

Leofric made her weakest of all, she thought. He'd saved her from the black place. He'd been with her while her blood burned and her skin screamed and she couldn't find the place that was real. In those days, he'd been the only constant that wasn't pain and fear.

When she saw him now, and he came every day, there was a part of her, the same part of her that feared the dark again, that wanted to run into his arms and feel them around her again.

She had never run into a man's arms in her life.

He'd been gentle when she'd forgotten that such a thing existed. He'd made her feel safe when all she'd known was terror and pain. She wanted to know his gentleness, she wanted to feel that safety, again. She wanted him.

She'd never needed such things from anyone but herself, but now she felt them only in Leofric.

And she hated him all the more for it.

Elfleda moved around the room, tidying up, taking away the tray from the morning meal. She didn't speak, because she knew Astrid wouldn't. She'd stopped trying days ago. She simply checked the chamber pot, checked the water ewer, fluffed the pillows, switched one bundle of slave clothes for another, collected the tray, and left the room.

Alone and aimless, Astrid sat down on a chair and tried to make her broken mind focus on how she would escape.

~oOo~

Leofric came in after the midday meal, and Astrid despised the trembling in her belly when she saw him. The weak little girl inside her that wanted to go to him.

She knew some words of this place now. A few. And with those few words, she had learned a few things. She knew that Leofric was the king's son.

That meant that he had power to put her in the black place and power to take her from it at any time. Or to leave her there for all the infinite time she'd been left there.

That meant that he had killed her friends, or ordered them killed, or been involved in that attack in some way.

That meant that he was her enemy. Not only her jailer, and her master, but her enemy in war.

And yet her mouth wanted to smile when he walked into her room. The room in which she was kept under guard. On his orders.

Why did he keep her here? What did he want?

If he wanted her enslaved, then what was it he wanted her to do? He hadn't tried to use her, though he seemed to want to, and she'd thought he would when he'd grabbed her.

He hadn't tried to make her work, even in this room. Others came in and cleaned and tended to her food and other needs. All she did all day was sit—and try to find ways to make her body strong again.

He tried only to talk to her. Every day, he tried. She knew he wanted to teach her his language—and he had, a little. But she had not given him back any of his words. She would not. Where she could assert her will, she would.

She didn't get up as he came into the room and closed the door. The short guard was on watch, she saw. She could measure time by the guards more easily than by the path of the sun.

When Leofric came to the room, the guards didn't turn and look at her.

He came and sat in the chair facing her. "Hello," he said.

She stared.

His eyes moved over her bare legs, and Astrid hated the feeling of embarrassment for how they looked. They looked as they did—skinny and scarred—because of what this man and his father had made happen to her. She had nothing to feel shame for. Not shame. Anger. She should feel anger toward him for the way she looked and the way she felt. But she did feel shame. She hadn't earned these scars in battle but in captivity. They were not scars of strength but of subjugation. They showed her weakness for all the world to see. And Leofric and his people had made them.

She didn't think he'd ever been in the black place—she had no memory of it if he had, until the day he'd saved her—but it was him nonetheless, she knew. Him and his father, the king.

And why? What purpose could their cruelty have had? Unless the cruelty was meant to make her malleable to their designs now.

Astrid had tried to think that possibility out, but her mind wouldn't connect the pieces. She thought of Hnefatafl, the game she played with Leif, and the way he would move to trap her, or to lure her, and then come in behind her and defeat her king. Strategy. Thinking ahead. It wasn't her strength on her best of days. She tried to imagine the black place being a strategy for something they wanted of her now, and she could not.

He talked at her, a string of words she didn't understand, but she heard "father" and "brother" and "language" and assumed that he was telling her he wanted her to learn. Possibly that his father wanted her to learn. And that he had a brother. He said something about "time," but she didn't know what.

Then he leaned forward and reached for her hands. His hands were big and strong, well shaped, with long fingers. They bore the scars of a warrior. They were good hands, and she knew their touch. She craved it.

She pulled her hands from his reach. If he touched her, that frightened child who wanted him so badly might take over.

"Please," he said. She knew that word. He said it often. It was like the *snälla* of her own tongue. He was pleading.

He patted his chest. "Leofric. Leofric."

He pointed to her and lifted his eyebrows. She knew exactly what he wanted. Her name.

When she kept her mouth closed and simply stared at him, he shook his head.

After a moment spent staring at her hands, he sighed and stood.

At the door, he said, "Forgive me."

She understood that as well.

There was more she understood. Something about his aspect while he'd been with her for so brief a time made her feel wary. He hadn't tried very hard today, and he'd seemed different.

He'd given up. And that was important in some way.

It was time to leave. Whether she was strong enough to do it, she didn't know, but something had changed again, and it was time for her to run. If she wasn't strong enough to get away, they would kill her. She would make sure of it. She wouldn't go back to the black place.

A tiny hope fluttered its wings in her heart—that Leif and Vali and Brenna and the rest were still alive, were still in Anglia, that it hadn't been the years it seemed to have been since she'd been with them. The part of her brain that had sense knew it was a fantasy. But at the least, the camp was the place she knew, a place where she could start, where she might find strength in the spirit of her friends and that small remnant of home.

And perhaps they would still be there after all, waiting for her. Those tiny wings fanned a small fire in her soul, and she knew she would try.

If only she knew how.

~oOo~

It came to her when the girl, Audie, collected the evening tray and spilled the bowl. She'd wiped up the meal that was like skause with part of her slave dress and then torn the stained part away and folded the fabric so that the tear wouldn't show.

Astrid was reminded how easily these dresses tore.

Once Audie had left, she knew she would be alone for the duration of the evening, and through the night, until the morning tray came.

She needed clothes—not that stupid dress that she had no idea how she would run in. She needed proper clothes. She needed a weapon.

The morning guard, who came on at the dawn. He was about her size. He carried the same weapon the other guards did— the steel spear. She was no good with a spear, and she'd never wielded one of steel, but it was better than her hands.

She knew how she would get it from him. His weapon and his clothes. If she were strong enough.

If she were brave enough.

There was a time when she had been both. She needed only to remember how it had felt to be brave and strong.

She grabbed the bundle of slave clothes and got to work.

~oOo~

She spent the night tearing the dress into strips and braiding them. The fabric was flimsy, so she braided strips and then braided the braids, until she had a length of strong rope about as long as she was tall. Enough to wrap well around her hands.

She rested a little—she would need all the strength she could muster. Even in her short sleep, her mind played out her plan.

It was a terrible plan, based on too many things she could not know. But it was the only thing she could think of.

As the sky lightened toward dawn, she heard the rustle and thump and quiet conversation that meant that the night's watch was giving over to the morning. The big man far too much for her to handle was going away, and the man about her size was standing outside the door.

The door they never locked.

She waited a few minutes—not too long, because she needed the quiet of dawn, before the castle was busy, to get away, but long enough that the night man had time to leave the corridor.

Astrid knew nothing at all about what was beyond the door. More than three feet from the threshold, all was a mystery, and she was in the hands of the gods.

All night long, she'd prayed to Tyr to help her find her courage and strength, and to know the rightness of her plan.

When she thought the time was right, she stripped the tunic off and tossed it to the bed. She braided her hair in one long, simple braid and used a scrap of dress to tie it off. She picked up the braided rope she'd made of the slave dress and coiled it around her hand, resting that hand on the small of her back.

She went to the door and opened it.

The guard turned, dropping his spear across the door to block her way. She saw his eyes take her body in, and she saw them take on that particular light that meant he was thinking of things he could do to her.

She had intended to smile, but her mouth wouldn't make one. So she did what she could to be alluring. She stepped slowly backward, toward the bed. Slow, small steps—she didn't want to be too far from him when he gave in to his urges.

He looked side to side on the other side of the door. What he saw—or didn't see—satisfied him, and he came into the room and closed the door.

She let him get close. She let him put his hands on her. She lifted one arm, then, carefully, the other, and put them around his neck.

As he leaned close, meaning to kiss her, she uncoiled the rope and looped it quickly around his neck.

Grabbing an end in each hand and coiling them around her fists as quickly as she could, while he fought against her, Astrid pulled, finding more might than she'd thought she had. He struggled and kicked, but she crossed her arms, crossing the rope over his throat, and then feinted and twisted until they were back to back. Planting her legs and bending her knees just right, she bent forward and yanked, as hard and sharply as she could.

The crack was so loud, she had a moment's unreasonable worry that someone elsewhere in the castle would hear it.

The man had stopped struggling. She dropped him.

He was still breathing. Interesting. She'd broken his neck but not killed him.

He blinked up at her, his jaw working like a fish as he sucked in garbled gasps of air.

Moving with haste and care, she stripped him of his boots and breeches. She would have taken his chestpiece, too, but she couldn't make out how it was fastened, so she grabbed the tunic Leofric had given her, and she dressed herself. She was smaller than she'd realized. The breeches were loose, and she had to draw the belt so tightly that the leather gathered in big clumps on her hips. The boots were too large and would make blisters quickly, but Astrid had learned a new level of pain in all things, and blisters were nothing.

All that mattered was never going back to the black place. Not ever.

She grabbed the man's spear—it was heavy and she would never be able to throw it well, but she might use it in close combat.

The man lay on the floor, still gasping, blinking at her, his body at an odd angle, now that she'd jostled it to undress him. It would be a mercy to stab him through the heart with his spear.

She left him where he lay.

~oOo~

The corridor was dark and plain. It reminded Astrid of the servants' quarters in Estland. Now that she thought of it, though it had felt to her like the height of luxury after the black place, the room she'd been in was not nearly as elegant

178

as her chambers in Estland, where there had been elaborate carpets and hangings, and furniture painted with gold, and other oddities of wealthy people.

She was in this castle's servants' quarters, then. That was her best guess. And that was good, because the entrances and exits would be tucked away so the nobles wouldn't have to see their own filth carried away.

But servants rose early. She could not dally. Astrid ran, as quietly as she could, letting her natural sense of direction lead her.

She came to an exterior door without meeting another soul, and she eased it open.

The outdoors. The full world. Fresh air. Her heart sang.

Reminding herself to stay calm and pay attention, she scanned the quiet grounds. A few men and women were out and about, and Astrid realized then that she would have been less noticeable if she'd worn the slave dress, with its stupid headpiece and flimsy shoes.

But she wouldn't have been able to move the way she needed to move.

At any rate, it was too late now. The woods were just ahead, on the other side of the castle wall. There was a small door in the wall, a few yards to the right.

Hoping the door would not be locked or watched, she ran.

It was locked, but from the inside. There was no watch on it. Astrid slipped through the wall and found herself ten feet from dense woods.

For days, she'd been drawing in her mind the map they'd used to plot their raid. She knew where they'd landed. She knew how long it had taken the soldiers to attack them from the time they'd overrun the little town. With those pieces of knowledge, Astrid guessed that she would find the shore if she went west, and if she moved quickly for most of a day.

She turned in that direction and she ran.

Would she find her friends still there?

A tiny flutter in her heart hoped she would.

~oOo~

The sun had moved well into the west before she finally found the camp. Exhaustion had turned her muscles to mush, and her knees shook with every step. But her aim had been true, and she'd never found herself circling in the unfamiliar forest. The sun had guided her all the day.

The camp was gone. The bodies of several horses were scattered around the tent perimeter, rotting into puddles of viscera, and little else left but bone and clumps of hair. So much more time had passed than she'd thought.

Burnt shards of the tent poles still stretched to the sky, and the spear fence jabbed out into the air at several points, but otherwise the camp was gone.

Her friends were gone. She had known it would be true, and yet it made her heart ache.

But grief wouldn't come. Something in her mind blocked her from mourning her friends. A question she felt but couldn't see.

She stood in the center of the camp she'd helped stake and tried to understand what was wrong with what she saw.

The horses. The horses were the only bodies. The soldiers were gone. So were the raiders.

If this king's men were the kind who would leave their horses to rot, would they bury their enemies?

Or would they take their heads and leave the bodies to rot?

She scanned the area more closely, forcing her legs to keep moving. She found an iron helm in the grass. A dented steel shield. An arm, rotted nearly to bone, but draped in mail.

All soldiers' leavings.

There was nothing left inside the camp. Not a broken shield, not a scrap of fur or a mead horn.

They had not been killed.

They had left.

They had left her behind.

No. *No.* They wouldn't. Leif would not have left her to the black place. Her friends would not have left her. If they had lived, they would have come for her. She saw in her mind Leif and Vali crashing through her cell door.

She'd *seen* it. Again and again, she'd seen it. She'd cleaved to that vision. She'd known it would be true.

She ran from the camp, toward the shore, careening through the tall grass and down the rise to the water.

There were no burnt remnants of their skeids destroyed. There was no sign at all that four mighty raiding ships had come to this shore.

They had sailed away.

They had left her.

Astrid's knees gave up their fight, and she dropped to the rough sand.

They had left her.

She was alone.

12

Dunstan had returned to court with his new countess, Winifred, and they joined the royal family for most meals, even in the private residence. The king seemed taken with the young girl, who was reserved and modest.

Or simply shy and immature. She was very young.

Only a few months past her first blood, and naïve. Possibly dull as well, though it was difficult to tell when so little came from her lips. On a morning when they broke their fast together, Leofric hid a smirk behind a mouthful of bread as he watched his friend try and fail to draw his bride into the table's conversation.

The marriage had been arranged with the king's blessing for its suitability of alliance, not for the compatibility of the couple. Dunstan was nearly old enough to be her father and vastly more experienced in the ways of all things. Vastly less pious as well, except for the ways in which one must show piety.

But the king doted on the young countess and found smiles and lightness for her. She was only six years older than Dreda had been and small enough of stature to seem younger than her age. Leofric thought the king was reminded of the daughter he'd lost. The reminder seemed to ease him and not cause him more grief, so Leofric and Eadric were glad to have the little mouse nearby.

Dunstan, however, was frustrated and unhappy. Over ale the night before, they'd both bemoaned their woman troubles— Dunstan's empty bed since his wedding night and the hurt he'd had no choice but to cause his young bride, and Leofric's inability to win the Northern woman's trust and cooperation. He'd been far more forthcoming with his friend about his failure than he had with his family, but he and Dunstan had always kept each other's secrets.

It mattered little, in any regard. The king wanted the woman brought to him soon. He wanted to see what progress was made in her healing and her usefulness. Leofric was all but out of time.

He was, in truth, entirely out of time, because the woman would not yield. It made no difference whether the king summoned her this day or next week or next year. The result would be the same. She would be put to death.

And he would not have learned even her name.

Taking pity on his friend, and needing something to do himself to keep his mind off the woman in the servant's quarters, Leofric inserted himself into a lull at the table and said, "Would you ride this morning, Dunstan?"

His friend greeted the offer with a wide smile. "Yes, Your Grace, that sounds like a fine way to spend a morning while the sun is yet warm."

~oOo~

They were in the stables a short while later when Elfleda's girl—Leofric couldn't remember her name—ran up to them, nearly crashing into him as she tried to hurry and keep her head respectfully low.

"Yer Grace!" she said, breathless.

184

He knew already that it was trouble with the woman. Before he asked, he took her arm and pulled her away from his horse and the stable workers. "What is it?"

"There's...Elfleda asks...Will you come?"

Dunstan was at his side. "Is there trouble?"

"It seems there is," he sighed. "If you would wait, we can ride out after I get this sorted."

"I'll come with you."

The refusal of his offer was on Leofric's tongue, but the girl's frantic eyes told him that there might be serious trouble, and he would not mind the support of his friend. So he nodded, and they followed after Elfleda's girl.

~oOo~

Leofric stared at the guard on the floor. Elfleda knelt at his side. She'd pulled linens from the bed to cover him, because he was all but bare below his waist. The odor in the air told that the man had soiled himself, but Elfleda seemed to have cleaned that up already.

He was alive, but pale and grey, a sheen of perspiration coating his forehead and the skin above his lip. All he could do was blink and gasp.

The woman had broken his neck and taken his boots and breeches. The rope she'd used to do it was still around his throat.

Not a rope. Linen. She'd torn into strips the dress she reviled and made a rope of them.

She'd run. She'd all but killed this man, a castle guardsman, and she'd escaped.

On foot.

"Your project is finished, Your Grace. The king will not give her more time after this." Dunstan was at his side, also staring at the man.

Leofric knew it was true, but it turned his stomach to acid. She'd done what any warrior would have done. She'd found a way to escape her captivity. Still weak, with no weapon but her own ingenuity, she'd bested a trained soldier and escaped. She was a marvel of will and perseverance.

He didn't want her to die.

But she had proven beyond all doubt that she would be no use to the realm.

Elfleda looked up. "There's nothing I can do for him, Your Grace. He cannot seem to speak, but I don't think he's in pain."

"Why is he in this room? The guards are on strict orders not to cross this threshold."

No one answered, because no one could know. But he could guess. Perhaps she'd used her body; he'd seen the guards try to catch glimpses of her when they thought he wasn't looking.

She'd lured him in and overtaken him—a nearly-naked, battered woman against an armed guard.

"His presence here is a breach of my order. He has no family, as I recall."

Elfleda's face showed a silent diatribe of shock and dismay as she quickly and astutely grasped what he meant to do.

Dunstan understood as well. "Your Grace, are you certain? Is your barbarian woman so important?"

His barbarian woman. Yes, she was that—and it was the crux of all his feelings regarding her and every situation around her. She hadn't left his thoughts since he'd gathered her up from the filthy cell floor, and she'd been a frequent presence before that, since the first day he'd gone into the Black Walls and watched his father watch her torment. Since he'd noted her determined silence against all manner of subjection.

She was his.

Though she wouldn't speak to him, wouldn't give him even her name, he remembered the feel of her trust and her need for him, and he had come to know her a little.

And he thought he knew where'd she run to. The only place in their world she knew.

Would she know how to get there?

He answered his friend's question by crouching down to the disabled guard's side. Feeling Elfleda's glaring disapprobation, Leofric wrapped his hands around the guard's neck and finishing the job the woman had started. His woman.

When the guard was dead, Leofric stared steadily into Elfleda's eyes until the healing woman dropped her own. Then he said, "I killed him. Did I not, Elfleda?"

"Yes, Your Grace," she muttered, staring at her hands.

"When I confronted him for his dereliction of duty, he attacked, and I killed him. Is that not what happened, Elfleda?"

A long pause. Leofric waited. Finally, in a voice much softer than her normal strident tone, she said, "Yes, Your Grace."

"The woman is in this room right now, is she not?"

Elfleda looked up at that, her eyes wide with surprise. When she faced Leofric's steady gaze, she nodded. "Yes, Your Grace."

He looked over his shoulder and gave her girl the same steady stare. "And you? What is your name?"

The girl curtsied. "Audie, Yer Grace."

"Audie, do you understand what has happened in this room?"

"Yes, Yer Grace. You wanna help the quiet lady, so yer gonna say the guard had at 'er and then you when you stopped 'im."

She was a smart one, little Audie. "And you will say so as well."

"Yes, Yer Grace. But…" she cut herself off.

Leofric stood. "Ask your question."

She dipped a little curtsey again. "Beggin' yer pardon, Yer Grace, but how can we say she's here when she's not? What if she's roamin' the halls lookin' for trouble?"

Smart indeed. But Leofric didn't believe for a moment that the woman was still within the castle. She would have fled through the first door she found. "Leave that problem to me. For now, you and Elfleda will put the room to rights and leave it closed. Go on with the day as usual." He turned to Dunstan. "I have an idea where she might have gone. Will you see to the guard—and be discreet? I don't want the king to know anything at all is amiss until I have her back."

"I am yours to command, Your Grace. But Leofric—how will this matter? Can you save her? And why?"

188

He didn't have a way to say the answer, so he simply met his friend's curious eyes and held them.

After a moment, Dunstan's expression changed. An understanding had dawned. "Oh, my dear friend. A child bride or a kitchen wench, either would be a preferable choice."

It didn't matter. "Will you help me?"

"Of course. Go find your wild woman."

~oOo~

As he ran to the stable, the warden of the dungeons stepped out from the shadow of an overhang. "Beggin' yer pardon, Yer Grace," he said, his voice stuffed and stunted by the leather band he wore where his nose had been. His words had been correct, but his attitude was devoid of all respect.

Leofric drew up short and glared at the man. "What is it?"

"If it's the northern bitch yer seekin', she ran out through the western wall. I's on me way to alert the guard."

The woman had run hours before. If the warden had seen her run, he'd known then that there was trouble. He'd waited. Why?

Because he'd been waiting for this—for him. He'd gambled that Leofric would go for her and not tell the king.

"What is it you want?" he asked, cutting through to the crux of the thing.

"Jus' a token, Yer Grace. Fer me trouble." He tapped the leather across his face.

Leofric sighed and looked around the bailey. They had no one's attention; the bustle of work left no time for wandering eyes and provided good cover as well. He nodded, then indicated that they should step into the shadows of the overhang. The warden grinned and moved back.

When they were tucked into the corner, Leofric reached as if he meant to take his purse. Instead, he pulled his dagger and shoved it up into the soft meat of the man's flabby chin.

He watched until the warden gurgled his last breath. Then he used the man's tunic to wipe the blood from his hands and his blade, and he left the body sagged in the corner. He returned to his purpose, going to the stable for his horse.

A warden of the dungeons had a long list of enemies, and, for that reason, only men without families were chosen for the position. Leofric knew no one would mourn for him or even wonder who had done the people such a service.

He even felt that he had exacted a measure of atonement for the harm done to the woman.

~oOo~

He rode through the wood on his grey charger, moving as quickly as he could while scanning the brush and low growth for signs of her. She was on foot and unfamiliar with the land, but the Northmen had a reputation for astute navigation. The day was clear and sunny, warm with a nip in the breeze that augured the end of summer. If she knew that they'd landed on the western shore, then she could find west easily, by simply looking upward. Even in midday, the chill in the breeze would have shown her which way was north, and thus which way was west.

So rather than take the more wending path of a true search, Leofric rode straight to the shore. To what was left of the barbarian camp.

The sun was low and straight in his eyes when he arrived. A remnant odor of rotting horseflesh weighted the breeze. He dismounted and set his reins. His horse shook forcefully, glad to be rid of his rider for a moment.

She wasn't here. Had he been wrong about her ability to make her way? Was she lost in the wood? Was she hurt? She wasn't fully recovered yet, not at her true strength. Had the attempt been too much?

He turned and considered the wood behind him, beginning to darken. If he returned now, the last part of his journey back would be in darkness. But it would be a night just past the full moon, and the sky was clear, so he wasn't worried. Not for himself.

The night would be cold, however, and unless she had found something warmer than the guard's breeches and his old tunic, she would freeze.

Or perhaps she wouldn't. She had gone weeks with no warmth or comfort and survived.

He had to get her back before the morning. He might find a way to buy more time if she were in her room and the truth of the day's events went unknown.

Perhaps in her attempt, this flash of hope, he could find a way through to her.

But where was she? He'd been so sure he'd find her here.

Staring off to the west, he could just see the greying blue of the sea beyond. The shore was at the base of a steep hill of thick sand and high grasses, and the barbarians had made their camp atop it.

Taking his horse's reins, he crossed through the charred remains of the camp, to the top of the hill.

There she was. On her knees at the water's edge, staring out at the sea. The tide was coming in; he could see the water lapping around her. Her flaxen hair was braided simply, hanging down her back in a single, thick plait. The sea breezes whipped loose strands around her head.

His tunic, all she wore over the guard's breeches, sagged off one thin shoulder. Even from this distance, he could see welts of freshly healed scars.

Every part inside him, from his heart to his sex, throbbed at the sight of her.

He set the reins and left his horse at the top of the hill, then made his way down. Though he didn't attempt stealth, she didn't seem to notice his approach. He got all the way to her, his boots in the lapping tidewater, and she never moved. The guard's lance lay ignored at her side.

He knelt beside her.

Though her face was expressionless, Leofric could see a straight track of gleaming wet down her cheek and the circle of wet on the tunic, on her breast, showing fair, scarred skin beneath it.

She was crying. Silently, passively.

He thought he understood. She'd been left behind, and she only now knew it. Had she not realized that she had? It had been months since they'd driven her people away.

But they'd seen to it that her people wouldn't wait for her or search for her, hadn't they? His father and Eadric had made it so her people thought her dead. She hadn't been abandoned.

He remembered the shock and outrage on her friends' faces, the way the biggest one had charged them in fury, even facing a line of drawn archers.

No, she hadn't been abandoned. She'd been mourned.

He couldn't tell her that, because she'd refused his words.

So he did what he could, and set his hand—gently, carefully, as if he reached out to a wild creature—on her shoulder. Still so very thin. Yet she had bested a castle guard.

She turned and looked at him. There was no contempt or fury in her blue eyes. No fight at all. She seemed empty.

"Forgive me," he said, unsure whether she understood even those words. "I wish you could know my regret for all of this." Absurd it was to feel remorse for things done to an enemy during conflict, yet Leofric couldn't remember if he'd ever felt anything but remorse where it came to this woman and her treatment.

She stood and picked up the lance. Leofric stood as well, warily. The only weapon he'd brought down the hill was the small blade at his side.

But she put the bottom of the lance in the sand and leaned it toward him, offering it to him. Confused, he took it.

Then she stepped back and spread her arms wide. "*Aldrig igen*," she said. "*Den svarta platsen—aldrig igen.*"

He didn't understand any of the words she'd said, but he understood her meaning nonetheless. She meant him to kill her.

Dropping the lance to the sand, he shook his head. "No. I will not hurt you."

"*Snälla! Snälla! Aldrig igen!*"

She lunged for the lance, but he caught her and closed her up in his arms. "You're safe with me. I'll keep you safe. Safe." She'd sagged in his hold, not fighting him at all. He slid his hand under her chin and lifted her face so he could see her eyes. "Do you understand? You are safe with me."

He was lying, but he didn't want to be. If only she would open to him, just a little, it could be true. He could keep her safe. But the dead eyes that looked into his and tore him up inside wouldn't give him more. Perhaps they couldn't.

"Leofric," he tried yet again. "I am Leofric."

His thumb brushed over the faint line of the old scar through her lips. "What is your name? Please tell me your name."

Yet again, she didn't answer. But after a moment, she dropped her head, letting it rest on his chest. She let him hold her, and when he took her hand, she let him lead her back up the hill. He left the lance lying in the sand.

She let him hoist her onto his saddle. She let him mount behind her.

She rode quietly, leaning back on his chest, his arms around her, back to the castle.

As much as his heart hurt to see this brave woman give up, Leofric felt the first flowering of real hope. After a rest, when she saw that he'd arranged for her morning activities to disappear, perhaps she then would warm to him again.

Perhaps she'd needed to lose all of her own hope before she could see the kind of hope he offered.

~oOo~

194

The moon shone brightly over the castle, making stark shadows over the bailey. Leofric rode into the stable and had dismounted and lifted the woman down before he was greeted by a sleep-addled stable boy. He left his horse in the boy's care and led the woman back into the castle, entering through the servants' entrance.

She went where he wanted, entirely meek. When they got to the corridor to her room, he pushed her gently into a shadowy nook and left her there, using his body to try to convey that he wanted her to stay there.

Then he went to the guard at her door and dismissed him. As the second son of the king, and the Duke of Orenshire, Leofric was not questioned. The guard nodded his respect and walked away, toward the far corridor, which would lead to the door to the guards' quarters.

When Leofric went back, the woman was exactly where he'd left her.

He led her to her room. As he ushered her inside, she paused, just a stutter in her step, and considered the empty space at the side of the door, where the guard had been standing moments before.

"No more guard," he said, without hope that she understood him. But he needed the words to be said. "You are no longer a prisoner."

She obviously hadn't understood; she simply walked into the room, reacting to his words not at all.

He came in with her and closed the door. There was no sign that a man had been killed on this floor. The room was warm and ready for her: torches lit, a small fire burning, a supper tray on the table with bread and cheese and a pitcher. Elfleda and Audie had done well today. Dunstan, too.

The woman turned and stood facing him, her arms slack at her sides.

The guard's breeches were far too big for her; they sagged and bunched at her hips, bottom, and knees. From the knees down, the leather had been darkened and stained by the salt of the tide she'd knelt in. The boots, too. His tunic had torn at some point during her day's travels, and, again, it hung off her shoulder, showing her pale skin and a few of the many scars that marred it.

He couldn't leave her after this strange, long day without trying one more time. When he stepped to her, she flinched back, her eyes wary, and he was glad to see it, even if it meant that she still saw him as a threat. At least it was not meekness. At least there was life in her eyes again.

Standing right before her, he patted his chest. "I am Leofric." He patted her chest, his thumb and fingers over the high ridge of her collarbones. "Who *are* you? I so want to know your name."

When she didn't answer, he cupped his hands around her face and kissed her forehead. "Sleep now. On the morrow we will try again, but we haven't much more time. Please help me keep you safe."

He turned and left the room.

The door was unlocked, and the guard had been dismissed. If she wished to go, she wouldn't need to kill anyone else.

He was down the corridor and about to make the turn that would lead him to the castle proper when he heard the crank and creak of a heavy door being opened on its iron hinges. Curious, he turned.

The woman stood in the doorway, searching the other side of the corridor. As he watched, she turned, found him, and stopped.

They stared at each other.

When Leofric took a step toward her, she didn't back away. Keeping his eyes on hers, he retraced his steps. She watched him come, standing firm.

He arrived at the door and stood before her. Then he simply waited. She had made this move, whatever it was, and he would wait for her to make the next one.

She studied his eyes carefully, her own narrowing as if to improve her focus. He tried to fill his head with all the thoughts he had of her, of his feelings for her and his true desire to care for her, in case she could see into his eyes and find those thoughts.

After a long moment of quiet consideration, she patted her chest and opened her mouth.

Leofric's heart leapt.

"Astrid." She patted her chest again. "Astrid."

He had no hope of controlling what he did next; his heart and body didn't give his mind the chance. He cupped her face in his hands again and kissed her on the mouth.

13

Astrid tried to remember Hnefatafl, to think of the game and the way that Leif would make her see victory and then snatch it away from her. Leif would concede something, give up a piece or a position, and she would see that he'd lost an opportunity. She'd be lured into believing he'd made a mistake, and leave herself vulnerable to an attack from the side she'd made blind as she'd chased a victory that hadn't truly been.

She'd always played like that, reacting to what was immediately before her.

Her body was reacting to what was immediately before her now—Leofric's mouth on hers, his hands gentle and warm around her face, his beard brushing her chin. She needed this; on a physical, primal level, she needed this tenderness. Her heart ached for the past she'd lost, and her belly was full of fear for the future, but in this present, his hands were strong, and his mouth was soft, and he'd been kind since he'd found her at the water.

He'd always been kind.

But she didn't understand. She'd never understood.

She'd killed one of his men that morning, and now, in the night, she was back in the same room, but without a guard. What did he intend? Was it a trick that she couldn't see, like Leif's stratagems in the game? Would she be lured and made more vulnerable?

Could she be more vulnerable than she now was? Alone in the world, weak, unarmed, at the mercy of an enemy she didn't understand?

No, she could not.

But this man had been kind and had asked only words of her. He'd taken her from the black place. He could return her there if he chose. Only he stood between her and that horror.

She'd begged him to kill her rather than take her back to the black place. She could never survive it again. For the first time in her life, she'd *begged*. She hadn't had his words to do it, and he didn't have hers, but she believed he'd understood nonetheless.

But he hadn't done what she'd asked. Instead he'd held her, and then he'd brought her back to this room. He'd removed her guard and left her alone.

All he seemed to want was her words.

And this, too. He wanted her body, too. She could feel that want in his hands and his mouth, and in his breeches.

When she pulled back, she could see it in his eyes, which were the color of a cloudy evening sky, dark blue shot with grey. And she saw something deeper in his eyes as well, something too deep for words.

She wanted what she saw in him, even what she didn't understand.

Staring down at her, his mouth still parted and wet from their kiss, he let go of her face and laid one hand at the top of her chest, his thumb and fingers framing her throat. "Astrid," he said in a voice silky and deep and gentle.

Then he lifted her hand and set it on his chest, over his heart. With both of his hands, he pressed hers into his heavy, soft chestpiece.

He wanted her to say his name.

More even than finally giving him her name, giving his back to him seemed as if she would be giving him everything. If she said his name, she would tell him that she would give him what he wanted.

But she didn't know what that was. Was it only her words? Her body? Was it more than that? Was it all a ruse to finish her undoing? She couldn't see.

What choice did she have? Her people had left her behind. She was alone in this place, where she would die—perhaps soon, perhaps not. If not, and if she wasn't returned to the black place, then she would have to make her way.

If sending the guard away meant that she was no longer a prisoner, did that mean she was not a slave?

There was no way of knowing. Not unless she could use words and ask.

She had no choice. The man holding her now was all she had. Until she could understand, she would have to give him what he wanted of her.

In his eyes, she saw no threat, only desire and kindness, and hope, and something deeper she didn't understand.

"Leofric," she said, making her voice clear and steady.

"Yes, yes!" He smiled and lifted her hand to his mouth. He kissed her fingers, his lips lingering long over each one. "Thank you. Astrid." His mouth moved over her skin as he spoke. He said more, said the word *safe* again, but she didn't understand more than that word.

He'd said the same words before; she recognized their sound, if not their meaning. She hoped he was telling her that she would be safe.

Astrid hated that she could no longer make herself feel safe, but she could not. That was one of the many things she'd lost in the black place.

She would give him anything he wanted if he would give her that.

With that in mind, she caught his hands in her own and backed into the room, leading him with her.

When she was standing in the middle of the room, she dropped his hands and began to remove the clothes she was wearing: the boots of the guard, then his breeches and belt, then the shirt Leofric had given her.

As she lifted the hem of the linen so she could pull it over her head, he set his hands on her shoulders and shook his head. He spoke words she didn't know, then smoothed his hands down her arms.

"Astrid," he murmured.

The shirt fell off her shoulder, drawn by his hand moving downward, and she saw his eyes fall on her bare skin.

He wanted her. He was being kind, but he wanted her.

It was only her body. A tool, nothing more. Not herself; no more than the thing that held her self. She could give it and lose little.

What was more, she wanted his touch. It soothed. When he held her, she felt sheltered.

Safe.

Shrugging her arms free of his hold, she pulled the shirt over her head and tossed it away. She stood, straight and still, as his eyes moved over her scarred body, which had lost most of its strong muscle. But the heat in his eyes didn't flicker.

He met her eyes again. "You want this?"

She understood those words. She wanted what he could give her, what he might give her if she had value to him. If she gave him what he wanted. She nodded.

"You understand?"

Again, she nodded. She understood enough: those words, and what he wanted, and what she needed.

He walked away from her, but only to close the door. Then he came back and brushed his fingertips over her cheek.

"Astrid."

Without his prompting this time, she laid her hand on his chest and said, "Leofric."

His face lit up in a broad grin, and he swept his arms around her waist, bending at the same time to kiss her. It felt like a claiming to Astrid, who had never followed a man's lead before. Always she had sought out a coupling, or at least been the one to make the first move that turned flirtation into contact.

She closed her eyes and tried to stop her thoughts, to simply feel the strength of his arms holding her, the softness of his mouth, the fervor of his tongue, the heat of his breath. He was taller than she by a few inches, and much broader than she. That wasn't unusual; she had always favored tall, strong men, and the men of her people were generally taller than most of the men of this place, as far as she'd seen.

What was unusual was her feeling of being overwhelmed by the man she was with. Leofric bent forward, cradling her in his arms, and she felt her braid swing loose behind her.

She didn't like it, couldn't be subjected, even as she tried to give him what he wanted. Her heart beating fast and loud in her head, she tore her mouth free of his and shoved on his chest until he stepped back and let her go.

Confusion wavered over his features. Astrid felt something strange in her arms and legs and realized with a jolt that she was shaking.

She was afraid. She was quaking with fear. Gods, how she despised this thing she had become.

No. She would not be subject to her fear. She was a shieldmaiden. She had fought many battles and killed men bigger than she and stronger. In coupling, she had taken what men had offered, not given them what they'd demanded.

Gathering up the memories of her strength, she took the steps that brought her back in contact with Leofric, and she reached up and grabbed handfuls of his dark hair. It was soft in her hands, and the loose waves curled over her fingers. She yanked sharply, forcing his head down to hers, and kissed him with force and intent, the way she'd kissed Jaan, and Ulv, and any other man she'd wanted. A kiss that said anything that happened would be on her terms, and he should be thankful she'd chosen him.

His grunt of hot surprise filled her mouth, and his arms were around her again, his hands filling themselves with her bottom, clutching her close. She could feel his need for her, hard and thick in his breeches.

Without breaking her kiss, she let go of his hair and worked at his chestpiece, seeking the fastenings. As she became frustrated by her lack of success, his hands let go of her and moved between them, taking over. He worked the fastenings and shook himself free of the garment, then drew his tunic up. When he tried to break away so he could pull it over his head, Astrid bit down on his bottom lip, sucking it into her mouth and holding him.

He groaned as if she'd done him real harm, but when she let go and he rid himself of his shirt, she saw the fire in his eyes and the stunned smile on his lips.

He was…he was beautiful, and for a moment Astrid forgot everything else. Her fear and self-loathing, her heartache and homesickness, her worry for the future, her weak body and uncertain mind. For one perfect moment, all she saw with the bare torso of the man before her. Visibly powerful. Sleek with muscle. Battle scarred. And heaving for her.

She set her hand on his chest. "Leofric."

"Astrid, please," he answered and gathered her into his arms.

A fire seemed to catch where her bare chest touched his, and she lifted onto her toes to claim his mouth again. To claim him. He groaned again, that sound of near pain, or of surrender, and a flicker of power rekindled in her heart. She was not giving up. She was not giving over. She wasn't kneeling at his feet and begging. She was standing toe to toe with him and taking as much as she was giving.

Cresting that rush of remembered strength, Astrid grabbed at his breeches and wrested them open. He helped her, changing his stance so that she could push them down his hips and release his sex.

But when her hand wrapped around his thickness to pull him free, her mind mutinied, and the room she was in was gone. Leofric was gone.

Everything around her, inside her, went black and cold.

She shook her head, and Leofric and the warm, golden room came back, but she jumped backward, away from him, feeling the deep despair and agony of the black place cramping her muscles and her mind again. She wrapped her arms around her body and crouched down, trying to hold herself together.

It was *that* which would undo her? What all those men had done with their sex? *That*? Not the lash or the fiery ointment, not the cane on her feet and across her knees, not the icy water dumped over her or the crumbs of maggoty bread shoved into her mouth? Not the shackles? Not the dark, the relentless dark?

The raping had been the least of it. As many times as it had happened, as many ways, that had been the least of the pain. It couldn't be that breaking her now.

"Astrid?" She felt him come close, could see his shadow move over her. She shook her head, and he didn't touch her.

He said something, a long string of words she didn't understand, and then he stepped away again. She heard the rustle of leather and the clomp of boots being dropped to the floor. He'd finished undressing.

He meant to take what she'd intended to give him. Even now, in the face of her cowering fear, he meant to take her.

This was the game, then, the move she hadn't seen. She was his to do with what he would, and he was no different from the rest.

"Astrid," he said, his tone coaxing. She would have called it kind just moments before.

When she didn't respond, he repeated her name. "Astrid."

She looked up.

He stood naked in the middle of the room. He wasn't hard; his sex hung heavily from its dark nest, between his muscled thighs. When she met his eyes, he smiled, but not with pleasure. With sorrow, if that was possible.

Then he spread his arms wide. She'd done the same on the shore, when she'd wanted him to run her through with the spear, when she'd begged him not to take her back to the black place. She'd opened her arms and made herself utterly vulnerable to him. Put her life in his hands.

As he was doing now.

She stood, and he didn't move. She walked to him, and he stood still, his arms spread wide. Only his eyes moved, tracking with hers.

Standing before him, looking up into his eyes, Astrid balled up her fist and punched him in the stomach.

He coughed out a burst of air, and he bent forward with the blow, but his arms stayed wide, and when he regained his breath, he stood straight again. His eyes on hers, he nodded, and she understood.

He was offering himself. He was atoning.

Atonement was not the way of her people. Her people settled their wrongs with vengeance. But the concept wasn't entirely foreign, and Astrid understood.

She punched him again, and, again, he stood straight when he could and waited for another blow.

With the next punch, thinking stopped and vengeance took over. It didn't matter that he was offering himself up for this of his own will. It didn't matter that he'd saved her from the black place and had taken care of her since. All that mattered was the hate and rage and pain that filled her blood with fire.

She punched and scratched and bit and kicked, and he took it all. She knocked him to the floor three times, and each time, he stood and spread his arms wide. She beat him until her arms shook from exertion and her body dripped sweat.

When she finally stopped, she heard herself for the first time. She was weeping. Great, loud, heaving sobs. She slapped her hands over her mouth and reeled backward.

She was a shieldmaiden. She didn't cry. Tears were weakness.

Leofric dropped his arms. His body was blotched with bright red, turning to purple. His nose was bleeding. His eye swelled. He came to her, reaching his arms out, meaning to hold her. She knew he meant to comfort her.

"No!" she yelled, her hands slamming his chest, shoving him away. "No!" She shoved him again. And again, until his legs hit the bed. She shoved him again, and he fell back onto the mattress. She dived at him, landing on him, straddling him, curling her hands into fists and slamming them again and again into his chest.

Still he didn't fight back. Again he spread his arms out and simply took what she gave.

She couldn't stop crying, and tears struck her fists and his chest as she slammed and slammed, infuriated by her weakness.

He went hard beneath her, his sex pressing against hers, and her body flinched away from it instinctually, enraging her even more. She would not fear that. *She would not.* It was nothing—nothing! Shouting, "No! It's nothing! Nothing!" she stopped hitting and grabbed the offending part of him. Holding it tightly, she shoved herself down on it.

Leofric made an earthy roar of surprise, but she didn't want to hear his grunts. She wrapped her hands around his throat to stifle him, pressing her thumbs deep, feeling the slowing of his blood and breath against her hands. And then she rode him as hard as she could, driving him deep again and again and again.

She told herself she was seeking the pain, wanting to find it and know it and draw its limits, to master it, but she didn't feel pain, not in her body. Her heart and mind were racked with it, but her body didn't hurt. What he was doing—what she was making him do—didn't hurt. With each driving surge on his hips, she was reminded of how it was supposed to feel.

Leofric's face had gone deep red, and then purple, but he still had not fought her. She realized, just as the first feeling of what might have become pleasure glimmered inside her, that he truly would let her kill him and never fight that end.

He had made himself subject to her. He had given her what she needed. He had taken nothing.

She let go of his throat, and at the same time that he heaved in his first great, desperate breath, he released, explosively, his hips leaping off the bed and nearly casting her off of him.

Comprehending too late that he'd spent inside her, Astrid threw herself to the far corner of the bed while his seed was still spilling, now over his belly and legs. She'd never let any man spend inside her before, under any circumstances. She wanted no children.

She was a shieldmaiden and wanted no ties to any other life.

She had been a shieldmaiden. What she was now, she didn't know.

210

14

Leofric lay on the bed, his arms splayed, dragging air through his aching throat. His body throbbed in every part.

He could not fathom all that he was feeling.

What had happened in this room, with this woman, was unlike anything he'd ever experienced in his life. He'd allowed her to beat him, to mount him, to nearly kill him, and never before had he let a woman take any kind of control over him.

And who would have? He was His Royal Highness, the Duke of Orenshire, the second son of the King of Mercuria, second in the line of succession. Women knelt before him; they gave him what he wanted. He'd never been cruel or rough or taken what hadn't been freely offered, but he'd never lain back, either. And he recognized that what was freely offered might not have been, had he not had power over the one who offered.

But this woman had never given him what he wanted. Not until this night.

Astrid. He finally knew her name, and it was lovely. She'd said his name, she'd touched him freely, without delirium. She'd offered herself to him.

He wasn't sure he fully understood her change of heart, but he'd thought it was that she'd given up, and he didn't want that. As she'd stood there offering him all he wanted of her, he'd not wanted it in that way. Not because she was broken. He wanted her to want him, to offer herself truly free.

Then she'd kissed him like she had—wildly, almost violently, grabbing and biting, her tongue thrusting into his mouth like a claiming—and he'd felt power and will in her again. He'd felt her desire for him. Never had a woman taken from him in that way before. When she'd touched his sex, wrapped her hand around him as though he were hers to take, the flame of his desire had burst into an inferno.

And then she'd reeled away. She'd *cowered*. Even in the Black Walls, she hadn't cowered.

Gasping confusion had clouded his thinking for a moment as his body and his mind had tried to catch up to each other, and then he'd seen the terrible truth. In his body, she remembered the Black Walls.

He'd thought of only one thing he could do to show her she was safe with him.

Though she was weaker than she'd once been, she was still a warrior, and in her rage and fire, she'd remembered that. He would bear the marks of her remembering for days to come. He would feel every strike.

For his part, never in his life had he felt a release like the one that had come in the moment when his life had been pulled back from the teetering brink of its end. The desperate ecstasy of it still sang in his bones and made his limbs shake.

Never had he spent in a woman before, either. He hoped he hadn't made her with child; he couldn't fathom the tangle of trouble that would cause them.

A small voice inside him cleared its throat then and suggested that no matter the tangle, if she bore his child, he could keep her truly safe. More than that, he could keep her in true comfort and ease. If he could persuade his father to acknowledge her, he might give her more yet than that. Make her royalty, even.

If he could convince her to agree to be baptized, he might move his father. The realm needed an heir. If Eadric could not provide one, perhaps he could.

Would he wed this woman if he could? A barbarian heathen whose name he'd known for less than an hour? A woman who refused even to wear clothes that would allow her to be seen in public?

Yes, he thought he would.

He thought he would wed her for love.

He found the strength to lift his head and bit back a groan as the ache in his throat sharpened with the movement. Astrid was sitting at the far corner of the bed, her arms crossed over her belly, staring at him.

Astrid. Oh, how he loved the shape and sound of her name.

When he sat up, he felt more keenly all the aches she'd made in him, but he felt no shame in taking this beating from a woman. Astrid was no ordinary woman, and this was no ordinary night.

What had transpired between them had been the most passionate experience of Leofric's life, but it had been intensely violent as well, and she had, he knew, felt no pleasure from it. So many things about her made his heart ache, but now, with her eyes wary and her posture closed, the greatest ache was that she wasn't feeling the things he was—the release, the ecstasy. The love.

He wanted to take from her the memories that had made this warrior woman reel away from him in fear. If she would allow him, he wanted to give her pleasure. Not in violence, but in tenderness.

He reached for her, but she tensed. "*Nej,*" she whispered, shaking her head. "*Det är inget.*"

She'd shouted those same words, cried them, as she'd ridden him. They were the last words she'd spoken. He didn't understand any but the first. *Nej* was her word for *No*, he thought.

He dropped his hand. "Astrid." His voice was rough, and the words came from his throat as if with sharp edges, but he swallowed and continued. "I want to show you pleasure. I want to take your pain away, if I can. Do you understand?"

She shook her head. Though she seemed to understand more words than he'd realized, there remained a dense space of ignorant silence between them. He wanted to be able to talk to her. Until he could, he didn't know how he could ease her mind or gain her trust.

"How can I make you understand?"

He didn't expect her to answer, and she didn't. She studied him, her eyes scanning over his face, coming to rest with his eyes. Then she twisted on the bed and put her legs over the side. She stood and walked away. Leofric sat where he was and watched her.

She went to the ewer and poured water in the bowl. As she picked up a cloth and soaked it, he studied her back—her straight shoulders, her slim hips, the long, disheveled pale braid that followed the path of her spine.

The red scars crosshatched over her alabaster skin.

Words or no, how could he earn her trust? The beating he'd allowed her to deal him was nothing in comparison to what she'd suffered. Nothing.

She wrung out the cloth and came back to the bed. As she sat near him again, closer than she'd been before, she held out the cloth to him.

Without understanding, he took it. He cocked his head, hoping she understood the gesture.

She did, and tapped her own nose, then nodded toward him. She spoke a sentence in her own language, and she nodded again.

He put his fingers to his nose and felt something sticky and wet; they came back bloody. Oh. He wiped his face with the cloth until no new red soaked in, and he found new aches he hadn't yet noted. As he wiped a final time, dragging the cloth over his cheek, he winced. By the next day, that eye would be purple, if it wasn't already.

She knew well how to punch.

The thought made him smile—and wonder of wonders, she answered it with a small one of her own. What a beautiful sight. She reached out and brushed her fingers over his sore cheek.

The touch was tender and possessive, and it gave him a fresh burst of hope. His heart swelling until his chest felt too small to hold it, Leofric caught her hand in his. He put it to his mouth and kissed her palm. "Can you forgive me?"

"Forgive," she said, her accent charmingly thick and her voice low but not hesitant. "*Förlåt.*"

The word was similar enough that Leofric thought she'd understood his word and had given him her own of the same meaning.

He pressed her hand to his chest. "Fur-lote?" he attempted and was rewarded with another scant smile.

"Can you, Astrid? Forgive?"

Her eyes were on their joined hands for a long time. "*Jag förlåter dig. Bara dig.*" She lifted her eyes to his to check for understanding, but though he'd listened closely, he hadn't understood. "You," she tried in his tongue. "Forgive you."

In her tone, and in her eyes, he saw that she meant that her forgiveness was for him alone. What that meant for her life beyond this room, he didn't know, but for now, on this night, Leofric was gladdened enough that she could forgive him.

But when he leaned toward her, meaning to kiss her, she freed her hand from his hold and pulled away.

Perhaps he should have let that be the end of it, but he couldn't. After the shocking violence of their coupling, they'd had this moment of understanding, and he wanted it to be more. He wanted her to know gentle pleasure. He wanted to give it to her.

So he reached for her, catching her hand before she could lock it again under her crossed arms. When he tugged against her resistance, fire ignited in her eyes, and she pulled more sharply. He tightened his hold but didn't hurt her.

"Astrid. Let me give you pleasure. Do you understand *pleasure?*"

She shook her head.

Rather than force her closer, he released her hand, rose onto his knees, and leaned toward her. Guarded, her forehead creased with a leery frown, she watched him come. When he took her chin in his hands, drawing his thumb down the line of the scar crossing her lips, she didn't pull back.

"Let me show you," he said and brought his mouth to hers.

She didn't fight him, but neither did she return the kiss. He eased his lips over hers, slowly, tasting her with the merest tip of his tongue. After a moment, she tipped her head away— not sharply, and not far. Just enough to put a breath between them.

"Det är inget," she whispered again. He wished he understood the words; she's said them over and over since they'd been bare in this bed together, and they seemed important. But, although he tried hard to make out each syllable, he couldn't discern their meaning.

"Ingenting."

"I do not understand, Astrid." But he thought he did, a little. It seemed like a statement of resistance or reluctance—in her posture and her tone, he thought he saw that much. She sounded as if she were trying to convince herself of something that she didn't believe.

She hadn't pulled much away, so he kissed her again. If she felt conflict, he wanted to help her resolve it. This time, he moved his mouth with more intent, taking her head in his hands, pressing his tongue against the seam between her lips.

Her hands came up and hooked over his shoulders, and Leofric thought he had her, but she shoved him away. Her eyes flashed hot, and she spoke a string of foreign words, far too quickly for him to make out anything but their music.

Then she surged forward and kissed him—hard, demanding, fierce, the way she'd kissed him before he was fully undressed. Before she'd jumped away from him and curled into herself.

Though it had been passionate and intensely erotic, Leofric didn't want that brutal coupling again. There had been too much pain in it—for them both. When she tried to shove him to lie back on the bed again, he grabbed her arms.

What he did next was a risk, but she seemed suspicious of his gentler actions. He brought her close in a firm embrace, overpowering the sudden tension in her body, and he laid her flat on the bed, beneath him.

She reacted exactly as he'd expected—full of fight, her expression tight with anger. "*Nej!*" she snarled, and spat out another string of furious words. Tired of being struck, he grabbed her wrists and held her still.

"I will not hurt you, Astrid. I want to be gentle. You are safe." She quieted at his last words, and he thought she understood at least that, so he said it again. "Safe."

In the space of her rigid quiet, Leofric bent to her and pressed his lips lightly to the corner of her mouth. He forged a path of kisses over her cheek to her ear, where he whispered "Safe," again and sucked her soft lobe between his teeth.

She took a cautious breath, and he felt a layer of tension melt from her body. That small victory charged his own body as if lightning had moved through it. He kissed her neck, letting his tongue taste her skin. Her shoulder, licking the length of a scar. The notch at the base of her throat, laving its deep recess.

Her chest. Each time he came upon a scar, he attended to it, tasting its full length, trailing his tongue over the smooth, raised new flesh.

By the time he arrived at her breasts, her breaths were deep and slow, and he thought if he released her arms, she wouldn't fight him. He lifted his head and found her watching him warily.

"Be at ease, love."

Her only response was the calm that came with another breath, and he took that as leave to continue.

Despite the scars crossing them—he thought of the cane and the lash tearing at such delicate flesh and wouldn't allow himself to shrink from the image—her breasts were lovely. Neither large nor small, they were round and full, and the peaks were of a pink so faint her skin seemed opalescent. All of her skin, except the scars, was fair and delicate. It was a stark contrast to the warlike woman inside it.

Her nipples were sharp points, and as he took in their beauty, that pale pink skin went tight under his gaze. It was the first clear sign of her arousal, the first true encouragement he'd had that forcing his point would not be their undoing.

Bending his head to her body, he tasted that puckered skin with his tongue. She drew in a sharp breath, and another when he sucked her nipple into his mouth. While he circled his tongue over her skin, he released her hands, wrapping one arm around her, under her back, and filling the other hand with her other breast.

Her hands went to his head; he felt her fingers sliding into his hair, and he smiled against her breast. She was with him. She would let him give her pleasure.

He attended fully to her breasts, traveling back and forth between them, taking his time, laving her gently, reveling in the way her body continued to relax by degrees. She gave few signs of her pleasure beyond that softening in his arms. She made no sound but the sighs of deep breaths released, and her hands in his hair didn't pull.

And yet he knew, he understood, that he was giving her something important. Each deep breath she took in came more quickly than the one before it, and he could feel her heartbeat throbbing throughout her body, making her blood rush and pulse. Her nipples took on a deeper pink as her skin flushed.

When his hand wanted to wander lower, over her belly, between her legs, Leofric forbore. He wanted to approach her slowly, with his mouth first. He didn't know if she'd ever been tasted like that—few women he'd been with had, and even the servant girls were often scandalized when he sought it—but he knew that it wouldn't have happened in the Black Walls.

Letting her breasts go, he continued his mouth's journey, over her sharp ribs, her concave belly, still lingering over each scar he came to. The worst of her scars spanned her belly, just below her ribs. The corruption had gone deep in that wound, and Elfleda had cut away a wide swath of flesh and then seared closed what remained. The only time he'd heard Astrid scream was when this wound had been treated. She'd been delirious with pain and fever, and the thin, pathetic sound had broken Leofric's heart.

Over this scar, he took especial care. Under the gentle attention of his lips and tongue, her skin twitched and quivered. "I will keep you safe now, I swear it," his whispered against the ridged skin.

He left the scar and traveled downward and felt no shocked resistance in her limbs. Pressing his mouth to her sparse, silky golden curls, he shifted his hold of her, widening her thighs and taking hold of the globes of her bottom. He drew his tongue lightly through her folds, over the pearl between them, tasting her deepest essence.

"*Åh,*" she gasped and lifted her hips, pressing herself to his face. Leofric's sex, hard and throbbing from the moment she'd first begun to find ease in his arms, leapt at the sound, and he groaned and sucked her pearl into his mouth.

She wasn't shocked or shamed or scandalized by this; she knew it, and that meant he wasn't the first to have tasted her in this way and given her pleasure. It didn't surprise him; she had made it quite obvious over these months that her people had a different relationship to their bodies than his people did. No woman—or man, for that matter—in this world would have been so unaffected by their own nakedness as Astrid had been.

It didn't surprise him, but it made a flare of disappointment in him. He wanted her to be his, only his. He wanted to be the only pleasure she knew. But if he couldn't be her only, then he would be her last.

And her best.

With that in mind, Leofric put his mind to making what he was doing explosive for her. He wanted her to cry out. He wanted to know her scream of ecstasy. This woman who would not reveal her pain, he would make revel in her pleasure.

He slid his arms farther under her, shrugging her thighs onto his shoulders and wrapping his arms around her so that he could take hold of her breasts as his lips and his tongue laved and delved deep over her most tender, most vulnerable place. Keeping every touch gentle, slow and devoted, he found the rhythm that brought up her deepest needs until her body writhed beneath his, within his.

His own need was so great that he couldn't keep himself from thrusting into the linens and furs, shoving his sex against the mattress. He needed to surge up and push her fully beneath him, to take her, to fill her sultry, honey-wet sheath, but he wanted her first pleasure with him to be only hers. When her fists tangled sharply in his hair and he heard her finally, finally moan, he nearly released into the linens. Her hips thrust frantically against him, and he tasted her release as it washed over his tongue.

Mercy, what a thing that was. To give this woman real pleasure. To know it was true. To feel it. To taste it.

Aching with need, he slid himself up, over her, until they were face to face—and he saw shock in her eyes. Not for what he'd done, but for what he'd given her. He didn't need words to know it. It was written in the sheen over her flushed face, in her glittering eyes, in her heaving breath. In the smile that blossomed before him.

"Knulla mig. Knulla mig."

Whatever the words meant, the voice that spoke them was husky and breathless, and her hand pushed between them and took hold of him. This time, she didn't fill with fear at the feel of him. This time, her eyes locked with his, she pressed him to her own sex and sighed.

She wanted him.

Holding those beautiful blue eyes with his own, Leofric flexed his hips and filled her full.

When she'd mounted him, he'd been too surprised and confused to feel anything more than the shock and the twisted, stabbing surge of sensation. He hadn't wanted that at all, no matter how intense his completion had been. He hadn't wanted the fear and fury that warred in her eyes, he hadn't wanted the pain for either of them. And then she'd nearly choked the life from him. No, he hadn't felt anything he'd wanted to feel.

Now, this time, he filled her and felt her body sliding over his, inside and out, felt the velvet of her sheath and the silk of her skin, ruched with scars. He felt the way she clutched around him, pulling him deeper. He felt her back in his hands, arching up, felt her breasts like soft pillows at his chest. He felt her hands—mercy, her hands, skimming over his back, her nails dragging lightly over his skin.

But all he saw was her eyes.

While their bodies moved together, their eyes stayed locked, and Leofric understood everything about her. For this moment, at least, he knew her completely. Knew what she wanted, what she needed. Who she was.

He loved this woman.

During his devotion to her pleasure, his own body had been strummed to a frantic pitch, and Leofric felt that tension fraying his control. But just as he began to truly fight his own finish, the light changed in her eyes, and she sighed.

"*Ja*. Leofric, *ja*."

At the sound of his name in her voice, and everything it meant, he surged hard, finding her deepest place, and she completed, sinking her nails into his back.

He flexed twice more to carry her to the end, and then, just as he was about to finally release his own tether, she shoved on his hips and tried to squirm from their connection.

She wanted him to pull out, not to spend in her.

But he'd decided he wanted her with child. It was the best way to ensure her comfort.

And, now that he'd let the idea take root in his mind, he wanted it. He simply wanted it. He flexed again, groaning harshly as his seed surged up.

"*Nej! Snälla!*"

That, he thought, was a plea, and he pulled out, just as his body could no longer be denied. He wouldn't, couldn't force her. Dropping his head to her chest, he grabbed his sex and helped his finish along, spasming with each pull, pining for the hot sheath he'd had.

When he was done and could focus again, he found clear blue orbs glinting suspicion at him.

She shook her head and spoke long in her language. Several sentences. None of the words but *nej* made sense to him. He assumed he'd just gotten a lecture about being careful where he cast his seed.

He would need much more language between them before he could persuade her to the merits of his will on the point. For now, he said something he knew she would understand—the word in her language that she'd taught him this night.

"*Förlåt?*"

As before, the attempt earned him a smile—this one packed with the clear message that there was only so much forgiveness to be had.

"*Förlåt*," she answered. Her pronunciation was different, far more nuanced. "*Gör det inte igen.* No…again."

"No, I won't. I promise."

She nodded. "Prom-ise." He could see her trying out the shape of the word in her mouth.

He was pleased beyond measure to find her trying to use the language he needed to teach her. There was so very much hope in this night, and when he'd come into this room in the morning and found the guard on the floor, he'd thought the end for her loomed heavily over them.

The torches were guttering and the fire turning to embers. A chill of a late night near the harvest had crept into the room. Leofric rolled to his back and pulled the fur up, drawing Astrid with him as he moved. When he tried to tuck her under his arm to lay her head on his chest, she pushed back, locking her arm on the bed, and frowned down at him.

Did she wish him to leave? That was a sour thought, but he'd go if she wished it. Her expression, however, wasn't one of impatience. She had that leery shadow again, like she was trying to understand what he was at.

Had she never slept in such a way before? No, she had—he'd held her like such when she'd been too ill to know it. But had she never chosen to? Had she never been close enough with another to have this?

He patted his chest, where he wanted her head to rest, and she finally relented.

Leofric fell asleep with her hand scratching lightly over his chest and belly, moving the hair there like a whisper.

~oOo~

He woke in pale sunlight to the creak of the door opening. Astrid had rolled away from him in the night and lay, apparently sleeping deeply, with her back to him. He was between her and the door, and he rolled and rose onto his elbow, blocking her from the view of whomever had entered.

His sleepy mind only registered that he was the one out of place, not Astrid, when Elfleda's wide-eyed, pinched-lipped face glared back at him. A compendium of judgment was written in every crease of the woman's expression.

"Good morning, Elfleda," he said, affecting a regal tone.

"Your Grace," she responded with the barest possible curtsey. "If I disturb, I shall return later."

He sensed Astrid stir and sit up behind him.

"No," he said. "Come in and do your duty."

He enjoyed the look Elfleda gave him then—she'd heard the rebuke he hadn't said and knew he meant to remind her of her place.

He needed to be careful how he pressed Elfleda. She had power among the servants. Not only a healer, she had charge of the women who served the castle, the scullions and chambermaids alike, and were she to let any word slip about what happened in this room, Leofric and Astrid would find their circumstances deeply complicated. Especially after the day before.

They were relying on the tight lips of too many people now. Once the story of the guard's death was widely known—the story, Leofric hoped, that they had concocted—then attention would be drawn to this room. The people who knew the truth must have no reason to share it.

The bed moved; Astrid had risen. He saw Elfleda turn a different look on her—protective, not censorious. Interesting. Despite Astrid's recalcitrance and Elfleda's complaints, the older woman had developed an interest in the 'shameless barbarian.'

He watched as Astrid, fully bare, went to Elfleda and put her hand on the healer's arm. Elfleda flinched with surprise but didn't pull away.

"*Tack*. Thank. Elf-Elfleda. Thank." Her tongue had trouble with the name, but not so much to be unclear.

Wonderment overtook the judgment on Elfleda's face, and Leofric thought he saw her eyes fill. She nodded and patted Astrid's hand. "You're welcome, dearie. It'll be all right now, I think."

She shot a look at Leofric, and that one said that if he didn't make sure it was all right, she'd find a way to make him sorry.

He grinned back. Their secrets were safe with Elfleda—and, therefore, they were safe.

Then the healer picked up the fresh bundle of folded clothes—she was nothing if not persistent—and held it out to Astrid. "Please, dearie. You must dress. It doesn't do for a lady to be as you are."

Leofric knew that was too many words for Astrid to understand, but she understood enough. The gist—trying to get her to wear a dress she did not want.

Instead of casting it away in a fit of pique this time, she turned to him. She patted her legs and spoke in her language. Then she heaved a sigh. "You. Like you."

He wished he could explain to her that his people—her people, now—felt differently about their bodies than she did. Bodies were to be kept private. Adam and Eve had been cast out of the Garden; they'd known their nakedness, and never since had bare bodies in public not been considered shameful.

A woman's body in particular. A woman in breeches was more than simply scandalous. A woman in breeches would be an outrage, an affront to God. A woman's legs were for no one but her husband and her attendants.

Or her lover, but such things were unspoken and unheard, and thus didn't exist. In this world, so much of propriety was keeping secrets rather than keeping faith. It wasn't the first time Leofric had had that thought.

The artifice didn't change the reality, however. Appearance mattered.

"I'm sorry. There is no other way." He got up. Elfleda gasped and turned away at his nakedness, which he hadn't even noticed. Astrid's nonchalance had affected him, it seemed. He grabbed his breeches and yanked them on. Astrid watched him. Then he went to her and took her hands.

"If you wear that"—he pointed to the bundle of clothes Elfleda yet held—"We can go out there"—he pointed to the windows, bright with sunlight.

She stared at the windows for a long time. Then she turned back to the clothes and Elfleda, who smiled and nodded like a mother encouraging her child.

She turned to him, a question in her eyes. He could see that the dress meant something profound, that she would give up something crucial to her if she were to agree. But he saw no other...

A ghost of an idea wisped through his mind. He needed time to think that out. For now, though, he squeezed her hands and said, "Please."

She studied him for a moment, her eyes narrow and keen, and then she blew out a slow breath and nodded.

As she picked the bundle up from Elfleda's relieved hands, her shoulders sagged. Leofric saw an unhappiness much deeper than some yards of woven fabric should delve.

"I'll let you dress. I must get to the residence before my father and brother break their fast. I'll be back as soon as I can, and we'll go outdoors today. Into the wood, if you'd like."

He was blathering, words she couldn't possibly understand, but he wanted to reassure her, and he hated to leave. He wanted her to know. Finally, he kissed her cheek and said, "Soon."

She nodded as if she understood, and he tore himself away from her and dressed as quickly as he could.

He had to get to his father and brother and manage the story of the dead guard and the warrior woman coming back to life.

And he had to visit the Keeper of the Wardrobe as well.

PART FIVE
INDUSTRIOUSNESS

15

Astrid despised the clothes women in the castle wore. She didn't understand how the women were able to work so encumbered. The sleeves were heavy and draped over the hands, the neck of the underdress bound at the throat, and the layers of skirts wound around the legs and made walking near impossible.

She still refused to wear the head covering. The women of her people covered their heads, too, but that was a matter of efficiency. These head covers were heavy, like the wings of great birds hanging over their shoulders.

She didn't need many words of this ugly language to understand that these people believed that women bore shame like they bore breasts—because they bore breasts—and did all they could to cover them up.

Except the rich ladies, who showed spans of their chest, between their shoulders. It was apparently only the common women who bore the shame, and likely bore it for the rich ones as well as for themselves.

After Astrid had suffered in these cumbersome dresses for a few days, Elfleda brought her one of the rich gowns in fine silks. She'd hated that even more. It squeezed her bosom and belly and bound her arms. If she ever had cause to fight in this place, she'd first need to tear such a dress off and go at her foe bare.

So she wore the rough-spun dresses in simple shades of brown and blue, and she braided her hair and tucked it up, making as little of it as she could, and Leofric pronounced it enough that she could be seen in this world.

Not that she wanted to be seen among these people. They all stared at her when she walked past. And they whispered. In her boiled leathers, she would scarcely have noticed, but in these odd, uncomfortable clothes, with no axe or shield in her hands, she heard and saw it all. Even if she only understood a stray word here and there, she knew the meaning of those whispers and stares.

They saw her as a beast tamed. And they saw Leofric as the one who'd tamed her. Her master.

Perhaps he had tamed her—or the black place had, and Leofric had simply picked up what they'd left. She no longer knew who she was. What she had been, where she had come from, all of that was lost to her now. This world covered its women up and made them helpless. There were no shieldmaidens here, and she was nothing else.

There was no place in this world from someone like her, and she had no other place.

It was why she stayed in this room when Leofric wasn't with her, though she was no longer under guard. There was nowhere for her to go, nowhere she understood.

Every day, when Leofric came to lead her from her room and into his world, she walked tall and resolute through the castle, and the grounds, and finally out into the wood. Only then, when they were alone again and she was in a world she understood, trees and ground and sky that she could almost believe might be home, could she set away the sense that she was lost.

In the wood, alone with Leofric, she found some ease.

She trusted him. A voice in her mind told her to remember the game, to look for trouble and betrayal on the edges of her sight, but he was the only thing here Astrid felt like she understood. Even without words, he seemed to know what she needed, and even without words, she believed she understood his intention.

He'd given himself up to her. Completely, on that first night. And then, while his face and neck swelled and his body purpled from the abuse she'd heaped on him, he'd treated her like a lover. Since then, he'd treated her always like a lover, and not only in bed. He touched her like a lover, even hooking her hand over his arm as they walked through the grounds, which seemed a scandalous thing, judging by the reactions of the people who saw them.

Astrid had never had such a relationship with any man before. She'd never before felt what she felt for Leofric.

She told herself to beware, to remember that it had been the king, Leofric's father, who'd put her in the black place, and possibly even Leofric himself. She tried to force herself to remember the deep despair she'd felt, the overwhelming pain, and to remind herself that soft feelings for the one who'd brought her back into the light did not mean love.

And yet, love was what she thought she felt. She felt it from him, in his touch, his look, his voice, and her heart returned the same feelings. It was love, or it was madness. Astrid had never felt either before.

But each time he came into the room and smiled at her, her mind went quiet, and her heart and body clamored. Each moment she spent with him, she felt calmed.

She didn't know who she was, or who she might become, or if she would have the chance at all, but she did know that Leofric was someone important to her, and she believed that she was important to him as well.

Perhaps she could learn to let that be enough. Perhaps she could find herself in his eyes.

Perhaps that woman would be comfortable in this place, in these clothes, with her hands empty and soft.

~oOo~

As Audie was clearing the morning tray, Elfleda came in with the day's dress. Since Astrid had agreed to wear the clothes, the old woman brought in something new each day, and a fresh, flowing sleeping dress each night.

Astrid enjoyed these two women, old and young. They did their work and made few demands, and they treated her like a person, not like a strange beast.

They were as yet the only people, other than Leofric, that she had cause to try to speak to. Their way of speaking was much different from Leofric's, thicker and broader, like the difference in accent between the people of Karlsa and of Geitland. The words were the same, but their sounds were little alike. It was not far different from learning two new languages at once.

They'd always been kind enough, but once she'd tried their words, they'd become friendly. Elfleda treated her like a mother—not her mother, but the gentle kind that others seemed to have. Audie seemed still a little fearful, but her curiosity and kindness were strong and turned that fear to awe. Audie was the hardest to understand, however, so they communicated in pantomime still.

Speaking this tongue had been a decision, and once Astrid had made it, she had few qualms about it. Wearing the clothes had been a concession, and that felt like a weakness. So she couldn't resist pulling a face at the new bundle of clothes. These would be wool, she knew. The weather had cooled in the past days. Even heavier fabric to weigh her down.

Elfleda, however, grinned broadly, showing a yellow smile missing two teeth. "Something special for you today, dearie."

Astrid frowned. She'd grown to like hearing herself called 'dearie,' but didn't understand one of the words. "Special?" The middle of the word didn't come out the way she'd heard it.

"Special, aye. Means you'll like it. Come see." She walked to the bed and set the bundle down.

It was wrapped in a piece of plain linen, and that was unusual. Normally, it was simply a neat stack of folded fabric. Elfleda began to open the linen, and Astrid went over to watch.

There was leather. On top, there was leather. She reached out and brushed her hand over it. Not boiled; soft. So not armor. But leather nonetheless. She picked it up.

Breeches. Gods, it was breeches! Astrid slapped her hand over her mouth to quash the odd sound coming from it.

There was more leather—a chestpiece, or something like one. Small, and artful, and still soft, but a good leather with give. The color matched the breeches: a deep, rich brown, like fallen leaves.

Under those glorious pieces was fabric, a lot of it, in a rich blue. It was different from the linens and wools she'd been wearing, or the silks she'd tried. She set her hand on it—it was wool, but so soft. Like Leofric's chestpieces. What he called *doublets*.

Elfleda picked that one up and shook it out. A gown. A fancy gown. The shine wore off Astrid's wonder at her new clothes. But then the old woman took hold of the skirt and lifted a piece.

It was split in front.

Elfleda laid the gown on the bed, spread neatly, and took the breeches from Astrid's hands. She set them on the dress, under the split, showing how to wear it. Then she closed the split. It didn't show. She set the chestpiece on the dress as well.

"His Grace had it made special for you, dearie."

Leofric had given her something she could wear and feel herself in, or at least a piece of who she'd been. He did know her—and he didn't expect her to give up all of herself. He didn't expect her to be tamed.

"Special," Astrid murmured and brushed her hands over the gown. "Special."

"Aye," Elfleda said, smiling. "Well, let's be getting you dressed, then."

~oOo~

There was a glass in the room. Astrid had never cared much for looking into a glass, except when she braided her hair in more than a single braid, but she couldn't stop looking into this one.

She'd let Elfleda braid her hair, and she'd done something almost like Astrid's style but more elegant. The plaits were not so tight at the scalp and seemed to be woven together into a pattern at the back. She hadn't been able to see that very well. But she could see her clothes.

The gown was soft, the wool like a cloud, and the blue made her eyes seem like light shone from them. The leather chestpiece over it—Elfleda called it a *corset*—was snug, but not uncomfortably so, and it had a high neck at the back. An ornate design of curls and sweeps was tooled into the leather. The gown itself had no adornment and needed none. Its wide neckline filled in the V of the corset—for *modesty*, Elfleda had cooed.

It was a word that seemed to have to do with women's shame in this place, but nothing could taint Astrid's pleasure at her new clothes.

The breeches fit her like skin. How had he known the fit of her body? His hands, good as they were, could not have been so deft to know that. If Astrid had had enough of their words, she would have asked if Elfleda had had something to do with this gift.

But she contented herself stalking around the room, feeling the leather over her legs, the wool of the gown swinging free and not catching around her calves.

It would be disappointing to put the silly thin shoes on her feet, beneath the breeches, but she didn't have boots. All of the clothes she'd been wearing when she'd been captured had been destroyed, she supposed.

Pushing that thought away, she sighed at the little shoes.

Before she could sit down and put the shoes on, the door opened, and her mind got quiet. Leofric stood there, looking as though his mind had gone quiet, too.

He stood and stared, his mouth slack. Then he blinked and came in. As he closed the door, Astrid saw that he held a pair of black boots in his hand. They looked very much like his own, only smaller. Her size.

Perhaps she could find her way in this place, if she had Leofric to guide her and to understand. Perhaps she could learn to be right in this place.

It was love, not madness, she felt in her heart.

A smile took over his slack features, and he crossed the room to her. "You are beautiful. So beautiful." He took her chin in his hand and drew his thumb over her mouth. It was a common gesture he made. A lover's touch.

She knew the word *beautiful*, and she smiled. "Thank." Remembering the proper phrasing, she repeated, "Thank *you*." She patted her chest, feeling calm in the leather. "This me."

"I know. And I think it's me enough as well. Understand?"

As had been the case in Estland, much of learning a new language was filling in the gaps between the words she knew with the context of the conversation. So Astrid thought she did understand. He'd found a way for her to be comfortable in his world. In her clothes, if in no other way.

She nodded, and he held out the boots. As she sat on the bed and slid them on—they were a bit too big, but she didn't mention it—Leofric sat beside her.

"I want to take you to my father today. We cannot put it off longer."

With one boot on and the other in her hand, she stopped and turned to him. Had he just told her she would see the king today? "*Fader? Kung?*"

He squinted, as if he were deciding whether he'd understood her words. "Yes. The king, my father."

She shook her head. The king had put her in the black place and left her there for what she now understood had been weeks. She would not meet that man without an axe in her hand.

Her axe hand hardened into a fist, and she felt Leofric lay his hand over it. "Astrid, yes. We must. For you to be safe, you

238

must go before him. He must see that you are trying. Do you understand?"

She understood enough. She shook her head.

He closed his eyes and took in a deep breath. "Show him...you." He pointed to her. "Show him..." He waved a hand over her clothes.

Had he dressed her up to show her off like a trinket? She lifted the skirt in a clutched fist. "This...him? Not me?"

"No. For you." He turned to Elfleda as if seeking help. Astrid looked at the old woman, too. She didn't understand, and she didn't like the cold fear she felt again. But Elfleda only shrugged, seeming sorry to do it.

Leofric turned back to Astrid. "Please. Important. For you."

Important for her. How? Because the king still held her life in his hands. Though she couldn't remember his face, she hated that man above all but one other. "No forgive king. You only. For king..." She didn't know the word for vengeance in this tongue, so she gave him her own. "*Hämnd.*" To make her point, she clenched a fist and held it up. "*Hämnd.*"

He covered her fist with his hand and brought it down to his lap. "Please. For me. I know your hate. But I need you—I need you safe. Please, Astrid. *Snälla.* For me."

"No forgive." But yes, she would meet this king, and she would know the face of her enemy. She nodded. "For you."

His relief filled the room. "Thank you."

~oOo~

She'd prepared herself to be led into a great stone hall like the one in the castle in Estland, where Prince Vladimir had attempted an ambush, but Leofric brought her instead to a smaller room—not small, by any measure, but smaller than her mind had conjured, and warmer as well. This room had a fire crackling in the fireplace, and the stone walls were draped with thick fabrics woven with images of people and plants and animals. Some seemed to tell a story.

The king sat in a massive chair behind a carven table. There were rolls of things arrayed neatly to one side. Seated, he seemed big enough, and well built. His hair was long, the waves curling at his shoulders, and white with dwindling streaks of black. His beard was white and artfully shaved. He had the eyes and nose of a hawk.

Even in that seat, in his rich clothes, threaded with gold that sparkled, Astrid knew him to be a warrior king. But he was old. He elicited no fear or worry in her. Only hate. Leofric's father or no, king or no, she wanted him dead at her hand.

There was a man seated nearby, also regally dressed. He stood when Leofric led her in, holding her hand at his arm. The resemblance between the two younger men was strong, and Astrid knew them to be brothers.

Leofric walked her to the center of the room, and both men, Leofric's father and brother, king and prince, one seated and one standing, stared at her. Even in her wonderful new clothes, she felt the sting of their curiosity and their contempt.

"Father, Eadric, I present to you Astrid, of the Northmen." He unhooked her hand from his arm and set his hand instead on her lower back. "Astrid, this is my father, Eadric, King of Mercuria, and my brother, Eadric, the Crown Prince."

She'd seen men and women dropping nearly to their knees in Leofric's presence often enough to know she was expected to do the same now. But she did not. She would not. Instead, she squared her shoulders and gave each man a simple nod. "*Hallo.*"

The brother returned her nod. The king did not. He stood and came around the table. He was not as tall as his sons, but Astrid had been right—even in his grey age, he had power in his body.

He walked right up to her and stared into her eyes, nearly scowling with concentration. His regard traveled downward, over her body, all the way to the floor. Then he walked a circle around her, studying her all the while.

She stood still and let him. Leofric had moved a step or two away to make room. He felt miles from her.

When he completed his circle and faced her again, the king asked, "How much of our language do you know? If we say you are a savage, do you know what we say?"

Leofric reacted to that, but she didn't need to see him in the corner of her sight to know she'd been insulted. *Savage* was a word she'd heard often in the black place. It was one of the first she'd come to understand.

"*Ja.* And know *cruel.* For you."

His eyes flared wide, and Astrid knew triumph. In the corners of her eyes, the younger men reacted to that—one worried and one angry. But after that first rush of surprise, something dark, a shadow, slid through the king's eyes.

He turned to his younger son and spoke a long time. Astrid understood little, except, "She can be nothing to you."

She turned to Leofric and saw his anger. He spoke a long time back at his father, and then his brother spoke. They were arguing fiercely, and no one was paying her any mind. The words she understood were upsetting—*savage, whore, die*; all words she'd learned in the black place—so she stopped trying to understand. Instead, she scanned the room for weapons. There were many, including a great broadsword on the wall above the fire. As the men fought, she sidled toward it, wondering how quickly she could get it down if she needed to wield it.

She would not be returned to the black place.

The door opened, and she spun in that direction, putting her back to the fire and the sword.

The man who walked in then made Astrid forget about the quarrel at her side and the sword at her back. He wore a white dress, and his hair was cut strangely, in a ring around his head. He was the one man she hated above the king, and the only face she could remember from her time in the black place. Their seer, who'd stood in the black place and watched all that had been done to her. Watched and enjoyed.

Without thinking of or seeing anything but the man before her, Astrid let loose her battle cry and leapt for him.

16

A shrieking roar split the air, and Leofric wheeled around, grabbing instinctually for a sword he wasn't wearing, just in time to see Astrid leap—she left her feet and nearly flew—at Father Francis, slamming her full weight into him and bringing him to the floor in a heap.

"Astrid, NO!"

As her hands went around the bishop's fat neck and heaved his head up, then slammed it back to the floor, Leofric ran to her, but not before the guards always stationed outside the door of the king's solar had crashed into the room and begun trying to pull her off.

She resisted mightily, shrieking like a wild thing, and Leofric just reached her, shouting "No! No! No!" as one of the guards sent his mailed fist into her face. She fell back, unconscious, and Leofric dropped to the floor and gathered her up.

A gash on her temple bled freely. He bent his head to her mouth and didn't breathe until he felt her breath caress his cheek. She lived.

"Take her to the dungeons," his father commanded behind him.

The guards moved at once to obey, and Leofric shrank back, tightening his arms and curling his body around hers.

"No! Father, no!"

Father and son stared hard at each other, and Leofric could feel the guards' confusion, but he knew that they wouldn't hesitate for long. "Your Majesty, please. She is only beginning to understand us. You know why she would attack Father Francis." He dashed a look at the bishop.

Eadric had helped him to his feet, and now the fat prat was making a show of his injuries.

He returned his attention to his father and saw that the king had also spared a glance for his spiritual advisor.

"You know, Father," Leofric repeated. Again, he held his father's stony look.

"Back to her room, then. Under guard. Until we have made a decision about her fate."

"Thank you, Father." Leofric moved to stand with Astrid in his arms.

"Not you. You shall stay." The king nodded at the guards, who both moved to wrest her from him.

He turned from their rough, grasping hands. "Gentle! You'll carry her gently."

Again, the men looked to the king, who, again, nodded. One of the guards, his expression perfectly blank but his eyes full of condemnation, held out his arms, and Leofric laid Astrid's inert form across them. "Gentle," he said again.

He watched as Astrid was carried away. Two new guards had already filled the posts outside the door, and they closed the door when the way was clear.

Now Leofric was alone with his angry family—and the bishop—and Astrid was alone with angry guards. The next moments could determine everything about her fate, and perhaps his as well.

With one last, loaded look at Leofric, the king went to the bishop. "Are you well, Father?"

Francis moaned pitiably and clutched at his head. "You must see, Sire. She is an animal. No amount of care can make her more than that."

"She has every cause to hate you, Francis," Leofric called, standing back from the others. "No one in this room can doubt why she would want to cause you pain. Father, *that* is what I know you see."

The king lowered his head, just a fraction, but enough that Leofric thought his father was feeling afresh the guilt he'd known for Astrid's suffering.

The bishop wasn't finished yet, however. He stopped swooning and sat straight up and glared at Leofric. "I do the Lord's work, Your Grace. It is not mine, nor yours, to question His ways."

"And who is there to question whether what you do is truly the Lord's work, or rather your own? The king." Leofric went to his father. "Father, I know you feel the wrongness of it. I knelt with you in the chapel. I stood with you in the Black Walls. You feel it."

He knew it was true. He'd seen his father's guilt and conflict, and it was the only explanation for the leniency he'd shown him until now. The weeks without seeing his captive, allowing himself to be put off again and again—if he'd truly believed in the bishop's counsel, then Astrid would have been killed, in the Black Walls or on the block, long ago.

Father Francis knew it was true, as well. His eyes were cold and shadowed under a deeply furrowed brow when he glared again at Leofric, but they softened upon turning to the king. "I speak the Lord's truth, Sire, and I do the Lord's work. I've given my life to that purpose. And I am telling you that the savage will never be anything but a savage."

"But Your Excellency," Eadric answered, frowning. He'd been observing silently until now. "She is human, is she not? And thus one of us? Is it not the apostle Paul's directive to bring the Light to the benighted? Would the Lord make any one of us incapable of salvation?"

Leofric saw a light leading a way out of this sudden darkness. His brother had found the crack in Francis that their father would really see. A break in his holy logic.

Indeed, the king saw it. "Father, you should have your head seen to."

Understanding that he was being dismissed, the bishop sputtered, "I'm fine, Sire, truly. She is feral, but not so strong to harm a man of God."

"Leave us." The king walked away, back to his desk, and gave the bishop no further word or notice.

It was a greater condemnation than any word might have been, and Father Francis knew it. He paled and gaped, his eyes going to king, prince, and duke in turn. Finally, he gathered up his dignity and bowed. "Your Majesty."

He backed from the room, and the family was alone. Leofric's father turned on him. "The truth remains: you cannot have this woman. She can be nothing to you, and whatever I decide for her, I want you out of it."

That was the argument they'd been having when Francis had come into the room. The king, astute about people, had seen today what Leofric knew he'd suspected: he loved Astrid. But the king did not see what Leofric did: the possibility for the match.

"She trusts no one but me, Father. You saw that yourself. Only I can bring her to our ways. Perhaps she might be baptized into the true Faith."

His father sighed. "And what do you think will happen if she is? You cannot marry a barbarian. What good is that alliance to the realm?"

Leofric took a terrible risk. "She might already be carrying my child." He didn't know if it was true; he'd only spent in her once, on that first night, and she'd pulled away before all his seed had been sown. But it was true that she might be. He hoped it was true that she was.

All air and sound seemed to leave the room in a rush. His father and brother stared at him, their eyes and mouths wide. They obviously didn't share his hope.

At last, the king sighed. "Your profligacies must stop, Leofric. You are not a boy. You have responsibilities beyond yourself. And why would you think such news cause to save the savage? Better I end her now, before such a complication can be known."

"Father!" Eadric cut in, his tone full of shock. "She might carry the seed of this house. We need an heir."

"And you shall provide one—more than one. You are the Crown Prince. We shall find you a princess, and you shall give the realm its heirs."

Eadric shook his head. "After burying three brides, no match I might make will be more suitable than Leofric's wild woman. No father will send his daughter to an alliance that will give him nothing but his daughter's death. That is what people all over believe of me. We've seen it to be true. Why not make a match with the warrior woman and show that she's been tamed into a lady of the court? Is that not another kind of victory over the barbarians? Does that not give us power over them, should they return?"

Astrid would despise this talk, if she'd heard and understood it. But in Leofric's ears and mind, it meant hope. This was what he wanted. Whether it was a victory for his father or not, he wanted Astrid at his side, on his arm, in his bed, wearing his crown. That was his victory, and hers, over everyone else.

His father railed often against his 'profligacies,' and he supposed the censure was merited. But since he'd brought Astrid up from the Black Walls, he had taken no other woman. He'd tried, in the days when she'd been strong enough to hate him, before he'd won her over, but he'd been unable. From the moment she'd curled against him for comfort in that bath, he'd wanted no other woman.

If he was profligate now, it was only in his extravagant love for that one woman, unlike any other he'd ever known.

"Father…" he began and then didn't know how to continue.

There was no need that he should; Eadric's argument had been persuasive. The king met Leofric with a different light in his eyes now. "Can she be brought to the right ways? Can she be trusted not to make further attempts on Francis, or on anyone else? On me? Will she renounce her people's licentious gods and accept the one true God as her Lord and Savior?"

"Yes," Leofric asserted, with all the confidence he could muster. "You have my most solemn vow, Father."

The king sighed. "If you are wrong, and you cannot control her, then you will both bear the burden of her actions."

His father had never made such a threat against him before, but it didn't sway him. "I understand."

"Very well. Then go to your woman and control her. And we shall see whether she can be made into a suitable match."

~oOo~

There were two guards on her door, the same two who'd come in and pulled her from the bishop. When Leofric sent them away, he was forced to assert that the order was from his father before they would go.

Privy to so many crucial details, castle guards were sworn to absolute secrecy, but those things which seemed especially salacious always managed to leak through. Leofric knew that the whole castle, and in short time the whole kingdom, would know that the barbarian woman he'd been escorting on his arm around the grounds and the wood had tried to kill the bishop of the realm. It was more than his father he'd have to convince of her change. It was everyone.

Including Astrid herself. She didn't want any of this. But what choice did she have? She could live as one of them—as one of the royal family—or she could die as a barbarian captive. There was nothing else.

The guards dismissed, Leofric opened the door. She was sitting near the fire, and she stood at once, her posture tense and defensive. She was still dressed in the clothes he'd had made for her, still stunning in that blue, like a warrior queen in the leather corset and the breeches peeking from under the skirt. She, or someone, had cleaned the blood from her face and tended her wound.

He went to her, and reached out to touch the bruise around the cut. She flinched lightly as his fingertips grazed the swollen flesh. Her eyes flashed with stoic interest.

"I die now," she said, as if it had always been her fate. There was no fear in the words, only certainty.

"No, my love. You are safe."

249

She frowned. "Safe?"

"Safe." He leaned in to kiss her, but she tipped her head back.

"No understand."

He closed his eyes and tried to think how he could explain in the few words they shared. When he lifted his lids again, she was still staring hard at him, as if she'd been trying to see through him to his thoughts.

"Be with me, Astrid. No more…" He tried to remember the word she'd used earlier in the day. Her own word. He'd only guessed at its meaning, but she'd said it with a tight fist. It meant something violent. Retribution, he thought. "No more *hämnd*. Live. Be with me."

She shook her head and began a string of her words. Then she cut it off with a frustrated huff and said, "Took me. Hurt me. Made me…" She faded out, and he saw her mind working, scrabbling through the words she had for one that would fit. Obviously, she didn't have one, so instead she made a gesture with both her hands, bringing them together, as loose fists, and then bursting them open and apart.

He understood. She was telling him that they'd made her nothing.

"No, my love. Not nothing. Everything. I love you, and I will keep you safe. If you allow it."

"In my place"—she tapped her chest sharply—"keep me own safe."

She'd kept herself safe in her own world. "I know. I'm sorry. Please, Astrid."

After a long moment of quiet, she asked, "Love?"

"Yes. Love." He put her hand to his chest and covered it with both of his. "Love."

She nodded. "Love."

It was the first time he'd considered that she might love him as well. He swept her into his arms. When he leaned down to kiss her this time, she was ready and waiting.

~oOo~

That night Leofric woke well before dawn, chilled to the bone and shivering. A strong, cold breeze blew over the bed, and he shrugged down under the furs and reached out to find Astrid's body. She always moved away from him at some point in the night, usually curling up with her back to him, but if he woke and moved to her, she didn't resist his embrace.

But she was not in the bed at all; the linens were cold with her absence. He sat up, the breeze becoming a wind in his face. On this night, winter shook the windows and announced its arrival. He grabbed a fur and heaved it over his bare shoulders.

The room was awash in the bright, limpid gleam of full moonlight. Astrid was at one of the windows; she'd flung it wide open, and she stood before it, as bare as she'd been when they'd fallen off to sleep. Her pale hair was loose, and waved back from her face with every gust. Her eyes were closed, her face tipped up into the wind and the moon, and her arms were stretched out along her sides, her palms up and her fingers splayed.

She seemed as if she were praying to the wind itself. Offering herself up to the elements. Leofric could only sit and stare at first, uncomprehending but enchanted.

In the moonlight, she seemed more than human. Lustrous and pale and wild, like a nymph of the night. Even her scars seemed to have faded away.

But the room was freezing, and the fire had dwindled to little more than a red glow. With the fur clutched around him, he went to her. Her nipples were tight knots, and her body prickled with the cold. He tried to wrap her up with him in the fur, but she shrugged free.

"Astrid, are you well?"

She turned her head slightly, not quite enough to look back at him, but enough to show that she'd heard him. "Lonely. For cold." Her hair blew across her face, but she gave it no mind. She simply turned to the window again, and it flew back with the next gust of angry wind.

Of course. Her people were from the North. It would be colder there. He wondered how much. He'd heard stories from traders of winters that lasted most of the year, snows as deep as a man was tall, and nights that lasted for days. Was she from such a place? What must she think of this place, where it rarely snowed and winter was only a colder, blander version of every other season?

Homesick. She was homesick. Of course she was.

He wanted to ask her, to talk to her about her loneliness, to ease it, but as he searched for a way to do it that she would understand, she spoke again.

"I...prisoner here."

Did she believe the king still meant to hold her for her attack on the bishop? "No, Astrid. No longer. Nevermore."

"*Ja*," she countered. "Always."

He put his hand on her shoulder and tugged lightly. She turned to face him without resistance. Her eyes were clear but sad.

"You are not a prisoner. You may come and go as you like. Wherever you like. With me, or on your own."

"Not home. Not go there."

"No. I'm sorry. But this can be your home now. With me." He pulled her close. "Let me make you with child. We will make a family, and you will see that this is your home." He set his hand on her flat belly to be sure she understood. "Please."

As usual, she'd made him withdraw from her earlier in the night; she did not want to be seeded. He wanted to be sure that she had been; any reservations his father might later raise about Astrid's fitness as a mate could be set aside at the thought of an heir—a legitimate heir. Moreover, he believed what he'd just told her: if she had a child, she could begin to grow roots here. It would calm her and open her to the truth of her life.

Also, he simply wanted her to bear his child.

But she shook her head. "No child. Prisoner."

"No, Astrid, you are not."

Her smile was sad and resolute. "*Ja.*"

She rested her head on his chest.

His heart aching, Leofric wrapped her up in his arms, under the fur, and set the matter aside. As long as she continued to learn their language and their ways, as long as she was his, and if she would agree to be baptized into the Faith, then it might even be preferable to wait until after they were wed to get her with child. In any event, she wasn't ready for that step. So if he hadn't already seeded her, he would spend his time making her ready.

He would help her see that she was home.

"Come back to bed, love." He felt her nod on his chest, and he reached up to close the window, but she caught his arm.

"Keep. Please."

"Open?"

"*Ja.*"

He smiled down at her and brushed silken blonde strands from her eyes. "Will you keep me warm?"

The smile she gave him was loving and real and eased his worry a bit. She slid her hand over his chest, down his belly, and took firm hold of his sex, which swelled full at her touch.

"*Ja.* Make hot."

He lifted her, and she hooked her legs around his waist. The fur fell from his shoulders, but there were others on the bed—and his woman was wrapped around him. They'd make their own heat.

He laid her down and tucked them both under cover, and as the new winter wind blew over them, Leofric set out to make her feel free.

17

Leofric preferred to sleep with his body around hers, their limbs wound together, but Astrid had rarely slept so close with anyone before. Moreover, since the black place—he called it the Black Walls, and it was apt, but she would never think of it as anything but the black place—she couldn't rest when she felt restrained.

So on those nights when he slept with her—which was nearly always, now that she had a room in the guest quarters, nearer his own—she lay until he fell asleep in the tangle that gave him ease, and then she loosed herself from his embrace and found ease of her own.

Often, in the wee hours, he found her again and wrapped her up, and she let him draw her close again, even if it meant that sleep for her was finished.

In her life before, when she had been a shieldmaiden, she never would have thought to give a man such consideration. Now, she barely had the thought to deny him.

Did love always change a person so completely? Or had she been changed already, in the black place, and simply loved the man who'd saved her from it? She'd never felt love before, and she understood the feeling less than she understood the world she'd been abandoned to. Both seemed to control her in ways beyond her ken.

Leofric spoke often about her safety—that she was safe, that he would keep her safe, that he swore it on his own life—as if that were his duty. He had saved her, so of course he would believe he always must. In this world, he was right. In this world, Astrid couldn't save herself. With no axe or shield, no friend but he, no standing of her own, she was only safe so long as he was there to protect her.

She loved him, but she hated that.

And she abhorred this place.

Winter had come, and with it chill northern winds and a loneliness that frosted her heart. Astrid had never known its like before. Not even in the black place had she missed home so very much. Then, she'd cleaved to hope that she'd see Geitland again someday. Now, she knew she never would.

There was no snow here. No blanketing of the world in brilliant, pure quiet. No snug fire in a longhouse pit, everyone gathered together to make warm merry, with mead and meat and laughter. Here, people hunkered down into their colorless clothes against the misting rain and drear, and they shambled about their day, then closed themselves up alone with only their blood families in the night.

When she'd raided in this world, she'd marveled at the dense foliage and the riot of different greens. She'd thought it beautiful. But all that color faded into nothingness when north winds blew.

The winter of home was dazzling white and blue, and the night sky often danced with wild color. Here, winter was simply grey. Grey and damp and dead.

Thinking those thoughts as she lay in bed and watched an indifferent dawn grey the windows, Astrid sighed.

This was the world she lived in now, and if she would live, then she must learn to do it here. This world had no place for shieldmaidens, so she would have to become something else. Find a new strength.

Leofric wanted to wed her. He wanted to make her with child and put a crown on her head. For him, it was the answer to everything.

He'd been disappointed when her blood had come, showing that his seed hadn't taken root that first night. Astrid had been relieved. She could think of no circumstance more telling of her lost self than making a child. All her years as a shieldmaiden, she had never wanted to bear a child. That had been the most clear truth to her: one could not be both shieldmaiden and mother.

Brenna God's-Eye was both, it seemed, or at the least had tried to be both. Perhaps if she had been raiding with them for the years she'd stayed home mothering, perhaps if she and Vali had not been protective of each other as parents of their children, they would have been stronger fighters against Leofric's father's soldiers.

A shieldmaiden voyaged in the world. A mother was bound to the hearth. A woman who tried to be both was split in twain.

But Astrid could not be a shieldmaiden in this place. Should she then be a mother? Was it less a prison if there was no other option? She lived in a world now where women were only slaves and broodmares.

No, it was no less a prison. But there truly was no other option—she would wed Leofric, or she would die.

Would she know how to show a child love? Or even tenderness? Or would she be a mother like her own?

She looked down at the strong hand resting over her belly. He had such good hands. Not the soft hands of one who'd known no work or strife. A warrior's hands. Scarred and rough and big. But also beautifully formed, and they touched her with love and tenderness the like of which she'd never before experienced.

He would know how to be loving and tender with a child. Perhaps she could learn from him, as she was learning everything else about this world.

Perhaps he could show her how to be content in a life here.

Warm and snug under the furs and in his arms, Astrid rolled to face him. He stirred and sighed but didn't wake, and she tucked her head under his chin, feeling the dark hair on his chest tickling her cheek.

His heart thumped its strong, steady beat. Steady. Strong. Leofric was these things. He seemed to know his mind and act without questioning his choices. She had been the same, in her own world.

He'd chosen her and hadn't wavered. He understood her; even when they'd had no words shared between them, he'd seemed to understand. He'd given her what she'd needed. He'd saved her and healed her and loved her. Now he wanted to give her a crown.

If only she could have taken those things for herself instead. In the way of her people.

Who had left her behind.

She sent a word to Skaði, goddess of strength and of winter, who had given Odin many children: *Skaði, I beseech you. Show me my strength. Let me see my way in this place.*

She kissed Leofric's strong chest, letting her tongue out to trail over the tickling hair until she found his nipple. As her hand slid downward, over his hip, across his belly, she sucked his nipple into her mouth and flicked her tongue over it.

He shuddered and flexed, and when she took hold of his sex, he was already hard. His hand came up and clutched the back of her head, holding her firmly, his fingers snagging in her hair.

"Astrid," he groaned, her name rumbling against her lips. His hand in her hair became a fist, and he pulled, bringing her head up to his. As she worked his sex, dragging her tight fist along his length, he claimed her mouth.

Before Leofric, Astrid had been indifferent on the topic of kissing. She'd found that more men were terrible at it than not, thrusting fat tongues far back in her mouth, leaving slobber all over her face. Kissing a man had been a way to lock in his attention and to signal her intentions, nothing more. Rarely had she truly enjoyed a man's mouth on her own.

A man's mouth elsewhere on her body was another matter. In those ways, she'd found ample pleasure.

Whether it was because of her feelings for Leofric or because he was simply more deft at the act, his kisses brought up all manner of sensations in her. He could bring her to great, writhing need simply with his lips on hers, his beard brushing her skin, his tongue meeting hers.

And the way he held her when his kissed her. It was claiming, it was possession, and yet nothing in her wished to resist it. There were times, when their bodies were so entwined, that Astrid felt as if she would crawl inside him if she could.

He tore his mouth from hers with a growl and rolled to his back, bringing her with him. "Mount me, love. I want to feel you have your way."

She did. Pushing the furs away so she could feel the cold, Astrid straddled him and settled onto his hot, thick sex, letting her head fall back with a moan as he filled her. He answered with one of his own, rough with need, and his hands clenched around her thighs.

She moved slowly at first, savoring the slide of him against her slick walls. Lifting up until only the tip of his sex was still inside her, she sat down slowly, tensing her legs, so that she could feel all of him, each vein and ridge, every inch, all the way in. Again and again, she moved in that determined fashion, twisting her hips slightly as she drew him in and out. The molten heat began to coil around her joints, and in her belly, and still she moved slowly, each exclamation of pained need from Leofric only focusing her more on her steady pace.

And then the liquid fire filled her too full to heed anything but on her own need, and she began to move with more speed, more force. She bent forward and clawed her hands into his chest as she drove herself onto him, harder and harder, feeling need throb into a flower of painful fire bursting at her core. Then Leofric filled his hands with her breasts and pinched her nipples, and she released, all at once, grunting out her surprise at the speed of it slamming through her after so much slow build.

When she could think and see again, she saw Leofric beneath her, his face a rictus of restrained need. He was trying not to release until she was done—until she could pull away and be free of his seed.

And she made a choice. She didn't let herself think more of it. She saw what was before her and acted.

"Let go, Leofric."

His eyes flew open, widening despite the tense furrow of his brow.

She bent forward and began to rock on him again. With her mouth on his, she whispered, "Let go." When he remained tense, she said it again. "Let go. Let go."

Finally convinced, he threw his arms around her, flipped them over, and pounded into her with wild abandon. He completed quickly, with a roar of utter ecstasy and satisfaction, and Astrid almost believed she'd felt his seed fill her.

What would it mean to her to bear his child? Who would she be?

As he dropped, exhausted, onto her, she pushed those thoughts away and held him close. This new world required a new self. She would have to find her way and find her strength.

When he'd gained his breath again, he gathered her close and lifted her onto his knees, setting her over his thighs. Staring up into her eyes, he brushed her hair from her face, and then simply gazed at her.

There was so much emotion in his eyes—love and relief and hope—that she could almost see her way in their light.

~oOo~

Astrid cocked her head at the small hut with a thatched roof. It was like the houses of the little villages in Mercuria, where the peasants lived, and much like the peasant homes in Estland as well. But it was deep in the wood, all on its own, with no land to farm or animals to raise.

"This place, it is what?"

Leofric swung off his grey horse and grinned up at her. "Privacy."

She didn't know that word. "What is that?"

"We will be alone here."

He took the reins of her horse, a smaller bay mare that he called a 'palfrey,' and held out his hand. She ignored it and dismounted. He always offered his hand to help her from her horse, and she always ignored it and helped herself. She'd had to learn how to dismount gracefully around skirts—she now had a wardrobe full of dresses with split skirts and leather breeches to wear under them—but now she managed it easily.

She adjusted the fur-trimmed cape she wore against what they called cold here. They didn't know cold here.

"It is a house?"

"A hunting cabin. A place to be warm and dry when we're too far from the castle. No servants, no guards, no one but us. Go and see while I put up the horses."

There was a small structure at the side of the hut, well back into a copse of trees. Leofric left Astrid at the hut's door and led the horses back to what must have been a small stable.

She grabbed the iron hasp and opened the door. It creaked on stiff hinges; it seemed to have been a while since anyone had used this cabin.

Inside, that became more clearly true. A light film of dust lay over everything, and the air bore a hint of the dank odor of a place left too long without life. But there was a full rack of wood near a deep stone fireplace, and when she pulled the covers from the furnishings, she found them to be cozy and sturdy. Four deep chairs clustered before the fireplace, a bed nestled into a far corner, and a solid table and four chairs stood near the door. An assortment of cooking tools hung on the wall and from the ceiling over the table.

Not like the castle, with its gilt and brocade, the furnishings of this hut were more humble and more pleasing for it.

She opened the windows and let light and air in. Leofric's tolerance for the cold was nothing like her own, so she knew there'd be a fire soon, and he'd want the windows closed, but for now, she smiled as motes of dust danced in the sunbeams stretched over the rough plank floor.

The door creaked open, and Leofric came in, his expression brilliant with smug pleasure. On the table, he set the panniers holding a meal of wine, bread, and cheese, and then he came to her and hooked his arms around her.

"Have you looked around?"

She swiveled her head to and fro and saw, she thought, all the cabin had to offer. "*Ja.* Is more?"

He wiggled his brows and let her go. Against one wall was a large chest of heavy, dark wood. She'd taken it for some kind of storage, possibly linens. He went to it and opened it, then reached into its depth. From her vantage, Astrid could only see more dark wood.

When he stood, he was holding two unstrung recurve bows and two quivers full of neatly fletched arrows.

He spun to her on his heel, with a flourish, his grin absurdly smug. "If you want meat tonight, we'll have to hunt it. Can you shoot?"

Not every word he'd said was one she knew, but over these months, she'd become adept at filling in the blanks and working backward from her understanding of the context to a grasp of the words themselves. He was asking her if she could shoot, and telling her that they were hunting today. Her whole body began to tremble. She went to him and took one of the bows into her shaking hand.

It was the first time she'd held a weapon since the day she'd killed the guard and stolen his spear.

"Astrid? If you don't know, I'll teach you."

"I know." Peering into the chest, she saw a coil of gut string and a basket of tools and supplies. She gathered it all up and went to the table. Then she sat down, shed her leather gloves, and got to work stringing the bow.

She would show him how well she knew.

With that grin on his face like it had frozen there, Leofric joined her and prepared his own bow.

~oOo~

Her cloak was made of deep crimson wool, but her dress was dark green and would make good camouflage, so she left the cloak behind and went into the winter wood. Leofric protested that she would be cold, but she only shook her head and strapped the quiver to her back.

A bow. Not her weapon of war, but one she had used all her life, even before she'd picked up a shield. Since it had been months, and her body thrummed with excitement and made her hands want to shake, she took a practice shot, aiming at a knot in a tree at about a hundred paces away.

The arrow struck true, with a thump, and Leofric lifted his eyebrows at her.

"Mayhap I'll wait here and make the hearth, and you will bag us our meal."

Feeling a happiness that wanted to burst through her skin, Astrid tipped her head at him and smiled. "If you like that."

"Mercy!" He laughed and caught her in his arms. "My warrior woman has learned to be coy. No, my love. I wouldn't miss seeing you bring down a great stag with an angry look and a single arrow."

She didn't know what 'coy' meant, or what a 'stag' was, but it didn't matter.

~oOo~

That evening, after a meal of wine, bread, cheese, and venison taken from the buck she'd killed—though Leofric hadn't even tried, which had made her punch him in the arm—they lay curled together on the floor before the hearth, bare and breathless and basking in an afterglow warmer than the fire itself.

He'd pulled all the furs and pillows from another chest, and the cushions from the chairs, and made for them a cozy nest. Now, Astrid reclined against his chest, holding one of his arms to her, under her breasts. His other hand combed lazily through her loose hair.

"Advent begins on Sunday," he murmured and kissed her head.

She looked back and up at him. "What is this?"

"It's a holy time of preparation. A time of fasting before we celebrate the birth of Christ."

"Fasting?"

"We eat little and revel not at all. I won't be able to be with you in the nights. My father turns his back often regarding us, but he'll not ignore that."

The king. Though she still hated him and trusted him not at all, Astrid understood his power and her need, so she was learning to be in the same room with him, on those rare occasions when Leofric said she must, and to give him signs of respect, though she had none for him.

They, in turn, had all learned to keep the bishop away from her. That man, she would not make nice for. That man, she never wanted to think of until the day she could kill him. But Leofric had brought up his god, and with his god came the bishop in her mind. She closed her eyes and shoved the image away.

Leofric had given her this perfect day and night because he had ill news to break with her. She focused on that, understanding that she would be all but alone while Leofric was on his knees in supplication to his god.

With a sigh, she returned her attention to the fire. "Your god no like life much well."

"What do you mean?"

"He wants you have shame and need always."

For a long moment, he was quiet, his breathing deep and his fingers moving through her hair. "Perhaps He does. What are your gods like?"

He'd never asked before, and the question sent a spike of loneliness through her heart. It was his season of 'advent,' but in her world, the solstice was almost upon them, and the season of *jul*. It was a time of revelry and hope, a sign that the darkest part of winter was coming to a close and the sun would return.

"Our gods, we not kill and hang on wood. They live. They fight and…*festa*…feast?" She looked back, and he nodded. "Feast and…*knulla*."

Not knowing the word in his tongue, she slapped her hand between her legs and thrust her hips with a grunt, and he chuckled, comprehending.

"They love and hate," she continued. "Make war and peace. They live."

"How are they different from us, then?"

She thought about that, and then shrugged, seeing the simple answer. "They are better."

Again, he was quiet, and then his arms snaked tightly around her and pulled her close. "Perhaps they are."

~oOo~

Leofric's people celebrated something like *jul* as well. At the end of their fasting, near the solstice, they feasted, celebrating the birth of their god's son, who was also their god himself. The same god whose same son hung naked and bleeding on crosses everywhere.

Astrid found that confusing and perverse, but her own gods did inexplicable things, too, so she set it aside as a strange god's strange ways.

Seemingly everyone who wasn't a servant—or her—was always engaged in prayer and introspection during this 'advent,' so she saw Leofric only brief times in each day, and rarely anyone else at all of note, except Elfleda, who made a point to visit every day. In this new room higher in the castle, Astrid had other attendants, and Elfleda came as a visitor, who could sit and talk.

She'd taken to going out on her own, riding her bay mare into the woods. Leofric said he wished she wouldn't go alone, but he wouldn't go with her, so she went. He gave her a dagger to keep at her belt, for safety, and it was the first weapon she could claim as her own in this place.

She was looking forward to the feast, and the end of this silly fasting season, when they all went several whole days in every week without anything but water, even though the castle larders swelled with plenty. Astrid was required to fast as well, if only for the fact that there was no food or drink prepared on those days.

Despite her weeks of starvation in the black place, or perhaps because of them, the fasting took its toll on her, and on some mornings, she felt nearly as weak as she had in the dark. As the weeks wore on, she was angered to find herself too tired to ride, and then she did little more than roam the castle halls until *that* was too tiring, and she went to bed.

By the morning of the feast, when she was awakened by Leofric sliding naked into bed with her, Astrid was sad, exhausted, and ill.

He pulled her into his arms and kissed her head. "Elfleda tells me you've been unwell."

She fussed in his embrace, trying to get the voluminous sleeping gown unwound from her legs—and to hide the shocking fact that tears had surged behind her eyes as he'd wrapped his arms around her. Was she so weak that his mere presence brought her an elation worthy of tears?

"Tired only. Days too many with no food." The idea of food didn't really appeal, however. She shuddered. Saliva filled her mouth, and she swallowed it back, feeling unsettled.

He chuckled and squeezed her more tightly. "I'm sorry."

He didn't sound sorry, and she huffed.

"Astrid, Elfleda also tells me you haven't had your blood during the fast."

She'd come from a world of little privacy, where people ate, drank, slept, rutted, everything in company. But she'd never had anyone so deeply involved in her personal rhythms before. Other people here knew as much as she did about the workings of her body. So bizarre it was that people who would cover themselves head to toe and pretend that they didn't have bodily workings or needs at all would so freely share the results.

Apparently, her attendants knew her body more than she did—because she hadn't thought about her blood lately. She'd had it twice since Leofric had been spending inside her, and she'd let the question fade away. And now it was again at the fore.

Was she with child?

Her mother was a healer, but not a midwife, and in any case, Astrid hadn't had the relationship with her to have been taught about such things. As a woman, she'd not had the interest to seek out knowledge about such things. She'd seen childbirth, and it was bloody and full of screaming. But she knew little about what came before, except that a woman's blood stopped while the child was inside her—and seemingly came out all in one rush with the child.

Her mouth flooded again, and she spun out of Leofric's arms. While the room whirled around her, she grabbed the pot from the floor and heaved into it. The day before had been a fast day, so there wasn't anything but a wad of foam to lose.

He was behind her, leaning over her, stroking her back, pulling her hair back and holding it. "My love, my love, my love," he murmured, sprinkling kisses over her shoulders and neck. "My love."

She was with child. She would be a mother. Nevermore a shieldmaiden.

As that truth finally settled with permanence in her heart, the tears that she'd denied earlier surged again. Astrid dropped the pot, laid her head on the bed, and wept.

~oOo~

Later in the day, when she felt stronger and more in control of her yawing emotions, Astrid walked, for the first time, into the great hall. Vastly different from the great halls of Geitland or Karlsa, or any other place of home, this was no long, cozy building filled with people and animals alike. This was vaster even than the hall in the Estland castle, and felt cold and stark to her, despite the great fires and festooned dark greens, and the long tables heaped with rich food and surrounded by fine people in beautiful garments.

On Leofric's arm, wearing a new gown of heavy, ruby-red silk, without a leather corset—but yet with her breeches and boots concealed underneath—she kept her spine straight and her head high while a legion of richly clad men and women stood and watched her walk across the front of the hall, up onto a higher part, like a block, where a smaller and much grander table was elaborately dressed. It faced the rest of the hall.

She could see that many of these people were whispering and trying not to show it. She knew she was a scandal, a source of prurient gossip—the wild creature the king's son had claimed and tamed. One foreign to all their ways, a savage, an animal, a beast, who'd been tortured in the dungeon and was now wearing silks and rubies and being led to the king's table on the arm of a prince.

Her grasp of the language was strong now and grew stronger every day. She knew enough words to understand what was said. So she smiled as Leofric led her to stand behind a chair, and she sought out those faces whose condemnation hadn't been so well concealed. She made sure to meet their gaze full on and hold it. None could withstand her.

Music played while they'd entered, a kind of music with no strong beat, played on instruments made of strings that sounded to her like cats crying.

Eadric stood there already, as did Leofric's friend Dunstan and his young wife, Winifred. Astrid liked Eadric well enough, and he seemed to accept her. He was patient talking with her and helped her learn some of the language.

She'd met Leofric's friend and his wife a few times but didn't know them well. Her impression of Dunstan was good—he was handsome and had a good humor. His wife was simply quiet. Like so many rich women here, she seemed good only at wearing clothes.

Astrid was not so good at wearing clothes. The bodice of the dress had no give at all, and her arms felt tied nearly to her sides. And her head itched with all the pins.

Elfleda had insisted on weaving dark leaves and rubies into her hair. She'd thought it silly, and had only conceded because her friend seemed so intent, but now she saw that all the women were dressed in such a way.

Also standing at the table was the bishop. Leofric had prepared her to see him, insisting that both his presence and hers was required on this day. So she would keep to the other end of the table and not sink her dagger into his eye at their *jul* feast, before so many of the king's people. But she would not tolerate him.

Astrid glared at him until he looked away.

The music changed, became more forceful, and Leofric's father entered the room, wearing an elaborate coat over his breeches and doublet and a high crown on his head. Leofric and Eadric wore crowns as well, but, though they were dressed elegantly, they wore no coat of golden threads and spotted white fur.

All around the hall, women and men bent their knees. Even Leofric and Eadric did. Leofric tugged lightly on her sleeve, and she attempted to do what she was supposed to do.

271

Elfleda had attempted to teach her this 'curtsey,' but it was more complicated than it seemed. Men were required only to go to one knee. That, she could have done—not willingly, but at least with some grace. But women were made to twist their legs and nearly sit on them.

It was beyond her, and she wobbled and would have fallen but for Leofric's steadying arm.

The king spoke, welcoming all to the meal, and the bishop, wearing a golden cowl almost as grand as the king's coat, spoke of their god. Then, at last, the king sat, and everyone else could.

These people had so very many ways to hold a few above the rest, and none above the dead-but-not-dead, son-and-his-own-father man hanging on the cross. All sought someone to abase themselves to.

She would never understand.

As the food was being served, Astrid's belly rolled at the smell of the meat, and she set her hand there as if she could calm it that way.

Leofric noticed at once and laid his hand over her other, which rested on the table. He said nothing, except with his eyes. She found a smile; she didn't want to think right now about what was inside her, not trapped in this rigid gown, with so many eyes on her.

"Are you well, child?"

The voice was the king's, and Leofric's head turned so quickly his hair flew. Astrid bent her head to see around him to his father. The king had never addressed her in so familiar a manner before.

"*Ja.*" She remembered the courtly manners she'd been taught, and added, "Your Majesty."

At that moment, a servant set some kind of dark meat on her plate and poured sauce over it, and Astrid was not well at all. She gripped the table and forced her rebellious organs back to their places.

When she could, she looked again at the king. "I well. Sire."

He smiled. He'd never smiled at her before. His eyes moved to Leofric. Astrid couldn't see what transpired between them, but the king's smile widened, and he returned his attention to her and gave her a courtly nod.

She understood what he had just learned.

Leofric turned to her, beaming, and, in full view of everyone in the great hall, lifted her hand and kissed it.

She'd given them all what they wanted, it seemed. Everyone was happy.

If only she could find a way to join them.

18

"As the babe grows, Your Grace," Elfleda reached out as if she meant to pat his arm, but remembered her station and thought better of it. "Soon, she won't be so ill, and soon after that will be the quickening. When she feels that life stirring inside her, then she'll change. You'll see."

Leofric sighed unhappily at the door he'd just closed. Behind it was a woman he loved with a power and depth that sometimes frightened him. Inside her was his child, who had been making her quite ill for weeks.

And she was desperately unhappy.

He knew exactly why. He would have known anyway, he understood his woman, but Astrid was not one to prevaricate her feelings. She'd been perfectly forthcoming: she wanted to be the woman she'd been in her world. She didn't know how to be anything in his world. She didn't know how to be a mother.

She wanted to be a warrior. And she had never wanted children.

The only women Leofric had known who seemed not to want children were bawd's house whores, and a fair number of those, in fact, had children. He'd believed it to be something built into feminine nature: with breasts and a womb came the desire to nurture life.

Even had it not been a natural impulse, bearing children simply wasn't a choice for women, certainly not at his station.

They made heirs. It was the purpose of noble and royal marriage—heirs and alliances.

But her world was different. In her world, it seemed women could make their way like men did and follow whatever paths they wanted. It had once seemed shockingly cruel that a world existed where men put their women at such risk, put swords in their hands and let them stand side by side with them and fight.

But now he knew Astrid, as strong-willed a warrior as he'd ever known.

He would have put her in armor and given her a sword if he could have. But women did not fight in his world. Which was now, and would evermore be, her world. Women were mothers and mates. She was his mate, and she would mother his children. There was simply no other choice.

The lethargic woman still lying abed behind that closed door, however—if she spent these long months with child dwindling, there'd be nothing left of her, as a mother or a warrior, or the woman he loved.

"I pray you're right, Elfleda."

"You'll see, Your Grace. You'll see."

~oOo~

The king set aside a scroll and nodded at a chair before his desk. As Leofric sat, his father said, "You swore that you would bring her to our ways, Leofric."

When he'd been formally summoned to the solar, he'd known exactly what his father had on his mind, but foreknowledge made the topic little easier. "And I will. I have. She carries my child. She's dined at the royal table, and

276

in the residence, and she's comported herself well. She knows our language and our ways. She has changed much in these months."

"And yet she remains unsaved. She will swell soon with your child, and yet there has been no marriage. Not even the banns can be called. There is scandal enough spinning around you, son. Legitimize her."

Astrid would not agree to be baptized, and they couldn't be married until she was. He couldn't marry a heathen. But she would not give up her gods, and the god Father Francis represented was absolutely repellant to her. She would never allow the bishop to touch her—another complication to the question of the marriage, if they could overcome the hurdle of the baptism.

Leofric hadn't managed to find an argument that might persuade her. In truth, he agreed with her on more points than he'd admit. Certainly that Francis was a terrible representative for the Lord.

When Leofric didn't answer in a timely manner, the king continued. "You promised me a moral victory over her people. A victory for the Lord our God. She must be baptized. There must be a wedding. Bring an heir with no question of succession into this line, Leofric. I gave you my approbation and allowed you a wide ground to act as you would with her. But the time for lust and licentiousness is over. Make her one of us."

"And if I cannot?"

"She would not be the first woman to weep at the altar and to kneel with stiff legs. But if you are not strong enough to force her, then you will forget her. We will find you a suitable mate, and we will put your mistress and your bastard away from us."

Leofric sagged back in his chair, his mouth gaping. For a few moments, as the full dimension of his father's words came clear, he could do little more than blink. "I believed that you had come to have affection for Astrid."

"I have. She is lovely, and I see how different she is from when I first saw her. I admire the strength of her will." He smiled. "I think Dreda would have been enchanted by her."

Leofric smiled as well, thinking of his sister. "She would have. She wanted to be a pirate."

The king gave a sad chuckle and then sighed. "I also know my own wrongness in how she was treated. I was ill-advised during a time of great grief, and I forgot my own way."

That was a near condemnation of Francis, and Leofric leapt upon it. "If God were not so closely aligned with the bishop in her mind, I could persuade her, Father. She despises Francis so. She remembers that he watched all that was done to her. She remembers that he smiled and"—he stopped, knowing that his father would not thank him for putting the baseness of the Black Walls into words.

But Astrid had spoken in detail about her loathing for the bishop, and his father needed to know. "He smiled and he panted, and he touched himself, Father. That is what she saw when she was being raped and tortured almost to death. What was done to her in the Black Walls excited Francis. In a way no man of God should be."

His words had a physical impact. The king's complexion deepened, and his cheeks twitched with his tensing jaws. Leofric waited while his father struggled to keep his composure.

"And I should believe a heathen's accusations against the bishop of this realm, a man who has many times sat at table with the Most Holy Father?"

Leofric didn't respond with words. He simply held his father's gaze and let his steadiness be answer enough. The king knew Francis well. There had been many signs. Leofric, who spent not nearly as much time in company with the bishop, had seen them. The Bishop of Mercuria was a man of many vices, many sins.

Finally, the king sighed. "And what is it that I can do?"

His father had already given them the answer, Leofric apprehended with a jolt. "Send him to Rome. On a pilgrimage. The weather is warming. He'll be gone months." The idea blossomed in his head. "Mayhap he won't return. Mayhap His Holiness will keep his friend Francis nearby and appoint a new bishop. Should you make such a request."

Astrid wanted to kill Francis, and held it as a plan she meant to accomplish, but such an act would end in her demise as well, whether she were married to him or not. Getting Francis out of Mercuria solved a host of difficulties, and his father knew it, too.

"Francis has been my closest advisor for many years," his father mused.

"Yes. And he's cultivated power over those years. Power beyond the castle. Power he's abused. Father, he was a good man once, but no more." Another great risk—underlying his words was a criticism: that the king had not recognized the failings of the one he trusted most. "Mayhap Rome will bring his goodness back to him."

The king considered for a long time. "Astrid will give up her resistance and join the Faith, if the bishop is gone from us?"

Leofric had no confidence in that at all. To do so still required her to give up her gods, and she cleaved to them as if they were a lifeline. And, of course, they were. Not only was her belief in them the last thing she still held of her past self, but they were her gods. For all Leofric's skepticism about men like Francis, and for all his own sins, he could not imagine giving up his faith in the Lord.

"Yes, she will," he assured his father.

~oOo~

Astrid was sleeping when he returned to her. Lately, she'd been sleeping through great portions of each day. Worried and frustrated, he kissed her forehead and left her to her rest.

For his part, rest was impossible, or ease of any kind. He couldn't decide whether he'd solved his dilemma with his father or only made it worse. So he went in search of Dunstan. He wanted to ride, and to talk with his friend.

A winter more than typically full of grey mists and heavy rains had shrunk back, leaving a soggy but brighter world behind. The trees had sprouted tender new leaves, and a watery sun dappled through them. It was a good day for a long ride.

Neither of them was in a particularly loquacious tendency on this day, so they rode with little chatter, focusing instead on driving their steeds apace—not racing, but not ambling, either. As always, the tension began to bleed out of Leofric as he pushed his charger down the road, leaning in, feeling the bond between horse and rider, their bodies finding the same rhythm.

They rode out well beyond the castle, into the countryside, and, when their horses were lathered, they stopped at a humble roadside inn. They'd dressed for a long ride, and didn't appear as anything more than nobles of no especial note. So they made themselves comfortable at a corner table, where no one could come up on their backs, and ordered ale and a meal of hearty stew and rye bread.

The companionable quiet between them lingered while they drank their first mugs, their exchanges limited to insignificant comments about the ride, the weather, the inn. But as their meal arrived with their second mugs of ale, Dunstan took a long draught and then groaned loudly after he swallowed.

"'Swounds, I needed this day."

"Aye, and I." Leofric lifted his mug, and Dunstan knocked it with his own.

"You and I, Your Grace, we seem to have gotten ourselves confused. You cannot make the woman who bears your child marry you, and I cannot make the woman I married bear my child. Somewhere between us is a good husband."

Leofric chuckled. Dunstan had been wed for months now, but had been denied the marriage bed since the wedding night. Not denied, exactly. More driven from it by his wife's terrified tears.

He chewed a hunk of bread soaked in stew. "No luck yet, eh?"

His friend rolled his eyes. "She is immune to my considerable charms, and I cannot find my way to force a sobbing child. She will not take drink, so I cannot make her agreeable in that way. I've even prostrated myself, offered to let her explore me as she would and have her way, and she is appalled at the thought of it. All she does is weep and pray and order clothes and jewels. At least I'll have no heir to concern myself with when she drives me to the almshouse."

"You've married the one female in the kingdom who doesn't want you," Leofric laughed, shaking his head. "Did her mother not come and speak with her?"

"Agh." Dunstan dropped his head to the table with a theatrical thump and then looked up. "Aye, she did, and all that accomplished was weeping for homesickness. And more praying. You are lucky, my friend. You may not have the marriage, but you have the important results—a willing woman in your bed, and your child in her belly."

Leofric's sex twitched and tingled at the thought of Astrid in his bed. In the months since he'd taken her from the Black Walls, her body had regained much of its sleekness, if not the astonishing contours of muscle she'd first had. Now, and especially since the child had begun to work on her form, she had a womanly shape and softness that his hands and mouth savored.

He resettled himself on the bench and took a healthy portion of his ale. "You know I need the marriage."

"Aye, I know. No progress in that regard?"

"She'll marry me. But she won't be baptized." Dunstan knew as much; this wasn't the first time Leofric had needed his friend's ear to work out the problem of Astrid.

"And not one without the other."

"No. But—" he looked around to be sure that there were no other ears close by. The innkeeper's wife met his eyes and offered a look to ask if they needed anything. He shook his head, and she nodded and went on about her work. "I spoke with the king today."

Dunstan's eyebrows went up, and he set his mug on the scarred table. "And?"

Again, Leofric looked around, trying not to appear to be someone who had a secret he didn't want heard. "I believe he will send the bishop to Rome. Mayhap to stay."

Dunstan's jaw dropped. "True?"

"Aye, I believe so."

"And how did you accomplish such a miracle?"

He hunkered down, close to the table, and Dunstan joined him. The savory aroma of the half-eaten stew wafted between them. "The king gave me the idea himself, as he was demanding I bring her in hand. Astrid will not allow the bishop near her, and my father knows well why. I told him details she's shared with me about her time in the Black Walls—and no, I'll not share them with you. But Francis is a repugnant pretender to piety, and I think today the king fully realized it."

"Well, we both know the bishop does not live as he would have his flock do, or as he would appear to his flock."

"No, he does not."

"And you think if Francis leaves, Astrid will give up her gods?"

The surge of blood he'd felt speaking of, and imagining, Francis' downfall slowed at Dunstan's question. "I don't know," he answered truthfully. "She doesn't find much use in ours."

"Need she?"

Leofric cocked his head. "What do you mean?"

Their mugs were empty, and Dunstan waved the innkeeper's wife over. She, in turn, waved someone else over, someone standing behind part of a wall.

The innkeeper's daughter, it seemed. A buxom, curvaceous young woman with a mountain of flaming curls came to the table, carrying the pitcher of ale. She gave Dunstan a feline smile and bent low to fill his mug, showing ample cleavage spilling from a dress immodestly too small for her.

Leofric got a similar show as she filled his mug, but her effect on him was scant. Dunstan, however, appeared to be in actual pain.

When the girl walked away, she rolled her hips dramatically with each step, and Dunstan groaned.

"We should have captured the other savage woman as well. One for each of us."

Leofric found no humor in his friend's jest. "You had a point to make."

Dunstan blinked stupidly for a moment. "Ah. May I blaspheme, Your Grace?"

Curious, not particularly concerned about blasphemy, and understanding that the question had been made at least partially with irony, Leofric nodded.

"Need she give up her gods in truth? So much of what we do at court is pretense. Appearance. You and I know that as well as most—not so very long ago, if we'd confessed all we'd done during the week, we'd never have had a chance to sin. We'd have been on our knees all day, every day. Even your father understands, or he would not have turned a blind eye to your arrangement with Astrid now. If it's not Francis, but another priest who puts her under the water, will she allow herself to simply bathe?"

"To swear an oath and not mean it?"

"Are you truly repentant for every chambermaid and kitchen wench you've speared? Every bawd's house you've visited? Every game of chance you've played? I am not repentant for any. And yet we say the words. We do our penance. And we go out and do it all over again." He chuckled. "Well, we did. The words aren't our faith. They're the appearance of faith. They're a show."

"You are a cynic, my friend."

"And you are not? Is not Astrid a cynic regarding our faith? If she makes the show, she can believe what she will. Would you disapprove?"

He loved Astrid as she was. He would give her a sword and a shield if he could—no, he'd give her an axe. That had been her weapon. Her gods interested him. They were so very many, and so very different from his singular Lord. "No, I would not."

"Then there's your solution. Don't attempt to persuade her to give up her faith and adopt one she hates. Persuade her to have a bathe and say some words in a tongue that's foreign to her anyway."

Would Astrid make a vow that was a lie? Perhaps, when it was so clearly the best of her options. He nodded, mulling over the question.

Dunstan laughed. "There's your problem sorted. I'm going to have a go at the wench." He grabbed his breeches between his thighs. "It's going to rot off if it doesn't get some use soon."

With a chuckle, Leofric waved his friend off to find his pleasure. He sat at the table and called over another mug of ale.

Would she do it? Was it so simple as a lie?

~oOo~

When he went to her room at dusk that evening, she was awake, sitting at the table near the windows and poking indifferently at a meat pie. As he closed the door, she set her spoon down and watched him cross the room to her.

He kissed her cheek, and she gave him a wan smile he disliked. She was terrible at hiding her emotions and making a good show—which could be a complication to Dunstan's idea. That idea had become a plan in Leofric's mind. Their best option, one that solved most of the problems between them.

Her supper had only been picked at, and he could tell by looking that it had gone cold. He pulled a chair close to hers and sat. "You must eat, my love. You'll not be well by starving yourself."

She wrinkled her nose. "The smell is bad." Pointing to a small, empty plate, she added, "I eat bread with…fruit soup?"

"Jam?"

"*Ja*. Cham. I eat that."

Not nearly enough. She was surviving on bread and milk of late, and Elfleda insisted that she needed meat as well. But he had one fight between them already in mind, so he would not start a second over food.

"Astrid, we must speak."

Her eyes narrowed until they were barely slits, glittering blue lines between her long, fair lashes. "No bishop talk. No more."

"If I have a solution?"

"What is 'solution'?"

He thought about how he could explain that word. "A way…a way out of the problem."

She frowned. He tried again. "A way to make the problem go away."

"Ah. *Ja?*"

"Ja—Yes. Perhaps. Will you listen?"

She nodded.

He took her hands in his. Her hands were not lovely; they showed the way she'd lived her life. Noblewomen had soft, pale, languid hands; it was a mark of wealth and status for a woman's hands to show no wear at all. Holding a noblewoman's hand was like holding a dead fish. Astrid's hands had wielded an axe and held a shield, and every battle seemed to show on them. They were scarred and coarse and darker at the knuckles. Her nails were ridged and flat. Holding her hands was like holding life itself.

People at court often remarked that Astrid would have been a spectacularly beautiful woman if not for all her scars. Leofric thought she was a spectacularly beautiful woman because of them.

"Much of what happens at court is done to be seen. Do you understand what I mean?"

She considered him. "You mean people are two faces. They make pretty one for king, but ugly one real."

He was impressed. Her grasp not only of their language but of their figurative ideas was solid, even if her speech wasn't quite fluent. "Yes. At court, for the most part, the pretty one is the one that matters."

Her response to that was a derisive snort.

"Wait. Perhaps that will work for us. Do you love me, Astrid?"

Now she was suspicious. "Why?"

"Do you?"

"*Ja*. I love you."

She rarely said it, and when she did, the words seemed to feel more foreign to her than any other, but he believed they were true. She wouldn't say them otherwise.

Which was also a complication to his plan. Lying had a bitter taste to her.

"And I you. Would you be my wife?"

Her frown turned into a scowl. "*No bishop.*"

"If not for that, would you be my wife?"

He'd surprised the frown off her face. She stared at him, her eyes peering deeply into his. "No"—she made a gesture he didn't grasp—"No water?"

Ah. Baptism. It was time for the difficult part of this discussion. But first he wanted an answer to his question. "If there were nothing else between us, would you wed with me?"

"*Ja.*"

Heartened by the scantiness of her hesitation, he pushed on. "Would you agree to be baptized if you didn't have to change what you believe?"

"No understand."

As strong as her comprehension had become, sometimes finding ways to say important things in words she could understand seemed almost beyond his skill. "Would you say the words for show and keep your gods in truth?"

"Swear a lie?"

"Yes."

"If lies so easy, how you know any word true?"

An excellent question, but he had an answer. "Trust. You know the truth of those you trust, and you keep your trust close."

She stood up and walked away, to the far window, and stared out at the deepening dark. Leofric stayed where he was and waited for her to say or do something.

"You take from me all. Home. Freedom. Strongness. Now you take truth."

Her words might as well have been shards of glass, for how deeply they cut. "Not I, Astrid."

"Father. Same as son."

Now he stood and went to her, but when she folded her arms across her chest, he didn't touch her. "I'm trying to let you keep what I can. The past cannot be undone, unjust as it was. This is your home now. You're free. You're alive, and you're with me. And, Astrid, there are other ways to be strong. Not only fighting. The women here are strong, too, even if they don't wield weapons. My mother was one of the strongest people I've ever known, and she was gentle. You wallow in your hate. That seems like a weakness to me. It takes will and might to let go of vengeance. Forgiveness is a strength."

He unwound her arms and pulled her close. She didn't resist him, though her expression was hardly welcoming. "Say the words, my love. You can keep your gods. I like them. There will be trust and truth between you and me always, and that is all that matters. My father will send Francis away, never to return, if you will say the words and make a show for the people."

"He goes?"

"He goes."

"If I lie."

"What better choice do you have?"

She thought about that for a long time, staring at his chest. He held her and waited. At last, her breast swelled with a deep breath, and then deflated as she let the air out.

"No choice," she muttered. "Ever."

PART SIX
PERSEVERANCE

19

Astrid had taken part in only two weddings before her own: those of Brenna God's-Eye and Vali Storm-Wolf, in Estland, and of Leif and Olga in Geitland. Both had been rituals of her own people, and she had understood the purpose of each part.

Beyond the ritual of the baptism, which had been accomplished in a stream near the castle, with Astrid, dressed in a gown like a heavy sleeping shift, submerged by a priest she didn't know, the rituals of the wedding seemed nearly nonexistent, at least on the parts of the people being married. Leofric had told her that the ceremony would be mainly in yet another language, and that they would kneel and listen for most of it.

Kneel before a priest. And swear empty vows to their god. Again.

If she could make her vows to Leofric alone, she could speak true. She loved him. He was all in this world that made sense to her. In his presence, the ground settled under her feet. In his arms, she knew herself.

Because all she was now was what he made of her.

Away from him on the day of their wedding, in the room that would no longer be hers after this day, while Elfleda wound her hair into artful braids, Astrid stared into the glass and tried to know this woman she'd become. A mother. A duchess. A woman of silks and jewels and leisure. Who bore the scars in body, mind, and spirit of another woman altogether.

Standing behind her, Elfleda patted her shoulder and leaned down to smile sweetly into the glass. "There now. You're lovely. Up with you, dearie, and let's get that gown on. Pray you haven't grown again since the last fitting."

Astrid stood and swept her hands over her breasts and belly, her palms skimming the soft linen of her underdress. Though she had no swelling belly yet, her body had changed with the babe growing inside her—and had done so almost daily in the two weeks that she'd been free of illness. The changes so far were in her breasts and hips, which were larger and rounder. They'd occurred mainly while her gown had been designed and fitted, and had harried the seamstresses to no end.

There were other changes, too, though not to her size. To touch—her skin felt different. More sensitive everywhere, and especially in her places of pleasure. Those changes, only Leofric knew about.

In one place, no change had yet occurred: her heart. Or perhaps it was her mind. She felt nothing for what was happening inside her. The debilitating malaise she'd experienced while the babe had made her ill had given way to an indifferent numbness. When she was away from Leofric, the strongest feeling she ever had for her own child, and that only rarely, was curiosity. Was this how her mother had felt, carrying her?

If so, Astrid knew she would have little to offer this child.

When Leofric was with her, she felt something good and real stir inside her for the babe. In her love for him, in his love for her, and in his devotion to, and wonder for, the life inside her, she could feel something like hope. Seeing him happy with the babe inside her eased her heart and made her want to feel the same.

Perhaps her love for the father would create love in her for their child.

Astrid sighed, and Elfleda clucked behind her. "Be still, dearie." She drew the lacings of the gown tight.

The gown fit as it should. It wasn't comfortable or easy to move in, but it was beautiful, and women here had only two roles: beauty and breeding. Astrid was no match for the women around her in beauty, but she could wear a pretty gown.

This one was, even to her skeptical eye, more than pretty. Made of silk in the palest blue she'd ever seen, and the creamiest white, it fit her body snugly across the chest and then fell gracefully away, skimming her sides and flaring out to pool at her feet and trail some distance behind her. The neckline was wide, just catching her shoulders, and the two-part sleeves fit her arms all the way to her hands and also flared wide to drape like wings at her sides. The neckline, bodice, and sleeves were accented by wide, intricate stitching in silver thread, and a braided belt made of silver thread looped around her waist and rested on her hips, trailing down the full length of the front.

The width and dip of the neckline showed several of her scars, back and front, most of which were remnants of wounds that had come in the black place. The seamstresses had been dismayed and ashamed at the first trial of the design, when they'd realized that fact. They'd bowed and fussed and promised a new design that would hide the scars.

But Astrid didn't want them hidden. She'd have wed in nothing but her skin, if she'd thought the wedding would occur while she was in that state. None of her scars were her shame. They were either her honor, earned in battle, or they were the king's shame, afflicted on her in the black place. She bore them all as one who'd survived.

She would wear these flowing silks as a mark of her survival as well.

There was no room for breeches and boots under such a gown. Astrid lifted her feet and let one of her army of maids help her into a pair of flimsy shoes in creamy leather.

When she was dressed, Elfleda stepped back and gave her a critical eye. She clapped. "Ah me, you're lovely, dearie. A proper duchess. Next we meet, I'll be droppin' a curtsey to you."

The thought appalled Astrid. "No, Elfleda."

"Aye. You'll be the Her Royal Highness, the Duchess of Orenshire, and you'll be due all the courtesies of the royal family."

A sharp rap on the door curtailed Astrid's protest. Elfleda went to open it. When she did, she dropped to the floor in a curtsey deeper than Astrid would have thought the old woman capable of. She bowed her head. "Your Majesty."

The door opened wide, and the king himself stood there, dressed in sparkling regalia. The three girls who'd been helping Astrid and Elfleda with the preparations dropped to the floor.

For her part, Astrid curtsied, too, though not so deeply. She had yet to perfect the movement. She tipped her head downward.

"Yes, very well. As you were." Everyone stood and went back to work, keeping their eyes from the king. He came straight to Astrid with a smile on his face. "I come to escort you to the chapel, if you'll take my arm."

The susurration of gasps around the room told Astrid that the king's offer was highly unusual and a great honor.

Leofric had spoken to her of the strength in forgiveness, and he'd made her see that perhaps she could be strong in a different way. If so, she hadn't gained the strength she needed to forgive the king. He'd ordered her to suffer the most horrific torments daily, for weeks, and for no purpose other than the torment itself. He hadn't wanted information. He hadn't taken all the raiders or any others. He hadn't wanted her death. He'd wanted only her pain. Her pain specifically. Only hers. For no reason. She had no way to understand that, thus she had no way to forgive it.

He was Leofric's father and the ruler of this realm. He would hold her life in his hands as long as they both had life, and she had no recourse against him. So she had found a way to be in his company and be calm. And he'd treated her kindly since Leofric had claimed her, especially since she carried the child. Though she meant to withhold forgiveness always, a tiny fissure had emerged in her intentions to hold hate for him in her heart all her days.

"I will."

His smile at her answer was warm, and she felt moved despite herself. "First, I have for you a gift." He snapped his fingers, and a boy in regalia came in carrying a leather-covered box on a velvet cushion. At the king's nod, the boy opened the lid.

Sitting in a swirling bed of dark silk was a silver circle of stones that dazzled like stars made of lightning. At the center of the circle was a blue stone, a larger mate to the one in the ring Leofric had given her during the betrothal ritual.

A crown. The king was giving her a crown.

"This is the Diadem of Æbbe. My grandmother. Your ring comes from her as well." He lifted the small crown from its silk bed. "You join our family now, Astrid of the North. You carry our heir. It would honor me if you would wear these family jewels when you meet your betrothed before God, and if you would claim them as your own."

She nodded, and he set the crown on her head. When he offered his arm, she took it, and the King of Mercuria led her through the castle to the chapel, where she would wed his son before his god.

~oOo~

A long swath of golden cloth split the chapel in two. All of the benches—there was a word for them, but Astrid couldn't remember it—were packed full of people in rich clothes, all of them standing and staring at her. At the very back, separated from the others, were the castle servants she knew: Elfleda and Audie and the others. Elfleda smiled and gave her an encouraging nod.

At the end of the aisle, the king lifted her hand to his lips. Then he let her go and walked alone down the golden aisle toward the altar. As he passed, a wave went through the crowd: people bowing and curtseying to their king. Then they all stood straight again and stared at her.

She stood alone and felt small and weak. At the head of that long aisle stood Leofric—she could see him, standing tall, his hands at his sides, dressed in dark leather breeches and a dark doublet, over his shoulders a cloak of golden and blue brocade trimmed with fur. He wore his crown, much higher and more elaborate than the one on her own head, and smaller and simpler than his father's or brother's.

He was smiling at her.

But she couldn't move. Between them were all these people she didn't understand, people who thought her a curiosity at best and an animal at worst, who whispered and japed and hoped for her to do something worthy of mockery. She hated that she had to pass through such a gauntlet to reach the one person in all this world she trusted.

As she stood there alone and unmoving, she heard the rustle of whispers moving through the crowd. She was already giving them something to laugh about behind their hands.

This was shame she was feeling, was it not? She rejected shame. These people could not make her feel shame; she would not allow it.

Just as she steeled her spine to take her first step—how absurd that she needed courage to do no more than walk in a straight line—Leofric's friend Dunstan turned from his place at the front of the chapel and strolled down the aisle straight for her. His smile was bright and sly—amused, but not at her expense.

When he arrived before her, he held out his elbow. "Might I escort milady to the altar?"

It felt like a rescue, silly as that was, and she was glad for it. "*Ja.* Thank you." She took his arm and walked, with her back straight and her shoulders square, down the golden aisle.

At the altar, Leofric held out his hand, and Dunstan set hers in it. Then he stepped back, and there was only Astrid and the man she loved. She barely even noticed the new bishop.

"You are beautiful," he murmured as he led her to kneel on a rail padded with silk. "You'll be happy, my love. I swear it."

With her hand in his, Astrid could nearly believe it.

~oOo~

That night, stripped to his breeches, Leofric unfastened the lacings at the back of Astrid's gown. He'd barred the door from the intrusions of revelers. That was something their people shared in common: the revelry after a couple were wed, and then jesting attempts to crowd in on their night together.

An attendant had taken their crowns and Leofric's cloak, and he'd wasted no time thereafter in shedding most of the rest of his clothes and coming for hers.

She was in Leofric's own chamber, a place she'd never before seen. It was a grand suite of vast rooms, each one far bigger than even her improved quarters had been. The bed was a mammoth thing draped in heavy black and red fabric. It was so high from the floor that there were steps leading up to it. The fireplace across from the bed was nearly tall enough for Astrid to stand in.

A table was laden so heavily with sumptuous foods and wines that it seemed they could stay in this room for weeks and never need be bothered.

She had her own suite of rooms as well now, adjoining his. The two of them had private space between them that might have housed half the people of Geitland.

As he loosened the gown and pushed it from her shoulders, she dropped her hands, one at a time, still busy finding all the vexing pins that had been holding her braids and their adornments in place. When she finally was able to let her hair fall down her back, he pushed the gown over her hips. It pooled at the floor, and he helped her step out of it.

"You were glorious today," he purred, sweeping her hair to the side. He tucked his head against her neck and brushed his beard over her skin. "Thank you."

She sighed and turned in his arms, sliding her hands into his hair, letting the cool silk of his loose curls coil over her fingers. "I yours now."

"And I am yours." He leaned back, and her hands fell to his bare chest. "You've made me happy, Astrid. I will help you find your happiness as well. I swear it."

"Between us, trust and truth, *ja?*"

"Always."

The day had not been so awful as she'd expected. Unlike the baptism, the words she'd had to swear at the altar had mostly been about Leofric, and those words had been true. She'd closed her mind to the words about his god. That had been much easier than when she'd been swearing to love a god that was not one of her own and never would be.

The rest of the ritual had been spoken in a language far beyond her knowing, and had required nothing more of her than her presence, so she'd turned her mind from it and studied the man at her side. A fine-looking man. A good man. Beloved. The only one she'd ever felt such a thing for. She would have chosen him if she had been free to make any choice.

Then there had been feasting and reveling, and she'd felt moments of true enjoyment. At the heart of her enjoyment was a single, simple truth: she loved this man, and now they were truly mated. There was more than safety in that. There was certainty. A space of solid ground in this world she stumbled through.

"I have happy with you," she said and bent her head forward to kiss his chest, at the spot over his heart.

His hands came up to frame her face, and he lifted her head. Searching her eyes, he asked, "Do you, my love?"

"*Ja.* With you."

"I'm glad. And you'll have more." He leaned down and kissed her, pulling her tightly to his body, enclosing her in his arms, and Astrid felt her body and mind let go of everything but him. It was always the way—in his arms, she belonged. She was home, and at ease.

If she could stay like this, closed off from all the rest of this world, only with him, she might imagine that she was the woman she was supposed to be.

His mouth left hers and drew along her jaw, leaving light nips to tingle her skin. She sighed and arched more closely, pressing the point of her desire to the point of his, little more than his breeches yet between them.

He groaned and dropped his hands to her hips. At her ear, he murmured, "I want to take you to the cabin in the morning. A few days for ourselves, to hunt and rut and feed each other, and not be bothered. A celebration of our own kind."

Their single night at the cabin was the happiest she'd been in this world. If she could live there always, she would. She took hold of his head and pulled him back so she could see his face. "You mean this?"

"Aye, I do. We can take a carriage."

"No, I ride!" Oh, the thought of that ride, of the wind in her face, her feet in the stirrups, racing Leofric as they rode through trees dappled with sunlight. She would not be cooped up in one of the closed-up boxes they called carriages.

"But the babe. Astrid, you must think of him."

"I'm well again. I ride." There was little more than usual of her belly yet. Nothing to get in her way.

He condescended with a smile. "Women shouldn't ride when they're with child, love."

That was absurd. "I not big yet. I ride."

"But—"

She stomped her foot. "Your women fall down at littlest thump and go to bed and cry. My people strong. Women ride until belly too big. We have big, strong babes. I ride!"

"You'll give Elfleda worry. My father, too."

Rather than repeat her demand yet again, she arched an eyebrow at him. She would claim this victory at least.

He laughed. "Very well. You ride—at my side. Only then." His grin growing, he grabbed her and brought her to his body again, pressing his hard sex to her. "Unless you wish to ride me. Then you'll be atop."

Feeling freer and happier than she'd been since the time they'd last spent at the cabin, Astrid laughed.

"Mercy, what a delight that sound is," Leofric said. "And rare indeed. When you laugh, I see our future." His expression turned hot and serious as he pulled loose the tie on her underdress. "Tonight, I would have you lie back. Let me attend to you, my wife. Lie under me and let me give you all the pleasure I know how to give. Let me lead you there."

Astrid rarely coupled passively. She liked a grapple, and she liked to win it. But when Leofric's hand slid along her side and he swept her up to cradle her in his arms, she was reminded of the feeling of being carried just this way, up from the dark, into the light, away from the black place where she'd been fighting against death and into a world she could learn to live in.

She looped her arms around his neck and kissed his cheek, nuzzling her nose in his dark beard. It was a more impulsively affectionate gesture than she might ever have made, but it didn't feel strange to make it. Leofric tipped his head into her touch and tightened his hold around her, and she could feel that she'd pleased him.

"I love you."

She'd pleased him even more; his smile shone over her. "You will always have my love, Astrid of the North."

Astrid of the North. She'd heard herself called that repeatedly in recent weeks, but it was the first time she'd heard it in Leofric's voice. Suddenly, cradled in his arms, as he stood in the middle of his magnificent bedchamber, Astrid realized that she had gained a name beyond that which her parents had given her. She'd cast off her father's name and sought one made of her own life, and she had it. She was Astrid of the North, a name that would have been meaningless in the world she'd had.

She was also a duchess now, but that was Leofric's title applied to her. Astrid of the North was her own. She had come to this world as a shieldmaiden. And a new thing dawned upon her: every time she'd been called by these people a savage or a beast, an animal or a barbarian, they'd been calling her a shieldmaiden—a word they did not possess. A woman they feared. She was beyond their understanding, beyond their language, beyond their capacity to define.

Whether she ever lifted an axe or a shield again, she would always be the sum of her own life. She would always be a shieldmaiden because she had lived as one.

She understood herself in ways they never would, and now she understood them as well, more every day. That she could now walk among them—that she had power over them, that they *bowed* to her—that was a victory.

She had won.

As Leofric climbed with her into his royal bed and laid her upon the thick heaps of soft silk covers, she smiled and spread her body wide. She would let her husband worship her, and she would trust him to give her all the pleasure there was to be had.

He must have seen her surrender, because he said her name like a prayer.

On his knees, he loomed above her, then pushed back and stood on the steps, his eyes locked on hers as he opened his breeches and shoved them away.

Need surged through her at the sight of his body. From the moment her eyes had grown used to light again, they'd wanted to look upon him. The mere sight of him had steadied her even when her own mind had seemed alien and strange.

And his touch—his touch brought her home.

Though he was tall among his people, among her own he might have been only average height for a man—a few inches taller than she, but not so tall that they couldn't meet face to face. And he lacked the stone-hewn breadth of shoulder that Leif or Vali or Ulv possessed. Yet he was beautiful. His face was handsome, his dusky blue eyes, straight nose, and strong brow framed by dark waves and a closely trimmed dark beard. His lips were full and his smile kind and sincere. He was lean and well-shaped, strong shoulders tapering to narrow hips, sleek muscle making curving contours under his skin. Light curls of dark hair covered his chest and belly, his legs, and his forearms.

And at the center of it all was his sex, standing proudly erect for her. None before him had given her the pleasure that he had.

Seeing where her eyes had traveled, Leofric chuckled and circled a hand around himself, stroking languidly. Astrid smiled back and touched herself, sliding her fingers through her folds, already wet for him. Even her own touch zinged more than usual, and she moaned and licked her lips.

Leofric growled like a beast and dropped onto the bed, crawling over her and pushing her hand away to make room for his own. At the touch of his bigger, rougher fingers, Astrid gasped and lifted her hips. She was glad of the babe for this if for no other reason—the way being full of his child had made her want him even more, had made his touch even more intense.

"Your pleasure is mine tonight." He slid a finger into her, and Astrid closed her eyes and, for this night, gave him dominion over her body.

As his finger probed, finding all the places inside her that could make her moan with need, he showered her with kisses, over her throat, her shoulders, her chest, her breasts, her sides, her belly, each kiss like a prayer, a moment of devotion, his tongue laving and savoring each piece of her. When he lavished her breasts, while his finger—now fingers—pumped into her, she couldn't be still. Hot charges of unmanageable sensation pulsed through her and drove her to writhe. She closed his head up in her arms and held him to her, her fingers dragging at his hair.

Again and again, he brought her to the precipice of completion, and again and again, he pulled her back, slowing his fingers and gentling his mouth until she could be still beneath him. When Astrid was moaning, virtually keening with frantic need, when she couldn't breathe enough to fill her lungs, when she could think of nothing but her desperate desire, his fingers left her completely, and she cried out a protest.

Flailing, she tried to grab his hand and put it back, but he only chuckled. "Close your eyes, love," he said. "Be still and let me move you."

When she did as he'd bid her, she felt his beard between her legs and then his tongue at her core. Clutching his head to keep him close, she completed almost at once, shocked at the force of it, and shocked more at the sound that erupted from her mouth. She screamed. And screamed. And screamed until the waves and waves of ecstatic release finally ebbed. He fed on her until she'd lost all control of her body, and even the will to control it, and her hands dropped from his head.

Gasping in great gulps of air, she wedged her eyes open and looked down her body to see him smiling at her, still nestled between her thighs. He laughed lightly, his eyes glittering with happiness.

"I've waited long for that, my love."

"For what?"

"To hear you scream in ecstasy. To know I reached so deep into your soul that I touched its fire."

She smiled and brushed a finger over his damp beard, his hot lips. "You make pretty words."

He scooted up and kissed her belly, lingering over the wide scar that slashed across it. "You give me a pretty life." His breath caressed her skin as he spoke. "I will worship you and our child—our children—every day I draw breath."

Her belly twitched beneath his mouth's adoration. She tugged on his hair and brought his attention back to her eyes. "*Knulla mig.*"

Understanding exactly what she wanted, he grinned and pushed himself over her, feeding himself into her as she brought her legs up and encircled his hips. He filled her full with a bestial groan and latched his mouth to hers. Tasting herself on his lips and tongue, she dug her hands into his back and felt his muscles flex as he took her with wild ferocity.

When he released, he threw his head back and roared up at the top of the royal bed, and seeing his tense, dark ecstasy brought Astrid to another release of her own.

She went to sleep that night snug in his arms, his fingers laced with hers. As she felt his body ease into rest behind her, she smiled.

She understood now. She'd been trying to define herself by what she'd known, but she was something new.

She was Astrid of the North, a woman stronger than this world could fathom. She had survived the worst suffering they could conjure, and she had risen to claim royalty. She was a shieldmaiden. And she was a duchess. She was a warrior. And she was a wife. She was a lover. And she was a mother.

She made her way in every world, in every life, in every self.

20

Leofric reached into the carriage, and Astrid took his hand. When she leaned through the door, he caught her around the waist and lifted her out, setting her gently on the ground at his side.

She glared up at him. "I climb from a carriage. Not too big."

Smiling at her vexed expression, Leofric set his hand on his wife's swelling belly. She wasn't big yet, it was true, but as the weather had warmed to true summer, she had finally begun to appear to be with child. He could scarcely keep his hands from her.

Better yet, she had begun to feel movement inside her: the quickening that Elfleda had foretold. The old woman had been right, it seemed. Often, he saw Astrid's hand on her swell, as if she'd felt the life inside her. And often, she smiled. A tiny smile, only for herself and the child.

In the few weeks since they'd been wed, even before her belly had suddenly popped forward, Astrid had seemed different, in all the ways that Leofric had hoped. She was calmer and more open. Rather than merely answer questions his father or brother put to her, she initiated conversations. Though she'd resisted everything he'd offered her, now that she had it, she seemed to be finally finding her place here. She was making this world her home.

Even the child. He'd waited until a child had been her own choice, but her carrying had vexed her from the start, and he'd begun to worry that she would never be happy to bear his child, or love it. She still didn't wish to talk about her carrying or to plan for the child, but those little moments he'd spied, those small, secret smiles, they gave him hope.

They spoke little about her life in her world; the memories pained her, and he was loath to remind her of what she'd lost. But she'd told him some about her kin, and knew they'd not been warm with her. He thought she worried whether she would know how to be warm with her own child.

He no longer worried. True, Astrid wasn't warm in aspect. She rarely made shows of love or affection, and she was far more likely to scowl than to smile. But her emotions burned wild and deep inside her. She loved, and when she did, she loved fiercely. She would be a warrior mother, and her love would be a shield over their child.

Taking her hand, he led her away from the carriage. Her head swiveled to and fro, taking in the sights of this place he'd brought her to for the first time: Eldham, a town on the southern coast of the kingdom. Two trading ships were moored in Eldham Harbor at the same time, and a usually lively market town had taken on the manner of a carnival. Not only the traders offered their wares, but the people of the town and its environs as well. Entertainers and musicians appeared from far and wide, drawn by news of a great gathering of people with money in their purses.

Astrid had been restless since her belly had grown and she could no longer ride. She'd fought and fussed, insisting that she *could* ride, but he'd allowed her to push the point too far already. The whole castle had been up in arms at the sight of the new duchess, carrying the only of the next generation of the royal family, sitting a saddle as if she were a man and trotting off into the woods. That Leofric was at her side only increased the scandal, because he was being derelict in his duty to wife, child, family, and realm.

He'd fought that fight to win it, and he had. Since then, she'd been in poor humor again, but a mood different from the apathetic indolence she'd fallen into during the early days of her carrying, or the guarded quiet of the time just after her captivity. This was a fit of pique, and he was its target. Leofric vastly preferred her temper to her torpor. If pressed, he might even admit he enjoyed sparring with her.

Still, he preferred her good spirits most of all, so when word came of the traders, he suggested a trip to the south, where she'd not yet been. Market days could be dangerous—cutpurses and blackguards reveled in the crush of people—and it was highly irregular to escort a lady to market while she was with child, but Leofric had married a highly irregular woman. A woman who knew well the use of the blade she carried at her side. He would stay at her side at all times, and they would have an adventure.

So as not to draw particular attention, they'd taken the simplest carriage and were dressed plainly, he in normal leathers, and she in a light wool gown in the blue he loved best on her. It made her eyes seem like the sky shone through them. Their child had grown too much for her to wear her breeches with the split-skirt gowns she preferred, but she'd become used to wearing gowns and complained little about dressing now.

He smiled at her interest in the town and its chaotic offerings. They stopped at every cart, every table, every basket, every window, and the footman who followed after them was soon laden with all manner of new acquisitions, none of which they had need of. All before they were in sight of the harbor.

They stopped and watched a puppet show, and Astrid's lovely face took on a glow of childlike wonder. He'd never seen such a look on her before, and his heart pulsed hard with love.

He leaned in and pressed his lips to her cheek, just at her ear. "Do you like this?"

"I never see before. How they make them move?"

"There are strings—you see?" He pointed, and she squinted.

"Ah. But how?"

"At the top of the strings, behind the curtain, men move the dolls. They act out stories. Those are puppets."

"Puppets." The people around them laughed and applauded, and Astrid moved her attention to the audience. "For make fun."

He laughed. In her inexpert phrasing, she'd struck on the real truth of it. "Yes. They make fun." Lifting her hand to his mouth, he kissed her knuckles. "Shall we go on?"

She nodded, but when he led her away, her head stayed turned to the puppet show until she couldn't see it anymore.

As they finally arrived near the docks, where the real wares were on offer, the exotic treasures from far-off places, Astrid stopped and frowned at the ships. Noticing that they had his wife's full attention, Leofric studied them, too. He wasn't a seafaring man, and he knew little of seacraft. All he saw were the masts and furled sails of trading ships like any other. From what he could see of their hulls, he knew they were different from each other, but not in a way he'd be able to describe when he was no longer looking directly at them.

"What is it, Astrid?"

"I know that ship."

Later, he would remember this moment and think that it was the one in which he might have changed the outcome. If he'd recognized the import of those four words. But when she said them, he was merely confused.

"What do you mean?"

Instead of answering him, she shook her hand free of his and stalked forward, her strides long and fast.

"Astrid!" He trotted to catch up with her, but the docks were crowded with sellers and buyers, and she blended quickly into the crush.

He knew real panic then. His wife, carrying his child, was alone on the docks, where all manner of bad men lurked.

"Astrid!" He pressed forward, trying to see her. She was taller than almost all the women, but not taller than most men. He was taller, however, and he peered over the heads of the people, trying to catch sight of her fair hair, braided prettily so that it laced across the back of her head. "Astrid!"

He caught up with her at the pier where the ship she'd been talking about was moored. Before she could walk to the gangway, he caught her arm. "Astrid!"

She stopped and turned to him. She was smiling. "I know this ship! The...*kapten*? I not know word."

"Captain?" Their words were apparently similar.

"*Ja*. Captain. He my friend's brother. This ship stop in my home. Make trade there."

The first wave of dread washed over Leofric's heart then. Did she mean to leave him? No. She wouldn't leave him—she loved him, and she carried his child. She wouldn't. She wouldn't.

That worry so filled his head and heart that he could think of no other.

But he didn't stop her from charging down the pier and stopping to speak to a rough-looking sailor at the end of the gangway. Leofric followed on her heels, wanting to keep her safe, and wanting to keep her with him.

The sailor showed obvious shock to have such a fine lady come up to him on her own. She spoke in her own language, and the man's shock didn't abate. But he nodded and called up to the ship, "Oi! Captain!"

Leofric looked up the gangway, trying to resist the urge to draw his shortsword from its scabbard.

A man with short, dark hair and beard and the ruddy skin that came of a life on the sea appeared at the top. He didn't seem to recognize Astrid, but she very much recognized him. She went to the gangway and put her foot on it. Leofric grabbed her arm and pulled her back. When she tried to pull her arm free, he held on.

"Stay with me, Astrid."

She frowned at him and turned back to the man, who was apparently the captain of this ship.

The man descended slowly, his brow furrowed. About halfway down, the furrow became gaping shock.

"Astrid?"

"*Ja. Ja!* Mihkel!" She spoke words in a different language entirely—one Leofric didn't understand but was obviously not her own. The captain spoke back in the same language. And then Astrid yanked her arm free and ran up to meet her friend. The two embraced, and Leofric wanted to draw his sword more than ever.

When they stepped back, they spoke again in that especially foreign language. Astrid soon seemed agitated, even angry, and Leofric tried to understand her bearing rather than her words.

Then she wheeled around and turned a look of shocked fury on him.

"Astrid?" He went to her, his hand out, and she shrank away.

"What you do?" she asked. Her tone topped over with stunned accusation. With betrayal.

"I don't know what you mean. I understand none of this."

"You make me dead. For my people. They leave me."

Now, too late, he understood the real danger. "Astrid, come. We'll talk."

The captain said something, and Astrid turned her head and considered him. She spoke again.

Leofric would have given much to know what they said.

Whatever it was, the conversation went on for a long time, and Leofric was helpless to act. Then Astrid nodded at the captain and walked down the gangway. When Leofric reached for her, she yanked her arm from his reach and stalked past him.

The captain watched her go, then turned to Leofric and said, in Leofric's language, "Her people mourned the loss of her. They will not take lightly that she was your prisoner, no matter if you've put a crown on her head and a child in her belly."

"Then do not tell them. Name your price."

The captain didn't answer. They stared at each other for a moment longer, and then he turned and walked back up the gangway. Leofric didn't follow; he had more pressing concerns. Astrid had folded herself into the crowd again.

He went to find his wife. His *wife*. *His*.

~oOo~

While he was searching, at the point at which he'd grown truly frantic, one of the footmen found him and told him she was waiting at the carriage. It hadn't occurred to him that she'd have simply returned there. He wasn't sure whether he should feel hope that she had, but at least she wasn't dead in the street—or standing on the trading ship, preparing to sail north.

He ran through the crowd back to the carriage. She sat inside it, staring out the far window.

"I was mad with worry, my love. I'm glad to see you safe."

She didn't answer or acknowledge him at all. When he tried to take her hand, she pulled away.

He sat across from her, feeling despondent and lost. "Astrid. Talk with me."

They'd spoken about her time in the Black Walls, because he'd asked her questions and she'd answered them. But she'd never asked any questions of her own. By the time she had the words to do it, her attention seemed to have turned to the matters of the present, not the past—nor the future, for that matter.

Now, she must have had questions, and she had the words to make them known. But she only stared out the window, her hands slack in her lap.

He knocked on the carriage wall and got them moving back toward home.

~oOo~

The ride was hours long, and they'd sat in tense quiet all the way, even when they'd stopped to water the horses and take a meal. Astrid had taken on that silent stoicism that spoke of deep pain—this of the heart and not the body.

Knowing that she wouldn't hear any word he might say, Leofric let her be quiet. He spent the ride lost in his own worries and pains.

About an hour or so from the castle, she finally spoke. "I not understand. I think and think, but I not see game."

"My love? What game?"

"Your game. Your father. I not see why you play with me."

He leaned forward, and she drew back. "I'm not playing with you, Astrid. I never have. What you see in me is truth."

She shook her head. "Why you take me? There no questions. Only hurt. Always hurt. Why? You take me and you make so no one come. So you hurt me all you want. Keep me alive for hurting. Why?"

He gave her the answer he hoped she could understand. "Vengeance."

Finally, she faced him straight on. "What for vengeance? How I earn that?"

"My sister. Dreda." He'd told her that he had a younger sister who'd died, but nothing more than that. It had been too painful to talk about, and too fraught. But now there was no avoiding it. "She was only nine years old, and your people murdered her and defiled her."

"No. No!"

"Yes. I held her body in my own arms. She was naked and bloody and torn apart, and she died worried that she'd been

317

bad. That is why you were made to suffer. My father wanted you to carry the sins of your savage people." His voice shook as he remembered the rending pain of Dreda's death.

Her brow creased with confusion. "There only peasant girl."

"That was Dreda. She often slipped into the woods to play. She was fascinated by your people and wanted to see. And you tore a little girl apart. Raped her bloody. Whether she was peasant or princess, only animals would do such a thing."

"No."

"Yes, Astrid. I never wanted what happened to you, but I understood it. Losing Dreda nearly killed my father. It nearly undid us all."

"No. She not raped."

"I saw her. She was bare. Her thighs and belly dripped with blood." His fists clenched at the memory.

"No! I stop him! His blood! His!" She slammed her fists on her thighs. "I find Vidar on girl. We not take childs or rape, but Vidar angry. Village have no treasure. He want take what he find. Girl fight—hard. She hit him with rock. Make him bleed bad. He bash her head before I can stop. His breeches still closed. I put my blade on his throat and take him back. He judged by us all and go to death. We not hurt childs! I take his head! My blade give her justice!"

As he understood the import of all her angry words, garbled by an accent grown thick with stress, his guilt for her suffering grew until it was a thunder in his head. "Astrid. My God."

"Your god cruel and petty! His priest watched all my hurt and...and...This why you took me? Why I lose all? Why my bones ache always and night too dark? This how you make vengeance? There no honor! You tell my people I dead and

318

leave me alone to hurt! You take everything! You—you know I think they leave me! You say there trust and truth with us, but you make lies! You make me yours and know it all lie!"

"It's not a lie! What's between you and me is not a lie! Astrid!" He couldn't stand being across the carriage from her anymore. He knew she found calm when he held her. He leapt to the other side and grabbed her, trying to force her to let him hold her. To let him love her and comfort her and find a way to make sense of it all. To force her to forgive him yet again.

But she fought with all she had, kicking and biting and punching. Then, somehow in their violent tangle, she got hold of the dagger he'd given her for safety. She brandished it in his face, and he let her go and threw himself back against the seat.

"There no truth in this place. Only pretty words."

Before he could fathom that she would dare do such a thing, she'd opened the carriage door and leapt out.

His wife, full of his child, had just leapt from a moving carriage. While holding a dagger. In the blink it took him to comprehend that horror, she was already out of sight of the wildly swinging door.

He pounded on the carriage wall. "HALT! HALT!"

Before it stopped, he lunged out the door after her, falling hard to his knees. She was running through a field toward the edge of the wood, her gown gathered in her fists and held almost up to her waist.

He'd never run faster in his life than in that moment. If she got to the wood, she was skilled and wily enough to disappear into the trees.

"ASTRID! NO!"

Wild and desperate as she was, her speed and grace was hindered by their child, and Leofric, equally wild and desperate, was able to close the distance between them. He caught up with her just as the shadows of the wood took over the field. She no longer had her dagger; she must have dropped it when she'd jumped from the carriage.

"Astrid! Please!"

Her head swung back, and she saw how close he was. She shrieked angrily and redoubled her efforts to elude him, adding inches between them just as he might have reached out and caught her.

And then she seemed to stumble, but the way was clear before her, as far as Leofric could see. She didn't fall, and she ran a few more steps, then stumbled again, doubling over with a cry. This time she did fall, and when she landed, she curled into a ball, grabbing her belly with both hands.

The babe. *Oh God, don't take our child.* "Astrid!"

He dived to his knees at her side, but when he tried to gather her up in his arms, she fought and struggled, trying to crawl from him. Again, a pain beset her, and she collapsed to the ground. This time, rather than cry out, she bit down on her bottom lip. When he took hold of her, she didn't fight.

"Is it the babe?" he asked, cradling her at his chest.

"*Ja*," she gasped. "I think."

Holding her snugly, he worked his way to his feet. "Don't fight me, wife. Let me get you home to Elfleda."

"No home here," she said, but she didn't fight him.

He went as quickly as he could back to the carriage. Astrid tensed hard in his arms three times more, but she didn't cry out again. She'd begun to shiver, trembling with such force that her body shook his.

The footmen ran up as he approached.

"Blankets! And hurry!" To the driver, he called up, "Make all haste to the castle. Her Grace is injured!"

He accepted a footman's help to get her into the carriage, and to wrap her up in light wool blankets. He instructed them to close up the windows.

Then they were closed into the carriage, alone in the dim.

She tensed again, and he bent his head to hers. "Forgive me, my love."

"No more forgive," she mumbled. Her eyes were closed, and though she shivered hard, her brow was damp with perspiration. The pain she felt must have been intense. But she was quiet in her torment, as ever. His stoic warrior.

The carriage rocked and rattled, moving at a speed beyond its usual purpose, and Leofric held onto his wife while she suffered, not knowing what else he could do. Then, when they must have been nearing the castle, she cried out, and her hands clutched at him as her body folded tightly.

Over his arm and thigh, through his leathers and the blankets, he felt a soaking of warm wet, and soon thereafter, he smelled the coppery tang of blood.

"Oh, my love," he murmured, knowing exactly what was happening, "Forgive me. Please forgive me."

She didn't answer. She lay slack in his arms, insensible.

~oOo~

321

Elfleda curtsied, then backed away, returning to her patient. Leofric sat hard on the chair he'd stood from when she'd come out of Astrid's bedchamber.

The babe was gone.

His father squeezed his shoulder and then left the room.

"You should go to her, brother," Eadric said after a while. Leofric had forgotten that he wasn't alone in the room. He'd been sitting there, staring into nothingness, his mind void of all but a single thought: on this day, he'd lost everything.

"I cannot. She despises me. All of us. What forgiveness she had for what we did was lost today."

While he'd paced and sat and paced and sat, waiting for news of his wife, his father and brother had kept company with him, and they'd made him say as much as he could about the events of the day.

Eadric sat at his side. "She is your wife. I've seen love in her eyes for you, and I know you love her. She is hurting. Abandon her in her pain, and you truly will lose what you had. Your love grew when you comforted her before. Comfort her now. Nurture the love, and another child will come soon enough."

Leofric didn't think the child was Astrid's most significant hurt. She'd only begun to warm to the idea of being a mother, and not yet in any way she'd spoken of. His grief for the child was, he had no doubt, far more acute than his wife's. Her pain was in the betrayal she saw.

"She thinks it all a lie. I cannot offer her comfort because I've lost her trust."

He should have told her long ago that her people hadn't abandoned her. He'd never meant to keep it from her. But when that pain had been most acute for her, they'd had no words between them to explain. When she might have understood, there'd been other things to talk about. He'd been focused on making her his wife, helping her accept her present, and she'd been reticent about her past. But how to make her believe that truth now?

In her mind, he knew, everything that had happened in the Black Walls had happened because she'd been left behind. She'd believed that her people would come for her if they had lived—and she was likely right. Whether they would have succeeded and rescued her or died in the effort, they would have come. It was the very reason they'd made a show of her death. To make it easier to drive the Northmen back. To give her people no reason to stay.

To give them cause to grieve.

And her to suffer.

She'd accepted this world, this life, even in the reluctant way she had, because she believed she'd been abandoned to it. Leofric and his family had made it seem that she had. But she had been mourned.

She had not lost her home. They had stolen it from her.

How on earth could she ever forgive that?

"To think she tried to save Dreda," Eadric mumbled, almost to himself. "And killed the one who did it."

"God!" Overcome with despair, Leofric buried his head in his hands.

He felt Eadric's hand on his back. "What can I do, brother?"

"Nothing. There is nothing."

His brother stood up. "Go to her, Leofric. She is your wife now. Don't let this fester. There is no change we can make to the past, and the future is in the Lord's hands. Only what you do now is in your own."

~oOo~

Only two sconces were lit, and the room had a faint golden glow. It was quiet. Elfleda and a young servant girl were gathering up bloody linens into baskets. Leofric averted his eyes from the sight.

They both curtsied.

"Your Grace," Elfleda said, coming over to him. "She sleeps now. I gave her a draught to keep her calm." The old woman looked up at him, catching his eye boldly. "She was in a state, Your Grace."

There was no greater guilt the woman could add; he was feeling all of it already. "I know." He went to the bed. "She's pale."

"Aye, she is. There is always much blood lost in a thing like this. She'll need to rest a goodly while and build her blood up. But she'll be well again, and ripe soon enough for another babe. It's not so unusual to lose the first. And she had such a hard spell before she was seeded."

Elfleda didn't know how Astrid had come to lose their child. She would soon; he expected that the footmen had carried the story all through the bailey, and it would soon roll through the villages: the barbarian duchess jumping from a moving carriage, running wild and reckless away from her husband.

"What was it? The child?"

"Your Grace..."

With a look, he demanded an answer, and Elfleda dropped her eyes. "A girl."

His father might know relief that Astrid hadn't lost a son, but Leofric could only think of his love for Dreda, the sweet delight she'd brought to them all, and mourn the loss of his daughter. "I want to be alone with her."

"Of course, Your Grace. We'll take these things away, and I'll be back to see to her later in the night."

With that, the servants took their leave.

Leofric went to her bed. She was nearly as pale as the white linens; her lovely lips seemed grey. Her hair was tangled. But her sleeping shift was clean and crisp, as were the linens she lay on and under. Her hands were at her sides on the sky blue silk coverlet.

He'd had her rooms made up especially for her as a wedding gift, hoping they would be to her liking. For all the fabrics, he'd chosen varying tones of blue to complement her eyes. He'd selected the Æbbe jewels for her for the same reason: because sapphires reminded him of her eyes.

This bed was smaller than his own but could still more than comfortably accommodate them both—and had. No step was required to reach the mattress. But Leofric didn't get into bed with her. He didn't want to disturb her rest. Instead, he knelt on the floor near the pillows and lifted her hand—cool and dry now—into his own.

She stirred, her hand coming to life in his hold. When he looked to her face, he saw her eyes.

They didn't focus well, but they were on him, and he took the moment he had. "I love you, Astrid. My vow to you is unchanged and unwavering. I will love you all my days, and I will make you happy. What's between us is more than words."

She closed her eyes again without speaking, but her fingers curled around his thumb.

He hoped that was a sign that there was still love for him in her heart.

21

Astrid woke and, before she opened her eyes, she knew she wasn't alone. In the way of her old life, the life that had been taken from her, she sent out her instincts and tried to understand her surroundings before she showed herself to be aware.

Her room in the castle. Her bed. No sound out of the ordinary. But the mattress curved with extra weight.

She opened her eyes. Bright moonlight washed through the windows and made a blue glow and long shadows. Leofric sat on her bed, watching her. His chest was bare, and she scanned down the rest of his body. He wore braies only—a garment he rarely wore under his breeches. She wondered how long he'd sat there.

"Astrid," he said, seeing her awake. "Please."

In the weeks since they'd gone to the market town and she'd seen Mihkel, since she'd discovered Leofric's deceit and she'd lost the babe, Astrid had kept to her own company as much as she could, and Leofric had respected her need for distance. His father and brother seemed chastened as well, and didn't press her hard. So Astrid had been left alone with her thoughts most of each day, sequestered in these rooms that were her ostensibly her own.

They adjoined Leofric's, and were located within the royal family's private residence, so she hadn't been able to avoid him, or any of his family, all the time. But Leofric had left her, as she wished, to sleep each night alone.

Until this night.

He reached out and wrapped his hand around hers. She didn't pull away. "I miss you. I'm going mad with this between us."

She missed him as well. She was lonely and sad, and she felt the loss of the babe more keenly than she'd have believed. In the last days of her carrying, she'd felt movement inside her, little flutters, and the import of what had been happening had flowered in her mind. Another life inside her own. Her body making it and nurturing it. A kind of fascination had dawned in her. She'd found herself talking to her belly when she'd felt movement.

But that was all gone now, and she was alone again in her body, in this castle, in this world.

She missed him. She loved him. But she looked on him now and remembered kneeling in the tide, crushed under the knowledge that she'd been abandoned to this horrible place, that her friends hadn't even tried to come for her.

Her love for Leofric had grown in that empty space. This new life she had had been built in that empty space. And that space was a lie. She hadn't been abandoned. The life she'd had was still there, in her true home. Leofric had known all this and kept it from her, pushing her to make a home in this place, within the very same walls where she had been rent apart in body and spirit.

Rent apart to feed a vengeance she hadn't deserved. All that she had endured, all that she'd lost, all of it had been taken from her as recompense for an evil she hadn't committed.

All these months, she hadn't understood. The capacity these people had for cruelty transcended anything she could comprehend. Not even Åke had engaged in the kind of purposeless depravity of her time in the black place. Its enormity had been so far beyond her understanding that she'd had to close it away, as far and as deep as she could. But every day, it was with her, in her body and in her mind.

Now she understood, but understanding brought no sense. Understanding was worse.

How could she love a man who'd been complicit in it all? How could she be part of his family?

But she did love him, and she was in his family now. He had let her stay in the black place for so long, but he had saved her from it. He'd been kind and gentle. He loved her. But he'd forced her into this life, let her believe that she'd been abandoned to it. Her mind couldn't reconcile so many conflicts. It spun and spun and made her feel sick and lost. And so very sad.

"My love. I will do anything you ask of me to earn your forgiveness."

"I not know what to ask. Not know to forgive."

For a moment as long as several breaths, they only gazed into each other's eyes. Astrid believed the pain and regret she saw in his. Forgiveness was a strength, he'd told her once. It seemed to his benefit above all others that he would want her to find such a strength.

"Will you allow me to hold you?"

She knew what she would feel in his arms, and she knew he knew as well. Since he'd gathered her up from the floor in the black place, she'd felt safe in his embrace, no matter her mood otherwise. His touch calmed her, and she'd sought it out again and again as she'd struggled to navigate this world.

She knew she would forgive him if she allowed him to hold her now. She could feel her body yearn for it, her heart crave it, her mind seek the calm he would bring. She could conjure the feeling of her cheek on his chest, her head tucked under his chin, his arms around her. She could smell the warm spice of his male scent. She could remember how calm rolled through her when she was nestled with him.

She would forgive him and ask nothing of him but that calm. Because she loved him, and love had made her weak.

She turned the covers back and accepted him into her bed.

When he was beside her, pulling her close and wrapping her tight, she tucked her head under his chin, felt the hair of his chest on her cheek, breathed deep of his scent. As calm rolled through her like smoke, she forgave.

~oOo~

"I wonder if you'd walk with me in the Pleasaunce after our meal, Duchess?"

Astrid looked up from her plate, where she'd been vying unsuccessfully with the carcass of some strange bird dressed up in fruit, too small to pull meat from it neatly. She wanted to pick the thing up with her hands, but that wasn't allowed at the king's table, not even this one, in the private residence.

It was the king who'd spoken. Astrid resisted the pull to turn to Leofric and check his reaction. Instead she faced his father straight on.

In her months living in comfort as his guest, and then in luxury as his family, Astrid's hatred of the king had cooled and become something akin to a grudging affection. He'd been kind to her while she'd carried his grandchild, and he'd continued kind—perhaps even more so—since the babe had gone. But she had never forgiven him. It was he who'd ordered her torture. Even knowing that he'd been grieving for his daughter, she couldn't find the strength in her heart to forgive him for what he'd made happen to her.

Her hatred hadn't reflowered, however, since she'd spoken with Mihkel. Only Leofric had felt the heat of her shock and pain. Only he had her love, thus only he had betrayed it.

"Why?" she asked, and everyone with them at table—Leofric, Eadric, Dunstan, Winifred, and Father Thomas, the new bishop—went still and quiet. She knew the cause of their shock: she hadn't addressed the king with respect.

For his part, the king only blinked but seemed to take no offense. "You and I have, I think, things to discuss." He smiled a smile that seemed only for her. She'd seen it often, directed nowhere else. It had a kind of fatherliness to it.

"I not—" Hearing a mistake she made often, she checked her sentence and tried again. "I *do* not understand. Your Majesty."

She had tested him as far as his patience would allow. "You'll join me in the gardens after our meal, Astrid."

Sitting at the family table with a mangled bird on her plate, dressed in a light wool gown, with silver threads woven into her braids and a large blue stone sparkling on her finger, Astrid was keenly aware of the limits of her power. Even the restoration of her leather breeches and sturdy boots couldn't armor her against the stabs of all the eyes around her.

She held his look for a few seconds more, and then, with a single nod, agreed.

~oOo~

The Pleasaunce was a large green space on the south side of the castle, where servants tended plants grown for no purpose but their beauty. Long paths of small, sparkling-white pebbles crossed through the patches of green. Some of the plants bore flowers in bright colors and others were only green, dozens and dozens of differing shades and patterns. At points along the paths were trees and wooden benches, and strollers could sit and do nothing but look on the beauty, feel the sun, and smell the rich tangle of scents in the air.

It was one of the first places she'd seen of the castle grounds. Leofric had brought her to the Pleasaunce shortly after she'd agreed to be dressed in the clothes of the women here. She liked it; it was quiet and pretty, and, although the nature had been forcefully arranged by human hands, it was the most natural place within the castle grounds.

Her arm was wrapped in the king's, and his other hand lay on hers, so that she felt almost bound to him. They walked along the white path, their feet crunching over the pebbles, and they were well into the garden, in privacy, before he spoke.

"I wish to tell you about my Dreda," he said without looking at her.

But she looked at him. She tensed, worried even more about the talk he wanted to have while they walked, and where it would lead them.

He patted her hand. "Fret not, child. I mean you no harm. Quite the other, in fact. I think you and I have air to clear between us."

Still he hadn't turned to her. He kept his eyes on the path before him.

"The queen, my beloved wife, was called Dreda as well. She died bringing our daughter into the world. Eadric and Leofric were already well grown, and Dreda was too far along in life to bear another child. We hadn't thought it possible, or we would have been more careful. Her final carrying was difficult, but she bore it with the graceful serenity and sweet spirit that was her nature. She was a woman of deep faith— not ostentatious, or for the eyes of others. Simply her own love of the Lord. I believe that the Lord let her live on in our daughter, whom I named for her. The instant I saw her eyes, exactly like her mother's, even while my dearest one lay lifeless on the bed, I felt a peace under my grief. I knew she was still with me, and that she was with our daughter."

He sighed and was quiet for a time. As they walked on, Astrid tried to understand his intention in opening himself so wide to her.

"As Dreda grew, I knew I was right. She had so much of her mother in her. Such a good heart and a kind spirit, such enthusiasm for life. And already, so young, she had a true faith. Not the kind that is learned, but the kind that is known. From the day of her birth, she lighted my way and kept me from the darkness of a life without her mother."

They came upon a bench, and the king gestured that Astrid should sit. She did, and he sat beside her. He picked up her hand. The diffuse sunlight of a partly cloudy day hit the stone in her ring and threw soft rays of light over them.

"When I lost my daughter, I lost my wife as well. The grief I felt…is my own, and I'll not describe it. But I felt an unspooling of my mind. All I knew was grief. And the way she died…I needed someone to know her pain and my own. That someone was you."

Astrid tried to take her hand back, but he clamped down, and she would have had to fight to free herself. She was prepared to do it; she did not want to talk about the black place with the man who'd put her there.

Before she could, he said, "Please."

She relented, but said, "I don't know why you tell to me this."

"Because I seek a forgiveness I have no right to have. What I did to you was wrong. Leofric showed me that, but knowing you has proved it. It was an affront to the Lord, and it was against my better judgment, and most of all, it was an abomination to the memory of my wife and child, in whose name I did it. I know what you suffered, and I am deeply sorry."

"You not—*do* not—know. You can't know."

"You're right, Astrid. I can't. But I can regret. Even before I knew that you tried to help Dreda, and that you held the man who hurt her to justice, I regretted. Now, my belly is on fire with remorse. My knees bleed from my prayers. The Lord has forgiven me. In His bounty, He asks only repentance. What would you ask of me?"

Oh, how she hated this god, who would forgive a man for a wrong not done to him and call it enough, who would not seek redress for the injured. As if no one mattered in the world but himself. Her gods would sanction vengeance. Would demand it.

"There is nothing."

The king's shoulders sagged. "You have no understanding in your heart for a grieving father?"

"Why you—*do* you—care? You are king. I have no power over you."

"You do, Astrid. You are wife to my son. You are my family. Leofric loves you with the fire that was my love for his mother. He loves you body and soul. I would have only love among us all. You have great power over all of us, Astrid of the North."

Before she could answer, a guard ran toward them. He stopped before them and bowed low, panting. "Begging your pardon, Your Majesty, but word has come from Garmwood. There are raiders at the western shore. Eight ships."

"Eight!" the king exclaimed.

"Yes, Sire." The guard's voice quavered. "They bear the same sails as before, and more besides."

Eight ships. They had come for her. Mihkel had told Leif, and her people had come for her. She knew it for a certainty. And they'd brought more than a raiding party.

They'd brought a war.

~oOo~

At the king's behest, Leofric asked Astrid to ride out and parley with the raiders, before they could advance on the castle. He knew what he risked to ask her, and it was a true risk. The thought that her people were again on the same ground with her, that they had never intentionally left her to her fate, and that they'd come for her at once—that thought drew her and made her ache for what she'd lost. She didn't know whether she'd ride to the camp to parley for her husband and his people or to rejoin her friends and her own.

But the king knew there was little other choice than to send the one person in his realm who could speak with an invasion of greater number than the soldiers he had in the castle battalion. If he sent the one they'd come for, they wouldn't strike.

Unless Astrid turned on the king once she reached the camp.

Leofric trusted that she wouldn't, but as she approached the camp, she wasn't sure what she'd do. She felt loyalty to both sides, but her draw was toward home.

She knew the king's soldiers followed her not so far behind. She couldn't see them, but she could hear them. They hadn't trusted her so far as that.

Dressed in a blue gown of light wool for warm weather, her leather breeches and good boots under its split skirt and a boiled leather corset over its bodice, Astrid rode her bay mare out of the castle wood and into the clearing near Garmwood. She carried no weapon; since losing her dagger on the day of the market, she'd had none to call her own. If she had need of defense, she supposed, there was an army at her back and another before her.

She heard the horn that announced the coming of a rider. Her.

The camp, twice the size of the first, was staked within sight of that burnt relic. Astrid understood this—to look on the memory of an outrage was to keep the fires of vengeance stoked. She saw the shields of Vali's people and of Leif's—and of the jarls between their lands as well: Ivar and Finn.

Raiders amassed near the camp entrance, and she saw Leif move through the crowd, looking as he ever did. Her heart beat so hard and fast in her chest that she could hear it in her ears. Leif. Her friend. Gods, how she'd missed him.

She didn't see Vali or Brenna, but they had to be there. Vali, at the least. Some of the raiders bore the shield of his people, with the red eye.

Jaan was there. And Ulv. Ulv, who disliked raiding, had come this time. For her.

She dismounted outside the camp boundary and set her horse's reins. Leif, his eyes wide and serious, came through the camp entrance. He held no weapon or shield. He walked straight to her and, with no word at all, enfolded her in his arms.

"We thought you in Valhalla." He spoke into her hair.

She clutched him close and swallowed her heart back to its place. "I know. I thought myself abandoned."

He let her go. "Never, Astrid. We'd have died to bring you home." He raised his voice so that the camp could hear. "And now we'll kill everyone who tore us apart!"

A roar went up among her people.

She saw Vali coming through the gathered raiders. He stopped at the entrance of the camp, leaving Astrid and her best friend to make their reunion. But he smiled at her, and she nodded in answer.

"The king's army followed me. I don't know how many, but as many as he had, I expect. The king fears I will turn on him and tell you all I know."

"And will you?" He leaned back and examined her from head to toe. "You don't seem ill used. Mihkel told that you are wedded and with child. I could not believe it, and to look on you, I can't know what is true. Have you made your home among these people?"

"I had no choice. I was alone, and very ill used. I will show you scars if proof you need. Now I'm wedded to the king's son. I lost the child before it could be born."

Leif had experienced the loss of many children. "I am sorry to hear that. It seems we have much to talk about, my friend." He hooked his big arm around her shoulders and led her into the camp.

When she got to Vali, he spread his arms wide, and Astrid went to hug him. His massive arms closed around her and squeezed. "Astrid, my friend. The gods are great to give you back to us."

She didn't think she'd ever hugged Vali before—or Leif, for that matter.

And then she was embraced by an entire camp, all of her old friends, and even people she didn't know, crushing in around her, celebrating her return to them.

Had she returned to them? Was she home? If she was, why didn't she feel the elation she'd dreamed of? Why hadn't calm security claimed her?

Why didn't she feel like she was home?

While her people still buffeted her with glad tidings, a horn blew—announcing the coming of the king's army. They all quieted and dispersed, seeking their weapons and shields. With no weapon to claim, Astrid stood alone near the camp entrance and watched the soldiers come—in formation, riders at the fore and marchers behind.

At the center of the riders was a grey charger. Astrid knew the horse and its rider well. Leofric. Eadric was at his side, astride his black steed.

Leif and Vali came up at her sides. Leif held her axe in his hand. Her axe. Her mouth watered and her eyes stung. Her axe.

He held it out for her to take, and her hand lifted. Her palm itched to feel its leather and wood. She wanted to run her fingertips over the honed blade and put them to her mouth to suck the blood away.

But if she took that axe in her hand while Leofric stood there on his horse, an army at his back, she would have made her choice. Was it the choice she wanted to make?

"ASTRID! WHAT NEWS?" Leofric called, as if he'd brought an army with him with no more intent than to get word of her parley.

She dropped her hand.

Leif's eyebrow cocked up. "Astrid?"

"That is my mate. Let me talk with him."

"Not without us at your sides," Vali answered with a growl. "They'll not take you again."

She loved these men. Her friends. Before her time in Mercuria, she hadn't known the feeling of love, any kind of love, enough to know even when she'd felt it. Leofric had given her that. He'd taught her how to love.

"Where is Brenna?"

Vali grinned. "In Karlsa. We have a new son. He's called Agnar."

"That is good news."

"Indeed. Is there good news for you as well?"

"No. I lost the babe."

Vali, too, knew that loss. "Ah. I'm sorry for you."

"ASTRID! WIFE!"

Vali turned a menacing sneer at Leofric. "Your man makes demands, it would seem."

"Yes."

Leif scanned the army before them. "We are greater in number than they. We need no parley. I say we call the archers forward and be done with them."

"No!" The thought sent a cold spike of fear through Astrid's heart. Fear for Leofric. She didn't want him harmed. To Leif's shocked expression, she said, "Let me speak with him."

Leif and Vali both gave her looks that said they didn't recognize her. She didn't recognize herself. There was so much conflict and uncertainty in her heart. There was no urge in her to fight. None at all. Never in her life had she known a feeling like this, like sickness in her heart and belly, in her mind. She wanted everyone safe. She just wanted to go home.

But where was home?

With her friends on either side, and many of the raiders following behind, she walked back out of the camp. Leofric and Eadric dismounted and walked toward them.

Despite his sharp shouts before, Leofric wore an aspect of perfect despair. As soon as they were close enough to speak normally, he said, "Please, my love. Don't leave me. Send your people away and stay. Here, where you belong. At my side. I beg you. We want no fighting."

"Then why bring an army?"

"That was my order," Eadric answered. "Leofric didn't want it, but I command the soldiers. I'm sorry, Astrid, but I couldn't leave the security of the realm to trust in one woman who has never been happy here."

She had been happy. With Leofric, in their times alone, she'd been happy. To Eadric, however, she offered a challenge. "Would you have happy in a place where people tore flesh from your bones, again and again?"

"No, I would not." He shook his head. "And that is why I brought the army."

"What is said?" Vali asked.

Behind them, the raiders became restless. Someone shouted, "KILL THE CHRISTIANS!" and another slammed his sword against his shield. Others picked up that battle rhythm, and Leofric and Eadric looked past Astrid, their eyes wary and alert.

From the corner of her eye, Astrid saw something zing past her, from the soldiers to the camp. She knew, without a clear view of it, that it had been an arrow, and she wasn't surprised when a shout went out among the raiders. One of them had been shot.

Leofric spun and faced the troops. "HOLD! HOLD!"

At the same time, Eadric fell, a spear through his throat.

And the war began.

Astrid found herself instantly pulled between two men: Leofric and Leif, each one with firm hold of an arm, dragging as if they meant to tear her in two. She shrieked and twisted, freeing herself from both.

When Leif threw her axe, she caught it. Leofric, his face a melting mask of grief, shouted, "Astrid, no!"

But they were surrounded on all sides by fighting men and women, and the time to parley was over.

She didn't know what side she fought on, and neither did anyone else. So she fought the fight in front of her. She defended herself from all comers and made no effort to advance either side.

Leif and Leofric stayed near her, keeping her safe.

PART SEVEN
FIDELITY

22

There were too many of them. The world seemed full to bursting with raiders, at least two, maybe more, for every one of the realm's men. Leofric stood between the inert body of his brother and the wildly fighting form of his wife, and knew the battle was lost. Perhaps the realm itself, if the castle fell before reinforcements could arrive.

The king's men were overrun; he could hear their death cries all around him. He knew he should—he *must*—jump deeper into the fray and lead his men, bring them together in a push forward. He was their leader now, with Eadric dead at his feet. But he couldn't leave his wife's side.

Astrid fought madly, striking down any who came for her—and fighters from both sides came. No one knew where she stood. Leofric didn't know where she stood. He only knew she must survive, or he would not. He couldn't lose her as well.

Her friend, the big blond, stayed near her as well, and even in the midst of such chaos, Leofric knew raging jealousy. The blond man was as protective of Astrid as he was—fighting off the king's men from her just as Leofric fought off the raiders. Had she been his woman? Was this for whom she had pined?

Leofric knew Astrid had been experienced with the pleasures of the flesh before him; underneath the trauma left by the Black Walls had been a considerable understanding of the ways men and women pleasured each other and themselves. Was this the man who'd given her that understanding?

Then he wanted to cut this man down before this fight was over.

But already it nearly was. His men lay dead and dying all around him, and the air shook more with the sounds of their suffering than with the clang of swords and shields. It was time to call a retreat, to lift Eadric's body and fall back, to return to the castle and mount a defense until reinforcements could arrive.

As he opened his mouth to call the order, he heard Dunstan shout near his side—a sound of great pain. His attention swung from Astrid, and he saw his oldest and dearest friend down, lifting his broadsword with one hand, trying to hold off a looming raider.

Leofric lunged forward with a whoop and slashed the raider across the back. He roared and turned, and Leofric slashed again, sinking his longsword into the man's head and pulling it through. The top half of his head slid away on a slant, and the raider fell dead.

Leofric ran to Dunstan. "You're struck!"

"A flesh wound only," Dunstan gasped with a strained grin.

Not a flesh wound. He was open from ribs to hip. He would die if he wasn't seen to right away; he would likely die regardless.

"RETREAT!" Leofric bellowed. "RETREAT!" He heard the call move through his men and could sense them already pulling back, glad for the permission. This battle was badly lost.

Crouching to lift his friend, he heard a wild, feminine roar, and a shadow fell over him. He twisted and saw Astrid right with him, her axe held in both her hands, crossways, blocking a blow from the giant raider.

The man's blood-drenched face was twisted with rage and hatred, and his fierce blue eyes were focused on Leofric. The blow Astrid had blocked had been meant for him. She was far smaller than the giant, but she held him off, straining against his force.

"*Nej! Nej*, Vali!" she grunted, and the giant shifted his attention to her. He backed off. They exchanged a few words Leofric didn't understand, and the giant stalked away.

There was shouting going on all around. Leofric swung his head back and forth, seeing his men retreating. The raiders seemed to be allowing it; the blond man so devoted to Astrid seemed to be calling them off.

Astrid crouched at his side. Her head and gown were splashed with blood. It dripped from her hair and down her face. "Go! Go now!"

"Come with me! Come home!" He grabbed her hand. She still held the axe that Eadric had dropped at the blond man's feet the year before. Her axe. "Astrid, please!"

She stared hard into his eyes. "I love you," she said.

He heard her farewell in her tone. "Come home, my love. Come home."

With one last hard look into his eyes, she stood. Turning her back to him, she walked toward the camp. To the blond man.

Dunstan groaned, and Leofric set aside his heartbreak and lifted his friend to his feet. As he dragged him toward the woods, few of his men were still near the camp. He had no choice but to leave his brother's body behind.

There was more heartbreak in this day than he could withstand.

~oOo~

The king took the news of Eadric's death and the realm's loss with stony calm and then sent out riders to neighboring kingdoms with requests for aid. The men who'd been stationed away from the castle, keeping the harbor and borders secure, had been called back and were arriving, but the losses in the battle had been so drastic that their own soldiers wouldn't be enough.

The raiders could not even be faulted. One of the king's own men had made the first strike, breaking a parley. Even the barbarians seemed to understand the sanctity of a parley, and to know the dishonor of breaking it.

They were not barbarians, in truth. Knowing Astrid, Leofric couldn't see them as the savages he'd believed them to be. They had a deep honor not unlike that which he himself held dear, and they had tight bonds among them. Those bonds were now tearing him apart.

Dunstan was inside the castle, still alive but on the very cusp of death. Winifred was on her knees in the chapel, doing her wifely duty by praying for his recovery. A true wife would have been at his side.

Until this day, Leofric had believed that Astrid would have been at his side, had he been injured. But she'd turned her back. She'd left him.

If he allowed the black thoughts to have sway in his mind, he would have been unmanned. So he kept his focus on duty and locked his losses away to be felt at another time. For now, he had to amass a force that could defend the castle from without. He turned his attention on the map before him, trying to anticipate how the raiders would move through the wood.

They would have Astrid to guide them, and Leofric had shown her all the secrets of the forest during their rides together. Those rides had been among the few times she had shown true happiness.

"Your Highness!" one of the officers called out nearby. When no one responded, he called out again, "Your Highness! Sir!"

Remembering that it was he being hailed, that he was now the Crown Prince, that his brother was dead, Leofric felt a chill through his heart. He looked up at the officer—a young man of noble birth, a third son. Officer of the King's Army was a worthy and honorable vocation for such a man.

"What is it?"

"A rider approaches. It is Her Gra...Her High...It is Astrid of the North, Your Highness."

He was at the man before he'd realized he'd moved from the table. He grabbed his arms. "Is she alone? Does she bring the raiders with her?"

The officer blinked. "I—she—"

"Answer!"

"She rides alone, sir! But she pulls a litter. She brings Prince Eadric home."

Around them, the men had gone quiet. Leofric looked west, the direction of the raiders' camp, and saw Astrid approaching. She rode his grey charger, and she had not cleaned the blood from her face.

Men lined up as she rode past. They didn't brandish their swords, but neither did they bow. The men who'd been in the battle had seen her fight for no side but her own survival. No one knew where her loyalty lay, so no one knew if she was still due the respect of a member of the royal family. But when the litter passed them, they dropped to one knee in honor of their fallen prince and commander.

Leofric walked into the path so that she rode directly at him. She pulled up his horse. He took hold of the reins as she dismounted.

She'd come unarmed and alone. He didn't know whether that was arrogance or trust.

He didn't know if she was staying.

"Are you here? Have you come home?"

In a rare gesture for her, she brushed her fingers over his cheek. "I bring Eadric home. Other dead wait for you to come for them. We not stop you. If you not attack, we not."

We. The pain he'd held off stormed inside him. "Astrid, are you going back home?"

"I not know where is home." She dropped her eyes, and Leofric saw that she was in almost as much pain as he was.

"With me. It's with me."

She turned and looked at all the men staring at her, their expressions carefully blank, but their hands on the pommels of their swords.

"Is it?" she asked when she turned back to him.

He hooked his hand around the back of her neck and dragged her close. She fought against his kiss at first, but he ignored her wish and claimed his own.

After a moment stiff in his arms, she gave in and returned his passion. She tasted like blood and sweat, and the memory of the battle swirled around them and made him feel desperate.

"It is," he whispered against her mouth. "It is. If there is a question in your heart, it's because you fear to make the choice. This is your home now. With me."

Her eyes held raw anguish, and Leofric's heart bled. He knew where her loyalty lay: in both places. With her people, and with him. She had no bond to his world; in his world, she had suffered horribly, and she was still, even with a crown on her head, a source of gossip and judgment. But she loved him. In her world, she was a leader, and she was admired. Her whole past was there. Her friends. Her life.

She had lost it all forever, and then it had been returned to her.

But she loved him.

He'd never lived anywhere but in the castle. He'd never known any other world but this one. His family, friends, memories—his life—were all part of the earth on which he stood. He couldn't imagine how the pull between her home and her love might rend her, but he could see in her eyes that it did.

The solution was to keep her with her love and return her to her home.

If he went with her—but no. He was the Crown Prince now. Even if he might have entertained such an idea before, even if her people would allow him to go to their world, now he could not. He was his father's only heir. He couldn't leave Mercuria.

So it was an impossibility, and the only solution.

"Come to the castle with me. We'll bring Eadric home together."

She nodded, and Leofric considered that a small victory. As long as she was with him, he had time to find a solution. There had to be one.

~oOo~

Winifred had fled from the chapel as soon as she saw the prince being carried in. When the king entered and walked slowly down the aisle toward the body of his son, Leofric and Astrid were alone with him.

He regarded Astrid's bloody face for an endless time, and Astrid stood quietly, her eyes on his, and let him. Leofric tried to interpret that silent stare. He could see no malice in it, from his father or his wife. Only sorrow and uncertainty.

"You are our only hope, Astrid," his father finally said. "You made a vow before God and are wedded. I know that you feel torn, but the answer is there. You have chosen your home. You have chosen this family. In this place, where we now stand, you made a sacred, unbreakable promise."

"Many promises broken here. Pretty words mean nothing here. You tell many lies." Her speech had lost some of the precision she'd achieved during recent weeks, almost as if she were shedding the duchess she'd become.

"Did you lie, Astrid? When you swore to love and honor my son and to be with him until death will part you?"

Leofric held his breath. He knew she'd spoken an empty vow at her baptism, but he didn't believe the words they'd said to each other had been empty, no matter if they'd sworn them to a God she didn't believe in. If she said now that she'd lied, he'd know that she'd decided where her home was.

Elsewhere.

She didn't answer his father. Instead, she turned her eyes to Leofric, and he saw that agonizing conflict. He took heart in it; in the deep pain in her beautiful eyes, he saw that her love for him was just as deep as his for her. She had made him a true promise at this altar.

But to be true to him, she would have to give up this magnificent gift that had landed on their shores: her past. Her friends. All the things she'd mourned so hard for throughout the year since Eadric had knocked her senseless and carried her away.

At the thought of his brother, Leofric turned and studied his body. The raiders had treated it well, setting his mail chestpiece so that the gaping wound in his throat was not so vicious to look upon. His face had been washed, and his eyes closed.

Astrid had done all of it; he knew it without asking. She'd treated his brother with good care. With loving care. And now, as he sighed at his brother's body, thinking of all that he'd lost, that he might still lose, Astrid came to his side and took his hand, sliding her fingers between his.

He could feel her sapphire ring, still on her finger.

"I not know how I give up my people. Or you. I not know how I can," she murmured, her eyes on Eadric.

"I know, my love. I don't know, either."

The king came up and stood at Leofric's other side, near Eadric's head. "You are all that is left of my family. You are all that is left of my hope. Astrid, you've felt powerless and exploited here, I know. But do you understand that you hold the future of the realm in your hands?"

She turned and looked past Leofric to his father. "Unless you kill me, *ja*?"

Leofric winced. It was a cold statement to make, especially here before Eadric's body—and it was the truth.

"A wise king would kill you rather than allow you to sail away and leave the death of his line in your wake. But I will not. You haven't forgiven me. Perhaps that is the penance you require—the true end of us." He smiled. "I would like to have quiet with my sons now. Will you wait without for Leofric? I would ask that you not leave without a proper farewell, if leaving us is what you intend."

"Night is fast upon us in any event. Stay the night, Astrid. At least that." Leofric squeezed the hand he yet held.

She squeezed back, but she shook her head. "They come, if I not go back. I must go, or they come to fight."

This was when he would lose her, then. Everything inside him seemed to die at once. "Astrid…"

Her other hand came up and cupped his cheek. "Love." It was with that single word that she'd told him she loved him for the first time. And, it seemed, for the last time.

She blinked, and tears dropped from her eyes. Then she unwound her hand from his and walked away.

When he would have gone after her, his father put a restraining hand on his arm. Leofric stood and watched her every step away from him. When the chapel doors closed with a hollow echo, he closed his eyes and let them swim in tears he couldn't shed.

"All is not yet lost, my son. As much as we've lost, even with Eadric gone from us and his body cold before us, the Lord shines a light in my mind and shows me hope. Let us leave the priests and women to attend the preparations for Eadric's rest. You and I must speak now and consider."

~oOo~

Late that night, his mind reeling and his heart aching, Leofric went to Dunstan's chambers. Elfleda answered the door, and curtsied deeply. Winifred was nowhere to be seen.

"Where is the countess?"

He saw the moue of contempt before the old woman could clear it from her wrinkled features. "The sight of suffering upsets her, Your Highness. She is in her room, at prayer."

"Ah. How is he?"

"He is blessed, sir. The wound did not cut deeply enough to rend inside. The hours to bring him back to the castle wore hard, and the wound will take long to heal, but there is a chance for him to be well again." She patted him on his arm—a more familiar gesture than was appropriate, but one Leofric appreciated nonetheless. "He has times of wakefulness and has been sorry to be alone. If it please Your Highness, he would be happy to see a friend's face when next he wakes."

On impulse, he caught Elfleda's hand and held it between his own. "You are a good woman, Elfleda. All my life, you've been here to take care of us all, and you've done so more than ably. Thank you."

The old woman's cheeks went bright red, and her eyes glittered with sudden tears. "It's a true honor to serve this family, Your Highness." As he let her hand go, she added, "Might I ask after your princess?"

"I think Astrid has left us."

She swallowed and took a deep breath. "Ah. I'm sorry to hear that. The poor dear."

"You're not angry?"

Elfleda gave him a quick study before she responded. "May I speak plainly, Your Highness?"

"As I've said before, you speak more plainly with your face than most people at court ever speak with their tongues, so please. Indulge yourself."

That earned him a secret smile. "She loves you true, but I don't think she ever understood how to cast off the Black Walls."

"What do you mean?"

"She wasn't here by choice, so nothing that came after was her choice. I know I speak far beyond my station, Your Highness—"

"I give you leave. Speak freely."

She bowed her head in thanks. "I see it in the way she studies herself in the mirror. She sees the prisoner lurking inside her. Her people are different from us. Even as she learned our ways, she didn't understand them. Where she was from, she could make of herself what she wanted. She could choose. Here, men choose little about their lives, and women choose nothing at all."

There was a tang of envy in Elfleda's last words. But Leofric heard something else in them as well, and he was suddenly glad that Astrid had not stayed. He knew her people wouldn't sail before later in the next day, if they meant to sail as soon as they could. He had time. Elfleda's words, and his father's stunning concession, gave him hope. It shone before him like a beacon now.

He might not yet have lost her.

But she had to choose to stay.

"Thank you for your frankness, Elfleda."

Hearing the thanks and the dismissal implied in it, she curtsied and took her leave.

Before he sat with his sleeping friend, Leofric went to the door that led into Dunstan's young wife's room. He didn't knock. When he entered, he found her at the window, kneeling on a pillow, her hands clasped together and raised to the night sky.

She leapt to her feet and whirled to face him, her hands clutched over her slight form as if the miles of sleeping gown covering her from chin to floor might have left something unseemly for him to see. Mercy, she was young. In that ridiculously modest gown, he could more easily imagine her giggling with Dreda than he could coupling with his wild friend.

She curtsied, dropping all the way to the floor. "Your Highness."

"Forgive me the intrusion, my lady, but I have a pertinent question for you."

"Yes, sir?"

"If you could leave the castle forever and retire to a nunnery, would you choose to do so?"

She paled and frowned. "I'm sorry, sir. I know that I have been a bad wife—"

He waved off the apology. "I am asking you to choose, Winifred. You are already wedded, so your choices are limited to two. Well, three, but I don't think you'd choose death over the others. So I want you to tell me honestly, before God. If you have a choice, would you prefer to be a good wife to your husband and lie with him as a good wife should, love

357

him with your body as well as your heart, and give him issue, or would you rather devote your life to the Lord?"

"You—I—my mother said—"

"Winifred. Answer the question."

Her voice was very small as she answered, "Since I was a child, I've wanted to give my life to the Lord. But my mother and father—"

Again, he waved her off. "If that is your wish, I will speak to your parents. And to your husband. And to my father. And to the bishop, to seek an annulment. But if you choose, be sure it is the life you truly want. We cannot undo things already done. Not more than once, at any rate."

The smile the girl gave him was the biggest and most sincere he'd ever seen on her face. "Yes, sir. Yes! I choose! I choose God!" She clapped her hands like a little girl getting a treat.

He smiled. "Very well. Go back to your prayers."

"I shall! And I shall thank the Lord every day for you, sir."

"Do not forget your prayers for the earl's speedy recovery."

"No, sir. I shan't."

He closed the door on a very happy young woman, and he went to sit by her husband's side. Dunstan would be glad as well, he knew. At least he could repair that damage.

Whether he could repair his own, he would know on the morrow.

Ah, Astrid. Choose this life. Choose me. He folded his hands and rested his forehead on them. *Please, Lord, let her choose her future and not her past.*

23

Astrid stood in the center of the camp and watched men and women strike tents and carry chests, bundles, and baskets to the shore, where the eight massive skeids were being laded. She had discarded her blood-drenched gown of the day before and wore her breeches and boots, with a tunic Leif had found for her.

A black pall of unrest loomed over the camp; the raiders were angry to be leaving a land where they had the clear advantage. They'd sailed for days, they'd lost nearly a score of raiders in the battle of the previous day, and they were returning with nothing but Astrid herself.

They all turned angry eyes on her as they passed her, and no one but the jarls would speak to her—because they all knew that she was the reason they would leave in ships emptier than when they'd arrived.

The night before, upon returning to the camp, she'd sat with Leif and Vali, and with Gunnar and Tollak, the leaders from the parties of Jarl Ivar and Jarl Finn, and she'd spoken as emphatically and desperately as she'd known how. She had no good reason to offer them for turning away without taking any spoils or wiping out the force that had struck during the parley—the same force that had attacked them the year before and nearly wiped out that raiding party, the same that had taken her and abused her.

Her only reason had been that she loved Leofric and couldn't abide the thought of overrunning the castle of his family. Watching the surprise and confusion playing over Leif and Vali's faces, she'd known that she was a different woman from the Astrid she'd been. The woman they'd known would never in a hundred years have suggested withdrawing from a winnable fight.

The woman they'd known had never known love. Now that she knew it, had it, the specter of losing it was like to rend her in two.

In the end, it was the great change in her, she thought, that had convinced her friends, and their much greater facility with persuasive speech had grudgingly convinced Gunnar and Tollak. They weren't going home empty-handed, Leif had argued. They'd come for Astrid, and they were returning with her.

The raiders had been deeply unhappy, and the discussion that morning had filled the misty air with shouts and snarls. And now she was a pariah among them.

Had she lost this home, too?

It was more than their anger with her now. As happy as she was to be reunited with her friends, Astrid had felt out of step in the camp from before she'd taken Eadric's body back to the castle. She'd killed one raider and injured another during the fighting. Both men had attacked her, and Leif had seen it, but it had thrown her loyalty into greater question, even though she'd also killed one of the king's soldiers.

No one knew where she belonged. She didn't know where she belonged.

The thought of watching the friends of her life sail away from her broke her heart. The thought of sailing away from Leofric broke her heart.

Standing in the middle of the dwindling camp, facing west, where the sea loomed blue and calm, Astrid felt a compulsion she'd never felt before in her life, not even in the black place. There, she'd wished for death often, but she'd never seriously considered bringing it about herself. She'd begged Leofric to kill her because it had been beyond her thinking to do it herself.

Now, the thought of simply walking into the sea until she drowned had her mesmerized. She couldn't sail, and she couldn't stay. The sea was the only place for her to go.

"Astrid."

A heavy hand shook her shoulder, and she turned around. Vali was there. He'd been striking a tent, and he was bare-chested and shining with sweat. New scars marred his chest, the remnants of the ragged wounds of several arrows. His back had scars to mirror these, which was likely why he'd survived. If the arrows had stopped inside him, the damage done in pulling them would probably have killed him. Or maybe not; the man seemed nigh immortal.

Astrid knew that he'd gotten these new scars during the king's lie about her death. She knew the story now about how they'd been fooled into thinking that there was nothing of her to rescue. She knew that Brenna had nearly died in the sneak attack on the camp, and that Vali had nearly died when Leofric and his brother had brought the mangled head of a woman to them and called it her own.

Now Jaan was dead, killed the day before in the battle of the broken parley. Ulv might lose his leg. And others were dead and wounded. The incursions into Mercuria had been costly, in so many ways.

"Astrid," Vali said again.

She blinked and focused on the man before her, and he smiled.

"They will forget this. You will be home, where you belong. We will raid again before the season is done, and we'll bring back bounty from a new place. All will be well."

Astrid nodded, but it was an empty gesture, without conviction.

With a firm pat on her shoulder, Vali left her and went back to his work. Astrid looked for a way to be helpful, but no one wanted her help. So she wandered around, awash in silent disquiet, thinking about the sea.

When the camp was nearly gone, a horn sounded, announcing a rider.

There was no reason for a rider to be approaching. The raiders were leaving. The king's men had arrived long before, at first light, to collect their fallen dead. The raiders had burned their own the night before. Astrid felt sick at the thought that she had weakened her people by convincing them to pack up the skeids and sail, and now they might be caught unprepared and insufficiently armed against another surprise attack.

Raiders still at the camp collected their weapons and grouped at the camp entrance, expecting more perfidy from the king. Astrid held her own axe at the ready.

A lone rider approached. Astrid recognized the big grey horse before it had cleared the wood.

Leofric stopped just beyond the range of an arrow. Leaving his horse there, he dismounted and walked forward. He was unarmed and unarmored, carrying no weapon or shield, wearing nothing stronger than a brocade doublet over soft leather breeches, all in black—their color of mourning. For Eadric.

Vali moved to Astrid's side. "That's your man, yes?"

"Yes."

"This must be a ruse, then. He wouldn't approach us without defense." He scanned the wood.

Astrid's eyes stayed on Leofric, whose eyes were on her alone. He stopped well away from the cluster of armed raiders, and he held out his hand. Though he was fifty paces away or more, and though he didn't raise his voice, when he said her name—only that, nothing more—Astrid heard him.

There was no ruse. He'd come to her completely vulnerable. She remembered the night of their first coupling, when he'd seen her fear and made himself entirely subject to her, not even stopping her when she would have killed him. He was doing it again, understanding her turmoil and offering himself to her.

"He's alone."

She could sense Vali at her side, reacting to that in disbelief, and she sensed Leif coming up between them. She felt his head at her ear, and she saw Leofric flinch and drop his hand as he watched Leif move in so intimately near her.

He was jealous. He thought she was staying for a greater love than she had for him.

"There was a time," Leif said in her ear, "when you might have been jarl of Geitland. When I was in Karlsa with Olga, I would have stayed, if she'd refused to go. Because I knew that my true home was with her. I would have given up the jarldom and the home of my birth, because I knew the thing I needed most in my life. It wasn't what I'd had—it was what I *would have*."

Astrid turned her head and met his eyes. She had no words with which to form a response, but she needed none. They already understood each other. Leif smiled.

She handed him her axe, and she walked through her people, away from the camp, toward her husband.

Leofric watched her approach, his eyes and expression rioting with wary hope. When she was nearly close enough for them to touch, he said, "Choose, Astrid. Choose me."

She gave him her answer by looping her arms around his neck and kissing him with all the fierce love she felt for him.

His love met hers with the same force, and he wrapped her up tight in his arms as their mouths moved wildly together. In that moment, Astrid understood that this was where she belonged. Nothing else mattered—not her past or his past, not the black place, not the lies and omissions, not anything but the peace she felt in his arms, the peace she'd always felt in his arms, from the first time they'd gone around her.

He turned his head, breaking the seal of their mouths. "Give me the words, Astrid. I need the words."

"I stay. Home is with you."

Even as she said the words and knew relief in their truth, a piece of her heart seemed to tear away. She was turning her back on all she'd ever known. She was rejecting this boon from the gods—her friends and life returned to her.

The pain was sharp and deep, but she couldn't live in her past. Too much of her had changed in this year. Despite the way this part of her life had begun, she'd gained more than she'd lost.

Leofric's hands slid up her back and into her hair. He clutched her head and kissed her again, bending her backward, taking control. She grabbed handfuls of his hair and returned the force.

He broke away again and touched a gentle kiss to the corner of her mouth. "I want to parley with your people. With your blond man and the giant."

"Not my man. My friend only. Always."

A new facet of happiness gleamed in his eyes. "Yes?"

"*Ja.* I love you only. Ever."

He smiled and squeezed her more tightly. "Can we go to your friends in safety?"

Leif and Vali would never hurt her, and Leofric would be shielded by that unless he struck out. "*Ja.* But why?"

"I came for more than the hope that you would choose me. I came because my father has an offer to make to your people. One that could mean you lose nothing today."

She couldn't fathom what he might mean. When she frowned her confusion at him, he laughed.

"Introduce me to your friends. All will be made clear."

~oOo~

The king's solar was the room in which he did most of his business. The great hall was for feasts, dances, and other celebrations, and, though Leofric had told her that meetings among the sovereigns of Anglia often occurred there, Astrid had never known such a thing to happen. In the year since he'd taken her from the black place, she'd never seen any event in the hall except feasting.

The solar was a fraction of the size and appointed in a style that more reflected the taste of the king himself—luxurious, but not ostentatious. Heavy wood, dark fabrics, hangings that displayed his love for his god, and weapons that displayed his might—including the magnificent broadsword over the fireplace.

When Leofric had held her hand and led Leif, Vali, Gunnar, Tollak, and a select few other of her people, including Bjarke, one of Vali's most trusted men, deep into the castle to the solar, Astrid had felt the tension all around her. The king had acted without honor more than once against the raiders, and they were on alert now lest he have such plans again.

Leif especially walked with a rigid gait, his hand twitching, ready to pull his longsword. Astrid remembered the day in Estland when the prince there had lured them to the castle for a parley and had instead presented them with the defiled head of Leif's son.

Einar had been on his first raid. The boy had shown promise, Astrid remembered. He'd been big and strong like his father, and serious, too. He'd been scouting with another young raider when they'd been taken.

Einar had been the sixth of Leif's children to die—the seventh, when Leif's first wife and unborn child were also considered in the sad accounting. He'd been the last of Leif's children, until Olga had given him Magni.

Leif had Olga and Magni at home. Vali had Brenna and four children. Jaan, who would not be going home, left behind a pregnant wife and an infant daughter. That wife was now twice widowed.

They had left all that behind and come for her. And they'd been willing to return empty-handed, except for her, despite the losses they'd suffered. For her.

But Leofric had convinced them that this parley, in the castle, was to their benefit. She had convinced them to trust him.

Now, eight raiders, Astrid, Leofric, and the king sat around a heavy table in the solar. The table was laden with food and drink, and Leif had flinched sharply when he'd seen a covered tray in the center. But there had been no head of his son on this tray, only an assortment of roasted meats.

As big as the room was, and as substantial the furniture, the entire space had seemed to shrink when Leif and Vali had come into it. The king, who'd never laid eyes on a raider except for Astrid, had seemed, for the briefest moment, stunned. But he was in full command of the meeting now, sitting at the head of the table. Leif, the jarl of the largest holding among those present, sat at the other end, with Vali on his right and Gunnar on his left.

Astrid was serving as interpreter, which was a task beyond her comfort. Her understanding of Leofric's language was sufficient for her needs of use, but to translate between two tongues took skill she didn't really have. She was doing the best she could, however, and she thought she'd conveyed the king's words to her people well enough.

But Leif frowned at Astrid. "I don't understand. Does your prince not understand that we would have left today with nothing?"

She'd told Leofric she was staying with him. He'd seen the struck camp. "He understands. It doesn't seem to matter."

Vali slammed his cup down and leaned forward. "It's a trick, then. They mean to lure us in and cut us down while our backs are turned. This is how they fight. Not face to face but underhand." His lip turned sharply up, and he growled at the king.

"They see trick," she translated for Leofric and the king. "They think you attack again when people not can fight."

The king nodded and leveled his eyes on Vali. "We understand why you would be wary of giving us trust. We have been enemies, and we have dealt each other grave losses. Our eldest son lies in the chapel now, awaiting his vigil. Our young daughter was killed by one of your men last year. And yet we offer you this, because you have something we value deeply. Some*one*. You came to our shores last year with the intent to wrest land from our realm. From you, instead, we wrested Astrid of the North."

His eyes shifted and held Astrid. "We would that she stay with us, as one of us. We have grown to love her, and she, we believe, loves us. But you are her people, and it pains her to be torn from you again. We owe her a debt, and we seek her forgiveness. You wish to settle, and we wish peace in our realm and across Anglia. So we offer you a stake. Five thousand arable acres along the northwestern coast of Mercuria. You will be part of the realm, with all the protections and obligations of such, and we will welcome a new duke at our court. In return, you will assist us and our allies in the fight against further incursions from the people of the North. There is no trick here. There is unity."

Her head spinning, Astrid attempted to translate all that and hoped she at least preserved the heart of it—she hoped she *understood* the heart of it. It confused her when the king spoke as he had, saying *we* rather than *I*. It was the second time he'd made the offer, and she hoped she wasn't mangling what she understood it to be.

They had first come to Mercuria with the intent to claim land here. The king was offering them the thing which had brought them to his shores in the first place. Astrid had the sense of a circle closing.

Tollak spoke first, after she was finished. "So we would be subject to this Christian king? Usch! We are freemen! We don't need his gift—we will take what we want!" He pounded his fist on the table.

"A settlement we claimed by force would be vulnerable to attack from any neighboring kings," Leif mused. "This would be protection for our settlers—farmers and families. Vali?"

Vali turned to Astrid. "What is your judgment of this king? I have no cause to trust him. Do you?"

She studied the king for a moment, then put her eyes on her husband. He nodded. She trusted Leofric completely. Her shock at the deceit about her taking had struck so painfully because her trust in him ran deep. But it hadn't been his deceit. He hadn't taken her. He hadn't tortured her. He'd saved her. He'd loved her. He'd given her what she'd needed.

"They wish they can trust you. They ask do I trust. I trust *you*. If you say the king be trusted, I believe."

Leofric gave her a small smile and turned to his father.

The king reached across the table and took her hand. "I swear this oath before God, Astrid of the North. I mean this to be my atonement to you. If you can forgive me, settle your people here and make us all strong."

Astrid pulled her hand back and considered the king, then turned to Leofric again. In his eyes, she saw a future. Here, in this castle, with his love. In the king's offer, she saw a chance for her divided self to be whole. She knew Leif and Vali would never stay and settle, but if the two worlds of her life were allied, then she would not lose either part of herself.

She trusted her husband, and he trusted his father. Astrid realized that she trusted the king herself. She had forgiven him. Even before this offer, she had.

She turned to Leif and Vali. "He is true. We can trust him. I swear it on my life."

24

The leaders of the Northmen returned to their camp that night to discuss with the others the king's offer. Astrid stayed with Leofric. When she'd said goodbye to their friends and they retired to the private residence, the king was waiting for them in the common rooms.

He held out his arms to Astrid, and, after a moment's hesitation, she allowed him to embrace her.

"Thank you, daughter," Leofric's father said as he set her back. "You fill me with hope. Do you remember what I told you, about Dreda giving me light in a dark time?"

"*Ja.* I remember."

"You are my light now. We put Eadric to rest on the morrow. I've lost two children with the passing of only a single year. Yet I hold hope and gladness inside my sorrow. I can see a future now. You give me that light."

Her eyes found Leofric's, and he saw in them uncertainty and discomfort. He smiled. She wasn't used to such effusions of emotion. From the king, indeed, Leofric wasn't, either. Only Dreda had known such pure softness from their staid father.

With a lift of her hand for a kiss, the king bid them good night and retired to his own rooms.

Leofric pulled his wife into his arms. "You were magnificent today."

"How? I only make bad talk in two tongues."

"No, you did much more than that. You brought two worlds together. Because neither could stand to lose you."

"If others say they want it."

"Will they?"

She played with the top fastenings of his black doublet. Her fingertips brushing across his throat left hot tremors behind them. "Leif make good talk. Vali also. They sway Gunnar and Tollak. So I think *ja*. They will." Her eyes came to his. "I stay if they want land, or if they not. With you, I stay."

He groaned and grabbed her hands, holding them against his chest. "Ah, Astrid. How I've prayed to hear that. To know that you love me, and that you would want to make your home with me. To hope that you might forgive us all."

"Forgive is done. No more past. Now we make future." She pulled on his hand and led him to his own room.

~oOo~

Once they'd shed their clothes, while Astrid climbed up into his bed, Leofric closed the heavy drapes around it—not for privacy, they wouldn't be disturbed on this night, but for the illusion of isolation. He wanted the world to fall away; he wanted to exist only with his beloved.

When he parted the drapes and joined her, she was lying back, propped on her elbows, the pearly tips of her breasts jutting forward like twin offerings. He crawled across the silks and loomed over her, taking one into his mouth and letting it pop free as he went for the other. She arched with pleasure, her head dropping back, as he suckled her, but when his hand went to the scant patch of silky gold between her thighs, she twisted and shoved, and he was on his back before he could do anything to resist.

She straddled him, and he groaned. "Yes. Ride me. Mercy, yes."

But she didn't take him into herself. Instead, she leaned down and sucked at his throat, then moved downward, over his chest, sucking his flesh into her mouth and nipping at him, tiny bites causing no pain but leaving a zinging that lasted well after she'd moved on. She suckled each of his nipples until they had gone tight and aching. She nuzzled her nose through the hair across his chest. She drew a line with her pointed tongue down the center of his belly, around his navel, and farther down, licking him like he was a sweet. With each touch of her tongue, each nip of her teeth, each brush of her nose or her lips or her breasts, skimming over his skin, Leofric felt a fresh flood of the heat pooling deep inside him. All of his muscles had hardened into rock, and he struggled to draw enough breath to feed the blood that rushed through him.

He needed to be inside her, but when he tried to take over, to grab her, to bring her hips back to his, she knocked him away and carried on with her playful enticements.

One of her breasts brushed the head of his sex, and he thought he'd release right then. She did it again, intentionally this time, liking the feel of it, and then she took him in hand and dragged him back and forth over her nipple. Leofric lifted his head to watch, and the sight of her own pleasure— her eyes closed, her teeth biting down on her lip—was more than he could bear. He dropped his head back to the mattress with a groan of desperate ecstasy.

"Please. Astrid, please."

She answered by sucking his sex into her mouth. She tongued his head and sucked him deep, back and forth, pulling away each time his hips rose up as his finish surged forth. On the fourth, or fifth, time—he'd lost count—that she refused him his release, he groaned in loud frustration, "Astrid!"

She laughed—and the sound of it would never grow old. "Not like this. Inside me. Soon."

He lifted his head again. She was nestled between his thighs, smiling up at him, her hands around his sex and that sweet, rare smile tantalizingly near his tip.

Someday, he would no longer think of her smiles or her laughs as rare treats. Someday, she would know such joy that all would know the music of her laughter. He knew that to be true, because now they had a lifetime of somedays to share.

"A child?" he asked. "You wish another child now?"

She nodded. "I raise her to be warrior."

He cocked an eyebrow at that, but she wasn't dissuaded.

"I think I change this place like this place change me. Our childs be warriors. Boys and girls."

He thought of Dreda, his young, sweet, wild sister, who'd wanted to be a pirate, whose untrammeled curiosity and enthusiasm had charmed his heart every day of her life. He thought of the daughter he and Astrid had lost and wondered if she would have had her mother's pale hair and sharp temper. Whether she would, as he did, and as Dreda had, have had his mother's eyes. He imagined a tiny Astrid, her brow drawn in ferocious concentration, wielding a wooden sword and learning the fighting arts as he had when a boy.

The image nearly impelled him to cry out with joy.

He sat up and caught Astrid's head in his hands, raising her up to face him. "I like that thought very much. They'll be brave and strong and fierce like their mother."

"And have kindness and honor like father."

He took her hips in his hands and drew her forward. Understanding him, she shifted, bringing her legs forward and around him, so she could sit on his lap. When he lifted her up, she took hold of his sex and guided him into her while he settled her back down as slowly as he could. They both gasped as he slid into her wet sheath and filled her.

"From this day," he murmured, tucking his face against her throat and breathing deep the alluring, natural scent of her. "From this day, we are one."

"*Ja*," she whispered back, pressing her lips to his cheek. "*Åh, ja.*"

~oOo~

The land his father had offered the Northmen—Leofric was making an effort now to stop thinking of them as raiders—was excellent land for farming. Most of the western edge of the kingdom was cliffs, so the usable shoreline of this holding was slight, but enough for them to land two, or possibly three of the ships like the warships they'd sailed here. The design of their ships fascinated Leofric. He knew little about them, but he did know that a ship that could sail shallow waters as easily as it sailed the open sea was an unusual thing indeed. Except, apparently, in the North.

Their ships were a substantial reason for the raid—the *Northmen's* success across Anglia, and elsewhere, most likely. They could pilot those beasts from the ocean straight up into the rivers feeding into it, and do so quietly, so they'd been able to invade far inland and surprise peasants and royalty alike.

And then, of course, they'd fought like nothing Leofric's people had ever seen before them. None of them feared death. In fact, they sought it. Now, he understood that their people believed that the true life came after a valiant death, when they would be welcomed into the hall of their gods.

Their Valhalla seemed not so different from God's Heaven in that respect. In other respects, they could not be more different. An eternity in Heaven was a time of peace. Valhalla seemed little different from life, except for the company.

He stood back now with his father and watched the Northmen leaders. Vali was the giant, Leif was the blond one too close to Leofric's wife, Gunnar and Tollak were the other two, who seemed less comfortable leading and looked to Vali and Leif for guidance. Bjarke—that name felt strange on Leofric's tongue—was clearly allied with Vali. All five stood talking with Astrid, on a hill overlooking most of the land they'd agreed to take.

Astrid's people had agreed to the alliance. They would make a settlement. This new duchy would be called Norshire, and Bjarke would be its first duke. He was staying behind, and Leif and the others would bring his family as well as settlers to build a village either later during this summer, if they could manage it before the weather turned, or at first chance when warmth returned.

Leofric would have to practice saying the man's name. While Bjarke practiced being a duke at court.

The nobles at court had had a great deal to say about a Northman being elevated all the way to the title of duke, eclipsing many of their own titles. Even Dunstan, the Earl of Tarrin, had raised a wan brow at that. But the king was firm. And he was right. This alliance would work because the Northmen would have power in the realm and the ear of the king.

A breeze blew up, catching the skirt of Astrid's sedate black gown and showing her leathers underneath. Leofric's breath caught at the sight of her, standing on that hill, her gown blowing back, her legs locked and strong.

That was his woman, and she was, finally, truly his. She had chosen their life together.

The group seemed to have come to a conclusion, and they all walked back to Leofric and his father. Leif came forward, straight to the king. Vali and Astrid were right behind him.

Leofric and his father both had to look up to meet the man eye to eye. "Land good green," Leif said.

Leofric remembered that Leif had been the one who'd been able to understand them when they'd thrown the governess's head at them and told them it was Astrid's.

"Yes," agreed the king. "I mean this as a true alliance. Not a trick. This land is good for farming."

Leif turned to Astrid, and she spoke in her language. After she was done, Leif nodded and turned back to the king. He held out his hand. "Friend."

The king clasped his arm in the way of warriors. "Friend."

Leofric looked to his wife, who was smiling. Yes, someday— someday soon—that would not be such a surprise.

~oOo~

The raiders sailed away a few days later, after Eadric had been buried and the alliance had been feted.

The loss of his brother wore a raw spot on his heart. They'd never been remarkably close, they had been too different in temperament and outlook for a deep bond, but neither had they been at odds much since their boyhood. Eadric had been a good man, they had spent their lives together, and Leofric would feel the loss of him always.

Yet his happy relief and ease in having Astrid with him truly, without reservation, for no other reason than her love of him, had blunted the pain of Eadric's death. He searched deep within himself and tried to find guilt for not grieving more acutely, but there was no guilt. He had too much peace for guilt.

He loved his brother. His brother had been a good man, a godly man. He was saved and with the Lord now. With their mother and sister and with his brides, the first of whom he'd married for love, and who had died with their son trapped inside her.

Leofric would miss him, but he could not mourn him.

He stood now at the top of the steep, reed-strewn rise below which were the Northmen's ships, fully laded and ready to sail. Astrid and Bjarke stood with their friends, saying their farewells. Leofric hadn't joined them; he had no place in their parting.

Astrid clasped arms with many of the men and women; whatever tension had been between them had been forgotten, it seemed. Her last and longest embrace was for Leif, and Leofric couldn't help the surge of jealousy he felt as he observed that lingering union and its reluctant end. Her love had been so hard to win; he wanted it all for himself.

Bjarke and Astrid stood on the shore as the ships shoved off. Neither of them waved, and Leofric saw no one on the ships wave, either. After a few minutes, when the rowers had moved into bluer waters in the bay, Bjarke and Astrid turned as one and climbed up the rise toward him. Bjarke nodded and walked on, back toward their horses. Astrid stopped at his side and took the hand he'd held out.

He could see that she was inexpressibly sad, but she twitched the corner of her mouth up in an attempted smile. He pulled her into his arms and turned her so her back was against his chest and she could see the ships.

"They'll be back. Mayhap in only weeks."

"No. Not before new summer. Need time for—to—make ready."

He squeezed her, offering, he hoped, reassurance. "But they'll be back."

"*Ja.* They will."

"And we will travel to them someday, and you can show me the world that made you."

She leaned back, resting her head on his shoulder. "I like that, *ja.* But it make part of me only. This world make me, too."

"I love you, Astrid of the North."

"Love," she whispered, nodding. Her eyes, though, were on the ships moving away.

"We can stay here and watch them as long as you like."

Again, she nodded. Leofric held her and rested his cheek on her head. While she watched her friends leave her again, he waited and hoped that she felt surrounded by the love she was staying to keep.

They stood like that until all eight ships had moved out of the bay and had unfurled their sails. As the ocean breeze filled them full, Astrid stood straight and turned in his arms to face him.

"Take me home," she said, her voice soft with sadness and with love.

EPILOGUE
HOSPITALITY

QUEEN

Leofric leaned into the carriage and held his hands out to her. She'd intended to ignore him and climb out on her own two legs, but when she tried to get herself off the seat, she failed.

He laughed and stepped back up so he could help her from the seat as well. When she was finally standing on the ground, he groaned dramatically and arched as if his back ached. "You get bigger each time, I think."

Astrid glared at her husband. "King or not, you should be careful with your words, lest they cost you your blood."

Leofric grinned down at the two children goggling up at them. "We jest, children. Your mother doesn't mean it."

"You'll see if I do not." But even the discomfort of the end of her third carrying couldn't keep her in poor temper on this day, and the grin took over her face before she finished the threat. Leofric laughed and kissed her hard. When he pulled back, she was breathless, but that was no rare occurrence of late.

The footmen and driver, and the villagers who'd stopped to watch the royal family exit their carriage, all remained in their bows and curtsies, pretending not to notice their exchange.

Leofric had been king, and Astrid his queen, for a year now. His father had died the year before, in his sleep, after celebrating with his family the day marking Eira's second year of life. The people of Mercuria were just beginning to accept Leofric's more relaxed style of rule. Eadric had been a good and fair king, but he'd been reserved and devout. Leofric enjoyed life more obviously than his father had, and he wasn't above teasing his wife and children in public. Or bending his queen back over his arm and kissing her as if he intended to do more right there.

"Godric, take your sister's hand and escort her to the docks, will you?"

"Yes, Papa." Their dark and serious son took Eira's hand, still round and soft with an infancy not so long past, and headed toward the docks.

Leofric offered Astrid his arm. "Come, my queen. We have guests to greet."

She took her husband's arm, and they followed their children to the Norshire docks, nodding as the people of the village bowed and curtsied.

The first settlers had come the summer after the alliance had been forged, when Godric had been just a new babe. In the six years since, Norshire had grown into a bustling and prosperous community.

Bjarke had used those first months, nearly a year, without his family to learn the ways of Mercuria and his responsibilities as a noble. He'd also marked out a place to begin the village of Norshire. Coming from a coast-dwelling people, he'd wanted the sea nearby, so the village spread from the small bay upward, fading into farmland at the top of a cliff. They'd made the buildings and streets meander down a hill. It was a lovely place, though the trek from the bay to the church was challenging for some.

The church. Every village had a church at its center, and Leofric and his father had both been adamant on that point. Bjarke had resisted, and the first settlers had as well. They'd finally conceded, expecting to ignore the structure that they thought of as the Christian treasure house.

But the Christian god had a way of sneaking in, and by now, many of the settlers had given up the gods of Asgard and had been baptized into the Catholic church. It had begun, Astrid thought, as a way to ease their business in this Christian world, but over the years, as the northern settlers began to meet, blend with, and sometimes mate with, other people of Mercuria, the faith of this place seemed to be taking true hold.

Godric and Eira had been baptized as babes, and they took instruction about the Christian god from Father Thomas, the realm's bishop. Astrid had fought and won many battles with Leofric over the years, but that was one she hadn't even tried to wage. His god was of this place, as were their children, so they should hold this god close.

But she told them stories of her people—of their marvelous living gods and of the mighty people who'd achieved great things. Warriors like Vali Storm-Wolf. Great leaders like Jarl Leif of Geitland. And shieldmaidens like Brenna God's-Eye and Astrid of the North.

For her part, Astrid, more than seven years after her baptism, could feel her gods fading away. She liked Father Thomas very much. He was kind and wise, a healer at heart, and she'd found herself going to him often when she had questions for which she could find no answers on her own. She attended Mass regularly because it was expected of her, and she found herself sometimes moved.

What she believed about the world beyond this one, she no longer knew for certain. She kept her mind on this world, and she knew what was true and important here: her husband, her children, her life.

And today, her life was full and complete. On the docks stood Leif, Olga, and their son, Magni, who had grown, at fourteen years, into a tall, fine-looking young man. Astrid noticed at once, before they were close enough to greet, that he wore an arm ring, so he was a true man indeed. Vali,

Brenna, and their oldest two children, Solveig and Håkon, were there as well, talking with Norshire men who'd been helping unlade the ship.

This ship had brought no raid, no war. This ship brought friendship, a renewing of an alliance that had grown strong and bountiful over the course of peaceful years.

Leif and Vali had visited three times since the alliance had been made. Brenna had joined them once before. Astrid and Leofric had visited Geitland twice as well. This was the first time that they'd brought any of their children with them, because this was the first time they'd made a trip primarily for friendship, without other business to attend.

Solveig, at fifteen years, looked so much like her mother that Astrid had the strange sense of looking into the past. The two were dressed alike as well, in leathers and braids. Solveig was taller than her mother, though—and Brenna was a tall woman, like Astrid.

Håkon favored his parents in equal measure, it seemed. He was—Astrid figured in her head—half a year younger than Magni, so near fourteen years, and taller than Magni already, and more broad. His size and darker coloring were of his father, but there was something in his aspect that showed his mother as well. A tendency to frown, perhaps—though Brenna, like Astrid, had found a life that made smiles fit more easily on her face.

It was the first time Olga had traveled since she'd first landed in Geitland, before Magni had been born—and, truthfully, she looked a bit worse for the trip. She was a woman who needed a good rest on steady ground.

The three families met together at the head of the docks, and there was a sudden wellspring of chaotic happiness, as hugs and handshakes were exchanged, and happy words said. They all spoke in the Northern tongue. Leofric had become fluent in Astrid's language, and they had taught their children from birth to speak in both ways.

Bjarke and his family came to the head of the docks. The Duke of Norshire, dressed to greet dignitaries, lifted a hand in greeting.

"Come!" Leofric called out above the group's gleeful babble, sweeping Eira into his arms. "Norshire has put on a festival to greet our dear friends, and tonight we shall feast in the great hall."

He met Astrid's eye, and she nodded. She was too far along with her third child to make it up Norshire's hill on foot, so they would proceed without her. Carrying Eira, he and Leif strode out ahead. Vali swept Godric into his big arms and followed them, holding Solveig's hand. Brenna followed with Håkon, and Olga, leaning a bit on Magni's strong arm, walked with Astrid.

When they reached Bjarke and his family, Leofric stepped back and let the greetings and welcome continue. Then Bjarke and his wife took the group up into the town. Astrid held back with her husband. Before Magni could lead his mother too far away, Astrid grabbed his arm.

"Olga, would you prefer to stay back here with us? We can sit under the canopy with Mayda and enjoy the view while we rest." Dunstan's wife was nearly as great with child as Astrid. She was posed prettily on a grassy patch that overlooked the sea, under a silk canopy.

Her friend, still pale with seasickness, nodded. "Go on, *kullake*," she said to her son. "I'll rest and be well soon."

With a nod, Magni led his mother to the canopy and helped her sit. Astrid had made her own seat before he or Leofric could help her. The king walked away to speak with Dunstan, and Magni gave the women a courtly nod and ran to catch up with the group.

Olga laughed as they watched him go. In his haste to miss nothing, he looked more like a boy than a man, his blond hair swinging over his back with each hurried stride. "You'd think I was gravely ill rather than simply woozy."

Astrid remembered the days when he'd been a small boy, and she had thought he would never be disciplined enough to follow his father. She'd been wrong. "He takes care of his mother."

"Yes, indeed he does. He's a good boy. A good man. Like his father."

Realizing that they were speaking in a language Mayda didn't understand, and that Lady Tarrin had never met Olga, Astrid switched to the language they could all speak. She made introductions, and the three women picked up the empty chatter that women made when they'd been left behind by their husbands.

Though Astrid had redefined what being a queen meant in Mercuria, there were some feminine courtly skills even a warrior queen couldn't escape, especially in a kingdom without war. Making pretty words of little import was one of them.

Leofric had explained to her the political importance of a queen who could smooth the social waters of the realm. He'd convinced her of the power in pretty words.

So she had set out to achieve greatness in her every role.

~oOo~

Feasting when Astrid's people came was not the same as feasting for special guests from elsewhere in Anglia. Despite their alliance and the influx of settlers into Mercuria, there had not yet been significant melding of their cultures. What had occurred was more of a sharing than a blending. Her people retained their egalitarian impulses and their earthy attitudes. They were suspicious of finery and pomp and found all the many layers of ritual and steps of respect unnecessarily complicated, but both ways had come to coexist.

Astrid had learned to accept that her adopted home found comfort in its regimens and rituals.

To their credit, Leif and Vali and the others had learned to moderate their behaviors in the great hall. They ate and drank and spoke in ways that mimicked the nobles at court. Leofric's attitude about feasting was considerably more lighthearted than his father's, and a middle place had been found between the courtly rigor of the kingdom and the emphatic revelry of their guests.

Over the years, the 'Wildmen of the North' had become more familiar to the people of Mercuria, and thus less wild and scandalous. By now, few tensions remained among all of Astrid's people.

There was dancing after the meal, because there was always dancing. Now, with a whole village of northern people residing in Mercuria, the dances and music Astrid had known in her life before had become part of the customs of the realm, and the musicians played music from both worlds. Her people hadn't learned so well the traditional dances of this place, but they were willing to try and to laugh when they failed.

Astrid was far too big and uncomfortable to dance, so Leofric took Godric and Eira onto the floor and danced with them both. Holding her belly as her babe danced inside her, Astrid smiled and watched all her people at play.

When the musicians ended a Northern circle dance and struck up a courtly tune, Leif bowed out and came to sit beside her.

"You look happy, my friend," he said in their language. He set his hand on her belly, and his eyebrows went up when the babe kicked hard at the spot. "He's dancing with us."

"Yes. He's been happy tonight, too. But there's not so much room in me for him to move so vigorously."

"It can't be much longer."

"No," she sighed. "Every morn I wake and hope it is the day, but he seems content where he is. More comfortable than I."

Leif chuckled, smiling down at her belly, his hand rubbing circles. Astrid scanned the dancers for her husband and found him. Their eyes met, but he had no more jealousy for Leif. He simply smiled and continued on with the dance.

"What makes you laugh?"

"I was thinking of the woman I knew in Geitland. The one who looked so sourly at Magni when he was playful and excited. I never thought to see a day like this one."

She smiled. Much of that woman was still inside her, but Astrid now understood that she had been incompletely formed. She had thought she needed no love or tenderness, no family or child of her own. She had thought the very idea of happiness was a tale for stories and that strength and will were all she needed to be her best.

In those days, she'd thought Brenna God's-Eye had given up her life to become a wife and mother. Now, she understood that she had enriched that life. It was, in fact, possible to be both a shieldmaiden and a mother. Because a shieldmaiden was more than the weapon she wielded. A shieldmaiden was a shieldmaiden in her soul foremost. In peace or at war, alone or in company, a true shieldmaiden's fire couldn't be doused.

And little was worth having or being if it couldn't be shared.

To Leif, she said, "They still say here that King Leofric tamed his wild woman and made her into a queen. It's become quite a story."

He grinned. "And you let them live? With all their parts?"

She returned the grin. "I let them think they're right."

~oOo~

A few days later, while their guests were still with them, Astrid pushed a fussing Audie away with a huff. "Enough, Audie."

"Forgive me, ma'am. I just want you to look your best."

"Do I not look well?" She cocked an eyebrow at her maid, and regretted her teasing when Audie went pale.

"You're beautiful, ma'am. The most beautiful—"

"I was teasing, Audie. I look a mess. I just brought this boy into the world, and the work is hard. I don't need to be beautiful today. I made a miracle. So go on—His Majesty will want to meet his new son."

In the world of her past, Leofric would have been with her, if he'd wished, but in this world, men were not allowed in the birthing room, and Leofric had looked quite ill at the thought of it, when she'd been carrying Godric. So she brought her children into this world with the help of friends, and Leofric met them after all the reality of it had been cleaned away.

Astrid looked down into the fat-cheeked face of her third child and second son. The many years of her life when she'd thought she would never want children seemed far away now. How odd that she'd believed that bearing children meant giving up strength and power.

Above the fireplace across the room hung her axe, and she thought of the talk she'd had with Leif on the night of the feast. For years, she'd fought valiantly with that weapon in her hands. Now, living a fuller life, she understood that the power to wield an axe well was not the only power there was. A life of battle was lonely and fraught. The power to build a future, though—that made a life rich and complete.

She hadn't been tamed. She had grown.

There was a knock on the door, and Elfleda, still bustling about the room, answered it and dropped immediately into a deep curtsey. Astrid smiled, knowing who would enter. Leofric came in, carrying Eira and holding Godric's hand. He brought their older children to her bed and helped them climb on.

"Be gentle, children. Your brother is but new, and your mother has worked hard today."

Smiling, she held out her free hand and welcomed Godric and Eira to come close. They sat at her side and peered curiously at the swaddled babe in her arms. When Godric stretched a tentative arm out, Astrid caught it and lay his hand gently on his brother's cheek. "See how soft? Always be slow and easy with him, or you could harm him without meaning it."

Godric smiled, and then Eira wanted a touch as well.

"What is he called?" Godric asked.

"He is Eadric," she answered, looking up at her husband, who nodded. They had discussed names before their son had arrived.

Leofric came to the side of the bed and looked down on his new son. "He's perfect, my love. Are you well?"

"He is, and I am. This was easier than the others. Each time, it seems easier."

"I'm glad. I hate for you to suffer." He kissed her forehead, then knelt at her side.

He couldn't understand, no man truly could, but Astrid had a vast knowledge of pain and of suffering and understood the differences. "To bring forth a child is pain, but not suffering. Suffering is empty of hope. This pain is full of it. It is joy."

They stared into each other's eyes for a long moment of perfect understanding. As it ended, he brushed her loose hair back and kissed her shoulder. "The solar is filled to the brim with friends wanting to see you and meet our son."

"Let them wait for now. I want this moment to be only for us."

"As do I. In this room, right now, you and our children—this is my whole heart and soul."

Astrid studied her children. Godric and Eira sat with uncharacteristic calm at her side, entranced by their new little brother. She turned to her husband, gazing on her with the love and devotion that took her breath each time she saw it.

"And mine as well."

Susan Fanetti is a Midwestern native transplanted to Northern California, where she lives with her husband, youngest son, and assorted cats.

Susan's blog: www.susanfanetti.com
Freak Circle Press blog: www.freakcirclepress.com

Susan's Facebook author page:
https://www.facebook.com/authorsusanfanetti
'Susan's FANetties' fan group:
https://www.facebook.com/groups/871235502925756/

Freak Circle Press Facebook page:
https://www.facebook.com/freakcirclepress
'The FCP Clubhouse' fan group:
https://www.facebook.com/groups/810728735692965 /

Twitter: @sfanetti

The Northwomen Sagas Pinterest Board:
https://www.pinterest.com/laughingwarrior/the-northwomen-sagas/

Printed in Great Britain
by Amazon

78401171R00224